(1859–1945) was born Ma... Melbourne, Australia, daughter of a vv... ... an Irish father. Her childhood was passed in New Zealand, Chile, Wales, Ireland and Germany. Chavelita tried nursing in London and various jobs in London and New York before joining a friend of her father's, Henry Higginson, a bigamist, and his present 'wife', Whyte Melville's widow, as travelling companion.

Chavelita and Higginson eloped to Norway in 1887 where they remained until Higginson's death two years later. While living in Norway, Chavelita read the work of Ibsen, Strindberg and Bjørnsen; she met and was influenced by Knut Hamsen, and began translating his novel *Hunger* on her return to London in 1890 (published in 1899). The next year she married a Newfoundlander, George Egerton Clairmonte, and moved to Ireland. It was here she wrote the short stories that were to create a sensation on their publication as *Keynotes* in 1893.

Early the following year George Egerton contributed to the first volume of *The Yellow Book*. *Discords* was published in 1894, succeeded by *Young Ofeg's Ditties* (1895), *Symphonies* (1897), *Fantasias* (1898), *The Wheel of God* (1898), *Rosa Amorosa* (1901) and *Flies in Amber* (1905).

Soon after the birth of her son in 1895, her marriage came to an end and 1901 she married her second husband Reginald Golding Bright, a drama critic fifteen years her junior. George Egerton now turned her attention to the world of theatre: she wrote a number of plays and adaptations which, however, were not successful. She died at her home at Ifield Park, Crawley, at the age of eighty-five.

Keynotes

by

George Egerton

With a New Introduction
by Martha Vicinus

Published by VIRAGO PRESS Limited 1983
20 Vauxhall Bridge Road, London SW1V 2SA

Reprinted 1995

Keynotes was first published in *The Yellow Book*
by Elkin Matthews & John Lane 1893
Discords was first published in *The Yellow Book*
by Elkin Matthews & John Lane 1894

Virago edition offset from first British editions

A CIP catalogue record for this book is available from the British Library

Printed and bound in Great Britain by
Cox & Wyman Ltd, Reading, Berks.

CONTENTS

PAGE

NEW INTRODUCTION, by Martha Vicinus ix

A CROSS LINE, ... 1

NOW SPRING HAS COME, ... 37

THE SPELL OF THE WHITE ELF, ... 68

A LITTLE GREY GLOVE, ... 91

AN EMPTY FRAME, ... 115

UNDER NORTHERN SKY—

    I. HOW MARIE LARSEN EXORCISED A DEMON, 124

    II. A SHADOW'S SLANT, ... 140

    III. AN EBB TIDE, ... 155

TO

KNUT HAMSUN

*In memory of a day when the west wind
and the rainbow met.*

1892-1893.

*Fancies are toys of the brain, to write them
down is to destroy them—as fancies! and yet . . .*

'*I gave him such a pretty toy to play with, and
he is breaking it up. When I say: "You are
very naughty, Biff; if you break it I shall whip
you!" he only says:*
'"*But I must, Mumsey, I must!*"'

FRAGMENT OF A LETTER, 1893.

INTRODUCTION

The publication of *Keynotes* in 1893 and *Discords* a year later made George Egerton one of the most famous—and notorious—writers of the 1890s. In a decade that encouraged originality and experimentation, Egerton seemed remarkably new and daring. The *Review of Reviews* praised her honesty, believing that 'some woman has crystallised her life's drama, has written down her soul upon the page'.[1] *Punch*, always on the look-out for the latest literary fad, parodied 'The Cross Line' as 'She Notes' by 'Borgia Smudgiton'.[2] But Egerton was not simply a literary *cause célèbre*. She was also in the vanguard of what more conservative critics dubbed 'erotomania', the unseemly display of sexual feeling on the part of women writers:

> The physiological excursions of our writers of neuropathic fiction are usually confined to one field—that of sex. Their chief delight seems to be in making their characters discuss matters which would not have been tolerated in the novels of a decade ago. Emancipated woman in particular loves to show her independence by dealing freely with the relations of the sexes. Hence all the prating of passion, animalism, 'the natural workings of sex', and so forth, with which we are nauseated. Most of the characters in these books seem to be erotomaniacs.[3]

London journalists had found it hard to swallow Thomas Hardy's *Tess of the D'Urbervilles* (1891) as the story of 'A Pure Woman', but the sudden popularity of writers such as Egerton seemed to indicate a terrible change in

1. *Review of Reviews*, 8 (December, 1893), p. 671.
2. *Punch*, 106 (1894), pp. 109, 129.
3. Hugh Stutfield, 'Tommyrotics', *Blackwood's Magazine*, 157 (June, 1895), p. 836.

England. Their dismay was not unreasonable. Women were revolting against their traditional role with utter disdain for male opinion.

During a brief space of three years the London literary world was rocked by women writers determined to expand the permissible topics in fiction. Egerton's daring was matched by others. Sarah Grand's *The Heavenly Twins* (1893) dissected the effects of venereal disease; Iota's *The Yellow Aster* (1893) analysed frigidity; Emma Brooke's *The Superfluous Woman* (1894) described the sexual and spiritual limitations placed upon an upper-class woman; Mona Caird's *The Daughters of Danaus* (1894) traced the sexual perils of an independent woman composer; and Ménie Muriel Dowie's *Gallia* (1895) analysed the social and sexual choices of an emancipated woman.[4] These 'New Women' revolted against what they saw as a totally unnatural upbringing, teaching them nothing about themselves or the opposite sex. Their fiction focused upon the extremes into which such an ill-trained creature could plunge, testifying to the sexual confusion, misery and frustration of the times. All confronted the very limited range of alternatives available to women with an honesty and anger that shocked and fascinated readers.

Egerton in particular felt compelled to describe with a new vehemence and confidence the importance of honouring women's sexuality. She opposed the demeaning notion that a woman's honour consisted in her technical virginity before marriage, and asserted through her characters that a woman must have a full life—

4. Grant Allen's *The Woman Who Did* (1895), George Gissing's *The Odd Women* (1893) and Thomas Hardy's *Jude the Obscure* (1896) all reflect this concern with woman's sexuality and her role in modern sexual relationships which was begun by women.

marriage, maternity and work. The reverse of these demands was an extreme distaste for any life that was less than its full potential. A cowardly refusal to follow one's soul-mate, as in 'An Empty Frame' or 'A Psychological Moment in Three Parts', met with condescending pity. Egerton, unlike other feminists, had no patience for respectability, considering it a male construct:

> . . . men manufactured an artificial morality; made sins of things that were clean in themselves as the pairing of birds on the wing; crushed nature, robbed it of its beauty and meaning, and established a system that means war, and always war, because it is a struggle between instinctive truths and cultivated lies . . . In one word, the untrue feminine is of man's making; while the strong, the natural, the true woman is of God's making.[5]

Egerton's disdain for conventional morality separated her from her contemporaries of both sexes. Even her mentors thought she might be a little more cautious in discussing sexual desire.[6] But Egerton was never interested in guilt or punishment; rather, her works celebrate the potential in women, not the possibly debilitating consequences of living the life of a New Woman in an old world.

Egerton has been labelled a realist and a naturalist because of her devastating descriptions of marriages gone awry in such stories as 'Wedlock' and 'Virgin Soil'. Certainly she shared with her female contemporaries a zeal (and zest) for describing the effects of sexual ignorance on women faced with venereal disease, or

5. 'A Cross Line', *Keynotes*, pp. 49–50.
6. See, for example, T. P. Gill's letter to her about 'A Cross Line', when he assumed that she was a man, *A Leaf from the Yellow Book: The Correspondence of George Egerton*, ed. by Terence de Vere White (London: The Richards Press, 1958), pp. 23–26.

alcoholism or gratuitous violence on the part of a careless man. But she differed from her contemporaries in her portrayal of solutions to these situations; she advocated not restraint and meaningful work, but sexual fulfilment and power. Throughout her work the highest compliment Egerton could give a woman was to declare her a witch, in the sense of being bewitching—someone who knew her sexual attractiveness and was willing to use it. She praised

> . . . the eternal wildness, the untamed primitive savage temperament that lurks in the mildest, best woman. Deep in through ages of convention this primeval trait burns,—an untameable quantity that may be concealed but is never eradicated by culture—the keynote of woman's witchcraft and woman's strength.[7]

Women were not boring carriers of society's social and moral standards, but mysterious creatures whom no man could understand; they were about to seize the leadership of society and reinstate the primacy of maternity and feeling. Men read her to find out about women, while women responded to her insistence upon freedom for the soul to grow and expand, no matter how much social convention might weigh them down.

By the 1890s Egerton had earned her optimism and her indifference to conventional morality; in her own life she balanced the two with adroitness. Born in 1859, Mary Chavelita Dunne was the oldest daughter of a ne'er-do-well Irishman who 'lived, with a large family, on air and other people for the greater part of his life'.[8] When she was fourteen-and-a-half her mother died, and

7. 'A Cross Line', p. 30.
8. de Vere White, p. 12. All biographical information comes from de Vere White's book.

the family broke up. Relatives helped out from time to time, but in such an unreliable fashion that her brothers received no schooling at all. 'Chav' was given sufficient money to attend a German school briefly, but she hated the idea of teaching. The other obvious option was nursing, which she tried for a short period in London. She then fled to New York, where she worked at a variety of low-paying jobs, living in a boarding house. Her novel, *The Wheel of God* (1898) and 'Gone Under' both provide glimpses into these lonely years. After two years she returned to England to eke out her living. Forced to make her way at an early age, Chav had few illusions, but many fantasies, about life, men and her own future.

In spite of occasional flashes of anger at her hopelessly impractical father, Chav remained close to him and deeply attracted to men of his charm. Her father taught her to fly-fish, a sport that was an abiding passion for both. Her father also treated her as an equal in a hearty male fashion that she never ceased to admire. Throughout her life Egerton considered the sportsman's outdoor life to be truer to male and female natures than the artificialities of the drawing room. She consistently moves her characters outdoors for moments of self-revelation or reverie. Men and women who fish meet as comrades-in-arms, recognising and appreciating each other's skill. Egerton did not equate Nature with woman's nature, but rather saw the outdoors as a freeing agent, providing the space and climate for personal growth. Thus, Nature never simply reflects a character's emotions or symbolises states of mind; it is a place of possibilities, but individuals must make the most of their own opportunities.

But Chav's father left her a more mixed dowry than just a love of the outdoors. Her attraction to his type of feckless charm led her into two nearly disastrous liaisons. In 1887 a friend of her father's suggested that she join him and his wife as a travelling companion. Henry Higginson was actually bigamously married at the time, but he was soon making love to Chav Dunne. The two fled to Norway, bought property and set up as a wealthy English couple. Higginson turned out to be a violent drunkard, as recorded in 'Under Northern Sky', but fortunately he lived only two years. These years were to be the most important in Egerton's life, for they gave her the experience and the tools to shape and fictionalise her life. Although she had had plenty of experience with men's lying and prevaricating, Higginson's brutality and neediness swept away any remaining illusions she might have had about finding a man to lean upon. Her two marriages were to lesser men in a dependent mother-son relationship. In her fiction she tended to idealise a similar relation, as in 'The Regeneration of Two' or 'The Cross Line', where the women clearly hold the reins of power.

Egerton learned Norwegian quickly, and was soon devouring the works of Ibsen, Strindberg, Bjørnsen, Hamsun and other lesser-known writers of Scandinavia. She was enthralled by what she read; they represented a kind of honesty and spirituality that she had found absent from Anglo-American literature of the time. Unlike other *fin de siècle* writers, such as George Moore, Oscar Wilde and Ernest Dowson, Egerton was not influenced by French Decadence, but by the virtually unknown Scandinavian realists. From them she absorbed the value of describing the minutiae of the moment—the tiny seemingly irrelevant impressions that remain after emotionally important events, such as the look of the grass or the pebbles on a path. She also adapted Hamsun's extended recreations of fluctuating states of mind in a character, acutely recording the inner reactions of sensitive women and girls. 'A Psychological Moment at Three Periods' is her most effective example in this style, describing with a fidelity new to English literature the painful promises of childhood. Given her infatuation with Norwegian literature, it is not surprising that she carried on an intense correspondence with Knut Hamsun, described in 'Now Spring Has Come'.

By 1890 Chavelita was back in London, working in the British Museum, translating Hamsun's novel *Hunger*, and seeking to recoup her fortunes. Then in 1891 she abruptly married an idle and penniless Newfoundlander, George Egerton Clairmonte. To save money they moved to Ireland, but soon their financial situation was so precarious that they considered emigrating to South Africa. Chav decided to try her hand at writing stories first. She sent a set of six to T. P. Gill, who ran an advice column for aspiring writers in the Dublin *Weekly Sun*. He wrote long and enthusiastic letters to her, recommending that she try Heinemann or the new publishing firm of Elkin Mathews and John Lane. After being summarily rejected by Heinemann, the stories were sent to John Lane, who was just beginning plans for *The Yellow Book* and a series of short works by new writers. Richard Le Gallienne, the reader, strongly recommended publication, but Chavelita had failed to include a name or return address. She finally turned up at the Bodley Head office, and was enthusiastically welcomed. *Keynotes* was published under her husband's first two names. Its success led Lane to name his new series 'Keynotes'. Launched at the head of what became a distinguished list of new writers, Egerton's life was transformed.[9]

9. For a full discussion of the 'Keynotes' series and Egerton's role, see Wendell V. Harris, 'John Lane's Keynote Series and the Fiction of the 1890's', *PMLA*, 83 (October, 1968), pp. 1407–1413.

In the mid-nineties Egerton was sought after by all the literary lights of London. Havelock Ellis, W. B. Yeats and George Bernard Shaw were only three among many who invited her to their homes. Richard Le Gallienne and John Lane had serious flirtations with her, if not affairs. They were heady years, but Egerton's later writings showed a discouraging falling off from *Keynotes* and *Discords*, and interest in her waned. After the birth of her son in 1895 Clairmonte became increasingly unreliable. He finally left for America and they were divorced; he died soon after. Then in 1899 Egerton met Golding Bright, an aspiring drama critic fifteen years younger than she. After the failure of an affair with a Norwegian (commemorated in the fictionalised *Rosa Amorosa* [1901]), Chav agreed to marry him. Bright went on to become a well-known and respected literary and dramatic agent, while she attempted under his influence to recoup her fading star by writing plays. In 1932 she explained her limited output,

> I could not take myself seriously. I was *intransigeant*, a bad seller of myself, but I had my standard and I could not be bought. I was a short-story, at most a long short-story writer. For years they came in droves and said themselves, leaving no scope for padding or altered endings; the long book was not my pigeon . . . Publishers told me bluntly: There is no market for short stories.[10]

She did not include her plays in the accompanying bibliography. Egerton's strength—the subtle transformation of personal experience—was also her weakness. Once she was settled into respectable marriage, she

10. 'A Keynote to *Keynotes*', *Ten Contemporaries: Notes Toward Their Definitive Bibliography*, ed. by John Gawsworth [Terence Armstrong] (London: E. Benn, 1932), p. 59.

could not develop new themes with the daring and excitement of her first stories.

However brief her fame, Egerton's stories live for us once again because she speaks to our renewed sense of the unspoken divisions between the sexes, and of the need for a specifically female voice to articulate how women feel about themselves and their most important experiences. Egerton pioneered in presenting English women's internal states of consciousness, capturing 'the eternal wildness' she saw there:

> I realised that in literature, everything had been done better by man than woman could hope to emulate. There was only one small plot left for her to tell: the *terra incognita* of herself, as she knew herself to be, not as man liked to imagine her— in a word to give herself away, as man had given himself away in his writings.[11]

Freed from the confines of respectability, yet resiliently optimistic, Egerton could frankly present a wife's desire to be rid of her husband in 'Under Northern Sky' as a positive virtue. Indeed, the mysterious heroine of 'The Regeneration of Two' might well be the wife of 'Under Northern Sky' recovered and seeking some outlet for her energy and money. Egerton sought to express women's needs, fears and strengths, regardless of who she shocked; her honesty and perceptive subtlety have not dated, though she no longer shocks us.

Egerton anticipated the modern short story.[12] She was among the first to employ ellipses, to refuse to give what had always been considered necessary background. She

11. Ibid., p. 58.
12. For a full discussion of Egerton's literary innovations, see Wendell V. Harris, 'Egerton: Forgotten Realist', *Victorian Newsletter*, 35 (Spring, 1968), pp. 31–35.

leaves unexplained, for example, how and why the woman in 'Under Northern Sky' came to marry a wealthy and brutal alcoholic, or why the woman in 'A Psychological Moment' is subject to blackmail. Causality is minimised, while impressions—fleeting moments, vital encounters, intuitive understandings—are emphasised. She was a master at capturing 'the infinitesimal electric threads vibrating' between woman and man, woman and woman. Although her use of the present tense can become at times a gratingly familiar device, at its most effective, its use captures precisely the mood, the moment, Egerton felt had been neglected by past writers. The sudden flash of recognition, of understanding, comes in virtually all of her stories. The coyness of 'The Spell of the White Elf' is redeemed by the growing friendship and respect between the two women; the hackneyed romanticism of 'Her Share' by the poignancy of the youthful moment described and the narrator's fidelity to the past.

Like so many writers at the end of the nineteenth century, Egerton tended to pour nonrealistic material into realistic forms. Struggling to express the previously unnamed aspects of themselves, women writers in particular experimented with remaking the traditional realistic novel. Olive Schreiner wrote a series of short allegories, expressive of the general seeking for new ideals, new relationships between men and women. Grand, Brooke and Iota created masculine, strongminded women who are forced to take over temporarily male responsibilities. Alternatively they invented fantasy interludes, in which a woman will dream of an entirely different world or will cross-dress, experimenting with the freedom available to boys and men. Within the conventional tale of courtship and marriage we have an effort to explain and analyse other, more inchoate desires and hopes of women. In our own times we have seen feminist writers turn to science fiction, prose poetry and personal journals as appropriate vehicles to express previously neglected aspects of women's lives and thoughts. In the 1890s Egerton used the short story as her best means of describing a woman's intuitive sensibility.

Egerton's women recognise two parts within themselves: their free soul and their need for self-fulfilment, usually through maternity. She endowed many of her heroines with money, time and sexual experience; ironically, Egerton herself never had the financial security she gave her characters until after her second marriage. Her women know their discontent, and are ready to see the world, to explore a range of experiences; they are eager to test their power. Under the guise of the realistic, Egerton wrote utopian fiction, a fiction that tries on different models of behaviour for different women.[13] In a fantasy interlude, the heroine of 'A Cross Line' imagines herself dancing before 'hundreds of faces' in a 'cobweb garment of wondrous tissue', giving 'to the soul of each man what he craves, be it good or evil'.

> One quivering, gleaming, daring bound, and she stands with outstretched arms and passion-filled eyes, poised on one slender foot, asking a supreme note to finish her dream of motion; and the men rise to a man and answer her, and cheer, cheer till the echoes shout from the surrounding hills and tumble wildly down the crags.[14]

Despite this keen sense of sexual power, the heroine gives up a spiritual friendship with a summer fly-fisher, not because she loves her husband, but rather because she

13. This same point is made more briefly by Patricia Stubbs in *Women and Fiction: Feminism and the Novel, 1880–1920* (Brighton: The Harvester Press, 1979), pp. 111–112.
14. 'A Cross Line', p. 28.

recognises the primacy of her pregnancy. Her maternity will keep her faithful, but it is a freely chosen fidelity to the forthcoming baby who will need her. Egerton never slips the burden of personal responsibility off her women characters, but assumes that they will make their choices freely, given their limited circumstances or unlimited imaginations.

Egerton's most extended utopia is the last story in this collection, 'The Regeneration of Two', in which a fatal moment, a single encounter with an honest man, turns a spoiled widow from her aimless life. Spurning social proprieties, she starts a co-operative in her country home, composed of all the fallen women of the area, working together in love and harmony. Her reward is the return of her poet, to be nursed back to health and love. When he recovers, she proudly tells him:

> You stung me to analyse myself, to see what was under the form into which custom had fashioned me, of what pith I was made, what spirit, if any, lay under the outer woman . . . I was sorry for myself, resentful because I had been reared in ignorance, because of my soul-hunger, but I had found myself all the same, and I said: From this out I belong body and soul to myself; I will live as I choose, seek joy as I choose, carve the way of my life as I will . . . Woman has cheapened herself body and soul through ignorant innocence, she must learn to worthen herself by all-seeing knowledge.[15]

They establish a free marriage of equals, which enables them to continue their respective work, but to draw nurturance from each other. Egerton, in common with her feminist contemporaries, insisted that women must regenerate themselves, without the assistance of male sympathisers. But unlike other women of her times, she

15. 'The Regeneration of Two', *Discords*, pp. 241–242.

could imagine the creation of a more equal relationship between the New Woman at her strongest and freest and an evolving 'New Man'. Her community of working mothers does not dissolve, but continues as a living testimony to a new power. Such a conclusion was obviously impossible in 1894, yet Egerton's fantasy still works. We are convinced because we, like her original readers, need to imagine a better world where women work together and men understand and keep their freedom too.

Egerton was unique in her positive expectations for women's natural superiority over men, and of her assumption that some men could overcome their sexism. But the gentleness and respect of the poet combined with the strength and independence of the widow are still goals feminists seek as the basis for better relationships and a better world. At the same time, Egerton was fearless in presenting the evil consequences of the continued ignorance and victimisation of women, though her portrayals of fallen women, injured wives and victimised women are more conventional, more predictably nineteenth century. The real excitement of reading Egerton comes from the discovery of self—the pushing outward of woman's potential in her stories. She refuses to accept less than the most complete life, the most complete freedom, the most complete soul for her women. Sometimes this means a traditional marriage, sometimes a free liaison, sometimes simple independence, but never does a woman deny her self without denying her soul. For Egerton the price of repression was always too high.

Martha Vicinus, Michigan, USA, 1982

A CROSS LINE

THE rather flat notes of a man's voice float out into the clear air, singing the refrain of a popular music-hall ditty. There is something incongruous between the melody and the surroundings. It seems profane, indelicate, to bring this slangy, vulgar tune, and with it the mental picture of footlight flare and fantastic dance into the lovely freshness of this perfect spring day.

A woman sitting on a felled tree turns her head to meet its coming, and an expression flits across her face in which disgust and humorous appreciation are subtly blended. Her mind is nothing if not picturesque ; her busy brain, with all its capabilities choked by a thousand vagrant fancies, is always producing pictures and finding associations between the most unlikely objects. She has been reading a little sketch written in the daintiest language of a fountain scene in Tanagra, and her vivid imagination has made it real to her. The slim, graceful maids grouped around it filling their exquisitely-formed earthen jars, the dainty poise of their classic heads, and the flowing folds of their draperies have been actually present with her ; and now ?—why, it is like the entrance of a half-tipsy vagabond player bedizened in tawdry finery—the picture is blurred. She rests her head against the trunk of a pine tree behind her, and awaits the singer. She is sitting on an incline in the midst of a wilderness of trees ; some have blown down, some have been cut down, and the lopped branches lie about; moss and bracken and trailing bramble, fir-cones, wild rose bushes, and speckled red 'fairy hats' fight for life in wild confusion. A disused quarry to the left is an ideal haunt of pike, and to the right a little river rushes along in haste to join a greater sister that is fighting a troubled way to the sea. A row of stepping-stones crosses it, and if you were to stand on one you would see shoals of restless stone loach 'Beardies' darting from side to side. The tails of several ducks can be seen above the water, and the paddle of their balancing feet, and the gurgling suction of their bills as they search for larvæ can be heard distinctly between the hum of insect, twitter of bird, and rustle of stream and leaf. The singer has changed his lay to a whistle, and presently he comes down the path a cool, neat, grey-clad figure, with a fishing creel slung across his back, and a trout rod held on his shoulder. The air ceases abruptly, and his cold grey eyes scan the seated figure with its gipsy ease of attitude, a scarlet shawl that has fallen from her shoulders forming an accentuative background to the slim roundness of her waist.

Persistent study, coupled with a varied experience of the female animal, has given the owner of the grey eyes some facility in classing her, although it has not supplied him with any definite data as to what any one of the species may do in a given circumstance. To put it in his own words, in answer to a friend who chaffed him on his untiring pursuit of women as an interesting problem :

'If a fellow has had much experience of his fellow-man he may divide him into types, and, given a certain number of men and a certain number of circumstances, he is pretty safe on hitting on the line of action each type will strike ; 't aint so with woman. You may always look out for the unexpected, she generally upsets a fellow's calculations, and you are never safe in laying odds on her. Tell you what, old chappie, we may talk about superior intellect; but, if a woman wasn't handicapped by her affection, or need of it, the cleverest chap in Christendom would be just a bit of putty in her hands. I find them more fascinating as problems than anything going. Never let an opportunity slip to get new data—never!'

He did not now. He met the frank, unembarrassed gaze of eyes that would have looked with just the same bright inquiry at the advent of a hare, or a toad, or any other object that might cross her path, and raised his hat with respectful courtesy, saying, in the drawling tone habitual with him—

'I hope I am not trespassing?'

'I can't say; you may be, so may I, but no one has ever told me so!'

A pause. His quick glance has noted the thick wedding ring on her slim brown hand, and the flash of a diamond in its keeper. A lady decidedly. Fast? perhaps. Original? undoubtedly. Worth knowing? rather.

'I am looking for a trout stream, but the

directions I got were rather vague; might
I——'

'It's straight ahead, but you won't catch
anything now, at least not here, sun's too glar-
ing and water too low, a mile up you may, in
an hour's time.'

'Oh, thanks awfully for the tip. You fish
then?'

'Yes, sometimes.'

'Trout run big here?' (what odd eyes the
woman has, kind of magnetic.)

'No, seldom over a pound, but they are very
game.'

'Rare good sport isn't it, whipping a stream?
There is so much besides the mere catching of
fish. The river and the trees and the quiet
sets a fellow thinking—kind of sermon—makes
a chap feel good, don't it?'

She smiles assentingly. And yet what the
devil is she amused at he queries mentally. An
inspiration. He acts upon it, and says eagerly:

'I wonder—I don't half like to ask—but fishing puts people on a common footing, don't it?
You knowing the stream, you know, would you
tell me what are the best flies to use?'

'I tie my own, but——'

'Do you? how clever of you! wish I could,'
and sitting down on the other end of the tree,
he takes out his fly book, 'but I interrupted
you, you were going to say?'

'Only,' stretching out her hand (of a perfect
shape but decidedly brown) for the book, 'that
you might give the local fly-tyer a trial, he'll
tell you.'

'Later on, end of next month, or perhaps
later, you might try the oak-fly, the natural fly
you know; a horn is the best thing to hold them
in, they get out of anything else—and put two
on at a time.'

'By Jove, I must try that dodge!'

He watches her as she handles his book and
examines the contents critically, turning aside
some with a glance, fingering others almost
tenderly, holding them daintily and noting the
cock of wings and the hint of tinsel, with her
head on one side; a trick of hers he thinks.

'Which do you like most, wet or dry fly?'
(she is looking at some dry flies.)

'Oh,' with that rare smile, 'at the time I
swear by whichever happens to catch most fish.
Perhaps, really, dry fly. I fancy most of these
flies are better for Scotland or England. Up

to this March-brown has been the most killing
thing. But you might try an "orange-grouse,"
that's always good here; with perhaps a "hare's
ear" for a change—and put on a "coachman"
for the evenings. My husband (he steals a side
look at her) brought home some beauties
yesterday evening.'

'Lucky fellow!'

She returns the book. There is a tone in his
voice as he says this that jars on her, sensitive
as she is to every inflection of a voice, with an
intuition that is almost second sight. She
gathers up her shawl. She has a cream-coloured
woollen gown on, and her skin looks duskily
foreign by contrast. She is on her feet before
he can regain his, and says, with a cool little
bend of her head: 'Good afternoon, I wish you
a full basket!'

Before he can raise his cap she is down the
slope, gliding with easy steps that have a strange
grace, and then springing lightly from stone to
stone across the stream. He feels small, snubbed
someway, and he sits down on the spot where
she sat and, lighting his pipe, says 'check!'

  *   *   *   *   *

She is walking slowly up the garden path.

A man in his shirt sleeves is stooping amongst
the tender young peas. A bundle of stakes lies
next him, and he whistles softly and all out of
tune as he twines the little tendrils round each
new support. She looks at his broad shoulders
and narrow flanks; his back is too long for
great strength, she thinks. He hears her step,
and smiles up at her from under the shadow of
his broad-leafed hat.

'How do you feel now, old woman?'

'Beastly. I've got that horrid qualmish
feeling again. I can't get rid of it.'

He has spread his coat on the side of the
path and pats it for her to sit down.

'What is it' (anxiously)? 'if you were a mare
I'd know what to do for you. Have a nip of
whisky?'

He strides off without waiting for her reply
and comes back with it and a biscuit, kneels
down and holds the glass to her lips.

'Poor little woman, buck up! You'll see
that'll fix you. Then you go by-and-by and
have a shy at the fish.'

She is about to say something when a fresh
qualm attacks her and she does not.

He goes back to his tying.

'By Jove!' he says suddenly, 'I forgot. Got something to show you!'

After a few minutes he returns carrying a basket covered with a piece of sacking. A dishevelled-looking hen, with spread wings trailing and her breast bare from sitting on her eggs, screeches after him. He puts it carefully down and uncovers it, disclosing seven little balls of yellow fluff splashed with olive green. They look up sideways with bright round eyes, and their little spoon bills look disproportionately large.

'Aren't they beauties (enthusiastically)? This one is just out,' taking up an egg, 'mustn't let it get chilled.' There is a chip out of it and a piece of hanging skin. 'Isn't it funny?' he asks, showing her how it is curled in the shell, with its paddles flattened and its bill breaking through the chip, and the slimy feathers sticking to its violet skin.

She suppresses an exclamation of disgust, and looks at his fresh-tinted skin instead. He is covering basket, hen, and all—

'How you love young things!' she says.

'Some. I had a filly once, she turned out a lovely mare! I cried when I had to sell her, I wouldn't have let any one in God's world mount her.'

'Yes, you would!'

'Who?' with a quick look of resentment.

'Me!'

'I wouldn't!'

'What! you wouldn't?'

'I wouldn't!'

'I think you would if I wanted to!' with a flash out of the tail of her eye.

'No, I wouldn't!'

'Then you would care more for her than for me. I would give you your choice (passionately), her or me!'

'What nonsense!'

'May be (concentrated), but it's lucky she isn't here to make deadly sense of it.' A humble-bee buzzes close to her ear, and she is roused to a sense of facts, and laughs to think how nearly they have quarrelled over a mare that was sold before she knew him.

       *   *   *   *

Some evenings later, she is stretched motionless in a chair, and yet she conveys an impression of restlessness ; a sensitively nervous person would feel it. She is gazing at her husband, her brows are drawn together, and make three little lines. He is reading, reading quietly, without moving his eyes quickly from side to side of the page as she does when she reads, and he pulls away at a big pipe with steady enjoyment. Her eyes turn from him to the window, and follow the course of two clouds, then they close for a few seconds, then open to watch him again. He looks up and smiles.

'Finished your book?'

There is a singular soft monotony in his voice; the organ with which she replies is capable of more varied expression.

'Yes, it is a book makes one think. It would be a greater book if he were not an Englishman. He's afraid of shocking the big middle class. You wouldn't care about it.'

'Finished your smoke?'

'No, it went out, too much fag to light up again! No (protestingly), never you mind, old boy, why do you?'

He has drawn his long length out of his chair, and, kneeling down beside her, guards a lighted match from the incoming evening air. She draws in the smoke contentedly, and her eyes smile back with a general vague tenderness.

' Thank you, dear old man !'

' Going out again ?' negative head shake.

' Back aching ?' affirmative nod, accompanied by a steadily aimed puff of smoke, that she has been carefully inhaling, into his eyes.

' Scamp ! Have your booties off ?'

' Oh, don't you bother, Lizzie will do it !'

He has seized a foot from under the rocker, and, sitting on his heels, holds it on his knee, whilst he unlaces the boot ; then he loosens the stocking under her toes, and strokes her foot gently.

' Now, the other !' Then he drops both boots outside the door, and fetching a little pair of slippers, past their first smartness, from the bedroom, puts one on. He examines the left foot; it is a little swollen round the ankle, and he presses his broad fingers gently round it as one sees a man do to a horse with windgalls. Then he pulls the rocker nearer to his chair and rests the slipperless foot on his thigh. He relights his pipe, takes up his book, and rubs softly from ankle to toes as he reads.

She smokes and watches him, diverting herself by imagining him in the hats of different periods. His is a delicate-skinned face with regular features; the eyes are fine, in colour and shape with the luminous clearness of a child's; his pointed beard is soft and curly. She looks at his hand,—a broad strong hand with capable fingers,—the hand of a craftsman, a contradiction to the face with its distinguished delicacy. She holds her own up with a cigarette poised between the first and second fingers, idly pleased with its beauty of form and delicate nervous slightness. One speculation chases the other in her quick brain; odd questions as to race arise; she dives into theories as to the why and wherefore of their distinctive natures, and holds a mental debate in which she takes both sides of the question impartially. He has finished his pipe, laid down his book, and is gazing dreamily, with his eyes darkened by their long lashes, and a look of tender melancholy in their clear depths, into space.

'What are you thinking of?' There is a look of expectation in her quivering nervous little face.

He turns to her, chafing her ankle again.

'I was wondering if lob-worms would do for——'

He stops. A strange look of disappointment

flits across her face and is lost in an hysterical peal of laughter.

'You are the best emotional check I ever knew,' she gasps.

He stares at her in utter bewilderment, and then a slow smile creeps to his eyes and curves the thin lips under his moustache, a smile at her.

'You seem amused, Gipsy!'

She springs out of her chair and seizes book and pipe; he follows the latter anxiously with his eyes until he sees it laid safely on the table. Then she perches herself, resting her knees against one of his legs, whilst she hooks her feet back under the other—

'Now I am all up, don't I look small?'

He smiles his slow smile. 'Yes, I believe you are made of gutta percha.'

She is stroking out all the lines in his face with the tip of her finger; then she runs it through his hair. He twists his head half impatiently, she desists.

'I divide all the people in the world,' she says, 'into those who like their hair played with, and those who don't. Having my hair brushed gives me more pleasure than anything

else ; it's delicious. I'd *purr* if I knew how.
I notice (meditatively) I am never in sympathy with those who don't like it ; I am
with those who do. I always get on with
them.'

'You are a queer little devil !'

' Am I ? I shouldn't have thought you would
have found out I was the latter at all. I wish
I were a man ! I believe if I were a man, I'd
be a disgrace to my family.'

'Why ?'

'I'd go on a jolly old spree !'

He laughs : 'Poor little woman, is it so
dull ?'

There is a gleam of devilry in her eyes,
and she whispers solemnly—

'Begin with a D,' and she traces imaginary
letters across his forehead, and ending with a
flick over his ear, says, 'and that is the tail
of the y !'

After a short silence she queries—

'Are you fond of me ?' She is rubbing her
chin up and down his face.

'Of course I am, don't you know it ?'

'Yes, perhaps I do,' impatiently ; 'but I want
to be told it. A woman doesn't care a fig for

a love as deep as the death-sea and as silent, she wants something that tells her it in little waves all the time. It isn't the love, you know, it's the being loved; it isn't really the man, it's his loving!'

'By Jove, you're a rum un!'

'I wish I wasn't then. I wish I was as commonplace as——. You don't tell me anything about myself (a fierce little kiss), you might, even if it were lies. Other men who cared for me told me things about my eyes, my hands, anything. I don't believe you notice.'

'Yes I *do*, little one, only I think it.'

'Yes, but I don't care a bit for your thinking; if I can't see what's in your head what good is it to me?'

'I wish I could understand you, dear!'

'I wish to God you could. Perhaps if you were badder and I were gooder we'd meet half-way. *You* are an awfully good old chap; it's just men like you send women like me to the devil!'

'But you are good (kissing her), a real good chum! You understand a fellow's weak points. You don't blow him up if he gets on a bit. Why (enthusiastically), being married to you is like chumming with a chap! Why (admiringly), do you remember before we were married, when I let that card fall out of my pocket? Why, I couldn't have told another girl about her. She wouldn't have believed that I *was* straight. She'd have thrown me over. And you sent her a quid because she was sick. You are a great little woman!'

'Don't see it! (she is biting his ear). Perhaps I was a man last time, and some hereditary memories are cropping up in this incarnation!'

He looks so utterly at sea that she has to laugh again, and, kneeling up, shuts his eyes with kisses, and bites his chin and shakes it like a terrier in her strong little teeth.

'You imp! was there ever such a woman!'

Catching her wrists, he parts his knees and drops her on to the rug. Then, perhaps the subtle magnetism that is in her affects him, for he stoops and snatches her up and carries her up and down, and then over to the window and lets the fading light with its glimmer of moonshine play on her odd face with its tantalising changes. His eyes dilate and his colour deepens as he crushes her soft little body to him and carries her off to her room.

*   *   *   *   *

Summer is waning and the harvest is ripe for ingathering, and the voice of the reaping machine is loud in the land. She is stretched on her back on the short heather-mixed moss at the side of a bog stream. Rod and creel are flung aside, and the wanton breeze, with the breath of coolness it has gathered in its passage over the murky dykes of black bog water, is playing with the tail fly, tossing it to and fro with a half threat to fasten it to a prickly spine of golden gorse. Bunches of bog-wool nod their fluffy heads, and through the myriad indefinite sounds comes the regular scrape of a strickle on the scythe of a reaper in a neighbouring meadow. Overhead a flotilla of clouds is steering from the south in a north-easterly direction. Her eyes follow them. Old time galleons, she thinks, with their wealth of snowy sail spread, riding breast to breast up a wide blue fjord after victory. The sails of the last are rose flushed, with a silver edge. Somehow she thinks of Cleopatra sailing down to meet Antony, and a great longing fills her soul to sail off somewhere too—away from the daily need of dinner-getting and the recurring Monday with its washing; life with its tame duties and virtuous monotony. She fancies herself in Arabia on the back of a swift steed. Flashing eyes set in dark faces surround her, and she can see the clouds of sand swirl, and feel the swing under her of his rushing stride. Her thoughts shape themselves into a wild song, a song to her steed of flowing mane and satin skin; an uncouth rhythmical jingle with a feverish beat; a song to the untamed spirit that dwells in her. Then she fancies she is on the stage of an ancient theatre out in the open air, with hundreds of faces upturned towards her. She is gauze-clad in a cobweb garment of wondrous tissue. Her arms are clasped by jewelled snakes, and one with quivering diamond fangs coils round her hips. Her hair floats loosely, and her feet are sandal-clad, and the delicate breath of vines and the salt freshness of an incoming sea seems to fill her nostrils. She bounds forward and dances, bends her lissom waist, and curves her slender arms, and gives to the soul of each man what he craves, be it good or evil. And she can feel now, lying here in the shade of

Irish hills with her head resting on her scarlet shawl and her eyes closed, the grand intoxicating power of swaying all these human souls to wonder and applause. She can see herself with parted lips and panting, rounded breasts, and a dancing devil in each glowing eye, sway voluptuously to the wild music that rises, now slow, now fast, now deliriously wild, seductive, intoxicating, with a human note of passion in its strain. She can feel the answering shiver of feeling that quivers up to her from the dense audience, spellbound by the motion of her glancing feet, and she flies swifter and swifter, and lighter and lighter, till the very serpents seem alive with jewelled scintillations. One quivering, gleaming, daring bound, and she stands with outstretched arms and passion-filled eyes, poised on one slender foot, asking a supreme note to finish her dream of motion. And the men rise to a man and answer her, and cheer, cheer till the echoes shout from the surrounding hills and tumble wildly down the crags. The clouds have sailed away, leaving long feathery streaks in their wake. Her eyes have an inseeing look, and she is tremulous with excitement. She can hear yet that last grand

shout, and the strain of that old-time music that
she has never heard in this life of hers, save
as an inner accompaniment to the memory of
hidden things, born with her, not of this time.

And her thoughts go to other women she has
known, women good and bad, school friends,
casual acquaintances, women workers—joyless
machines for grinding daily corn, unwilling
maids grown old in the endeavour to get
settled, patient wives who bear little ones to
indifferent husbands until they wear out—a
long array. She busies herself with questioning. Have they, too, this thirst for excitement,
for change, this restless craving for sun and
love and motion? Stray words, half con-
fidences, glimpses through soul-chinks of suppressed fires, actual outbreaks, domestic cata-
strophes, how the ghosts dance in the cells of
her memory! And she laughs, laughs softly to
herself because the denseness of man, his
chivalrous conservative devotion to the female
idea he has created blinds him, perhaps happily,
to the problems of her complex nature. Ay,
she mutters musingly, the wisest of them can
only say we are enigmas. Each one of them sets
about solving the riddle of the *ewig weibliche*

—and well it is that the workings of our
hearts are closed to them, that we are cunning
enough or *great* enough to seem to be what
they would have us, rather than be what we are.
But few of them have had the insight to find
out the key to our seeming contradictions. The
why a refined, physically fragile woman will
mate with a brute, a mere male animal with
primitive passions—and love him—the why
strength and beauty appeal more often than
the more subtly fine qualities of mind or heart
—the why women (and not the innocent ones)
will condone sins that men find hard to forgive
in their fellows.   They have all overlooked the
eternal wildness, the untamed primitive savage
temperament that lurks in the mildest, best
woman.   Deep in through ages of convention
this primeval trait burns, an untameable quantity
that may be concealed but is never eradicated
by culture — the keynote of woman's witch-
craft and woman's strength.   But it is there, sure
enough, and each woman is conscious of it in
her truth-telling hours of quiet self-scrutiny—
and each woman in God's wide world will deny
it, and each woman will help another to conceal
it—for the woman who tells the truth and is

not a liar about these things is untrue to her sex and abhorrent to man, for he has fashioned a model on imaginary lines, and he has said, 'so I would have you,' and every woman is an unconscious liar, for so man loves her. And when a Strindberg or a Nietzche arises and peers into the recesses of her nature and dissects her ruthlessly, the men shriek out louder than the women, because the truth is at all times unpalatable, and the gods they have set up are dear to them. . . .'

'Dreaming, or speering into futurity? You have the look of a seer. I believe you are half a witch!'

And he drops his grey-clad figure on the turf. He has dropped his drawl long ago, in midsummer.

'Is not every woman that? Let us hope I'm, for my friends, a white one.'

'A-ah! Have you many friends?'

'That is a query! If you mean many correspondents, many persons who send me Christmas cards, or remember my birthday, or figure in my address-book? No.'

'Well, grant I don't mean that!'

'Well, perhaps, yes. Scattered over the

world, if my death were belled out, many women would give me a tear, and some a prayer. And many men would turn back a page in their memory and give me a kind thought, perhaps a regret, and go back to their work with a feeling of having lost something— that they never possessed. I am a creature of moments. Women have told me that I came into their lives just when they needed me. Men had no need to tell me, I felt it. People have needed me more than I them. I have given freely whatever they craved from me in the way of understanding or love. I have touched sore places they showed me and healed them, but they never got at me. I have been for myself, and helped myself, and borne the burden of my own mistakes. Some have chafed at my self-sufficiency and have called me fickle—not understanding that they gave me nothing, and that when I had served them, their moment was ended, and I was to pass on. I read people easily, I am written in black letter to most——'

'To your husband !'

'He (quickly)—we will not speak of him ; it is not loyal.'

'Do not I understand you a little?'

'You do not misunderstand me.'

'That is something.'

'It is much!'

'Is it? (searching her face). It is not one grain of sand in the desert that stretches between you and me, and you are as impenetrable as a sphinx at the end of it. This (passionately) is my moment, and what have you given me?'

'Perhaps less than other men I have known; but you want less. You are a little like me, you can stand alone. And yet (her voice is shaking), have I given you nothing?'

He laughs, and she winces—and they sit silent, and they both feel as if the earth between them is laid with infinitesimal electric threads vibrating with a common pain. Her eyes are filled with tears that burn but don't fall, and she can see his somehow through her closed lids, see their cool greyness troubled by sudden fire, and she rolls her handkerchief into a moist cambric ball between her cold palms.

'You have given me something—something to carry away with me—an infernal want. You ought to be satisfied. I am infernally miserable.'

'You (nearer) have the most tantalising mouth in the world when your lips tremble like that. I . . . What! can you cry? You?'

'Yes, even I can cry!'

'You dear woman! (pause) And I can't help you!'

'You can't help me. No man can. Don't think it is because you are you I cry, but because you probe a little nearer into the real me that I feel so.'

'Was it necessary to say that? (reproachfully). Do you think I don't know it? I can't for the life of me think how you, with that free gipsy nature of yours, could bind yourself to a monotonous country life, with no excitement, no change. I wish I could offer you my yacht. Do you like the sea?'

'I love it, it answers one's moods.'

'Well, let us play pretending, as the children say. Grant that I could, I would hang your cabin with your own colours; fill it with books, all those I have heard you say you care for; make it a nest as rare as the bird it would shelter. You would reign supreme; when your highness would deign to honour her servant I would come and humour your every whim. If

you were glad, you could clap your hands and
order music, and we would dance on the white
deck, and we would skim through the sunshine
of Southern seas on a spice-scented breeze.
You make me poetical. And if you were angry
you could vent your feelings on me, and I would
give in and bow my head to your mood. And
we would drop anchor and stroll through
strange cities, go far inland and glean folk-
lore out of the beaten track of everyday tourists.
And at night when the harbour slept we would
sail out through the moonlight over silver seas.
You are smiling, you look so different when you
smile ; do you like my picture ? '

'Some of it ! '

'What not ? '

'You ! '

'Thank you.'

'You asked me. Can't you understand where
the spell lies ? It is the freedom, the freshness,
the vague danger, the unknown that has a
witchery for me, ay, for every woman ! '

' Are you incapable of affection, then ? '

' Of course not, I share ' (bitterly) ' that crowning disability of my sex. But not willingly, I
chafe under it. My God, if it were not for that,

we women would master the world. I tell you
men would be no match for us. At heart we
care nothing for laws, nothing for systems. All
your elaborately reasoned codes for controlling
morals or man do not weigh a jot with us
against an impulse, an instinct. We learn those
things from you, you tamed, amenable animals ;
they are not natural to us. It is a wise dis-
position of providence that this untameableness
of ours is corrected by our affections. We forge
our own chains in a moment of softness, and
then ' (bitterly) ' we may as well wear them with
a good grace. Perhaps many of our seeming
contradictions are only the outward evidences
of inward chafing. Bah ! the qualities that go
to make a Napoleon—superstition, want of
honour, disregard of opinion and the eternal I—
are oftener to be found in a woman than a man.
Lucky for the world perhaps that all these
attributes weigh as nothing in the balance with
the need to love if she be a good woman, to be
loved if she is of a coarser fibre.'

'I never met any one like you, you are a
strange woman !'

'No, I am merely a truthful one. Women
talk to me—why, I can't say—but always they

come, strip their hearts and souls naked, and let me see the hidden folds of their natures. The greatest tragedies I have ever read are child's play to those I have seen acted in the inner life of outwardly commonplace women. A woman must beware of speaking the truth to a man ; he loves her the less for it. It is the elusive spirit in her that he divines but cannot seize, that fascinates and keeps him.'

There is a long silence, the sun is waning and the scythes are silent, and overhead the crows are circling, a croaking irregular army, homeward bound from a long day's pillage.

She has made no sign, yet so subtly is the air charged with her that he feels but a few moments remain to him. He goes over and kneels beside her and fixes his eyes on her odd dark face. They both tremble, yet neither speaks. His breath is coming quickly, and the bistre stains about her eyes seem to have deepened, perhaps by contrast as she has paled.

'Look at me !'

She turns her head right round and gazes straight into his face. A few drops of sweat glisten on his forehead.

'You witch woman! what am I to do with myself? Is my moment ended?'

'I think so.'

'Lord, what a mouth!'

'Don't, oh don't!'

'No, I won't. But do you mean it? Am I, who understand your every mood, your restless spirit, to vanish out of your life? You can't mean it. Listen; are you listening to me? I can't see your face; take down your hands. Go back over every chance meeting you and I have had together since I met you first by the river, and judge them fairly. To-day is Monday; Wednesday afternoon I shall pass your gate, and if—if my moment is ended, and you mean to send me away, to let me go with this weary aching . . .'

'A-ah!' she stretches out one brown hand appealingly, but he does not touch it.

'*Hang something white on the lilac bush!*'

She gathers up creel and rod, and he takes her shawl, and, wrapping it round her, holds her a moment in it, and looks searchingly into her eyes, then stands back and raises his hat, and she glides away through the reedy grass.

*　　*　　*　　*　　*

Wednesday morning she lies watching the clouds sail by. A late rose spray nods into the open window, and the petals fall every time. A big bee buzzes in and fills the room with his bass note, and then dances out again. She can hear his footstep on the gravel. Presently he looks in over the half window.

'Get up and come out, 'twill do you good. Have a brisk walk!'

She shakes her head languidly, and he throws a great soft dewy rose with sure aim on her breast.

'Shall I go in and lift you out and put you, "nighty" and all, into your tub?'

'No (impatiently). I'll get up just now.'

The head disappears, and she rises wearily and gets through her dressing slowly, stopped every moment by a feeling of faintness. He finds her presently rocking slowly to and fro with closed eyes, and drops a leaf with three plums in it on to her lap.

'I have been watching four for the last week, but a bird, greedy beggar, got one this morning early—try them. Don't you mind, old girl, I'll pour out my own tea!'

She bites into one and tries to finish it, but cannot.

'You are a good old man!' she says, and
the tears come unbidden to her eyes, and trickle
down her cheeks, dropping on to the plums,
streaking their delicate bloom. He looks un-
easily at her, but doesn't know what to do,
and when he has finished his breakfast he
stoops over her chair and strokes her hair,
saying, as he leaves a kiss on the top of her
head—

'Come out into the air, little woman; do you
a world of good!' And presently she hears
the sharp thrust of his spade above the bee's
hum, leaf rustle, and the myriad late summer
sounds that thrill through the air. It irritates
her almost to screaming point. There is a
practical non-sympathy about it, she can distinguish the regular one, two, three, the thrust,
interval, then pat, pat, on the upturned sod.
To-day she wants some one, and her thoughts
wander to the grey-eyed man who never misun-
derstands her, and she wonders what he would
say to her. Oh, she wants some one so badly to
soothe her. And she yearns for the little mother
who is twenty years under the daisies. The
little mother who is a faint memory strengthened
by a daguerreotype in which she sits with silk-

mittened hands primly crossed on the lap of
her moiré gown, a diamond brooch fastening
the black velvet ribbon crossed so stiffly over
her lace collar, the shining tender eyes looking
steadily out, and her hair in the fashion of
fifty-six. How that spade dominates over
every sound! And what a sickening pain she
has; an odd pain, she never felt it before.
Supposing she were to die, she tries to fancy
how she would look. They would be sure to
plaster her curls down. He might be digging
her grave—no, it is the patch where the early
peas grew; the peas that were eaten with the
twelve weeks' ducklings; she remembers them,
little fluffy golden balls with waxen bills, and
such dainty paddles. Remembers holding an
egg to her ear and listening to it cheep inside
before even there was a chip in the shell.
Strange how things come to life. What! she
sits bolt upright and holds tightly to the chair,
and a questioning, awesome look comes over
her face. Then the quick blood creeps up
through her olive skin right up to her temples,
and she buries her face in her hands and sits
so a long time.

The maid comes in and watches her curiously,

and moves softly about. The look in her eyes is the look of a faithful dog, and she loves her with the same rare fidelity. She hesitates, then goes into the bedroom and stands thoughtfully, with her hands clasped over her breast.

She is a tall, thin, flat-waisted woman, with misty blue eyes and a receding chin. Her hair is pretty.

She turns as her mistress comes in, with an expectant look on her face. She has taken up a night-gown, but holds it idly.

' Lizzie, had you ever a child ? '

The girl's long left hand is ringless, yet she asks it with a quiet insistence as if she knew what the answer would be, and the odd eyes read her face with an almost cruel steadiness. The girl flushes painfully and then whitens, her very eyes seem to pale, and her under lip twitches as she jerks out huskily—

' Yes ! '

' What happened it ? '

' It died, Ma'm.'

' Poor thing ! Poor old Liz ! '

She pats the girl's hand softly, and the latter stands dumbly and looks down at both hands, as if fearful to break the wonder of a caress. She whispers hesitatingly—

' Have you, have you any little things left ? '

And she laughs such a soft, cooing little laugh, like the churring of a ring-dove, and nods shyly back in reply to the tall maid's questioning look. The latter goes out, and comes back with a flat, red-painted deal box and unlocks it. It does not hold very much, and the tiny garments are not of costly material, but the two women pore over them as a gem collector over a rare stone. She has a glimpse of thick crested paper as the girl unties a packet of letters, and looks away until she says tenderly—

' Look, Ma'm ! '

A little bit of hair inside a paper heart. It is almost white, so silky, and so fine, that it is more like a thread of bog wool than a baby's hair. And the mistress, who is a wife, puts her arms round the tall maid, who has never had more than a moral claim to the name, and kisses her in her quick way.

The afternoon is drawing on ; she is kneeling before an open trunk with flushed cheeks and sparkling eyes. A heap of unused, dainty lace trimmed ribbon-decked cambric garments is scattered around her. She holds the soft scented web to her cheek and smiles musingly. Then she rouses herself and sets to work, sorting out the finest, with the narrowest lace and tiniest ribbon, and puckers her swarthy brows, and measures lengths along her middle finger. Then she gets slowly up, as if careful of herself as a precious thing, and half afraid.

' Lizzie! '

' Yes, Ma'm! '

' Wasn't it lucky they were too fine for every day? They will be so pretty. Look at this one with the tiny valenciennes edging. Why, one nightgown will make a dozen little shirts—such elfin-shirts as they are too—and Lizzie ! '

' Yes, Ma'm! '

' Just hang it out on the lilac bush ; mind, the lilac bush ! '

' Yes, Ma'm.'

' Or Lizzie, wait—I 'll do it myself! '

NOW SPRING HAS COME

A CONFIDENCE

'When the spring time comes, gentle Annie, and the flowers are
  blossoming on the plain!
Lal, lal, la, la, la, lallailalla, lal, lal, lal, la, la, la, la, la,
When the spring time comes, gentle Annie, and the mockin' bird is
  singing on the tree!' . . .

'I DON'T believe that mocking-bird line belongs to the song at all, Lizzie, you never do get a thing right!'

The words have a partly irritated, partly contemptuous tone that seems oddly at variance with the size of the child who utters them. She is lying flat on her stomach on the floor, resting her elbows at each side of a book she is reading, holding her sharp chin in the palms of her hands, waving her skinny legs in unconscious time to the half tired, half feverish lilt of the nurse as she jogs the baby in time to the tune. She gazes, as she speaks, at the girl with a pair of unusually bright penetrating eyes. This mocking-bird line never fails to annoy her.

'Troth, an if I cud get the young limb to slape I wouldn't care if 'twas mockin'-birds or tom-cats!' is the indifferent answer.

*   *   *   *   *   *

Strange how some trivial thing will jog a link in a chain of association, and set it vibrating until it brings one face to face with scenes and people long forgotten in some prison cell in one's brain; calling to new life a red-haired girl, with sherry-brown eyes, and a flat back, pacing a nursery floor in impatient endeavour to get a fractious child to sleep—ay, her very voice and her persistent mixing of mocking-birds and spring time. So muses the child twenty years after, as, past her first youth, with only the eyes and the smile unchanged, she lies on a bear-skin before the fire on a chilly evening in late spring, and goes over a recent experience. A half humorous smile with a tinge of mockery in it plays round her lips as she says—

'Twenty years ago.   Queer how it should fit in after all that time!'

*   *   *   *   *   *

'Tell you how it was?   That is not very easy, pathos may become bathos in the telling.   Let me see.   Of course it was chance, or is there

any such thing as chance? Say fate, instead.
The three old ladies who spin our destinies
were in want of amusement, so they pitched
on me. They sent their messenger to me in
the guise of a paper-backed novel with a taking
name. I was waiting in a shop for some papers
I had ordered when it struck me. I took it up.
The author was unknown to me. I opened it
at haphazard and a line caught me. I read on.
I was roused by the bookseller's suave voice.

'That is a very bad book, Madam. One of
the modern realistic school, a *tendenz roman*, I
would not advise Madam to read it!'

'A-ah, indeed!'

I laid it down and left the shop, but the
words I had read kept dancing before me, I
saw them written across the blue of the sky,
in the sun streaks on the pavement, and the
luminous delicacy of the Norwegian summer
nights. They were impressed on my brain in
vivid colour, glowing, blushing with ardour as
they were. Weeks passed; one afternoon time
hung heavily on my hands, and I sent for the
book. I read all that afternoon; let the telling
words, the passionate pain, the hungry yearning,
all the tragedy of a man's soul-strife with evil

and destiny, sorrow and sin, bite into my sentient being. When the book was finished I was consumed with a desire to see and know the author. I never reasoned that the whole struggle might only be an extraordinarily clever intuitive analysis of a possible experience. I accepted it as real, and I wanted to help this man. I longed to tell him in his loneness, that one human being, and that one a woman, had courage to help him. The abstract ego of the novel haunted me. I have a will of my own, so I set to work to find him. It was not so easy. None of my acquaintances knew him, or of him. He was a strange meteor, and as the book was condemned by the orthodox I had to feel my way cautiously. Isn't it dreadful to think what slaves we are to custom? I wonder shall we ever be able to tell the truth, ever be able to live fearlessly according to our own light, to believe that what is right for us must be right? It seems as if all the religions, all the advancement, all the culture of the past, has only been a forging of chains to cripple posterity, a laborious building up of moral and legal prisons based on false conceptions of sin and shame, to cramp men's minds and hearts and souls, not to speak of women's. What half creatures we are, we women! Hermaphrodite by force of circumstances. Deformed results of a fight of centuries between physical suppression and natural impulse to fulfil our destiny. Every social revolution has told hardest on us : when a sacrifice was demanded, let woman make it. And yet there are men, and the best of them, who see all this and would effect a change, if they knew how. Why it came about? Because men manufactured an artificial morality, made sins of things that were as clean in themselves as the pairing of birds on the wing ; crushed nature, robbed it of its beauty and meaning, and established a system that means war, and always war, because it is a struggle between instinctive truths and cultivated lies. Yes, I know I speak hotly, but my heart burns in me sometimes, and I hate myself. It's a bad thing when a man or woman has a contempt for himself. There's nothing like a good dose of love fever (in other words, a waking to the fact that one is a higher animal with a destiny to fulfil) to teach one self-knowledge, to give one a glimpse into the contradictory issues of one's individual nature. Study yourself, and what

will you find? Just what I did; the weak, the
inconsequent, the irresponsible. In one word,
the untrue feminine is of man's making, whilst
the strong, the natural, the true womanly is of
God's making. It is easy to read as a primer;
but how change it? Go back to my poet!
Well, at length an old bookseller I knew gave
me surer information. My intuition was not at
fault, the experiences were wrung from the
man's soul. As the old superstition has it, a
dagger dipped in a man's heart-blood will
always strike home, so no wonder they pierced
me with their passion, despair, and brave endurance. What the old fellow wrote to him I
know not, but I got an unconventional pretty
letter from him, and it ended in our writing to
one another.

As my time to leave drew near, the desire to
see him became overpowering. I could afford
it; he could not. It ended in our arranging to
meet at a little town on the coast. It is strange
how the idea of a person one has never seen
can possess one as completely as this did me.
I, who, as you know, think as little of starting
alone for say, Mexico, as another woman
of going to afternoon tea, who have trotted

the globe without male assistance, felt as
tremulously stirred as at confirmation day.
There are days that stand out in the gallery of
one's remembrances clean painted as a Van
de Hooge, with a sharp clearness. I slept on
board, and early the next morning, it was
Sunday, I stood on deck watching the coast as
we glided through the water that danced in
delicious September sunshine. I was happily
expectant. At dinner hour we passed a fjord,
a lovely deep blue fjord winding to our right
as we passed, with the spire of a church just
visible amongst the fir trees round the bend.
Boats of all kinds, from a smart cutter to a
pram were coming out after the service. The
white sails swelled as they caught the breeze,
flapped as they tacked, hung listlessly a second,
and then dashed with a swerve, like swift snowy-
winged birds, through the water. I had not
troubled with church-going of late years. Why?
oh, speculation—weariness of soul that found
no drop of consolation in religious observance,
maybe that might be the reason. But all those
honest simple folks in their Sunday bravery, fair-
haired girls with their psalm-books wrapped up
in their only silk kerchief, the ring of laughter

echoing across the water, the magic of sun
and sky, mountain and fjord, made me feel
that I, too, was church-going, and I felt
strangely happy. It is the off-moments that
we do not count as playing any part in our
lives that are, after all, the best we have. I am
afraid it would be impossible to make you see
things as I felt them. I went up to the hotel
when I landed ; I had the reputation of riches,
the hotel was at my service. I inquire for
him, go down to my sitting-room, send him my
card, and wait. I wait with an odd feeling that
I am outside myself, watching myself as it were.
I can see the very childishness of my figure,
the too slight hips and bust, the flash of rings
on my fingers ; they are pressed against my
heart, for it is beating hatefully ; ay, the very
expectant side-poise of head is visible to me
somehow. It flashes across me as I stand that
so might a slave wait for the coming of a new
master, and I laugh at myself for my want-wit
agitation. A knock. . . . 'Come in !' . . . The
door opens, and I am satisfied. In the space
of a second's gaze I meet what my soul has
been waiting for,—ah, how long ? I think
always : Have I lived before in some other

life, that no surprise touches me? That it is just as if I am only meeting the embodiment of a disintegrated floating image that has often flashed before my consciousness, and flown before I could fix it? Has this man or some psychical part of this man been in touch with me before, or how is it? I stand still and stretch out my hand. I check an impulse to put out both. I feel so tremulously happy. I know before he speaks how his voice will sound, what his touch will be like before he clasps my hand. It is odd how the most important crisis of our lives often comes upon us in the most commonplace way. It is the fashion to decry love, yet the vehemence of the denials, the keenness of the weapons of satire and scepticism that are turned against it, only prove its existence. As long as man is man and woman is woman, it will be to them at some time the sweetest, and possibly the most fatal interest in life. Thrust it aside for ambition or gain, slight it as you will, sooner or later it will have its revenge. I had felt no breath of it as maid, wife, or widow, my heart had been a free, wild, shy thing, jessed by my will. Sometimes, by way of experiment, I let it fly to some one for an hour, but always

to call it back again to my own safe keeping.
Now it left me. We sat and talked, rather I
talked, I think, and he listened. He said my
going to see him even on literary grounds was
eccentric, but then it seemed I had a way of
doing as I pleased without exciting much comment. How did he know that? Oh, he had
heard it! Was I really going away? How
tiresome it was, really awfully tiresome! What
was he like? Well, an American bison or a
lion. You might put his head amongst the
rarest and handsomest heads in the world. Pre-
judiced in his favour! No, not a bit. His
hands, for instance, are great labourer's hands,
freckled too; I don't like his gait either, indeed
a dozen things. What we talked about? well,
as I said, he listened mostly, laughed with a
great joyous boyish laugh with a deep musical
note in it. He has a deferential manner and a
very caressing smile; a trick, too, of throwing
back his head and tossing his crest of hair.
Why he laughed? well, I suppose I made
him. I told him all about myself, turned myself inside out, good and bad alike, as one
might the pocket of an old gown, laughed at my
own expense, hid nothing. An extraordinary

thing to do, was it? I suppose it was—but
the whole thing was rather unusual. He got
up and walked about. Sometimes he thrust his
hands in his pockets and exclaimed 'The Deuce,'
etc. I fancy he learnt a good deal about me in
a few hours. You see it was not as if one were
talking to a stranger, it was as if one had met
part of one's self one had lost for a long time
and was filling up the gaps made during the
absence. You can't understand. I think we
were both very happy. He admired—no, that
is not the word—he was taken with me, that is
better. He said my hands were ' as small as a
child's,' the tablecloth was dark red plush
that made a good background. He pointed
timidly, as a great shy boy might, to one of my
rings. You see they don't as a rule wear many
rings up there. I suppose they gave an impression of wealth. ' That one is very beautiful!'
I laughed, I was so glad my hands were pretty ;
pretty hands last so much longer than a pretty
face. I laughed too at his finger, it had such a
deferential expression about it, and I called
him a great child. I think we were both like
two great children, we had found a common
interest to rejoice in—we had found ourselves

Every moment was delightful, we were making
discoveries, finding we had had like experiences,
had both hungered, both known want, were both
of an age. We were both unconventional, and
were shaking hands mentally all the time. I
don't remember now what it was he said, but
I remember I was obliged to drop my head,
and I felt I was smiling from sheer delicious
pleasure. He cried laughingly : 'You say I am
a great child, you are a child yourself when
you smile !' He was to have supper with me,
and he went away for an hour. After he left I
walked over to a long mirror and looked at myself. Tried to fancy how *he* saw me ; that might
be different, you know. I had colour, life, eyes
like stars, trembling, smiling lips. There was
something quivering, alert about me. I scarce
knew myself. Of course the same hips, figure,
features were reflected there—it was something
shining through that struck me as foreign.
Do you know what I did ? I danced all round
the room. Shows what an idiot an old woman
can be. By the way, he denied that I was old.
I was like a little girl—but a remarkable little
girl. No wonder people always noticed me, as if I
were a somebody. How did he know that ? oh,

he had heard it, for that matter seen it too, at
the pier. He knew the moment I stepped off
the boat that it was I. Yes, people always
stared at me, but how could he know? Ah!
presentiment perhaps. So he was on the pier?
why did he not come and meet me? No audible
answer, but a slow reddening up to the roots
of his fair hair. I do not know quite how he
conveyed it, but I had the sensation, a charming one, of being treated as a queen. But to
go back. I sat or rather lay in an arm-chair at
the window and watched the water and the
ships. It was getting dusk, the luminous dusk
of the north, as if a soft transparent purple veil
is being dropped gently over the world. The
fjord was full of lights from the different crafts
at anchor, and the heaven full of stars, and the
longer one looked up there, the more one
saw myriads of glimmering eyes of light, until
one's brain seemed full of their brightness, and
one forgot one's body in gazing. Long silvery
streaks glistened through the heaving water,
like the flash of feeding trout, and lads and
lasses in boats rowed to and fro, and human
vibration seemed to thrill from them, filling the
atmosphere with man and woman. And the

silken air caressed my face as the touch of cool soft fingers. I had a feeling of perfect well-being; one does not get many such moments in one's life, does one? I think I just was happy, rehearsing the hours that flew too quickly, recalling every look, tone, gesture, and smile. The *jomfru* came in to lay the table. She knew me from a previous visit and began to talk, but I wanted to be alone with my thoughts. So I went up stairs, washed my hands and puffed them with sweet-smelling powder, and then when I went down again and sat and waited, I clasped them up over my head to make them white. He came back, flung his hat on the sofa out of sheer boyish delight at being back, came over and stood and looked down at me and I laughed up to him. If I were to talk until Doomsday, I could not make you understand what I cannot yet understand my-self. After supper, at which I just sipped my tea and watched him, we sat at the window and looked out at the purple world. I had told him he might smoke. . . Well? well, we talked, and we talked when we were both silent, and he, I mean his thinking self came to me, and I, well, I believe, from the moment he came into the room, all the best of me went straight to him. The lights out in the harbour twinkled, a star fell, and I wished—well, wishes are foolish. I think he must have been watching my face, for when our eyes met, he smiled as if he understood. Sometimes he jumped up and stood rocking a chair backwards and forwards. He was sorry I was going away! Yes? oh, we might meet again! That might be difficult! Indeed? I should have thought *he* would be the last person in the world to say it was difficult to meet. He laughed at that, with a quick sidelong look he has, like a Finn dog; and said I was sharp, awfully sharp, as if he liked being caught. By the way, he occasionally used strong language, said I must forgive him, he wasn't very used to ladies' society.

At ten I said I would say good-night for conventionality's sake. He begged, humbly it struck me, for a little longer. I was to leave by the steamer at eight in the morning—would be down at seven—he might come to me. Would I give him a portrait of myself? Yes, I would get one specially done. As much in profile as possible, he thought that would be happier.—Yes.—He came to the top of the stairs with me, and when we bade good-night he took my hand and held it curiously as if it were something fearfully fragile, and stood and watched me down the corridor. And will you credit it? I felt inclined to run like an awkward little school-girl. I said prayers that night, thanked God—I don't quite know what for—I suppose I did then—perhaps for being happy. I looked at my foreign self in the glass too— and when the light was out. . . . Yes? . . . I did what you and every other woman might do, I cuddled my face to an imaginary face, rubbed my cheek to an imaginary cheek, whispered a God bless you! and fell asleep.

I was down before seven, paid my bill, and sat waiting, with the little tray, with its thick white cups and lumpy yellow cream before me. He came. Such a glad man, with glad eyes, glad smile, and outstretched hands. And I, I was so glad, too, that I could have shouted out for very joy of living. I might have been drinking some magic elixir instead of coffee.

'It is tiresome!' he said impatiently.

'What is tiresome? You have said that so often.'

'It is tiresome when a person one wants so

badly to keep in the country is going out
of it.'

'Supposing I were to stay in it, you would
probably be in one place and I in another. It
is only a question of a little dearer postage!'

We both laughed at that. It takes such a
little thing to make one laugh when one is
happy. Then the steamer came in sight, and
we walked down through the bright morning to
the pier, and went on board. He stood silently.
We only looked at one another. It did not then
strike me as odd—it does now. The first bell
rang! I felt a chill steal over me. 'It is tiresome, it is hateful!' His smile had flown ; and
old deep lines and traces of past suffering I had
not noticed before showed plainly. . . .

'I will come back,' I said, 'when the winter
is over!'

'Ay, but winter is long, or it used to be!'

'No matter, I will come with the spring!'

The second bell rang. . . . Ah, why can't we
do as our hearts bid us? We have one short
life, and it is spoiled by chains of our own
forging, in deference to narrow custom. I
shivered. There was after all an autumn chill
in the air. I hate the sound of a steamer bell

now. . . . The third bell. . . . We turn, and I
tighten my small fingers in his great hand, and
I say good-bye and God bless you ! Not from
a purely religious conception of God. Unless it
be that God, and I think it does, means all that
is good and beautiful, tender and best. I might
have said 'The best I can think of befall you !'
A second later and the steamer rail separates
us. I look into his soul through his eyes, and
see it is sorry, regretful ; as sorry as I am glad
it is so—he is sorry I am going from him, and
in that short concentrated gaze his soul comes
to me as I would have it come to me.

'When spring comes !' I whisper as I lean
over to him, whilst the steamer glides out. He
follows it to the end of the pier, and stands
there as long as we are in sight. If he had
held out his arms and said : 'Woman, stay with
me !' I would, I fear, have jumped down and
stayed. Didn't know anything about him !
No, that is true, only that I had been waiting
for something ever since I was old enough to
have a want, and that he was that something,
that I was nearly thirty when I found him, and
. . . life is short !

I was so glad, in spite of leaving him, that I

believe I thought the sun shone differently—I almost asked some people on deck if they did not think that the day was quite the loveliest day that ever dawned since the world was a world; if there was not something peculiarly and singularly delicious in the very air? I found a quiet sofa, and lay with closed eyes and lived it over again.

The rest is more difficult to tell you. . . . I was insanely happy, then I was intensely miserable. I sent him my portrait and a letter, and counted the days and the hours to a reply. It came. I stole away to read all the warm meaning ill concealed under the words of it. Slept with it under my pillow, carried it in my bosom, and answered it straight from my heart. Why try and tell you of the aftertime? I would not go through that winter again for anything in the world. Hope, fear, suspense, joy, despondency, all the strongest feelings that can torture or wear out a heart, were mine. I longed to be up on a high mountain alone with my dream. I wonder does a man ever realise the beauty there is in a woman's thought of him. What kind were the letters? Warm, passionate, yet with a *reservatio mentalis* that hurt me, but always with a 'When spring comes!' in them. It is amazing to what depths of folly a human being can descend. I had his photograph on my table. I greeted it as a Russian peasant his household saint. . . . It would be hard to find my match in idiocy. I felt a letter coming, and waited with strained ears and fever-racked nerves for the postman's knock. Do you know there is something touchingly pitiful in the way one finds out all the tender bits in a letter and re-reads them. I have kissed a thumb-mark on the paper. Heavens, how the days dragged! I was ill with yearning thought. Night brought no rest but the comfort of being alone. All the years of my life were not as long as that weary winter. Sleep fled, and nervous pain took its place. . . . It was foolish, exceedingly foolish, because it was fatal to my looks. At the rare times I looked at myself I got a glimpse of a thin waxen yellow face with dark ringed eyes, and I was certainly older-looking. Thinking of it all dispassionately, I am inclined to believe I was hysterical. How many of the follies and frailties of women are really due to hysterical rather than moral irresponsibility, is a question. You see there is no time of sowing wild oats for women ; we repress, and repress, and then some day we stumble on the man who just satisfies our sexual and emotional nature, and then there is shipwreck of some sort. When we shall live larger and freer lives, we shall be better balanced than we are now. If what I suffered is love, all I can say is I would not ask a better sample of the conventional hell's pain. Hu-s-sh! Very well, I won't say those things!

It is bad enough to be a fool and not to know it, but to be a fool and feel with every fibre of your being, every shred of your understanding that you are one, and that there is no help for it ; that all your philosophy won't aid you ; that you are one great want, stilled a little by a letter, only to be haunted afresh by the personality of another creature tortured with doubts and hurt by your loss of self-respect. . . . A-ah! it was a long winter! Then the New Year came and went, and time dragged slowly but surely. At length the Almanacs said it was spring-time, and the girls at the street corners called : 'vilets, sweet vilets!'; and the milliners marked down guinea bonnets to 12s. 11d., and I watched each token of its coming with a fearsome joyous expectation

. . . 'Go on,' ah yes, I 'll go on, where was I ?
Oh, Spring was coming, wasn't it ? I do not
laugh as I used to, eh ? How used I laugh ?
I forget. Well, I won't laugh if it hurts you,
dear, not even at myself.

Well, once again, I was standing at a table
in an hotel room waiting. It is the simple
things that are so hard to describe, and that
are most complicated in their effects. I said
again 'Come in !' held fast to the table with
my left hand and smiled—to be accurate, began
a smile. Spring is later up there, perhaps
some of the winter's frost was still in the
atmosphere, for something froze it on my lips.
I felt a curious stiffening in my face, and the
touch of his hand did not thaw me. Feel
happy ? No, I was numb in one way and
yet keenly alive to impressions. I felt as if
my nerve-net was outside my skin, not under
it, and that the exposure to the air and surrounding influences made it intensely, acutely
sensitive. I seemed to see with my sense of
feeling as well as my sight. You know how
in great cold you seem to burn your hand
with an icy heat if you suddenly grasp a
piece of iron ; well, I felt as though I was

touched by glowing shivers; that sounds nonsense, but it expresses the feeling. Why? I
don't know why. I was analysing, being analysed, criticising, being criticised. It was all so
different, you see. Supposing you had just
sipped a beaker of exhilarating, life-giving,
rich wine with an exquisite bouquet, and a
glow that steals through you and witches
and warms you; and suddenly, without your
knowing how it happens, the draught is transformed into lukewarm water, or 'Polly' without
the 'dash' in it. What did he say? Let me
think. Oh yes, I was wretchedly thin. Odd
how things strike one. I once saw a repre-
sentation of Holberg's Stundeslöse in Copen-
hagen. One of the characters is an ancient
housekeeper, with a long money-bag, who is,
as they term it, 'marriage-sick.' A match is
arranged between her and a young spark in
the village. The scene is this:—whilst the
monetary part of the affair is being arranged
by the notary, etc., he says to her:—'Permit
me to pass my hand over your bosom, mistress?'
She simpers, and I shall never forget the
comical expression of dismay with which the
suitor rolls his eyes and drops his jaw as

he turns aside. I felt rather than saw the comprehensive look which accompanied his comment on my thinness, and that scene flashed across my inner vision. Odd, was it not? A sort of sympathetic after-comprehension. It was as if I, too, were having a hand passed across the flatness of my figure.

'Yes, I have got thin'—silence—had I been very ill? Yes, very! Was that why I was so pale? It was fearful, not a tinge of warm colour in my face. One would be afraid to touch me. I felt as if I were being totted up. Item, so much colour, item, so much flesh. . . . Had I been worried? I had lost that buoyant childishness that was so attractive. Ah, yes, I had dwelt too much on a trouble I had. Did I sleep? not much! That was foolish! I ought to eat plenty too. I looked as if I didn't eat enough, my eyes and cheeks were hollowed out. Ah, yes, no doubt I did look older than in Autumn! I was not contradicted. I would have told a little lie to spare a man's feelings. Men are perhaps more conscientious. What else? I am rehearsing it all as best I can. Oh, my hands were altered, he thought they were not so small,

eh? . . . Might be my wrists were less round,
that made a difference! Did it? They certainly
were larger, and not so white. . . . Did he kiss
me? Oh, yes. You see I wanted to sift this
thing thoroughly to get clear into my head
what ground I was standing on. So I let
him. They were merely lip kisses; his spirit
did not come to mine, and I was simply
analysing them all the time. Did I not
feel anything? Yes, I did, deeply hurt. Ah,
I can't say how they hurt me; they lacked
everything a kiss, as the expression of the
strongest, best feeling of a man and woman,
can hold. How do I know? My dear woman,
have you never dreamt, felt, had *intuitive experiences*? I have. I am not sure that I had
not a keen sense of the ludicrous side of the
whole affair, that one portion of my soul was
not having a laugh at the other's expense.
I do not quite know what I had been expecting.
'Tis true he had written me beautiful letters.
You see he is too much of a word-artist to
write anything else. Treated me badly? . . .
No, I am not prepared to say that he did.
I am glad he was too honest to hide his
startled realisation of the fact that Autumn

and Spring are different seasons, and that
one's feelings may undergo a change in a winter.
I do not see why I should resent that. Why,
it would be punishing him for having cared
for me. To put it in his words: 'I came as
a strangely lovely dream into his life.' Probably the whole mistake lay in that. He
thought of me as a dream lady with dainty
hands, idealised me—and wrote to the dream
creature. When I came back in the flesh,
he realised that I was a prosaic fact, with less
charming hands, a tendency to leanness, and
coming crow's feet. His look of dismayed
awakening was simply delicious. I wish I
could catch and fasten the fleeting images that
flit across my memory, you would grasp my
mental attitude better. In the midst of all my
pain, I was sitting next him, and he was stroking my hand mechanically, I noticed a glass
case on the wall containing an Italian landscape
with ball-blue sky and pink lakes. Pasteboard
figures of Dutch-peasant build, with Zouave
jackets, Tyrolese hats, and bandaged legs,
figured in the foreground. You wound it up,
and the figures danced to a *varsoviana*. I
was listening to him, and yet at the same time

I caught myself imagining how he and I would look dressed like that, bobbing about to the old-fashioned tune. I could hardly keep from shrieking with laughter. He had a turn-down collar on ; he ought always to wear unstarched linen—it and his throat didn't fit. You cannot understand me ? Dearest woman, I do not pretend to understand the thing myself.

Did we not talk about anything ? Of course we did. Tolstoi and his doctrine of celibacy. Ibsen's Hedda. Strindberg's view of the female animal. And we agreed that Friedrich Nietzche appealed to us immensely. You must make allowances. Here was a man passionately attached to his art. His art that he had been treating churlishly for months, for the sake of a dream. The dream was out, and he feared her revenge. That is the one potent element of consolation for me. If one has made an idiot of one's-self, it is at least self-consoling to have done so for a genius. He chose the better part, if you come to think of it. The man or woman who jeopardises a great talent, be it of writing, painting, or acting for marriage's sake, is bartering a precious birthright for a mess of pottage—mostly indifferent pottage. And even if it were excellent, it is bound to pall, when one has it every day. There never was a marriage yet in which one was not a loser ; and it is generally the more gifted half who has to pay the heavier toll. . . . I believe he was intensely sorry for me ; I asked him once you know, half playfully, half maliciously, if he had meant something ; something deliciously tender which I quoted out of one of his letters. He paled to his lips, closed his eyes for a second, and I saw drops of sweat break out on his forehead. I sprang up and turned aside his answer. I remember when I was a little child I never would pick a flower. I always fancied they felt it and bled to death. I used to sneak behind and gather up all those my playmates threw down on the road or fields, and put them, stalks down, into the water in the ditch or brook—even now I can't wear them. I did not wish to hurt him either, he could not help his passion-flower withering. I suppose it was written that my love should turn, like fairy gold, into withered leaves in my grasp . . . What, dear ? a white hair ! oh, I saw several lately. How did it end ? Oh, he said that he was going away to glean material for a new

book ; that he would burn my letters ; it was
safer and wiser to burn letters. No, I did not
ask him, he volunteered it. He asked me, did
I not think so ? I said Yes. But is it not
marvellous how dazzlingly swift our thoughts
can travel ; like light. Whilst I was saying ' yes,'
one often regretted not having burned letters ;
receipts, receipts for bills were really the only
things of importance to keep. I was thinking
and crying inwardly over my letters. Such
letters. One only writes once like that, I think.
All the perfume of the flowers I ever smelt, all
the sun-glints on hill and sea, all the strains of
music and light and love I had garnered from
the glad fresh young years, when I tossed cowslip balls in the meadows, were crystallised
into love-words in those letters of mine. It
seemed to me often that the words burnt
with a white flame as I wrote them, and I was
shy when I saw them written. And he said : ' I
shall burn them !' much as you might say : ' I
shall take the trimming off that last summer hat
of mine.' I did not like to think of his burning
them, perhaps with his old washing bills. Do
you know, if I had a finger or toe cut off, I
wouldn't like them to take it away, I 'd like to

bury it. A sort of feel, I suppose. . . . Well, we said good-bye ! I felt as if I had a sponge with a lot of holes in it, instead of a heart, and that all the feeling had oozed away through them. He was glad to go, I think ; he felt a brute, I daresay, yet how could he help it ?

＊　　　＊　　　＊　　　＊　　　＊

Were you ever at the Scandinavian church in the Docks ? I went one Sunday after I came back. I like those blue-eyed, seafaring folk ; and the priest wears a black gown and stiff ruff like Luther of mixed renown. An apple-tree outside the open door was struggling to open its delicate pink blossoms ; each petal had a tinge of soot ; it reminded me of the pretty cheeks of a grimy maid-of-all-work. I sat still. A sunbeam came in and pierced Judas's heart, as he sat at his section of the Last Supper table, and it wrapped me up in a sun haze, so that all was misty around me. The sermon only struck my ear with a soothing, drowsy roll, something like the wave-note of the in-curling sea in the Mediterranean, a *legato* accompaniment to my thoughts ; and I had a grand burial all by myself. I dug a deep grave and laid all my dreams and foolish wishes and sweet hopes in it. A puff of wind rustled through the riggings of the ships and set the flags with their yellow cross fluttering, and scattered a few of the tender blooms over it . . . and, ah well . . . it seems hard to realise now Spring has gone!

Do you really think that crinolines will be worn?

THE SPELL OF THE WHITE ELF

HAVE you ever read out a joke that seemed excruciatingly funny, or repeated a line of poetry that struck you as being inexpressibly tender, and found that your listener was not impressed as you were? I have, and so it may be that this will bore you, though it was momentous enough to me.

I had been up in Norway to receive a little legacy that fell to me, and though my summer visits were not infrequent, I had never been up there in mid-winter, at least not since I was a little child tobogganing with Hans Jörgen (Hans Jörgen Dahl is his full name), and that was long ago. We are connected. Hans Jörgen and I were both orphans, and a cousin—we called her aunt—was one of our guardians. He was her favourite; and when an uncle on my mother's side—she was Cornish born; my father, a ship captain, met her at Dartmouth—offered to take me, I think she was glad to let me go. I

was a lanky girl of eleven, and Hans Jörgen
and I were sweethearts. We were to be
married some day, we had arranged all that,
and he reminded me of it when I was going
away, and gave me a silver perfume box, with
a gilt crown on top, that had belonged to his
mother. And later when he was going to
America he came to see me first; he was a
long freckled hobbledehoy, with just the same
true eyes and shock head. I was, I thought,
quite grown up, I had passed my 'intermediate'
and was condescending as girls are. But I don't
think it impressed Hans Jörgen much, for he
gave me a little ring, turquoise forget-me-nots
with enamelled leaves and a motto inside—a
quaint old thing that belonged to a sainted aunt
—they keep things a long time in Norway—
and said he would send for me; but of course
I laughed at that. He has grown to be a great
man out in Cincinnati and waits always. I
wrote later and told him I thought marriage a
vocation and I hadn't one for it; but Hans
Jörgen took no notice; just said he'd wait. He
understands waiting, I'll say that for Hans
Jörgen.

I have been alone now for five years, working away, though I was left enough to keep me before. Somehow I have not the same gladness in my work of late years. Working for one's-self seems a poor end even if one puts by money. But this has little or nothing to do with the white elf, has it?

Christiania is a singular city if one knows how to see under the surface, and I enjoyed my stay there greatly. The Hull boat was to sail at 4.30, and I had sent my things down early, for I was to dine at the Grand at two with a cousin, a typical Christiania man. It was a fine clear day, and Karl Johann was thronged with folks. The band was playing in the park, and pretty girls and laughing students walked up and down. Every one who is anybody may generally be seen about that time. Henrik Ibsen—if you did not know him from his portrait, you would take him to be a prosperous merchant—was going home to dine; but Björnstjerne Björnson, in town just then, with his grand leonine head, and the kind, keen eyes behind his glasses, was standing near the Storthing House with a group of politicians, probably discussing the vexed question of separate consulship. In no city does one see such characteristic odd faces and such queerly cut clothes. The streets are full of students. The farmers' sons amongst them are easily recognised by their homespun, sometimes home-made suits, their clever heads and intelligent faces ; from them come the writers, and brain carriers of Norway. The Finns, too, have a distinctive type of head and a something elusive in the expression of their changeful eyes. But all, the town students, too, of easier manners and slangier tongues—all alike are going, as finances permit, to dine in restaurant or steam-kitchen. I saw the *menu* for to-day posted up outside the door of the latter as I passed—'Rice porridge and salt meat soup, 6d.,' and Hans Jörgen came back with a vivid picture of childhood days, when every family in the little coast-town where we lived had a fixed *menu* for every day in the week ; and it was quite a distinction to have meat balls on pickled herring day, or ale soup when all the folks in town were cooking omelettes with bacon. How he used to eat rice porridge in those days ! I can see him now put his heels together and give his awkward bow as he said, 'Tak for Maden tante !' Well, we are sitting in the

Grand *Café* after dinner, at a little table near
the door, watching the people pass in and out.
An ubiquitous 'sample-count' from Berlin is
measuring his wits with a young Norwegian
merchant; he is standing green chartreuse; it
pays to be generous even for a German, when
you can oust honest Leeds cloth with German
shoddy. At least so my cousin says. He
knows every one by sight, and points out all
the celebrities to me. Suddenly he bows pro-
foundly. I look round. A tall woman with very
square shoulders, and gold-rimmed spectacles
is passing us with two gentlemen. She is
English by her tailor-made gown and little
shirt-front, and noticeable anywhere.

'That lady,' says my cousin, 'is a compatriot
of yours. She is a very fine person, a very
learned lady; she has been looking up referats
in the university bibliothek. Professor Sturm
—he is a good friend of me—did tell me. I
forget her name; she is married. I suppose her
husband he stay at home and keep the house!'

My cousin has just been refused by a young
lady dentist, who says she is too comfortably
off to change for a small housekeeping business,
so I excuse his sarcasm. We leave as the time

draws on and sleigh down to the steamer. I
like the jingle of the bells, and I feel a little
sad. There is a witchery about the country that
creeps into one and works like a love-philter,
and if one has once lived up there, one never
gets it out of one's blood again. I go on
board and lean over and watch the people.
There are a good many for winter-time. The
bell rings. Two sleighs drive up and my compatriot and her friends appear. She shakes
hands with them and comes leisurely up the
gangway. The thought flits through me that
she would cross it in just that cool way if she
were facing death ; it is foolish, but most of our
passing thoughts are just as inconsequent.
She calls down a remembrance to some one in
such pretty Norwegian, much prettier than
mine, and then we swing round. Handker-
chiefs wave in every hand, never have I seen
such persistent handkerchief-waving as at the
departure of a boat in Norway. It is a
national characteristic. If you live at the
mouth of a fjord, and go to the market town
at the head of it for your weekly supply of
coffee beans, the population give you a 'send
off' with fluttering kerchiefs. It is as universal

as the 'Thanks.' Hans Jörgen says I am anglicised and only see the ridiculous side, forgetting the kind feelings that prompt it. I find a strange pleasure in watching the rocks peep out under the snow, the children dragging their hand-sleds along the ice. All the little bits of winter life of which I get flying glimpses as we pass, bring back scenes grown dim in the years between. There is a mist ahead; and when we pass Dröbak cuddled like a dormouse for winter's sleep I go below. A bright coal fire burns in the open grate of the stove, and the *Rollo* saloon looks very cosy. My compatriot is stretched in a big arm-chair reading. She is sitting comfortably with one leg crossed over the other, in the manner called 'shockingly unladylike' of my early lessons in deportment. The flame flickers over the patent leather of her neat low-heeled boot, and strikes a spark from the pin in her tie. There is something manlike about her. I don't know where it lies, but it is there. Her hair curls in grey flecked rings about her head; it has not a cut look, seems rather to grow short naturally. She has a charming tubbed look. Of course every lady is alike clean, but some men and

women have an individual look of sweet clean-
ness that is a beauty of itself. She feels my
gaze and looks up and smiles. She has a rare
smile, it shows her white teeth and softens her
features :

'The fire is cosy, isn't it ? I hope we shall
have an easy passage, so that it can be kept
in.'

I answer something in English.

She has a trick of wrinkling her brows, she
does it now as she says :

'A-ah, I should have said you were Norsk.
Are you not really ? Surely you have a typical
head, or eyes and hair at the least ? '

'Half of me is Norsk, but I have lived a long
time in England.'

'Father of course ; case of " there was a sailor
loved a lass," was it not ? '

I smile an assent and add : 'I lost them both
when I was very young.'

A reflective look steals over her face. It is
stern in repose ; and as she seems lost in some
train of thought of her own I go to my cabin
and lie down ; the rattling noises and the smell
of paint makes me feel ill. I do not go out
again. I wake next morning with a sense of

fear at the stillness. There is no sound but a lapping wash of water at the side of the steamer, but it is delicious to lie quietly after the vibration of the screw and the sickening swing. I look at my watch; seven o'clock. I cannot make out why there is such a silence, as we only stop at Christiansand long enough to take cargo and passengers. I dress and go out. The saloon is empty but the fire is burning brightly. I go to the pantry and ask the stewardess when we arrived? Early, she says; all the passengers for here are already gone on shore; and there is a thick fog outside, goodness knows how long we 'll be kept. I go to the top of the stairs and look out; the prospect is uninviting and I come down again and turn over some books on the table; in Russian, I think. I feel sure they are hers.

'Good-morning!' comes her pleasant voice. How alert and bright-eyed she is! It is a pick-me-up to look at her.

'You did not appear last night? Not given in already, I hope!'

She is kneeling on one knee before the fire, holding her palms to the glow, and with her figure hidden in her loose, fur-lined coat and the light showing up her strong face under the little tweed cap, she seems so like a clever-faced slight man, that I feel I am conventionally guilty in talking so freely to her. She looks at me with a deliberate critical air, and then springs up.

'Let me give you something for your head! Stewardess, a wine-glass!'

I should not dream of remonstrance—not if she were to command me to drink sea-water; and I am not complaisant as a rule.

When she comes back I swallow it bravely, but I leave some powder in the glass; she shakes her head, and I finish this too. We sat and talked, or at least she talked and I listened. I don't remember what she said, I only know that she was making clear to me most of the things that had puzzled me for a long time; questions that arise in silent hours; that one speculates over, and to which one finds no answer in text-books. How she knew just the subjects that worked in me I knew not; some subtle intuitive sympathy, I suppose, enabled her to find it out. It was the same at breakfast, she talked down to the level of the men present (of course they did not see that it might be possible for a woman to do that), and made it a very pleasant meal.

It was in the evening—we had the saloon to ourselves—when she told me about the white elf. I had been talking of myself and of Hans Jörgen.

'I like your Mr. Hans Jörgen,' she said, 'he has a strong nature and knows what he wants; there is reliability in him. They are rarer qualities than one thinks in men, I have found through life that the average man is weaker than we are. It must be a good thing to have a stronger nature to lean to. I have never had that.'

There is a want in the tone of her voice as she ends, and I feel inclined to put out my hand and stroke hers—she has beautiful long hands—but I am afraid to do so. I query shyly—

'Have you no little ones?'

'Children, you mean? No, I am one of the barren ones; they are less rare than they used to be. But I have a white elf at home and that makes up for it. Shall I tell you how the elf came? Well, its mother is a connection of mine, and she hates me with an honest hatred. It is the only honest feeling I ever discovered in her. It was about the time that she found the elf was to come that it broke out openly, but that was mere coincidence. How she detested me! Those narrow, poor natures are capable of an intensity of feeling concentrated on one object that larger natures can scarcely measure. Now I shall tell you something strange. I do not pretend to understand it, I may have my theory, but that is of no physiological value, I only tell it to you. Well, all the time she was carrying the elf she was full of simmering hatred and she wished me evil often enough. One feels those things in an odd way. Why did she? Oh, that . . . that was a family affair, with perhaps a thread of jealousy mixed up in the knot. Well, one day the climax came, and much was said, and I went away and married and got ill and the doctors said I would be childless. And in the meantime the little human soul—I thought about it so often—had fought its way out of the darkness. We childless women weave more fancies into the " mithering o' bairns " than the actual mothers themselves. The poetry of it is not spoilt by nettle-rash or chin-cough any more than our figures. I am a writer by profession—oh, you knew! No, hardly celebrated, but I put my little chips into the great mosaic as best I can. Positions are reversed, they often are now-a-days. My husband stays at home and grows good things to eat, and pretty things to look at, and I go out and win bread and butter. It is a matter not of who has most brains, but whose brains are most saleable. Fit in with the housekeeping? Oh yes. I have a treasure, too, in Belinda. She is one of those women who must have something to love. She used to love cats, birds, dogs, anything. She is one bump of philo-progenitiveness, but she hates men. She says: "If one could only have a child, ma'm, without a husband or the disgrace; ugh, the disgusting men!" Do you know I think that is not an uncommon feeling amongst a certain number of women. I have often drawn her out on the subject. It struck me, because I have often found it in other women. I have known many, particularly older women, who would give anything in God's world to have a child of "their own" if it could be got just as Belinda says, "without the horrid man or the shame." It seems congenital with some women to have deeply rooted in their innermost nature a smouldering enmity, ay, sometimes a physical disgust to men, it is a kind of kin-feeling to the race dislike of white men to black. Perhaps it explains why woman, where her own feelings are not concerned, will always make common cause with woman against him. I have often thought about it. You should hear Belinda's "serve him right" when some fellow comes to grief. I have a little of it myself (meditatively), but in a broader way, you know. I like to cut them out in their own province. Well, the elf was born, and now comes the singular part of it. It was a wretched, frail little being with a startling likeness to me. It was as if the evil the mother had wished me had worked on the child, and the constant thought of me stamped my features on its little face. I was working then on a Finland saga, and I do not know why it was, but the thought of that little being kept disturbing my work. It was worst in the afternoon time when the house seemed quietest; there is always a lull then outside and inside. Have you ever noticed that? The birds hush their singing and the work is done. Belinda used to sit sewing in the kitchen, and the words of a hymn she used to lilt in half tones, something about 'joy bells ringing, children singing,' floated in to me, and the very tick-tock of the old clock sounded like the rocking of wooden cradles. It made me think sometimes that it would be pleasant to hear small pattering feet and the call of voices through the silent house. And I suppose it acted as an irritant on my imaginative faculty, for the whole room seemed filled with the spirits of little children. They seemed to dance round me with uncertain, lightsome steps, waving tiny pink dimpled hands, shaking sunny flossy curls, and haunting me with their great innocent child-eyes; filled with the unconscious sadness and the infinite questioning that is oftenest seen in the gaze of children. I used to fancy something stirred in me, and the spirits of unborn little ones never to come to life in me troubled me. I was probably overworked at the time. How we women digress! I am telling you more about myself than my white elf. Well, trouble came to their home, and I went and offered to take it. It was an odd little thing, and when I looked at it I could see how like we were. My glasses dimmed somehow, and a lump kept rising in my throat,

when it smiled up out of its great eyes and
held out two bits of hands like shrivelled white
rose leaves. Such a tiny scrap it was; it was not
bigger, she said, than a baby of eleven months.
I suppose they can tell that as I can the
date of a dialect; but I am getting wiser,' with
an emotional softening of her face and quite a
proud look. 'A child is like one of those wonderful runic alphabets; the signs are simple but
the lore they contain is marvellous. "She is very
like you," said the mother. "Hold her." She
was only beginning to walk. I did. You never
saw such elfin ears with strands of silk floss
ringing round them, and the quaintest, darlingest
wrinkles in its forehead, two long, and one short,
just as I have,' putting her head forward for me
to see. 'The other children were strong, and
the one on the road she hoped would be
healthy. So I took it there and then, "clothes
and baby, cradle and all." Yes, I have a collection of nursery rhymes from many nations;
I was going to put them in a book, but I say
them to the elf now. I wired to my husband.
You should have seen me going home. I was
so nervous, I was not half as nervous when I
read my paper—it was rather a celebrated paper,

perhaps you heard of it—to the Royal Geographical Society.   It was on Esquimaux marriage songs, and the analogy between them and the Song of Solomon.   She was so light, and so wrapped up, and my *pince-nez* kept dropping off when I stooped over her—I got spectacles after that—and I used to fancy I had dropped her out of the wrappings, and peep under the shawl to make sure'—with a sick shiver —' to find her sucking her thumb.   And I nearly passed my station.   And then a valuable book— indeed, it is really a case of MSS., and almost unique—I had borrowed for reference with some trouble, could not be found, and my husband roared with laughter when it turned up in the cradle.   Belinda was at the gate anxious to take her, and he said I did not know how to hold her, that I was holding her like a book of notes at a lecture, and so I gave her to Belinda. I think the poor little thing found it all strange, and when she puckered up her face, and thrust out her under lip, and two great tears jumped off her lashes, we all felt ready for hanging. But Belinda, though she doesn't know one language, not even her own, for she sows her h's broadcast and picks them up at hazard, she *can* talk to a baby. I am so glad for that reason she is bigger now; I couldn't manage it, I could not reason out any system they go on in baby talk. I tried mixing up the tenses, but somehow it wasn't right. My husband says it is not more odd than salmon taking a fly that is certainly like nothing they ever see in nature. Anyway it answered splendidly. Belinda used to say—I made a note of some of them—"Did-sum was denn? Oo did! Was ums de prettiest itta sweetums denn? oo was. An' did um put 'em in a nasty shawl an' joggle 'em in an ole puff-puff, um did, was a shame! Hitchy cum, hitchy cum, hitchy cum hi, Chinaman no likey me!" This always made her laugh, though in what connection the Chinaman came in I never *could* fathom. I was a little jealous of Belinda, but she knew how to undress her. George, that's my husband's name, said the bath water was too hot, and that the proper way to test it was to put one's elbow in. Belinda laughed, but I must confess it did feel too hot when I tried it that way; but how did he know? I got her such pretty clothes, I was going to buy a pragtbind of Nietzsche, but that must wait. George made her a cot with her name carved on the head of it, such a pretty one.'

'Did you find she made a change in your lives?' I asked.

'Oh, didn't she! Children are such funny things. I stole away to have a look at her later on, and did not hear him come after me. She looked so sweet, and she was smiling in her sleep. I believe the Irish peasantry say that an angel is whispering when a baby does that. I had given up all belief myself, except the belief in a Creator who is working out some system that is too infinite for our finite minds to grasp. If one looks round with seeing eyes one can't help thinking that after a run of 1893 years, Christianity is not very consoling in its results. But at that moment, kneeling next the cradle, I felt a strange, solemn feeling stealing over me; one is conscious of the same effect in a grand cathedral filled with the peal of organ music and soaring voices. It was as if all the old, sweet, untroubled child-belief came back for a spell, and I wondered if far back in the Nazarene village Mary ever knelt and watched the Christ-child sleep; and the legend of how he was often seen to weep but never to smile

came back to me, and I think the sorrow I felt
as I thought was an act of contrition and faith.
I could not teach a child scepticism, so I
remembered my husband prayed, and I re-
solved to ask him to teach her. You see (half
hesitatingly) I have more brains, or at least
more intellectuality than my husband, and in
that case one is apt to undervalue simpler,
perhaps greater, qualities. That came home to
me, and I began to cry, I don't know why, and
he lifted me up, and I think I said something
of the kind to him. . . . We got nearer to one
another someway. He said it was unlucky to
cry over a child.

'It made such a difference in the evenings. I
used to hurry home—I was on the staff of the
World's Review just then—and it was so jolly
to see the quaint little phiz smile up when I
went in.

'Belinda was quite jealous of George. She
said "Master worritted in an" out, an' interfered
with everything, she never seen a man as knew
so much about babies, not for one as never 'ad
none of 'is own. Wot if he didn't go to Parkins
hisself, an' say as how she was to have the milk
of one cow, an' mind not mix it." I wish you

could have seen the insinuating distrust on Belinda's face. I laughed. I believe we were all getting too serious, I know I felt years younger. I told George that it was really suspicious ; how did he acquire such a stock of baby lore ? *I* hadn't any. It was all very well to say Aunt Mary's kids. I should never be surprised if I saw a Zwazi woman appear with a lot of tawny pickaninnies in tow. George was shocked—I often shock him.

'She began to walk as soon as she got stronger. I never saw such an inquisitive mite. I had to rearrange all my bookshelves, change Le Nu de Rabelais, after Garnier, you know, and several others from the lower shelves to the top ones. One can't be so Bohemian when there is a little white soul like that playing about, can one? When we are alone she always comes in to say her prayers, and good-night. Larry Moore of the *Vulture*—he is one of the most wickedly amusing of men, prides himself on being *fin de siècle*—don't you detest that word?—or nothing, raves about Dégas, and is a worshipper of the decadent school of verse, quotes Verlaine, you know—well, he came in one evening on his way to some music hall. She's a whimsical little thing, not without incipient coquetry either; well, she would say them to him. If you can imagine a masher of the Jan van Beer type bending his head to hear a child in a white "nighty" lisping prayers, you have an idea of the picture. She kissed him good-night too; she never would before; and he must have forgotten his engagement, for he stayed with us to supper. She rules us all with a touch of her little hands, and I fancy we are all the better for it. Would you like to see her?' She hands me a medallion, with a beautifully painted head in it. I can't say she is a pretty child, a weird, elf-like thing, with questioning, wistful eyes, and masses of dark hair; and yet as I look the little face draws me to it, and makes a kind of yearning in me; strikes me with a 'fairy blast' perhaps.

The journey was all too short, and when we got to Hull she saw me to my train. It was odd to see the quiet way in which she got everything she wanted. She put me into the carriage, got me a footwarmer and a magazine, kissed me and said as she held my hand, 'The world is small, we run in circles, perhaps we shall meet again, in any case I wish you a white elf.' I was sorry to part with her ; I felt richer than before I knew her ; I fancy she goes about the world giving graciously from her richer nature to the poorer-endowed folks she meets on her way.

Often since that night I have rounded my arm and bowed down my face and fancied I had a little human elf cuddled to my breast.

*   *   *   *

I am very busy just now getting everything ready ; I had so much to buy. I don't like confessing it even to myself, but down in the bottom of my deepest trunk I have laid a parcel of things, such pretty tiny things. I saw them at a sale, I couldn't resist them, they were so cheap ; even if one doesn't want the things, it seems a sin to let them go. Besides, there may be some poor woman out in Cincinnati. I wrote to Hans Jörgen, you know, back in spring, and . . . . Du störer Gud! There is Hans Jörgen coming across the street.

A LITTLE GREY GLOVE.

EARLY-SPRING, 1893.

'The book of life begins with a man and woman in a garden
and ends—with Revelations.'   OSCAR WILDE.

YES, most fellows' book of life may be said to
begin at the chapter where woman comes in;
mine did.   She came in years ago, when I was
a raw undergraduate.   With the sober thought
of retrospective analysis, I may say she was
not all my fancy painted her; indeed now that
I come to think of it there was no fancy about
the vermeil of her cheeks, rather an artificial
reality; she had her bower in the bar of the
Golden Boar, and I was madly in love with
her, seriously intent on lawful wedlock.   Luckily
for me she threw me over for a neighbouring
pork butcher, but at the time I took it hardly,
and it made me sex-shy.   I was a very poor
man in those days.   One feels one's griefs more
keenly then, one hasn't the wherewithal to
buy distraction.   Besides, ladies snubbed me
rather, on the rare occasions I met them.   Later

I fell in for a legacy, the forerunner of several ;
indeed, I may say I am beastly rich. My tastes
are simple too, and I haven't any poor relations.
I believe they are of great assistance in getting
rid of superfluous capital, wish I had some!
It was after the legacy that women discovered
my attractions. They found that there was
something superb in my plainness (before, they
said ugliness), something after the style of the
late Victor Emanuel, something infinitely more
striking than mere ordinary beauty. At least
so Harding told me his sister said, and she had
the reputation of being a clever girl. Being an
only child, I never had the opportunity other
fellows had of studying the undress side of
women through familiar intercourse, say with
sisters. Their most ordinary belongings were
sacred to me. I had, I used to be told, ridiculous high-flown notions about them (by the
way I modified those considerably on closer
acquaintance). I ought to study them, nothing
like a woman for developing a fellow. So I
laid in a stock of books in different languages,
mostly novels, in which women played title
rôles, in order to get up some definite data
before venturing amongst them. I can't say I

derived much benefit from this course. There
seemed to be as great a diversity of opinion
about the female species as, let us say, about
the salmonidæ.

My friend Ponsonby Smith, who is one of the
oldest fly-fishers in the three kingdoms, said to
me once : ' Take my word for it, there are only
four true salmo ; the salar, the trutta, the fario,
the ferox ; all the rest are just varieties, sub-
genuses of the above; stick to that. Some
writing fellow divided all the women into good-
uns and bad-uns. But as a conscientious stickler
for truth, I must say that both in trout as in
women, I have found myself faced with most
puzzling varieties, that were a tantalising blending of several qualities.' I then resolved to
study them on my own account. I pursued
the Eternal Feminine in a spirit of purely
scientific investigation. I knew you'd laugh
sceptically at that, but it's a fact. I was im-
partial in my selection of subjects for obser-
vation,—French, German, Spanish, as well
as the home product. Nothing in petticoats
escaped me. I devoted myself to the freshest
ingenue as well as the experienced widow of
three departed ; and I may as well confess

that the more I saw of her, the less I understood her. But I think they understood me.
They refused to take me *au sérieux*. When
they weren't fleecing me, they were interested
in the state of my soul (I preferred the former),
but all humbugged me equally, so I gave them
up. I took to rod and gun instead, *pro salute
animæ*; it's decidedly safer. I have scoured
every country in the globe; indeed I can say
that I have shot and fished in woods and
waters where no other white man, perhaps,
ever dropped a beast or played a fish before.
There is no life like the life of a free wanderer,
and no lore like the lore one gleans in the
great book of nature. But one must have
freed one's spirit from the taint of the town
before one can even read the alphabet of its
mystic meaning.

What has this to do with the glove? True,
not much, and yet it has a connection—it
accounts for me.

Well, for twelve years I have followed the
impulses of the wandering spirit that dwells
in me. I have seen the sun rise in Finland
and gild the Devil's Knuckles as he sank behind
the Drachensberg. I have caught the barba

and the gamer yellow fish in the Vaal river, taken muskelunge and black-bass in Canada, thrown a fly over *guapote* and *cavallo* in Central American lakes, and choked the monster eels of the Mauritius with a cunningly faked-up duckling. But I have been shy as a chub at the shadow of a woman.

Well, it happened last year I came back on business—another confounded legacy; end of June too, just as I was off to Finland. But Messrs. Thimble and Rigg, the highly respectable firm who look after my affairs, represented that I owed it to others, whom I kept out of their share of the legacy, to stay near town till affairs were wound up. They told me, with a view to reconcile me perhaps, of a trout stream with a decent inn near it; an unknown stream in Kent. It seems a junior member of the firm is an angler, at least he sometimes catches pike or perch in the Medway some way from the stream where the trout rise in audacious security from artificial lures. I stipulated for a clerk to come down with any papers to be signed, and started at once for Victoria. I decline to tell the name of my find, firstly because the trout are the gamest

little fish that ever rose to fly and run to a
good two pounds. Secondly, I have paid for
all the rooms in the inn for the next year,
and I want it to myself. The glove is lying
on the table next me as I write. If it isn't in
my breast-pocket or under my pillow, it is in
some place where I can see it. It has a delicate
grey body (Suède, I think they call it) with
a whipping of silver round the top, and a
darker grey silk tag to fasten it. It is marked
$5\frac{3}{4}$ inside, and has a delicious scent about it,
to keep off moths, I suppose; naphthaline is
better. It reminds me of a 'silver-sedge'
tied on a ten hook. I startled the good
landlady of the little inn (there is no village
fortunately) when I arrived with the only
porter of the tiny station laden with traps.
She hesitated about a private sitting-room,
but eventually we compromised matters, as
I was willing to share it with the other visitor.
I got into knickerbockers at once, collared a
boy to get me worms and minnow for the
morrow, and as I felt too lazy to unpack
tackle, just sat in the shiny arm-chair (made
comfortable by the successive sitting of former
occupants) at the open window and looked

out. The river, not the trout stream, winds to the right, and the trees cast trembling shadows into its clear depths. The red tiles of a farm roof show between the beeches, and break the monotony of blue sky background. A dusty waggoner is slaking his thirst with a tankard of ale. I am conscious of the strange lonely feeling that a visit to England always gives me. Away in strange lands, even in solitary places, one doesn't feel it somehow. One is filled with the hunter's lust, bent on a 'kill;' but at home in the quiet country, with the smoke curling up from some fireside, the mowers busy laying the hay in swaths, the children tumbling under the trees in the orchards, and a girl singing as she spreads the clothes on the sweetbrier hedge, amidst a scene quick with home sights and sounds, a strange lack creeps in and makes itself felt in a dull, aching way. Oddly enough, too, I had a sense of uneasiness, a 'something going to happen.' I had often experienced it when out alone in a great forest, or on an unknown lake, and it always meant 'ware danger' of some kind. But why should I feel it here? Yet I did, and I couldn't shake it off. I took to examining the room. It was a common-place one of the usual type. But there was a work-basket on the table, a dainty thing, lined with blue satin. There was a bit of lace stretched over shiny blue linen, with the needle sticking in it; such fairy work, like cobwebs seen from below, spun from a branch against a background of sky. A gold thimble, too, with initials, not the landlady's, I know. What pretty things, too, in the basket! A scissors, a capital shape for fly-making; a little file, and some floss silk and tinsel, the identical colour I want for a new fly I have in my head, one that will be a demon to kill. The northern devil I mean to call him. Some one looks in behind me, and a light step passes up-stairs. I drop the basket, I don't know why. There are some reviews near it. I take up one, and am soon buried in an article on Tasmanian fauna. It is strange, but whenever I do know anything about a subject, I always find these writing fellows either entirely ignorant or damned wrong.

After supper, I took a stroll to see the river. It was a silver grey evening, with just the last lemon and pink streaks of the sunset staining

the sky. There had been a shower, and somehow the smell of the dust after rain mingled
with the mignonette in the garden brought
back vanished scenes of small-boyhood, when
I caught minnows in a bottle, and dreamt of
a shilling rod as happiness unattainable. I
turned aside from the road in accordance with
directions, and walked towards the stream.
Holloa! some one before me, what a bore! The
angler is hidden by an elder-bush, but I can see
the fly drop delicately, artistically on the water.
Fishing up-stream, too! There is a bit of
broken water there, and the midges dance in
myriads; a silver gleam, and the line spins out,
and the fly falls just in the right place. It is
growing dusk, but the fellow is an adept at
quick, fine casting—I wonder what fly he has
on—why, he's going to try down-stream now?
I hurry forward, and as I near him, I swerve to
the left out of the way. S-s-s-s! a sudden sting
in the lobe of my ear. Hey! I cry as I find I am
caught; the tail fly is fast in it. A slight, grey-
clad woman holding the rod lays it carefully
down and comes towards me through the
gathering dusk. My first impulse is to snap
the gut and take to my heels, but I am held by

something less tangible but far more powerful than the grip of the Limerick hook in my ear.

'I am very sorry!' she says in a voice that matched the evening, it was so quiet and soft; 'but it was exceedingly stupid of you to come behind like that.'

'I didn't think you threw such a long line; I thought I was safe,' I stammered.

'Hold this!' she says, giving me a diminutive fly-book, out of which she has taken a scissors. I obey meekly. She snips the gut.

'Have you a sharp knife? If I strip the hook you can push it through; it is lucky it isn't in the cartilage.'

I suppose I am an awful idiot, but I only handed her the knife, and she proceeded as calmly as if stripping a hook in a man's ear were an everyday occurrence. Her gown is of some soft grey stuff, and her grey leather belt is silver clasped. Her hands are soft and cool and steady, but there is a rarely disturbing thrill in their gentle touch. The thought flashed through my mind that I had just missed that, a woman's voluntary tender touch, not a paid caress, all my life.

'Now you can push it through yourself. I

hope it won't hurt much.' Taking the hook, I push it through, and a drop of blood follows it. 'Oh!' she cries, but I assure her it is nothing, and stick the hook surreptitiously in my coat sleeve. Then we both laugh, and I look at her for the first time. She has a very white forehead, with little tendrils of hair blowing round it under her grey cap, her eyes are grey. I didn't see that then, I only saw they were steady, smiling eyes that matched her mouth. Such a mouth, the most maddening mouth a man ever longed to kiss, above a too pointed chin, soft as a child's; indeed, the whole face looks soft in the misty light.

'I am sorry I spoilt your sport!' I say.

'Oh, that don't matter, it's time to stop. I got two brace, one a beauty.'

She is winding in her line, and I look in her basket; they *are* beauties, one two-pounder, the rest running from a half to a pound.

'What fly?'

'Yellow dun took that one, but your assailant was a partridge spider.' I sling her basket over my shoulder; she takes it as a matter of course, and we retrace our steps. I feel curiously happy as we walk towards the road; there is a novel delight in her nearness ; the feel of woman works subtly and strangely in me ; the rustle of her skirt as it brushes the black-heads in the meadow-grass, and the delicate perfume, partly violets, partly herself, that comes to me with each of her movements is a rare pleasure. I am hardly surprised when she turns into the garden of the inn, I think I knew from the first that she would.

'Better bathe that ear of yours, and put a few drops of carbolic in the water.' She takes the basket as she says it, and goes into the kitchen. I hurry over this, and go into the little sitting-room. There is a tray with a glass of milk and some oaten cakes upon the table. I am too disturbed to sit down ; I stand at the window and watch the bats flitter in the gathering moonlight, and listen with quivering nerves for her step—perhaps she will send for the tray, and not come after all. What a fool I am to be disturbed by a grey-clad witch with a tantalising mouth! That comes of loafing about doing nothing. I mentally darn the old fool who saved her money instead of spending it. Why the devil should I be bothered? I don't want it anyhow. She comes in as I fume,

and I forget everything at her entrance. I push
the arm-chair towards the table, and she sinks
quietly into it, pulling the tray nearer. She has
a wedding ring on, but somehow it never strikes
me to wonder if she is married or a widow or
who she may be. I am content to watch her
break her biscuits. She has the prettiest hands,
and a trick of separating her last fingers when
she takes hold of anything. They remind me of
white orchids I saw somewhere. She led me
to talk ; about Africa, I think. I liked to watch
her eyes glow deeply in the shadow and then
catch light as she bent forward to say something in her quick responsive way.

'Long ago when I was a girl,' she said
once.

'Long ago?' I echo incredulously, 'surely
not?'

'Ah, but yes, you haven't seen me in the
daylight,' with a soft little laugh. 'Do you
know what the gipsies say? "Never judge a
woman or a ribbon by candle-light." They
might have said moonlight equally well.'

She rises as she speaks, and I feel an overpowering wish to have her put out her hand.
But she does not, she only takes the work-

basket and a book, and says good-night with an inclination of her little head.

I go over and stand next her chair ; I don't like to sit in it, but I like to put my hand where her head leant, and fancy, if she were there, how she would look up.

I woke next morning with a curious sense of pleasurable excitement. I whistled from very lightness of heart as I dressed. When I got down I found the landlady clearing away her breakfast things. I felt disappointed and re-solved to be down earlier in future. I didn't feel inclined to try the minnow. I put them in a tub in the yard and tried to read and listen for her step. I dined alone. The day dragged terribly. I did not like to ask about her, I had a notion she might not like it. I spent the evening on the river. I might have filled a good basket, but I let the beggars rest. After all, I had caught fish enough to stock all the rivers in Great Britain. There are other things than trout in the world. I sit and smoke a pipe where she caught me last night. If I half close my eyes I can see hers, and her mouth in the smoke. That is one of the curious charms of baccy, it helps to reproduce brain pictures.

After a bit, I think 'perhaps she has left.' I get quite feverish at the thought and hasten back. I must ask. I look up at the window as I pass; there is surely a gleam of white. I throw down my traps and hasten up. She is leaning with her arms on the window-ledge staring out into the gloom. I could swear I caught a suppressed sob as I entered. I cough, and she turns quickly and bows slightly. A bonnet and gloves and lace affair and a lot of papers are lying on the table. I am awfully afraid she is going. I say—

'Please don't let me drive you away, it is so early yet. I half expected to see you on the river.'

'Nothing so pleasant; I have been up in town (the tears have certainly got into her voice) all day; it was so hot and dusty, I am tired out.'

The little servant brings in the lamp and a tray with a bottle of lemonade.

'Mistress hasn't any lemons, 'm, will this do?'

'Yes,' she says wearily, she is shading her eyes with her hand; 'anything; I am fearfully thirsty.'

'Let me concoct you a drink instead. I have lemons and ice and things. My man sent me down supplies to-day; I leave him in town. I am rather a dab at drinks; learnt it from the Yankees; about the only thing I did learn from them I care to remember. Susan!' The little maid helps me to get the materials, and *she* watches me quietly. When I give it to her she takes it with a smile (she *has* been crying). That is an ample thank-you. She looks quite old. Something more than tiredness called up those lines in her face.

*   *   *   *   *

Well, ten days passed, sometimes we met at breakfast, sometimes at supper, sometimes we fished together or sat in the straggling orchard and talked; she neither avoided me nor sought me. She is the most charming mixture of child and woman I ever met. She is a dual creature. Now I never met that in a man. When she is here without getting a letter in the morning or going to town, she seems like a girl. She runs about in her grey gown and little cap and laughs, and seems to throw off all thought like an irresponsible child. She is eager to fish, or pick gooseberries and eat them daintily, or sit

under the trees and talk. But when she goes to
town—I notice she always goes when she gets
a lawyer's letter, there is no mistaking the
envelope—she comes home tired and haggard-
looking, an old woman of thirty-five. I wonder
why. It takes her, even with her elasticity of
temperament, nearly a day to get young again.
I hate her to go to town; it is extraordinary
how I miss her; I can't recall, when she is
absent, her saying anything very wonderful,
but she converses all the time. She has a
gracious way of filling the place with herself,
there is an entertaining quality in her very
presence. We had one rainy afternoon; she
tied me some flies (I shan't use any of them); I
watched the lights in her hair as she moved, it
is quite golden in some places, and she has a
tiny mole near her left ear and another on her
left wrist. On the eleventh day she got a
letter but she didn't go to town, she stayed
up in her room all day; twenty times I felt
inclined to send her a line, but I had no excuse.
I heard the landlady say as I passed the
kitchen window: 'Poor dear! I'm sorry to
lose her!' Lose her? I should think not. It
has come to this with me that I don't care to

face any future without her; and yet I know nothing about her, not even if she is a free woman. I shall find that out the next time I see her. In the evening I catch a glimpse of her gown in the orchard, and I follow her. We sit down near the river. Her left hand is lying gloveless next me in the grass.

'Do you think from what you have seen of me, that I would ask a question out of any mere impertinent curiosity?'

She starts. 'No, I do not!'

I take up her hand and touch the ring. 'Tell me, does this bind you to any one?'

I am conscious of a buzzing in my ears and a dancing blurr of water and sky and trees, as I wait (it seems to me an hour) for her reply. I felt the same sensation once before, when I got drawn into some rapids and had an awfully narrow shave, but of that another time.

The voice is shaking.

'I am not legally bound to any one, at least; but why do you ask?' she looks me square in the face as she speaks, with a touch of haughtiness I never saw in her before.

Perhaps the great relief I feel, the sense of joy at knowing she is free, speaks out of my face, for hers flushes and she drops her eyes, her lips tremble. I don't look at her again, but I can see her all the same. After a while she says—

'I half intended to tell you something about myself this evening, now I *must*. Let us go in. I shall come down to the sitting-room after your supper.' She takes a long look at the river and the inn, as if fixing the place in her memory ; it strikes me with a chill that there is a good-bye in her gaze. Her eyes rest on me a moment as they come back, there is a sad look in their grey clearness. She swings her little grey gloves in her hand as we walk back. I can hear her walking up and down overhead ; how tired she will be, and how slowly the time goes. I am standing at one side of the window when she enters ; she stands at the other, leaning her head against the shutter with her hands clasped before her. I can hear my own heart beating, and, I fancy, hers through the stillness. The suspense is fearful. At length she says—

'You have been a long time out of England ; you don't read the papers?'

'No.' A pause. I believe my heart is beating inside my head.

'You asked me if I was a free woman. I don't pretend to misunderstand why you asked me. I am not a beautiful woman, I never was. But there must be something about me, there is in some women, "essential femininity" perhaps, that appeals to all men. What I read in your eyes I have seen in many men's before, but before God I never tried to rouse it. To-day (with a sob), I can say I am free, yesterday morning I could not. Yesterday my husband gained his case and divorced me!' she closes her eyes and draws in her under-lip to stop its quivering. I want to take her in my arms, but I am afraid to.

'I did not ask you any more than if you were free!'

'No, but I am afraid you don't quite take in the meaning. I did not divorce my husband, he divorced *me*, he got a decree *nisi*; do you understand now? (she is speaking with difficulty), do you know what that implies?'

I can't stand her face any longer. I take her hands, they are icy cold, and hold them tightly.

'Yes, I know what it implies, that is, I know the legal and social conclusion to be drawn

from it,—if that is what you mean. But I
never asked you for that information. I have
nothing to do with your past. You did not exist
for me before the day we met on the river. I
take you from that day and I ask you to marry
me.'

I feel her tremble and her hands get suddenly
warm. She turns her head and looks at me
long and searchingly, then she says—

'Sit down, I want to say something!'

I obey, and she comes and stands next the
chair. I can't help it, I reach up my arm, but
she puts it gently down.

'No, you must listen without touching me, I
shall go back to the window. I don't want to
influence you a bit by any personal magnetism
I possess. I want you to listen—I have told
you he divorced me, the co-respondent was an
old friend, a friend of my childhood, of my girlhood. He died just after the first application
was made, luckily for me. He would have
considered my honour before my happiness. *I*
did not defend the case, it wasn't likely—ah,
if you knew all? He proved his case; given
clever counsel, willing witnesses to whom you
make it worth while, and no defence, divorce is

always attainable even in England. But remember : I figure as an adulteress in every
English-speaking paper. If you buy last week's
evening papers—do you remember the day I
was in town ?'—I nod—' you will see a sketch
of me in that day's ; some one, perhaps he, must
have given it ; it was from an old photograph.
I bought one at Victoria as I came out ; it is
funny (with an hysterical laugh) to buy a
caricature of one's own poor face at a news-
stall. Yet in spite of that I have felt glad.
The point for you is that I made no defence to
the world, and (with a lifting of her head) I
will make no apology, no explanation, no denial
to you, now nor ever. I am very desolate and
your attention came very warm to me, but I
don't love you. Perhaps I could learn to (with
a rush of colour), for what you have said to-
night, and it is because of that I tell you to
weigh what this means. Later, when your care
for me will grow into habit, you may chafe at
my past. It is from that I would save you.'

I hold out my hands and she comes and
puts them aside and takes me by the beard
and turns up my face and scans it earnestly.
She must have been deceived a good deal. I

let her do as she pleases, it is the wisest way with women, and it is good to have her touch me in that way. She seems satisfied. She stands leaning against the arm of the chair and says—

'I must learn first to think of myself as a free woman again, it almost seems wrong to-day to talk like this; can you understand that feel?'

I nod assent.

'Next time I must be sure, and you must be sure,' she lays her fingers on my mouth as I am about to protest, 'S-sh! You shall have a year to think. If you repeat then what you have said to-day, I shall give you your answer. You must not try to find me. I have money. If I am living, I will come here to you. If I am dead, you will be told of it. In the year between I shall look upon myself as belonging to you, and render an account if you wish of every hour. You will not be influenced by me in any way, and you will be able to reason it out calmly. If you think better of it, don't come.'

I feel there would be no use trying to move her, I simply kiss her hands and say:

'As you will, dear woman, I shall be here.'

We don't say any more; she sits down on a

footstool with her head against my knee, and I just smooth it. When the clocks strike ten through the house, she rises and I stand up. I see that she has been crying quietly, poor lonely little soul. I lift her off her feet and kiss her, and stammer out my sorrow at losing her, and she is gone. Next morning the little maid brought me an envelope from the lady, who left by the first train. It held a little grey glove; that is why I carry it always, and why I haunt the inn and never leave it for longer than a week; why I sit and dream in the old chair that has a ghost of her presence always; dream of the spring to come with the May-fly on the wing, and the young summer when midges dance, and the trout are growing fastidious; when she will come to me across the meadow grass, through the silver haze, as she did before; come with her grey eyes shining to exchange herself for her little grey glove.

AN EMPTY FRAME.

IT was a simple pretty little frame, such as you may buy at any sale cheaply; its ribbed wood, aspinalled white, with an inner frame of pale blue plush; its one noticeable feature, that it was empty. And yet it stood on the middle of the bedroom mantel-board.

It was not a luxurious room, none of the furniture matched, it was a typical boarding-house bedroom.

Any one preserving the child habit of endowing inanimate objects with human attributes might fancy that the flickering flames of the fire took a pleasure in bringing into relief the bright bits in its dinginess. For they played over the silver-backed brushes, and the cut-glass perfume-bottles on the dressing-table; flicked the bright beads on the toes of coquettish small shoes and the steel clasps of a travelling bag in the corner; imparting a casual air of comfort, such as the touch of certain dainty women lends to a common room.

A woman enters, a woman wondrously soft and swift in all her movements. She seems to reach a place without your seeing how, no motion of elbow or knee betrays her. Her fingers glide swiftly down the buttons of her gown; in a second she has freed herself from its ensheathing, garment after garment falls from her until she stands almost free. She gets into night-dress and loose woollen dressing-gown, and slips her naked feet into fur-lined slippers with a movement that is somehow the expression of an intense nervous relief from a thrall. Everything she does is done so swiftly that you see the result rather than the working out of each action.

She sinks into a chair before the fire, and, clasping her hands behind her head, peers into the glowing embers. The firelight, lower than her face, touches it cruelly; picks out and accentuates as remorselessly as a rival woman the autographs past emotions have traced on its surface; deepens the hollows of her delicate thoughtful temples and the double furrow between her clever irregular eyebrows. Her face is more characteristic than beautiful. Nine men would pass it, the tenth sell his immortal soul for it. The chin is strong, the curve of jaw determined ; there is a little full place under the chin s sharp point. The eyes tell you little ; they are keen and inquiring, and probe others' thoughts rather than reveal their own. The whole face is·one of peculiar strength and self-reliance. The mouth is its contradiction— the passionate curve of the upper lip with its mobile corners, and the tender little under lip that shelters timidly beneath it, are encouraging promises against its strength.

The paleness of some strong feeling tinges her face, a slight trembling runs through her frame. Her inner soul-struggle is acting as a strong developing fluid upon a highly sensitised plate ; anger, scorn, pity, contempt chase one another like shadows across her face. Her eyes rest upon the empty frame, and the plain white space becomes alive to her. Her mind's eye fills it with a picture it once held in its dainty embrace. A rare head amongst the rarest heads of men, with its crest of hair tossed back from the great brow, its proud poise and the impress of grand confident compelling genius that reveals itself one scarce knows how ; with the brute possibility of an untamed, natural man lurking about the mouth and powerful throat. She feels the subduing smile of eyes that never failed to make her weak as a child under their gaze, and tame as a hungry bird. She stretches out her hands with a pitiful little movement, and then, remembering, lets them drop and locks them until the knuckles stand out whitely. She shuts her eyes, and one tear after the other starts from beneath her lids, trickles down her cheeks, and drops with a splash into her lap. She does not sob, only cries quietly, and she sees, as if she held the letter in her hand, the words that decided her fate—

'You love me; I know it, you other half of me. You want me to complete your life as I you, you good, sweet woman. You slight, weak thing, with your strong will and your grand, great heart. You witch with a soul of clean white fire. I kiss your hands (such little hands! I never saw the like), slim child-hands, with a touch as cool and as soft as a snow-flake! You dear one, come to me, I want you, now, always. Be with me, work with me, share with me, live with me, my equal as a creature; above me as my queen of women! I love you, I worship you, but you know my views. I cannot, I will not bind myself to you by any legal or religious tie. I must be free and unfettered to follow that which I believe right for me. If you come to me in all trust, I can and will give myself to you in all good faith, yours as much as you will, for ever! I will kneel to you. Why should I always desire to kneel to you? It is not that I stand in awe of you, or that I ever feel a need to kneel at all; but always to you, and to you alone. Come—I will crouch at your feet and swear myself to you,'—and she had replied 'No!' and in her loneliness of spirit married him who seemed to need her most out of those who admired her. . . .

The door opens and he comes in. He looks inquiringly at her, touches her hair half hesitatingly, and then stands with his hands thrust in his pockets and gnaws his moustache.

'Are you angry, little woman?'

'No' (very quietly), 'why should I be?'

She closes her eyes again, and after five minutes' silence he begins to undress. He does it very slowly, watching her perplexedly. When he has finished he stands with his

back to the fire, an unlovely object in sleeping suit.

'Would you like to read her letter?'

She shakes her head.

'I suppose I ought to have sent her back
her letters before, you know. She hadn't
heard I was married.'

'Yes,' she interjects, 'it would have been
better to start with a clean bill; but why
talk about it?'

He looks at her a while, then gets into bed
and watches her from behind the pages of
the *Field*. It seems unusually quiet. His
watch, that he has left in his waistcoat pocket,
thrown across the back of a chair, seems to
fill the whole room with a nervous tick.

He tosses the paper on to the floor. She
looks up as it falls, rises, turns off the gas-jet,
sinks back into her old position, and stares
into the fire. He gets up, goes over, and
kneels down next her.

'I am awfully sorry you are put out, old
girl. I saw you were when I answered you
like that, but I couldn't help feeling a bit cut
up, you know. She wrote such an awfully
nice letter, you know, wished'——

'you all sorts of happiness (with a snap) and hopes you'll meet in a better world?'

He rises to his feet and stares at her in dumb amazement. How could she know? She smiles with a touch of malicious satisfaction, as she sees the effect of her chance shot.

'It's a pity, isn't it, that you both have to wait so long?'

He imagines he sees light, and blunders ahead like an honest man.

'I wouldn't have sent those things back now if I had thought you cared. By Jove, it never entered my head that you'd be jealous!'

'Jealous? (she is on her feet like a red white flash). I, jealous of her? (each word is emphasised). I couldn't be jealous of her, *Nur die Dummen sind bescheiden!* Why, the girl isn't fit to tie my shoe-strings!'

This is too much; he feels he must protest.

'You don't know her (feebly). She is an awfully nice girl!'

'Nice girl! I don't doubt it, and she will be an awfully nice woman, and under each and every circumstance of life she will behave like an awfully nice person. Jealous! Do you think I cried because I was jealous? Good

God, no! I cried because I was sorry, fearfully sorry for myself. She' (with a fine thin contempt) 'would have suited you better than I. Jealous! no, only sorry. Sorry because any nice average girl of her type, who would model her frocks out of the *Lady's Pictorial*, gush over that dear Mr. Irving, paint milking-stools, try poker work, or any other fashionable fad, would have done for you just as well. And I' (with a catch of voice) 'with a great man might have made a great woman—and now those who know and understand me' (bitterly) 'think of me as a great failure.'

She finishes wearily, the fire dies out of eyes and voice. She adds half aloud as if to herself:

'I don't think I quite realised this until I saw how you took that letter. I was watching your face as you read it, and the fact that you could put her on the same level, that if it had not been for a mistake, she would have suited you as well, made me realise, don't you see? that I should have done better for some one else!'

He is looking at her in utter bewilderment, and she smiles as she notes his expression; she touches his cheek gently and leans her head against his arm.

'There, it's all right, boy! Don't mind me, I have a bit of a complex nature; you couldn't understand me if you tried to; you'd better not try!'

She has slipped, whilst speaking, her warm bare foot out of her slipper, and is rubbing it gently over his chilled ones.

'You are cold, better go back to bed, I shall go too!'

She stands a moment quietly as he turns to obey, and then takes the frame, and kneeling down puts it gently into the hollowed red heart of the fire. It crackles crisply, and little tongues of flame shoot up, and she gets into bed by their light.

*　　*　　*　　*　　*

When the fire has burnt out, and he is sleeping like a child with his curly head on her breast, she falls asleep too and dreams that she is sitting on a fiery globe rolling away into space. That her head is wedged in a huge frame, the top of her head touches its top, the sides its sides, and it keeps growing larger and larger and her head with it, until she seems to be sitting inside her own head, and the inside is one vast hollow.

UNDER NORTHERN SKY

I

HOW MARIE LARSEN EXORCISED A DEMON

THERE has been a mighty storm, it has been raging for two days. A storm in which the demon of drink has reigned like a sinister god in the big white house, and the frightened women have cowered away, driven before the hot blast of the breath upon which curses danced, and the blaze of ire in the lurid eyes of the master. Only the pale little mistress has stood unmoved through the whirlwind of his passion. Who knows? Maybe that roused him to higher, madder paroxysms of impotent rage; for he abuses her most when he loves her most, a way man has, he being a creature of higher understanding.

All yesterday the bells jangled, until one by one a violent jerk snapped the connecting wire, and hurled them with a last echoing crash on the hall floor. The serving-men kept out of it as men do. The horses cowered to the sides of their boxes and set their hind legs hard, and pointed their ears when they heard his halting step. The great hounds shrunk shiveringly into their boxes, and refused to come forth to his threatening call ; and when he lashed their houses in his rage they winced at each blow, and showed their fangs when he turned away.

Night brought little rest, for lamps and candles were lit in every room ; champagne replaced brandy, then brandy champagne, and then both mingled in one glass. And in measure as the liquid fire was tossed down the poor parched throat, the brain grew clearer ; the intellect, with its Rabelaisque fertility of diseased imagining, keener ; the sting the tongue carried more adder-like, and the ingenuity of its blasphemies more devilish. The tired women crept to bed at midnight, to start in their sleep at the hoot of every night-owl, the flitter of every bat, and the whistle of every passing steamer ; all save the little mistress of the great house, with its stores of linen and silver ; its flower-filled garden ; its farmyard with lowing sleek kine ; its meadows in prime heart, heavy with the sweetness of red clover ;

its line of brown nets pegged down to catch the incoming eager salmon at the mouth of the fjord; and the wood with its peaceful nooks of cool green, and its winding paths with their brown carpet of last year's fir-needles and pine cones. She sits wearily in her low chair with her thin hands clasped on her sharp knees, and her shawl drawn round her shoulders, for in spite of the fire the first hour of the morning sends its chill breath into the room. He is lying on the sofa talking to himself, emphasising his words with his heavy stick. A table with decanters and glasses stands next him.

'Women, ay, women, man's curse. At the end of the race they beat us always. We get one soft spot with our mother's milk and well they know it, well they know it. What a man I would have been' (a rising growl) 'if it hadn't been for women! Do you hear, you white-faced spawn! Yes, I mean it. God! when I look back. But' (chuckling) 'I paid them out, the brutes!' And curse follows curse, and worse than that; as from the lips of the step-daughter in the fairy tale, the words that drop from his lips are the toads and vipers of filth.

'If one could forget. There was one, one long ago. I might have spared her, she pleaded hard against me. Why do I think of her to-night? it is years, years ago. Ah, but I was big and beautiful in those days! She, she was an innocent little thing. I fascinated her like a snake, and I can see her eyes. They were blue with long lashes. I *can see them now*, curse them! She and the child, jibbering idiots both! oh' (groan), 'curses on you for a devil to plague me thus! Keep away! I say, keep away! How the ghosts dance about the room! There is another one I had forgotten. Light more candles, more!' (a shriek) 'more! I say all round the room—make a damn wake of it.'

Mutter, mutter—a sordine epic of Hades. She closes her eyes. The stick whirls past her, striking a vase off a table near her; she gets up, hands it to him without a word; he hiccoughs and laughs, and then he heaves one sob and cries bitterly with the great tears gushing forth in jets. She picks up his handkerchief and puts it into his hand, and he looks at her with a piteous softening of his wild eyes, and he says quietly, hiccoughing all the while like a child tired after a fit of passion—for man in all his passions has a little of the inconsequent child, it is only woman who sins with clear seeing.

'I am a brute, I know it, but you don't know what it is to see the ghosts of sins stirring in a man's soul like maggots in a dead rat. And the children, that is the worst of all. O God, my poor little girls! What will become of them? Oh! Oh!'

'But you settled for them!' soothing with her weary voice. 'But you settled for them all right!'

'O yes, the money's all right. O Lord, yes! I settled, I settled,' with the reiteration of drunken gravity, 'I settled that. But the mother was a brute, a heartless brute; and she was a lady too, ay, in her own right. And she never asked a word about them, not one word. It was I, I, poor disreputable brute, that put them to nurse; and I loathed her for it. Ah! if you women knew what a hold simple goodness has on us! I met her once, I had one at each hand; I used to go to see them. Oh, they don't know, they don't know, God forbid! And she lay back in her victoria and looked at us, curse her! She has children now, legitimate ones, and my little girls don't know I'm alive.

Oh, my poor little girls! They are so pretty. Mind you bury that locket with me, don't open it. Yes, yes, I know, don't think I don't trust you,—only woman I ever trusted in the world. But I'm afraid for them; curse this water in my eyes' (sob); 'don't you imagine I'm crying, I'm not! It's whiskey, pure unadulterated' (hiccough) 'whiskey, but I can't help thinking of them. The others, ay, Lord! how many others? I don't care about them, I settled for them, *they weren't ladies*, they'll get on well enough; but these, my pretty little ones. I'm afraid for them, afraid for them. I, who spared no man's daughter, how can I tell if some brute won't hurt mine? Oh God, oh God, how can they be good with such a father and such a mother?'

He drinks as he speaks, and pours out in grief and rage a wild torrent of prayers and curses.

'Ay, verily, it's reaping the whirlwind! How the faces crowd round! they always come with the grey morning light! women's faces, girls' faces, child-girls' faces, oh, damn you, hide me from them! Hold me tight and keep them away, put your arms right round me. You are clean—a clean little thing, they can't come through you.'

And she holds the throbbing head in her arms, and hides the wild eyes in her breast, and she feels as if there is a rustle of trailing skirts about her, and waving hair, and a feel of women. And then he tears himself out of her clasp, and she falls bruising herself sorely, and he throws over the table with a shatter of falling glass, and bounds up the stairs, snatching a riding-whip out of the hall. He beats its gold head into jagged shreds of glitter on the maids' door, and shouts to them to rise and come down. He 'll show them he is master in his own house. He has eaten nothing all day, no, nor for many days; down at once or he 'll know why, and cook—cook his dinner and light fires—yes, fires everywhere. What does he pay them for, lazy sluts, what does he keep house for? . . . And so, man, the master mind of creation, asserts his authority, and the maids troop down, heavy-eyed and stupid with sleep; and bake, and roast, and giggle hysterically under their breath; and tell stories of other masters they have served, and goings on; and grind fresh coffee beans, and have white bread, and lump sugar, and cold fowl, for there is no one to say them nay, and the larders are full of good things ; and only the pale little mistress knows how near the grand place is drawing to bankruptcy.

Morning came, and the table was decked and the dinner served, and taken out again untasted ; and another storm simmered all through the sunny forenoon to burst like a hurricane over the house at noon.

The kitchen is empty and the fire has gone out; a wreck of crockery shows where the storm raged worst. The girls flew before the thunder of voice and flash of whip ; the Swedish gardener left his birthright of song untouched and followed them ; he is skylarking with them now up in the great loft; they have pulled up the ladder, and are pelting one another with last year's hay. The cow-girl, a wench from Hittedal, lured the cattle and goats and long-legged, heifer calves deeper into the woods with her quaint Lokke song, calling :

'Come, sweet breath, come cowslip, come rich milk,
Aa lukelei aa lura, lura, luralai ! '

Only the housemaid, who is consumptive, and who stays for the little mistress' sake, her own days in the land being numbered, has taken her Bible up to the look-out in the wood, and laid it open on the stone table. She is crushing the Linnae as she kneels into a fragrant incense; rocking to and fro to the sombre rhythm of the last book of Ecclesiastes.

And the master of them all is sitting exhausted in his big chair, and Marie Larsen and he are doing battle. She came on the scene just as the grand retreat was sounded, and took the enemy by stratagem. She lifted the little mistress bodily up, and carried her up-stairs, leaving him, as she puts it, to ramp like a bull of Basan below. She lays her on her bed, takes off her shoes, pulls down the blind, and pours out some drops out of a little blue bottle she carries in her pocket, talking as she might to a child: 'There, Tulla, take naphtha drops, very good drops, you go sleep, good sleep, Marie mind him, Marie not afraid,' and with a final pat she goes down. He is laughing between his oaths at the stampede of petticoats, and he holds out his arms when she comes in.

She is a little square woman, between fifty and sixty, with a ruby button of a nose and hair, that oil and age has robbed of its brilliant red, drawn smoothly back into a tight screw at the back of her broad head. Her eyes are a fishy green grey, the left eyelid droops; when she thinks you are not looking, a sly elusive gleam brightens them, her pursed lips loosen, and if you happen to see it, you think that there may be something after all in the stories the gossips whisper of Marie Larsen. Her dress is exquisitely neat, her apron snowy. No one in the district can make such a *suprême* of fish as Marie; no one beat her at roasting a capercailzie and serving it with sour cream sauce; or brew such caudles and possets for a lying-in, or bake such meats for a funeral-feast. And what if there be an old-time tale of a brat accidentally smothered? And what if the Amtmanden (superior magistrate), he who had the sickly wife, did send Marie to Germany to learn cooking? Well, he had money to spare and was always freehanded. And if Nils Pettersen did write home and say that he saw her in Hamburg at a trade—well, other than cooking —sure Nils Pettersen was a bit of a liar anyhow, and good cooking covers a multitude of frailties. And if her nose was red and her breath smelt of cloves, who could say they ever saw her buy a bottle of akavit, and that was more than could be said of all the other temperance leaguers.

She had a nice cottage, with marigolds and curly-mint and none-so-prettys nodding down the garden paths, and if you went inside it was very respectable; and you could not fail to notice the large brass-bound Bible on a crochet-square on top of the mahogany chest of drawers, with a sprig of palm marking the gospel of the previous Sunday. And no one answered the responses more loudly, or confessed more openly at revival times, or quoted scripture more aptly to the confusion of a neighbour than Jomfru Marie Larsen. And then she had seen life too, and told them round the oven in winter over a cup of good coffee 'tales that were human,' just to warn them what risks they might run if they should be tempted to stray to the ungodly cities of the wicked world outside.

She stands and smiles at him.

'Arcades ambo! Blackguards both!' quotes he, pointing to a glass. She pours him out a measure and blinks, and fills a wine-glass with raw spirit for herself, and clinks glasses and sips like a connoisseur. And then she takes out her knitting and sets the needles flying. So they sit a while; his last grand charge has taxed him, but the quiet maddens him.

'Where's the Frue?' he asks, 'the Frue?'

She lays her head sideways on her hand and closes her eyes, saying in English: 'No can have Fruen, she sick, no can have her, be good, Marie tell you a tale.'

She gets up and shuts the doors; he roars at her and tries to rise, but his knees fail him; he sinks back into the chair and begins to swear. She knits away and commences in Norwegian a sing-song recitative like the drowsy buzz of a fly on a pane.

'Yesterday we had a bazaar, a bazaar in the school-house, a bazaar for the poor black heathens in Africa. For the poor black heathens lost in the darkness of unbelief, and ignorant of the saving of the Lamb—oh, it was a blessed work!'

A savage roar from him, but she goes on unheeding with her narrative.

'And there were tables with lots of things to be sold, and there were tables with refreshments, and there were wreaths and flags upon the walls, and godly texts and paper roses, yellow and red;' she draws out each word to spin the yarn longer, and he curses her for a Jezebel and foams with rage, and she sips her cognac with a deeper droop of eyelid and slower click of needle and proceeds with her tale :—

'And we had hymns, and the kapelan (curate) played the harmonium, and then he held a little edifying discourse, and the school children sang, and Marie had to hand round refreshments, and oh, it was a rousing day! And there was Frue [1] Magistrate Holmsen, and Frue Assessor Schwartz, and Frue Custom-house Chief's lady and her sister Fröken Dase, she of the long nose and pinched waist, and her engaged, the Candidat. And there was Frue Doctor Barthelsen, and Frue general dealer Steen and daughter, with a high frill to hide the evils in her neck, and Frue Insurance Agent. . . .' She dodges a glass adroitly, and raises her voice to drown his shriek of what the merry devil she means. 'Insurance Agent Hansen, and the Kaptein of the *Sea Gull*. . . . S-s-s, you be quiet, Marie tell you tale—there was Ma'm Sörensen and fat Ma'm Larsen ; she's going to have her twelfth, and Larsen only

---

[1] The title Frue is properly borne by the wives of officials, but all the professional men's wives bear it. Madam is used by the small shopkeepers or lower burgher class, but the distinction is dying out. A Frue's daughter is Fröken, Madam's Jomfrue.

third mate, and Ma'm Johnsen and all the young gentlemen and ladies, and oh, it was a glorious sight!' She starts a key higher, for he is purple with fury and exertion, 'and, and we had coffee two pence a cup, and chocolade,' with a long-drawn stress on the 'lade' 'and Brus-selzers and lemonade and fruit juice and temperance beer. . . . No, no, you be quiet, Marie tell tale!'

He is struggling till the veins stand in cords to get out of his chair, but in vain; he points to his glass in desperation. She refills it and her own . . . 'Yes, temperance beer, a penny a glass, and we had white bread and brown bread and currant buns and Berlin kringels and ginger nuts and little cakes with hundreds and thousands on top! And oh, it was grand! . . .'

She is yelling louder and louder, and he is swearing deeper, and the battle shows no signs of ceasing.

'And then we sold all sorts of things, and drew numbers, and had a lucky bag; and Hans Jacobsen played on the melodeon, and missionary Hansen told us about the poor blacks, and all his blessed work, and how the Lord guided his footsteps through the sandy wastes, and how he baptized a chief and all his wives in the waters of faith. And Nils Pettersen says, they took out more raw alcohol and spent gunpowder and spoilt cotton goods than the fear of God ; and that the *Bird o' Faith* cleared 100 per cent. on her freight. But Nils Pettersen was always a liar ; and oh, it was a blessed thing to do all that for the heathen blacks ! And then the kapelan spoke again, a touching discourse !' And she refills her glass, dodging his stick and watching him out of the tail of her eye as she turns the heel of her stocking, and repeats the whole of the sermon. His vocabulary is exhausted, and he is inventing the weirdest oaths, hurling them forth, a deep accompaniment to her shriller sermon, with its sanctimonious sing-song tune and unctuous phrasing ; for she is, perhaps unwittingly, mimicking the kapelan to the life. He is getting tired and drowsy, the cognac is rising to her head, and even a kapelan's sermon must draw to a close. And as a mother will change her lullaby into a quick hushoo, and pat mechanically with a drowsy nod as the child drops to sleep, so Marie puts her knitting tidily into her apron pocket, and folding her withered old hands, breaks into a hymn. He opens his eyes languidly, and protests feebly with a last damn, but Marie has exorcised the devil this time. His jaw drops, and muttering softly, he falls into heavy sleep—and she sings on till her head too droops on her breast, and her quavering old woman's voice dies away in an abortive hallelujah!

And the motes dance in the golden bar of a waning sun ray that pierces the room and crosses the motionless figures—and above stairs the little mistress is wrapped in rare, delicious, dreamless slumber. And I like to think that the recording angel registered that sleep to the credit of Jomfrue Marie Larsen!

II.

A SHADOW'S SLANT.

IT is a sunny afternoon in mid-summer. A phaeton drawn by a pair of sturdy grey Stavanger horses, whose dainty heads and the mark of St. Olaf's thumb on their throats tell their race, is dashing along at a break-neck pace. The whip curls over them and the vehicle sways a little to one side. Two great hounds bound along on the right of it.

A strip of blue fjord and a background of dark mountains, with the cool ice-kisses of the snow queen still resting on their dusky heads, can be seen at intervals through the fir and pine trees. A squirrel scrambles up a rowan tree, and a cattle bell tingles far in the woods. Nature has ever a discordant note in its symphony. A little brown bird is fluttering in helpless terrified jerks; it emits, as it rises and falls, a sharp sound between a chirp and a squeak—a hawk is swooping over it—a poise—

a dip—a few feathers float with the breeze, and the hawk soars up with its prey in its claws.

The red-brown eyes that gleam out of the small sallow face of the woman who sits on the left side of the phaeton close for a second; the delicate nostrils quiver, the lips tighten over a sigh—then the lids rise again, the eyes are darker, the pupils have a trick of dilating; a smile subtle in meaning, for much of mocking pain and bitterness is expressed in its brief passage, flits across her face.

A savage jerk—the horses stop.

'Kiss me!' says the man who is driving, his voice is harsh and the eyes that scan her face have a lurid light in them, and as he speaks a smell of spirit mingles with the smell of the pine chips. Her lips tighten still more; she turns to obey. She has to rise up a little, he is very tall. His nose is powerful like a hawk's beak, and his beard is stirred by the breeze, and his eyes peer out from under their fringe of black lashes with a cruel passionate gleam. She almost touches his face but falls back from a rough shove—

'No, keep your kiss and be damned to you!'

A savage whoop, the whip curls out and the

reins jerk, and the quivering horses that know
the voice too well dash on ; and the hounds
that have felt the whip-cord sting, as the
strike of a snake on their flanks, bay savagely
as they join in the race.

On the right of the narrow winding road a
great lake lies hundreds of feet below ; the
wheel is not half a foot from the edge, and the
vehicle jolts and leans that way, and the lash
coils round and it flicks her ear, and leaves a
sorry sting, and she never winces at it. But her
small hands clench, and her lips part, and the
red light flashes in her eyes, and something akin
to exultant expectation steals over the thin
small face as they court death, each wheel-
turn in their mad career.

*   *   *   *   *

The stable door opens and the horses turn
their heads.   She, it is she, goes over and passes
her fingers gently over the swollen stripes that
make little ridges in the close-clipped hair.
Once she lays her cheek caressingly upon a
cruel furrow and whispers, ' Poor little Ola, if I
had only governed my face better, you would
not have been so punished ; ' and Ola turns
his satiny muzzle, softer than the daintiest

lady's breast, and rubs it against her, to coax
for the apples that always follow. She goes
from one to the other and coos to them and
rubs her chin against their soft noses, and when
the stripes are very bad her jaws set; and one
can see the mark of the teeth through her thin
cheeks.

*   *   *   *

'Come here! I want some brandy! . . . .
Now put the glass down and come back.
What's that mark on your cheek?'

'Only the whip touched me.'

'And you were too damned proud to say so,
eh? By the way, I saw some gipsies in the
park. Johann can do the translating, they are
coming here to play. One of them is a thunder-
ing fine girl, I'd like to . . . . what? what's
that you said?'

'I did not make any remark!' a fine scorn
trembles about her pale lips, and her face is a
shade greyer.

A pause.

'Where are your rings?'

'Up-stairs!'

'Go and fetch them! Blast it! I don't buy
you rings to leave them up-stairs.'

She comes back with them on, and he takes up the slim fingers laden with jewelled bands, spreads them out on his palm, then closes his thumb and finger round her wrist, and laughs a rasping laugh.

'Did any mortal man ever see such a hand? You witch! with eyes that probe into a fellow's soul and shame him and fear nothing!' and he tightens his grip and she winces at his roughness. 'There' (with a softening of voice), 'did I hurt you? you poor little thing, you queer little womany! Come closer' (with fierce, impatient tenderness); 'put down your little old head, a head like a snipe, on my breast. There, great God, I'm very fond of you!' a tremor runs through his voice. 'You queer little thing. You are no beauty, but you creep in, and I, I love every inch of you. I'd kiss the ground under your feet. I know every turn of your little body, the slope of your shoulders, I that always liked women to have square shoulders—the swing of your hips when you walk. Hips! ha, ha! you haven't got any, you scrap! and yet, by the Lord, I'd *lick* you like a dog' (slower, with emphasis), 'and *you* don't care for me. You obey me, no matter what I ask.' . . . .

He is holding her face against his breast, and stroking her head with clumsy touch. 'You wait on me, ay, no slave better, and yet—I can't get at you, near you; that little soul of yours is as free as if I hadn't bought you, as if I didn't own you, as if you were not my chattel, my thing to do what I please with; do you hear' (with fury) 'to degrade, to—to treat as *I please*? No, you are not afraid, you little white-faced thing, you obey because you are strong enough to endure, not because you fear me. And I know it, don't you think I don't see it. You pity me, great God! pity *me*—me that could whistle any woman to heel—yes, you pity me with all that great heart of yours because I am just a great, weak, helpless, drunken beast, a poor wreck!' and the tears jump out of his eyes, eyes that are limpid and blue and unspoiled; and he sobs out: 'Kiss me, take my head in your arms, I am a brute, an infernal brute, but I'm awfully fond of you, you queer little gipsy with your big heart and your damnable will. I! I! I who hated women like poison, who always treated them as such— I could cry when I look at you, like a great puling boy, because your spirit is out of my grasp. Smooth my head; no other little hand in the world has such a touch as yours. I'd know it amongst a thousand—my poor little thing! Don't ever leave me, promise even if I go mad, promise you'll stay. Get a man to mind me, but stay, won't you? Stay!'

'I'll stay.'

'Did any Christian man ever have such an atom for a wife? I believe you are a gipsy; your hair curls at the ends like a live thing, and there are red lights in its black, and your eyes have a flash in them at times and a look as if you were off in other lands! Oh, oh! Get me a little brandy, quick, quick!'

*   *   *   *   *   *

Merrily twang the guitars, and the tambourines rattle as they are swung aloft by slender curving wrists. The wild cries of a Zingari dance ring out. Black eyes gleam, and brown skins shine under orange and scarlet kerchiefs. The grace of panthers and the charm of wild untamed natural things is revealed in every movement. Colour, vivacity, dirt, and rhythm.

Wild the music, wilder the dance, and he sits in his chair on the veranda, the clean, clear air and the fresh breeze blowing in from the sea,

stirring the white hairs in the curls at his
temples, and listens and looks with no eye or
ear for aught of its beauty—only a ribald jest
as their petticoats rise, or their bosoms quiver
in the fling of the dance . . . . and she with a
crimson shawl drawn round her spare shoulders,
and a splash of colour in her thin cheeks holds
one hand tightly pressed over her breast—to still
what? What does the music rouse inside that
frail frame, what parts her lips and causes her
eyes to glisten and the thin nostrils to quiver?
Is there aught in common between that slight
figure with its jewelled hands and its too heavy
silken gown, and those tattered healthy Zingari
vagabonds? . . . . who knows?

The whole tribe are gathered round him,
begging and screaming with one voice, and he
throws silver lavishly to them and thrusts his
hand with a coarse jest into the open bodice of
the girl nearest him. A brown hand goes to the
knife of a swarthy youth with gold rings in his
ears; but at a few strange words from the oldest
woman in the group the girl steps back, and
with the quickness of lightning the hag takes
her place and answers his jest in his own tongue.
The girl looks curiously, pityingly, respectfully

at the other girl, she is a little more than a girl
as she stands dumbly by during all this scene.
Eye seeks eye—sympathy meets sympathy—
what affinity is between these two creatures?

'Kan de rokra Romany?' she asks with a
smile that visits her face as the ghost of a
vanished beauty; and her voice is sweetly soft
as she asks it. A flash of eye, a hurried backward word thrown to the old woman who joins
them on hearing it. She stands between with
a smile at their wonder, and she holds out her
hand, and one slim ivory-tinted hand rests
palm upwards in a no less slim but browner
one. The old woman peers into the lines and
crosses, and as she scans them a look of wonder
creeps up to her usually inscrutable face. She
exchanges words in an undertone with the
gipsy girl at her side.

'I speak Romany too, Deya! An evil fate,
isn't it, mother?'

'A mole on your cheek, and a free Romany
heart in your breast, your spirit fights to be
free as the Romany chai. Seven suns rise and
seven moons, and the flag is half-mast, and the
cage opens and the bird . . . .' an impatient
curse cuts short her words, and they turn to him.

'Here, you old Jezebel! Send these vagabonds of yours down there, there's plenty to
eat.'

The servants are bearing beer and food to
the lawn.

'Shall I go blind? I daresay you know as
much as those infernal doctors, eh?'

'No, your eyes, and pretty eyes they are, and
many a soul they've lost, they'll last your time,
my lord! I see a journey to England, it lies
before you, and no return. Seven times the
moon will rise, and the Romanies go to the
South, but the bird. . . .'

'Get to blazes out of this! Help me in,
ducky, oh damn it, be quick. Get me some
brandy, quick, quick,—not all brandy, a little
milk in it!'

    *   *   *   *   *   *

The moon is high in the heavens, and the sea
is running into the creek with a silver sheen on
its back; the blinds are drawn up in the four
windows of the bedroom, and the northern
night is like unto day disguised in a domino of
silver-grey crape.

He is sleeping. She is standing motionless
at the window. The red of her dressing-gown

and the moonlight make her face look more ghostlike as she leans her head wearily against the window-frame. She is gazing seawards ; a steamer has just passed, and the beacon in the lighthouse on Jomfru-land gleams like a great bright eye. In how many dreary vigils has it not greeted her and seemed to say : 'Courage, I too am watching, you are not alone.'

At the end of the wood two tents are pitched, and she can see two figures outlined against the white palings. The Romany girl and the youth with the gold ear-rings. He is holding her in his arms. The dog-chains rattle now and then ; something brown and stealthy creeps about the duck-house ; the white mists in the marshy bit of meadow lying next the creek dance like spirits, and beckon to her with shadowy arms, and a faint yellow streak appears in the East. How many more nights must she stand alone and watch the morning herald a new day of bondage ? She moves noiselessly away, and goes into the dressing-room, and walks over to the mirror. She shakes her dusky elf locks round her face, and catching up a yellow scarf lying on a chair, winds it round her head, and then peers at herself in the glass. . . . A deft twist turns down the white frills of her night-gown, she has a gold chain round her neck, and she laughs a childish noiseless laugh at her own image. 'How strangely my eyes gleam, and what a gipsy I look! No one would know, no one would dream of it. I would soon get brown!' and she looks wistfully out towards the camp again. In an hour they will go . . . a heap of fern to lie on, scant fare, and weary feet; but the freedom, ah, the freedom! The woods with their wealth of shy, wild things, and the mountains that make one yearn to soar up over their heights to the worlds above. Free to follow the beck of one's spirit, a-ah to dream of it, and the red light glows in her eyes again; they have an inward look; what visions do they see? The small thin face is transformed, the lips are softer, one quick emotion chases the other across it, the eyes glisten and darken deeply, and the copper threads shine in her swart hair. What is she going to do, what resolve is she making? A muttered groan, a stir in the bed rouses her, and throwing aside the scarf, she glides swiftly to his side. She stands and looks down. What a magnificent head it is, and how repellent! The tossed black locks with their silver streaks lie scattered on the pillow. The ear suggests vigorous animalism, the nose is powerful, the broad forehead shines whitely, and the long lashes curl upward as those of a child. The sensual-lipped mouth with its cruel lines shows more cruel as the head is thrown back. She looks at it steadily, no line escapes her ; looks from it to the hands, nerveless, white. The long thin thumbs have a hateful expression, and the backs are short with an ugly joining to the wrists. He stirs, and a lewd word escapes his lips. . . . She shudders. Again her eyes wander out with an appealing look (to whom do they appeal, to part of herself, to some God of convention ?) towards the camp. They are stirring, she can see the Finn dog run to and fro. She steps away . . . irresolution is expressed in her face, her head is thrust forward, her fingers spread out unconsciously. . . . She glances across the floor, some shelves are to be nailed up, one of them is leant against the wardrobe door. As she hesitates she notices that the shadow of it and the half-closed door throws a long cross almost to her feet. She folds her hands involuntarily —a whimper from the bed, a frightened call—

'Come to me! Where are you? Don't leave me a second, oh God, don't leave me! What's that there? Give me a drop of brandy, quick, oh quick! . . . Kneel down, dearie, close, close to me, lay your little old cheek against mine, and say a little prayer, no psalm business, just one out of your own little head' (sob) 'to suit a poor devil like me!'

*   *   *   *   *

The sun is saying good-morning to the moon. She is wan from watching. The birds are awake, but the man still sleeps; and the little red-gowned figure crouched at the bed-side, her left hand with its heavy gold band clasped lightly in his, is sleeping too. A half-dried tear is held in the dark hollow under the closed eyes. The nose looks pinched in the morning light, and a grey-green shadow stains mouth and chin, but a smile plays round the dry lips.

The caravan is winding slowly round the curve of the road, and three plump geese are stowed inside. The Romany lass is humming a song, a song about love, and dance, and song; and the soul of the sleeping girl floats along at her side in a dream of freedom. She of the song looks up: 'Six moons will rise, then you will be free!' she mutters to herself as she passes on ; and the sun mounts higher, and the shadow of the cross is lightening with the coming dawn —who knows ?

III.

AN EBB TIDE

On right and left with flight of light,
  How whirled the hills, the trees, the bowers!
With light-like flight, on left and right,
  How spun the hamlets, towns, and towers!
Dost quail? The moon is fair to see;
  Hurrah! the Dead ride recklessly!
Beloved! Dost dread the shrouded dead?
  Ah let the dead repose! she said.'
                    James Clarence Mangan's *Anthology.*

IT is a sunshine Sabbath morning. The sea quivers under an armour of silver scales and laps, laps with a laugh as it runs into the creek. The sails of the ships glisten whiter than any snow. The sun distils the scent from the clove carnations and the sweetbrier leaves; and coaxes the pungent resin through the cracks in the bark, until the air is heavy with a smell that would cease to be perfume, were it not filtered through the salt ooze of the incoming sea-breeze that flutters the flags on the tall white poles, and tempers the ardour of the young year's sun.

The kariol bearing the specialist whose skill

is of no avail in the face of a pressing call from the great God Death, has just wound round the pine wood in a whirl of dust. The dogs, unbound, lie on the back veranda with their black snouts resting on their fore paws, and they watch him depart without a growl. They have not barked for days past, nor chased the plucky badger, nor yapped impatiently as the cheeky squirrels flirted through the branches. Even beggars have come and gone without a snarling protest. But all last night they howled and bayed and cowered together as if they could see the passage of invisible guests. A peculiar stillness seems to brood over the great place. The maids are sitting in their gowns of Sunday black, with open psalm-books on their laps; they are listening and whispering with the disturbance of expectancy.

The housekeeper is talking to the leech woman, quaint survival of older days, whose business in life is to keep the slimy suckers lively and apply them. She looks as if she fed them between-times on herself, so bony and colourless a creature is she. They are negotiating the last ghastly offices that may soon be needed—speculating as to the changes and their effect on the village. The vicar, she tells, is about to make the departing life the text of his sermon. Every one in the district is coming to hear it. Why not? A sermon of warning, with a smack of the Pharisee in it, a 'Lord, I thank Thee I am not like unto this man' note, especially if you know the publican in question, cannot fail to be attractive; it has an up-to-date interest that the parable of the far-away-time sinner necessarily lacks.

Up-stairs the cow-girl is crouching like a faithful dog outside his bedroom door; she is listening to the murmured Latin service of the mass that comes from inside. The windows of the room are wide open, and the sea stretches away and melts into the horizon in an infinity of blue and silver. He is lying still on the ebb of his last tide, and when his eyes open they wander from the little priest before the extemporised altar, to the bowed head of the woman kneeling beside him.

'Pax Domini sit semper vobiscum!' intones the priest.

'Et cum spiritu tuo!' she utters in response, in dead, dull tones, and when she chimes the little silver bell she does it in a mechanical way.

And all the time he holds her one hand to his breast. When the mass is read and the extreme unction administered, the little priest reads the prayers for the dying. He listens attentively, and she listens too, with eyes dry as horn, and tightened lips. She scarcely hears what he reads.

'My feet have gone astray in the paths of vanity and sin, now let me walk in the way of Thy commandments. . . . Forgive me, O Lord, all the sins which I have committed by my disordered steps. . . .' 'Steps!' that means feet, 'eyes seen vanities,' that means sight. . . . 'Tongue hath in many ways offended,' speech ; why he is going through all the seven senses, or is it seven? or five? She must give him the envelope with the cheque in it before he leaves. . . . She hasn't a black frock, not one ; he liked her in colours, light girlish colours with a silken waist-band to match. Must she wire for a coffin? What a beast she is to think like this? But how can she help it ? Her tear-bags—what is their right name? lachrymal glands?—are exhausted, even her lashes have thinned, yet she never shed a tear, at least only inwardly, with a choke.

He sobs and she looks up; the tears are trickling down his cheeks, she puts up her free hand and wipes them off gently.

'To Thee I resign my heart! Into Thy hands, O Lord, I commend my spirit!' reads the priest in broken English, and when the, from its point of view, beautiful prayer has drawn to a solemn close, the man sobs out in genuine heartfelt conviction with a force of epithet that is habit, not irreverence.

'That is a damn nice prayer! I was always afraid of death, always (with a sob) a coward, but when it comes to the point that vanishes too!'

And the boyish priest purses his cheque, and takes it with him, and leaves his blessing instead, and follows in the wake of the town doctor.

'Send Johann to me, dearums, let me get dressed, I'll have a try to die in the sunshine. Get your own little bed carried down to the veranda, and your own little white pillow; mind, the one you put your head on last; and lend them to me for this turn.'

And so the maids take it down, and she stands at the head of the stairs as they carry

it, two at the head, and two at the foot.
As she hears their cautious backward steps
and the rest at the turn, she fancies it sounds
like the bearing out of a coffin. And then he
follows slowly out, leaning on his big stick,
and his beard divides into patches and shows
the purplish skin, and his breathing is laboured,
but he steps more firmly than he has done
for a long time past. He leans on her frail
shoulders, and when they reach the dining-
room he calls in the maids and the men who
serve him, and bids them charge their glasses;
and he thanks them, and says he is sorry for
all the trouble he has given them, and shakes
hands with each one; and they courtesy and
say Skaal! (a salutation when drinking) and
troop out crying. They are mostly women,
and women forgive easily and forget everything—to a man! Only the cow-girl stops
behind crouched near the door crying: 'O-ah,
o-ah!' He fills his own glass with champagne and sips it, but nature sets a limit to
the alcohol a man may absorb, and he has
passed it. He cannot get it down, so he lays
his hand on her head and smooths it gently,
and says—

'Your luck, little one, your very good luck! Oh, my poor little one, I am afraid for you! I ought to have . . . well, it's no good regretting . . . and with a last flame of the old fierce fire he cries—

'I have had my last drink, and no man shall drink after me;' and he shivers the glass against the wall, and purple shadows, the 'skreigh' of another dawn, chase one another over his swollen face, and he leans heavily on her and says faintly—

'Lay me down, I am tired!'

When they reach the veranda, the leaves of the virgin-vine are strewn in dancing shadow leaves and fluttering tendrils at their feet. He looks at them and mutters: 'Shadows—only shadows!'

Suddenly he searches her face intently and asks—

'Is there no hope, little one? none?'

He reads the answer in her wistful eyes.

'When? Don't you be afraid to tell me, when did he say?'

'Inside twenty-four hours—'

There is a long silence, and the shadow leaves dance, and the bees whirl buzzing past, and the strong young life of midsummer mocks dissolution in a subtle arrogant way.

'One good clean year, one clean year, one year's home for a finish. Just as I learnt to know what it meant to leave it all! It's hard to look on a day like this' (sob) 'and know that to-morrow I rot. A long life as lives go, and nothing to show for it. Well, I always wanted to die in the sunshine with the birds singing, and, since I knew you, with you near me—oh, my dear, my poor dear little one!'

He reels, and she clutches him, but he steadies himself by a supreme effort, and says through his ground teeth—

'Now I am going to say good-bye to the world, and, by God, I'll say it standing. I have had good days in it, wild, glad days, drunk with the lust of love and wine, but I never saw good or beauty in it till you showed me how. Oh, oh, oh! Let no man write my epitaph!'

He stands leaning on her shoulders looking seawards, drinking his fill of sun and sea, sea that was a rapture to him, that he loved as the greatest, and strongest, and cruellest thing he knew; the only thing that responded

to the wild moods in his soul, and struck a
rushing strain of song in his stormy heart,
that made him rejoice with a fierce delight.
The tears fall and splash on her hands, and
then she helps him to lie down, and she feels
his feet, and they bring hot bottles, for they are
getting cold, and he lies with his eyes closed;
the village doctor comes and goes, but nothing
can be done, the sands are running out fast. 'If
the Lord be merciful' (the sermon is working in
him) 'He will take him before morning, otherwise he will suffer much,' he whispers to her.
She does not answer, only kneels silently at
his side, and he holds her hand. There is a
strange smell that has a chill uncleanness in
its breath about them. The people pass by
on the road above and peer down through
the palings. The maids give audience to inquisitive or interested callers at the back.
The housekeeper is busy at the linen press,
sorting out sheets and things that may be
needed, and as she moves about with noiseless tread, and folds and lays aside, she
mentally remodels her wardrobe. If she take
out the flower in her black summer hat,
and put in some curled tips, it will serve

nicely. Mistress will surely bring her a dress from England, and the merino they hang the rooms with, she will get it cut the proper lengths, will do for the maids. Uf! that nasty wine gave her a headache! she will get some fresh beans roasted, and have a good cup with fresh cream; that will do her good. How Gudrun (the cow-girl) takes on! He was a devil to serve, but there were advantages, ay, many pickings that would not fall to one's share in better-regulated Christian households, not to speak of the distinct comfort of having a mistress whose time is taken up elsewhere. Poor thing! Well, it's best for her, she has money, she'll marry again. But *that* Gudrun! it is odd. Why should she carry on so? Or could there be a reason? He always took great notice of Gudrun; she used to laugh and grin and go on, when he went out in the yard, and never was afraid. And then there was that anonymous letter the mistress got. Uf! Men folk, God save us! Even with a leg in the grave it's hard to trust them! There's no smoke without fire, that's sure. There, that's all ready. 'Well! what is it?'

This to the second housemaid. She is a fat girl, with a restless twitch about her mouth and half-closed eye-lids, that curl upwards at the outer corners. One gets the impression somehow that her solid physique is but a mask to cover an emotional soul with a dangerous sense of humour.

'The Bible reader, Morten Ring, wants to know if he may read for a while, now that the Popish priest has gone and left the dying sinner without any one to direct his thoughts heavenwards.'

There is an imitative note in her voice, and a mocking gleam shoots from her eyes.

'Uf! is he here again? That's the third time. Mistress told him no before, and strong enough too; I should think that ought to have been more than enough for him.'

'Yes, but he says the whole village thinks it shocking and he is like sent up, and that you might put it to her!'

'Indeed, then I won't. When I did last time she told me to tell him to go down to the weighing place on the wharf, and ring a bell, and call the population together and read out to them all the places in the Bible that refer to hypocrisy, lying, and scandal; the sins of adultery, fornication, and the begetting of bastards. That she 'd be willing to pay him treble his fee for the charity of it ; they need it so much. It might teach them to begin at home and let other folks alone.'

' Shall I tell him that ? ' (eagerly.)

' Are you mad ? No, tell him Mistress is reading herself, and ask him to stay and have a good cup of coffee and sweet rusks. I want to get the truth out of him about the magistrate's girl's illness ; he was up there, and I don't believe a sniff in her sprained foot. . . .'

And down below the rosebuds opened into roses, and nodded with the effrontery of assured beauty to the Sun God ; and the birds hushed them for their noon siesta ; and he lay with shut eyes and held her hand tightly ; and sometimes he spoke to her and sometimes he muttered to himself (she caught the words) a line of his favourite Mangan :

> ' Sleep ! no more the dupe of hopes and schemes,
> Soon thou sleepest where the thistles blow ;
> Curious anticlimax to thy dreams,
> Twenty golden years ago ! '

The odd unpleasant smell seems to hang about

them as if too heavy to diffuse itself in the
thin clear air; the smell of cow-sheds that
clings to the cow-girl's clothes, is perfume to it.
It attracted the flies and they gathered like
swarming bees on the window panes and door
posts; and buzzed and hummed and stung like
Bushmen, carousing over a find of dead meat;
and they crept over the bed and stuck in his
hair, and she tried to keep them off his face,
and when one of them crawled up her own
with tickling, clinging feet, she paled and
shuddered.   The cow-girl stepped out of her
clogs and went into the drawing-room and
brought out a gaily-painted palm-leaf fan and
stationing herself at the head of the bed, set it in
motion.   His breathing is getting laboured, and
at times an ugly flush crosses his face.   Once
when it is deeper than usual, the girl cries: 'O
Lord God, Lord God!'   He hears her and looks
up.

'Ah, Gudrun, is that you? good girl, good
girl!'

She sinks on to her knees and moans and
rocks herself, and then she looks at his closed
eyes and says to her—

'Mistress, may I?   It can't harm you!'

She nods her head wearily ; she is fanning awkwardly with her left hand, and she says with her tired tender voice—

'Gudrun wants to say good-bye, dear !'·

He opens his eyes, and for a moment the charm of his rare smile returns. The girl stoops and leaves a kiss upon his forehead, and then rushes away and flings herself down on the long lush grass, that is never cut, under a big chestnut tree. He looks at her and lifts her hand to his lips—

'Always a big heart, always a great little woman !' (with a groan) 'and now I am to lose you, and it is the best thing could happen to you. Ay, there's the sting ; leave you to some brute ; that is my punishment. O little one, don't you think too hardly of me (he talks with effort), I meant to be better than I was to you. You'll never find another man love you as I did ; remember that and forget all the rest if you can. You *have* forgotten all, I might have known you would . . . where am I drifting to? no man ever came back to say. Do you believe in hell' (eagerly), 'do *you* believe in it ?'

She looks at him pityingly, with a flash of past

energy in the lift of her head and a curl of scorn on her pale lips.

'The hell of the priests or parson? No, I do not. Is that worrying you? Don't you let it, old man, don't you let it. Wherever you are going, whatever after-existence your poor troubled soul is fighting its way to, it *is not to their hell.*' The girl has come back and taken up her former position, and fans steadily, for the flies are gathering in greater numbers every hour. The veranda seems airless and close, and uncanny with unseen things; the doctor comes and goes; the servants peep out; and the hours seem to hold many hours in their embrace. She seems to live all her life over again. Things she has forgotten completely come vividly back to her. An old Maori man, who used to sell sweet potatoes, and quaint ring shells for napkin rings to the Pakeha lady in Tauranga Bay, floats before her inward vision as tangible as if he were next her. And a soldier servant; she can hear his voice; he used to sing as he pipe-clayed—

'But kaipoi te waipero, Kaipoi te waiena
For Rangatira Sal, Bob Walker sold his pal,
But he's now at the bottom o' the harbour.

Why did the stupid chorus come back to her now, what chink of brain did it lie in all these years? Oh what a brute she is and how callous! She ought to read prayers, or say things; in a few hours it will be too late to ever say a word more. She finds herself beating time with her foot to a jig tune, a bizarre accompaniment to the words 'too late.' She would give all she possesses to cry, yet she cannot; and so the day wears on.

Later on she bends her head to him and asks:

'Are you dozing or are you thinking? What are you thinking of?'

He smiles. 'Of zoo, dearums, of zoo!'

'Have you said your prayers; shall I read you any?'

'Finished them long ago! I am just waiting, lying thinking of you, dearie, thinking of you. Happier than ever I was since I left off "taw in the lay" and pegging tops.'

Her question was a concession to a past religious conscience; she feels as she puts it that as for herself if she should die as she sits there, she would not trouble to pray—it would be well to drift out. There is another weary hour's silence, then he looks up at her and shivers slightly, and tightens his clasp of her hand.

'Kiss me, duckums, kiss me! Now lay your little old phiz on the pillow close to mine, you dearest and best in the world! Close, close to mine.'

The wind is changing, and the sun hides his face decently behind a great white cloud; there is a hoarse rattle in his throat, and his breathing is difficult. The doctor comes and stands quietly behind her; the crowd at the gate above gets denser; the servants huddle together in the dining-room and cry. The Swedish gardener pats them all in turn, but most gently the fat housemaid. A sudden blast of wind blows a strand of her hair loose and it touches his lips, and he mutters, 'My little one!' She lifts her face and looks at him, a strange purple colour vibration is waving over his face, and she calls affrightedly—

'Dear, oh dear man, look at me! Can you see me, do you know me?'

He lifts his heavy lids and looks at her steadily with half-dead eyes, and says with stiff, barely articulate speech—

'Of course I do, my dearie, I'm all rig . . . !'

She feels his fingers close more tightly over hers—once—twice, then relax. His chin falls, and the doctor passes his hand over his eyelids and puts a handkerchief to his lips. The cow-girl drops with a cry to the ground and throws her apron over her head. At the gate above a child calls 'mammy' in frightened tones. The lad who has been sitting up on the slope at the foot of the flag-staff, slides the Union Jack half-mast, and the big white house is without a master.

*   *   *   *   *   *

She is sitting in an old garden, a retired place in the village, right on the fjord. They have driven her down there away from the house that seems haunted by his spirit; infected with the loathsome odour of rapid dissolution that nothing can overcome, that seems to ooze out and taint the very flowers. And then the myriad flies that crawl and creep, as if sick or drunk, over everything; and make one loathe and turn from the very sight of food and drink, for dread of where they have been; make one long to scream hysterically to drown their hateful buzzing; and rush away and plunge into the sea—were it not that it too seems to whisper in undertones of dead men and lost sweethearts, drowned mariners with swollen grey-green faces and tangled locks floating like sea sedge behind them, as they toss on the swift undercurrents beneath its treacherous smiling surface.

It is with her, sitting there, as it is with most of us when numbed in mind and heart by some great trouble; her senses are more alive to outward sounds and scenes. It is as if when one's inner self is working with some emotion, wrestling with some potential moral enemy, crying out under the crucifixion of some soul-passion—eyes and ears and above all sense of smell are busy receiving impressions, and storing them up as a phonograph records a sound, to reproduce them with absolute fidelity if any of the senses be touched in the same way by the subtle connection between perfume and memory. She will, in all time to come, never forget that old garden. She is rocking unconsciously to and fro. Her thoughts, and the emotions belonging to them, cross one another rapidly; flash past as the landscape seen from a mail train, so that she cannot fasten any of them. The weary vigils of many months, the

details of days and hours are ticked off as the
events on a tape. The look in his eyes, press
of his fingers, the quiet face with the awful look
of peace—the rapid changes to a thing to be
hidden away as swiftly as hands can coffin it;
the clasped fingers never to be lifted in tender
caress or angry gesture; the future to face
without even the rough protection of his
passionate wayward affection—all these con-
flicting images and reasonings dash through
her brain and yet not a detail of her surroundings escapes her. The strips of blue fjord with
the pilot boats with their numbered sails in the
immediate foreground; and the prams, turned
bottom up on the miniature wharf for a fresh
coat of paint. The dip of the white sail of a
pleasure-boat in the distance, and the gleam of
the scarlet cap of a girl steering. Bright flecks
on the black-green shadows of the trees in the
near background, that stand out distinctly from
the misty blue of the distant mountains; misty
with the purple light that only clothes the
northern heights. Not a detail of the quaint
garden escapes her. It is a garden of surprises.
Fruit-trees from strange lands, dwarf shrubs of
foreign birth, curious shells gathered on the

beach of far-away islands flourish promiscuously with indigenous plants. A painted lady (the figure-head of some effete sailing craft), who has cloven the storms through many seas with her mighty breasts, and commanded the rising waves with her upraised hand, and faced the storm with a smile ghastly in its wooden fixity, has come here to rest. She leans next to an old sun-dial in the shade of an ancient lilac bush. The sense of beauty, and the bump of utility of successive owners is manifested at every turn. The even drills of potatoes are disturbed by the tombstone of a favourite dog. A plaster Mercury, and a shrub, cut in the form of a bulgy tea-pot, spoil the symmetry of a bed of carrots. Strawberries carrying their ripe red fruit right bravely fill the background of one bed. A tangled profusion of pinks, pansies, and gillyflowers, forget-me-nots, and fragrant lavender spikes have a long straight line of leeks running amidst their sweet irregularity as a pungent line in a dainty sheaf of verse. She is conscious of a vague pleasure as she notes these things, and a sort of wondering pity at the pathos of her own quiet figure. She fingers her black cashmere gown and the heavy silk

fringe of her shawl. She never wore a shawl
before, but they had nothing else black. Her
mother used to wear a shawl, a white Indian
silk with raised flowers. Her shoulders sloped
too, like Eugénie's. Funny to wear a shawl like
an old lady! She has a bag with money, papers,
certificate of death for the customs. What a
nuisance all these formalities are! Lum tum, te
tum, te tum . . . ! The dead march in Saul! No,
she mustn't hum that. She remembers once in
the long ago, before the flood, her flood, she had
a sweetheart, a boy officer. She wonders did he
get fat; they always chaffed and said he would.
Once she was humming it and he stopped
her, saying: 'Oh don't! when any one hums
that, a poor soldier dies somewhere.' Superstition of course, but she won't hum it all the
same, just for the old sake's sake. Why should
she kill a soldier? She used to like all soldiers,
tum tum! . . . Is she going mad? How does
one go mad? . . . She turns her head in relief
at an approaching step. The little doctor stands
bowing, hat in hand. She notices that he is
wearing his dress suit, and adds mentally, 'they
wear dress clothes on solemn occasions; christenings, weddings, funerals.' Why, of course

it's the funeral! She even smiles at the con-
junction of a swallow-tail with elastic side
leather boots with high heels. His trousers
too must have been made before he grew stout;
they ruck up at the knees, and show the end line
of his under-drawers quite plainly. She feels
inclined to laugh. She hasn't really laughed
for a long time; well, why shouldn't she laugh?

'Will Fruen come now?' he queries. There
is a subtle blending of the soothing professional
tone he uses to lady patients, and the gravity
befitting a solemn occasion. She takes up her
bag, gathers her shawl mechanically into graceful folds over her arms and follows him. They
go up through the wood past the poorhouse to
a side entrance. She notices as she looks down
over the town that the flags are all half-way
down the staffs, and that the village is crowded
with folk; and that outside the house there are
groups of black-coated men; like ants crawling
about a white stone, she thinks. The little
housekeeper meets her at the door; the other
girls are crying; she bows to people without
recognising them. Then there is a tramping
of feet, and some one leads her out; the bell is
tolling up from the church, and she sees that

they have covered the grey cobs with black palls, and attached a black canopy to the cart, and outlined the spokes of the wheels with fir needles, and smothered the rest of it with branches and flowers, wreaths and crosses, and harps and lyres; he hated music too. The coffin—what an ugly black thing, with an exaggerated stomach and garish silver ornaments! —is resting upon the Union Jack. A crowd of faces that she does not know meets her. She places herself behind the cart, and the maids follow her, and all the dogs gather round her but never growl once as they move on, and the crowd follows. She can see the green road; they have covered it according to custom with branches of fir and pine, a green river, a grass-green river winding to the left. And the sea, the sea he loved! it seems to her that there is a cadence of pity in the eternal note of its quiet sadness. How tired her feet are; it's quite half a mile yet; she has no ankles; how funny! Just stilts made of her will. She trips. The cow-girl pushes past the housekeeper, and watches her steps. 'Lord God, how stony-faced she is!' whispers the doctor's wife, 'and she never cried once.' It is a long way, she keeps thinking.

Where are they going anyway? Oh yes, to the
tug, the tug that is to bear them away on a
glorious lonely death-ride, out of the sunny
fjord to the glistening sea, away to where the
rainbow ends. At the end of the rainbow
you 'll find a pot of gold. But first they must
pass through the wide wooden gate; it is open.
What is that they say about a wide wooden
gate? No, it 's about a road, it 's the wide road
that leads to destruction. They have decked
the gate with green too. The gate through
which the children used to peer with inquisitive
frightened child-eyes, up to the house where
the wicked man dwelt. How they used to
scamper away with half-real, half-acted terror
at a cry of, 'the man is coming!' the man
who was a bogie-man to them, a name with
which to threaten them when naughty; about
whom their elders told dreadful tales in subdued voices. She remembers this, and smiles
half sadly to see as they reach the narrow street
how the children swarm to meet his coming.
There is no school to-day, and they get under
the horses' hoofs, and crowd round the car, and
point with dirty chubby fore-fingers, and clasp
hands and cluster together in groups of twos

and threes, and gaze with awe-struck eyes, and whisper, and follow. And one whispers to his comrades how he once got a drive and a silver piece from 'the man,' and another how he gave little Tulla a piece of cake. And she thinks of the train that danced in the wake of the pied piper, and of his own little ones who know him not. Perhaps they are dancing and laughing to-day. To-day, when the father who gave them no name is being borne along to the tuneful patter of little feet that are not of his kith nor his kin. She seems to feel that that thing in the coffin is not he. He is walking next her, laughing with the rare humour of his best moments; chuckling at the grand funeral they are giving him; him the bad man, of whom they had naught but evil to say. How hard it is to go down hill slowly! She tells herself that later on in the ages to come, when the little ones here have gone to their last homes as withered elders, the tales of the bogie-man of their child days may have grown into a saga of a wild Angle-man with great wealth, who landed and made himself a home on their coast, and drank and caroused and bought the strangest things; who took mad sails in a boat right into the teeth of

coming gales that the pilots feared to brave,
when the white-crested horses leaped high over
the rocks, and the sea dragons roared below,
and the grey mews shrieked shrill warnings to
the fishers to hasten them home. Who turned
the night into day and took wild hag-rides with
his baying and galloping horses at midnight,
and how he used to crack his whip and urge
them on with exultant oaths; and never let his
little wife out of his sight, but called for her if he
missed her till the woods rang with her name.

They reach the wharf, the tug *Bully-boy*, with
black funnel and hissing steam is lying taut to
the pier. Her head is really spinning. How
stupid those eight men are! they haven't
backed the horses enough. Hats off! They
lay him on the deck, they have put the old flag
under him and piled the posies on top. She
pats the dogs and bids them stay, and lets the
women kiss her, and walks up the plank; one
plank, surely there should be four—

> ' For thee it is that I dree such pain
> As when wounded even a plank will,
> My bosom is pierced, is rent in twain,
> That thine may ever bide tranquil.
>   May ever remain
> Henceforward untroubled and tranquil.'

No, that's not the verse, she can't get it.

'I heard four planks fall down with a sad-dening echo? . . . with a hollow echo?' She stands by the side of the coffin and gazes quietly at the crowd. Looks at the men with their uplifted hats, at the black-draped horses—Puck is biting Olla in the neck—at the children, and the group of dogs. And all the staring eyes seem to melt into one monster multi-coloured eye, that pierces her through and through; can't they see she is hollow? the fools!

They loosen the hawser and cry all right; and *Bully-boy* swings round, and they steam seaward and she sits and dreams; and the tug dances, and splutters, and fusses through the sunlit sea, past fjord mouths and hamlets, and boats with singing children and yapping dogs, and she never thinks of the future, nor of the steamer she is to meet at the city, nor makes any plan; simply sits and lets her fancies run riot through her tired brain. Sits under a canopy of clear air and listens to the strange conceits that arise in her thinking self. She is a Viking's bond-maid of olden days; she hid on his bark whilst they built up his funeral pyre and laid the old warrior down. She watched them touch the flaming pine knot to his fiery mausoleum, and set him adrift to the strain of a fierce exultant chant of victory, to sail out on his last voyage for a handigrips with the grim foe Death. Ay, he too was a primitive man, with the primæval passions of untamed nature, surging up and eating their way to his soul's core, as restless breakers hollow a place on the coast. And now he is going to rest.

The sun sinks in a superb, audacious blending of hues—orange and scarlet, pink and blue, and lemon-yellow streaks, with splotches of intensest purple, are hurled from a palette of fire in a frenzy of colour. The fishers pause and look curiously at the silent little figure keeping vigil next the flower-decked coffin as she passes them in the pearl-mists of the summer night. Pearl-mists that wrap her in a chilly shroud ; and she fancies that spirit hands spread the canopy of starred blue over them as they glide on ; and the moon peers down and nods to her ; and another moon runs seawards on a shining silver river. And the foam in their wake ripples together like frothing diamond chisps, and the dew falls on the withering flowers, and bathes her pale face, and moistens her dry lips. And the

night breeze sings sadly to the thrumming of unseen harps, and soothes her troubled spirit with
tender whisperings that only the stricken in soul
can catch in snatches from the spirit of nature.

The boy takes the wheel, and the captain
brews her some coffee. They have forgotten
at the house, in their care for the funeral, to
provide her with food or rugs. She is too
deliciously weary (there is no new effort either
to make unless she chooses) to care. When he
brings it to her she swallows it gratefully, and
follows him to the stuffy little cabin, and lies
down as he suggests, with her head on a pilot
coat, and he covers her tenderly with another;
she is so small and frail it takes but little.
Somehow, it smells 'homey' with its mingled
odour of tobacco, and brine, and man, and
touches her chilled lone soul like the honest
clasp of a warm human hand with a promise of
rest and shelter to come; and under its homely
spell she falls asleep. And so these two poor
human souls, tossed together for good or ill for
a brief space, sleep their last together through
the summer night. He, to no mortal awakening; she, perchance to a brighter dawn.

DISCORDS: BY
GEORGE EGERTON

VIRAGO

TO

T. P. GILL

'Here . . . . . carry this to my Gossip'

'Light, seeking light, doth light of light beguile.'

CONTENTS

PAGE

A PSYCHOLOGICAL MOMENT AT THREE PERIODS—

        THE CHILD, ... 1

        THE GIRL, ... 8

        THE WOMAN, ... 20

HER SHARE, ... 67

GONE UNDER, ... 82

WEDLOCK, ... 115

VIRGIN SOIL, ... 145

THE REGENERATION OF TWO, ... 163

A PSYCHOLOGICAL MOMENT
AT THREE PERIODS

I.—THE CHILD

THE lamp on the nursery table is yet unlit, and the waning daylight of the early spring throws the part of the room near the window into cold grey shadow. The fire burns with a dull red glow in the lower bars ; it has been slacked ; just one little bubble of gas seethes like a ball of molten jet and flickers into a bluish flame.

The quick patter of little feet, and the sound of quarrelling child voices, broken by the deeper note of a woman's voice raised in gentle chiding, comes up from below stairs.

A child is crouched on the old hearthrug, holding a book to the firelight. Her eyes run greedily along the lines, one little red hand holds the top of the right-hand page in eager readiness to turn it over ; her long, tangled elf-locks catch a ruddy glint each time her head moves.

A bit of coal drops, and the flamelet goes out ; she lifts her head and draws a deep breath ; she is trembling with excitement, for she has been holding it unconsciously. She makes a move to

stir the fire, but a shade passes over the questioning child-face as the inner voice that she
alone knows of, of which not even the tender
little mother has an inkling, begins its warning
and reproach.

'Shut the book now—now, just when the exciting part begins. No, you may not read to the
end of the page—no, not even a line more. If
you want to be brave, if you want to be strong,
sacrifice ; sacrifice, mortify yourself. If you don't
want to ! No, you are weak, you cannot do that,
not even that small thing, for God. No, not after
supper ! Not until to-morrow, to-morrow evening——' The small head with the straight white
parting bends over the closed book, and a sobbing
sigh floats out into the room full of shadows.

She rises slowly and puts the book away, high
up on a shelf on the old bookcase, and then looks
fearsomely round her. If she were only round the
next lobby, past the closed door of the empty
room where the coffin once stood, where the chill
air seems to rush out and play down one's back
like the cold, cruel taps of long, clutching fingers.
She steals out hurriedly, tip-toeing unconsciously,
and whispering with throbbing breathlessness,
'Guardian angel, O dear guardian angel ! take
care of me !' leaving a space for the angel on the
side next the door. A flying jump, a clutch at
the balusters, and the lobby where the tall clock
mounts guard is safely reached. The light streams
up from the hall below, and the cheery rattle of
the milk-boy's can on the steps, and the smell of

rice slightly burned, strike warmly to her heart.
But the face of the old clock seems to look mock-
ingly down at her, and its tick-tock speaks with a
jeering voice to the panting child—the house is
full of voices. 'You be a Grace Darling! you be
a Maid of Orleans! Afraid! afraid! Coward!
coward! go back right to the nursery door—yes,
to the very door, and count ten outside of it.' She
is rolling her holland 'pinny' into a mass of hopeless creases, and the look on the grave small face
is half defiant, half pleading. 'Tick, tock, afraid,
afraid! Leave you be? No, you must be strong.
God wants you; you must be strong! Offer it up
for a poor soul!' The little shrinking figure goes
wearily up again, halts outside the closed door,
and kneels. Then she comes down backwards,
resolutely facing the dreaded door.

.   .   .   .   .   .

'Summer, the wanton youth, is carrying all before him.'

The playground of a girls' school is thronged
with laughing pupils; snobbery, toadying, gossip
and backbiting, all the vices of matured society,
flourish there in miniature. The daughters of the
prosperous pawnbroker are snubbed and patron-
ised by the shabbily-clad offspring of the half-pay
captain, who owes two quarters' schooling and had
the bailiffs in last week; the girl with the most
pocket-money and the prettiest frocks is courted
and flattered to her face, and made fun of behind
her back, as they mimic her important, 'Me uncle
the Bishup o' Durry!'

Under an old elm-tree in a corner a group of
girls is gathered. Four of them are listening
intently to the fifth, a diminutive thing, class-
mate by virtue of brains not years. Her voice is
peculiar, and she speaks without a trace of accent,
whereas the anæmic-looking girl next her has
Doblin in every vowel. The two, with arms
entwined, are sworn to inseparable friendship ;
they wear a bit of each other's hair in silver
lockets under their frocks, and think of each
other every evening when the clock strikes nine.
All follow the speaker's words with rapt attention,
for as she warms to her narrative one telling
expression trips up the other, and they break into
laughter, with the shrilly giggling zest of early
girlhood at a supremely daring climax. Only the
fourth, a square-faced girl with steady pale-grey
eyes, thin lips, and smooth, foxy hair dragged
back from a broad forehead, gazes questioningly
at her. The little one flushes as she catches the
look, and when the bell rings she tucks her hand
coaxingly under the other's arm, and adds an
unnecessary detail, a stronger touch, as if to
compel her belief.

She talks until they gain their places at the
desk, and silence is commanded. The pale-grey
eyes study her face curiously, and an almost im-
perceptible smile plays about the thin mouth ; the
same may be seen any day on her father's face in
the Green Street Court-house, when he pins a
witness under cross-examination.

'Tired, childie?'

'Yes, mumsy, awful tired.'

'Perhaps you ran about too much in the heat, dearie?'

'No, mumsy, I didn't! It's not that way—I am tired *in me*. Does everybody think, I mean, ask about things, in one? I want to know so many things—I think such a lot, and'—with a half-sob—'oh, oh, I wish I didn't!'

The mother draws her down to the heart under which she lay cuddled long before thought came, and smooths back the dusky hair from the hot forehead with tender fingers, needle-pricked over tiny garments for ever-coming human problems.

'Tell mother, dearie!'

'Ah, there's so much, mumsy, there's so much pain in the world. It's everywhere! Those horrid Chinese with their torturing, and all the poor animals; oh, I can't bear it! Why did God make us when He knew we'd be wicked? when He knew we'd go to hell? and when we want so hard to be good, and there's always something inside making us do bad things—oh! why did He? why did He?'—sob—'I can't think it was right of Him!'—with passion—'Oh, oh, it wasn't!'

'H-u-ssh, childie!' says the mother, and she rocks her slowly to and fro, and whispers softly:

'It's best not to question, lovey—far best. Just trust God, as you trust me when I tell you something is for your good. Keep on and do what you believe to be right yourself. Mother's own dear little girl, her own little one!'

There is a singular look on the child's face, a look of resolute repression ; and when she raises it and kisses the worn, lovable face above hers, the spirit that looks up out of her eyes is older than the spirit that looks down out of the mother's.

And when the city clocks are pealing forth the midnight chimes, and the weary mother folds up the mended socks and puts them away, and goes her nightly round, and bends over each tiny cot, she stays longest at the bigger white bed, and makes, Spanish fashion, the sign of the cross with her thumb on the child's hot forehead, little dreaming that the lonely little soul has cried herself to sleep with the knowledge of having grown beyond her help.

Noon the next day—a hot, bleached noon.

Under the elm-tree three of the same girls are waiting. She comes out through the school-house door. Two sparrows are picking up crumbs on the flagged walk. A stump of pencil is lying next an orange peel. Every detail of that big yard, with its groups of chattering girls, pieces of greasy lunch paper, and the three figures waiting under the elm-tree in the corner, bites into her brain, a mind-etching never to be effaced.

She slips quickly down the path, and although every nerve is braced to support her in a tremendous resolve, although she feels a sick, cold, sinking weight in her stomach, she avoids treading on the joinings of the flag-stones, and takes two short steps where the space is very big. They are waiting for her, for is she not the most gifted, the most daring, the most individual amongst them ? Perhaps the set, unsmiling whiteness of her face strikes them as unusual. They stop talking ; they just wait.

She stands before them ; opens her mouth ; but something rises in her throat and checks her speech ; she masters it :

'You know what I told you yesterday,' she says ; 'well, it was untrue, every, every bit of it— no ; at—at least there was a little true, but I added all the rest, made it up, just lied for the sake of lying.'

There is a silence, at least it seems to her that they are standing inside a silent circle and that the long giggling scream of 'Tagg' of a triumphant catch comes to them from some far-off place. The friends search one another's eyes ; the same ex- pression is in both, not shocked, not a bit, but as folks look away from a mad person, half afraid ; they cling a little closer to one another and turn away in silence. The anæmic girl shifts her feet irresolutely and presses her hands together until the knuckles crack, and says with her weak monotonous voice, with a nervous desire to con- sole :

'Never mind, dear ; ma says you can't help exaggeratin'; for pa says your father's the biggest loiar out ! '

Then she, too, goes away, and the child leans her head against the trunk of the old tree. She feels that grinding her forehead into its rough bark would be a relief, her cheeks are so hot, and her eyelids smart so. She bites her tongue in her self-abasement. She had hoped they would have understood how much it cost her to tell them the truth—and yet—in between it all, had there not lurked an idea that they would think it nobly done of her? How the poor little soul cringes as this fresh bit of self-knowledge strikes home to her! Well, she has promised that she would punish herself, that she would tell each girl to whom she had lied the truth. She turns at the sound of a heavy step behind her, to face the cold grey eyes in the square face—'Her too, her too!' craves the voice. All the exalted spirit that spurred her on has fallen flat, only a sick feeling of useless shame remains, weighing heavily on the poor puzzled child-soul. Well, she will drain the chalice to the dregs, so she begins quaveringly:

'You know wh——'

'I know; they told me. Come and wash your face. I think you were a fool to do it.'

II.—THE GIRL

YELLOW sunshine flooding an autumn world, gold-brown leaves falling like shivered mica on the great highway that is straight and dusty and long, crossed by other straight and dusty roads, running as the squares of a chess-board across the flat landscape.

The road is flanked on each side by alternate

poplars and beeches, and their foliage honeycombs the white dust and the grey-green grass with flecks of quivering shadow.

Here and there at great intervals a clump of trees clusters about a villa, or an orchard, or forms a leafy square at the back of a farmhouse, or a long line of pollard willows defines a dyke. At the vanishing-point of the double line of trees flanking the highway, red-tiled roofs, a spire, and the tops of some canvas tents form a trefoil, and away across the flat brown land windmills lean against the horizon, with their sails at ease, like giant moths asleep on outstretched wings.

The scene, with its absolute serenity and subtle suggestion of delicate decay, suggests a Cuyp, an autumn study in quiet yellows and browns.

A child-girl is herding some lean cows that crop the dusty herbage under the trees at each side of the wide road. She is a thin, unformed thing of unlovely angles, with dirty flaxen hair clubbed short at her neck under a close-fitting cotton cap. Her dingy green stuff bodice and homespun skirt hang loosely, and her check apron is patched with newer brighter pieces. Her footless stockings just reach her ankles, and their strong bones and her shining red heels peer out of her wooden shoes. She is knitting a coarse stocking, and she presses the needle tightly against her flat, childish bosom as she knits off the stitches. Tink! tink! the bell-cow jangles a cracked bell as it stoops. Her eyes look wistfully towards the tents in the village; she can see the bright flutter of a flag. Her needles stop, and she stands still unconsciously, lost in dreams of the glorious future when she may go to service in the town, perhaps at the Burgomester's, when she will be free to visit the Kermesse and to ride in the carousals and see the dwarfs and all the sights that make it such a place of wonder. Ah! how much would she not give for a glimpse of the tigers and lions; the tigers above all, great striped cat-like things—she has seen them on a print on the school-house wall— and sometimes at night when the great farmhouse is quiet and her straw pallet over the cowshed is shrouded in gloom, and the snoring, laboured breathing of the cattle seems to fill the close air with a smell of warm milk, and a benighted glow-worm flits through the loft, she cowers down and thinks of a tiger breathing and staring at her with gleaming eyes. Ay, down there boys and girls are dancing and buying fairings, and pepper cakes baked in fantastic shapes, and chocolates and 'images' of 'the saint' stamped on wafers, and at the acting booths a lovely *meisje* with short skirts dotted with silver stars, and a glistening crown on her head, like the wooden Virgin in the village chapel, stands and invites one to enter with an engaging smile and wave of wand. Tink, tink, tink, clinks the bell-cow, springing with awkward leaps and high-swung tail to one side as a crowd of laughing *jonge jouvrouws* and 'sösterjes' from the great pensionnat come down the road.

They are laughing and talking gaily, for the

sisters are favourites and number many 'flames' amongst the crowd of girls filled with sickly sentiment, '*schwärmerei*,' and awakening sexual instinct. They are genuinely in love. If their favourite leans over their shoulder to correct a theme, and happens to touch their arm, it calls forth a blushing disturbance in even the most stolid of the pupils. They colour quickly if she speaks to them suddenly, and touch furtively her scapular or the great cross at the end of her beads. Some of them cherish a scrap of her writing, and scramble for a flower she has carried in her hand, and if, on turning up the corner of her veil where her number is neatly marked in white silk letters, say 693, they are lucky enough to possess a number that will divide into it without remainder, it is a matter of ecstatic happiness.

They are on their way to the Kermesse, and the competition to walk next the sisters has been keen, and the cause of stratagems and heartaches. The sister in the rear musters her flock, turns her head quickly (some couples are straggling behind) and draws her straight brows sharply together under her snowy guimpe—a girl is talking to the little peasant, a disobedience without parallel.

'You must walk in front,' she calls sharply, 'and not two together, please.' Her eyes meet the amused look and scornful twist of lip of the girl who looks round at her voice, and who turns back coolly and slips something into the herd-girl's hand, and the latter, who has started tremblingly at the *sösterje's* voice, bobs her an awkward curtsey.

The girl is a tall anæmic-looking thing, but she carries her head well and steps along like a thoroughbred filly. The sister stands and waits with her satellites on each side ; but her eyes stay with the girl. The latter is too sharp-tongued, too keen-eyed, too intolerant of meanness and untruth to be a favourite with her classmates—too independent a thinker, with too dangerous an influence over weaker souls to find favour with the nuns.

'You must postpone your practice in flirtations, meine Fräulein; join the ardent flames instead and burn at the shrine,' she says laughingly to the other girls as they move on.

Tête-a-têtes are strictly forbidden ; friendships are discouraged ; two girls seen together a few times are warned sharply, if necessary separated in all recreations. Perhaps this adds to the piquancy of a flirtation with a chum of one's own sex. A clasp of hand in the crush on the great staircase, an embrace in the golosh room, a billet-doux with sentimental verses and a Cupid with a dart-pierced heart or wreath of pink forget-me-nots are the usual result.

The worst trouble is with the girls from fourteen up ; if they fall in love with a 'sister' and become a flame, the matter is simple ; she will know how to blow hot and blow cold, and keep them where they are to remain. This girl will none of it.

She walks about with her hands clasped loosely behind her back ; and her sombre eyes dwell dreamily on the Dutch landscape.

They are bound for the little village of Gend-ringen, in Guelderland; and as they draw nearer to it, the strains of instruments mingle with the desultory tink, tink of the cattle bells behind them. The little cowherd watches them disappear, with surprised light filling her eyes and a wondering smile playing round her lips, and a silver thaler, a thick bright wonderful coin clutched in her hand.

The sister watches the careless swinging step of the girl ahead with rising colour; the ready scornful obedience, the indifference stings her. She draws out a little worn pocket-book and sets a mark against her name, Isabel, No. 7. The dowdily made convent gown of unbecoming material sits loosely on her unformed figure; she has twisted a crimson scarf round her neck, and one end flutters and shakes its fringe over her shoulder like a note of defiance, thinks the sister. For to the subdued soul of this still young woman, who has disciplined thoughts and feelings and soul and body into a machine, in a habit, this girl is a *bonnet-rouge*, an unregenerate spirit, the embodiment of all that is dangerous, and never fails to call forth whatever of the narrowness and the small jealousy of the world still clings to the religieuse. She cries sharply:

' There is no need for you to walk alone, Isabel, because I tell you to comply with the rules.'

This time the girl shrugs her shoulders impatiently and slips her arm into that of a half-witted girl, Katrine, the daughter of rich Zeeland peasants—the butt of the finer Fräulein.

'Will you have me, Trine?' she asks with a confident smile. Trine's dull eyes brighten and a slow mottled blush creeps up into the stupid face; she admires the clever elder girl, who is so indifferent to blame and who has so often helped her with her hopeless French themes, in a dumb animal wondering way, and loves her passionately, for she is almost the only one who has ever given her a kind word. The girl smiles as she notes her pleasure, and draws her by skilful questioning into a stammering, delighted tale of her home life— the five hundred cows she will inherit and the gold coif and filigree ornaments, and the quaint customs at weddings and christenings.

The little village is irregularly built. A hideous white-washed church with stucco angels holding palm branches keeps one end of it. The streets are cobble-stoned and spotlessly clean, even the two trees that stand in front of each house of importance are hosed free from dust; they are cut too in fantastic shapes, such as a lion-couchant, a griffin, or perhaps a teapot. One sister steps to the front, one to the rear, the flock in between. As they enter the village, the Burgomester, the notary, and the curate greet them. The latter is young; his neat legs, set off to advantage by silk stockings and square-toed shoes with plated buckles, are a source of envy to such of the girls as are afflicted with thick ankles. There is a quaint crowd of peasants in holiday dress, but they seem subdued, and take their pleasure stolidly; later on after dusk they will enliven to a coarser sort of merry-making.

The girls flit about in groups of ten, an enfant-de-Marie in charge of each, they flock round the booths like bees in search of honey, buying anything good to eat. They cluster at the roundabout with the fancifully painted pagoda and the tarnished trappings in the middle, its round of gaily painted steeds, as apocryphal as the unicorn, and its gaudily painted cars and gilded state coach to hold six. The sisters speak to the red-faced German who runs the show, and he cries lustily to the crowd at the entrance :

' All seats engaged for the next half hour ! All engaged !'

And when the hurdy-gurdy and the bells stop, and the plebeian equestrians are dispersed, the young ladies clamber up and strive to sit gracefully in their saddles and lean back in the phaeton —glorious opportunities for being together.

Katrine looks wistfully on, and whispers pleadingly to her silent companion :

' Will you come with me, oh, won't you come ? '

' Would you like to '—with a smile—' well, get up then.'

' No, they wouldn't like me to.'

' Nonsense, go on !' She helps the great-hipped clumsy girl into a saddle, where she sits humped up in delighted expectation.

Two München girls, high spirited, stylishly dressed, come laughingly along in search of places.

' Get down, Trine, we want these horses, you look like a great toad.'

An obstinate piteous look clouds the girl's dull face.

'Do you hear? Get into the car instead.'

'Stay where you are, Trine. We want these horses,' cries the girl mounting the companion steed, a liver-coloured impossibility with flowing scarlet mane. 'You can get into the car instead!' with a malicious grin over her shoulder at the others. They flush and look disdainfully at the patched boot she is thrusting through the stirrups. It is their only means of retaliation, she has worsted them too often to risk an encounter of wits. The hurdy-gurdy in the pagoda strikes up a polka, well known through Holland and South Africa as 'Polly Witfoet,'—and with many preliminary creaks and strains the roundabout starts in a giddy circle

'Lal, lal, la, la ; lal, lal, la, la, lallallallallalla.'

over and over again, and the gaudy tassels toss in the autumn breeze ; and the many-coloured manes and tails stream out ; and the pensionnaires giggle and scream and pretend to slip off ; and the great axle creaks and strains like a ship in the trough of a heavy sea, and the music seems to ring with the same feverish haste.

The girl's keen eyes note that at one point in the round, the breeze blows aside the trappings of the pagoda ; she peeps idly in, but each time after that her eyes seek it with a look of shrinking fascination. Her thin nostrils quiver, and her pupils dilate, and an indignant flush dyes her face in a beautiful way as she gazes—Why ?

An idiot lad is turning the handle of the hurdy-gurdy. He is fastened by a leathern strap round his middle to the pole in the centre of the tent.

His head is abnormally large, the heavy eyelids lie half folded on the prominent eyeballs so that only the whites show, his damp hair clings to his temples and about his outstanding ears. His mouth gapes, and his long tongue lolls from side to side, the saliva forming little bubbles as the great head wags heavily as he grinds—indeed every part of his stunted, sweat-dripping body sways mechanically to the lively air of white-footed Polly.

'Polly Witfoet, Polly Witfoet, lallallallallala!'

And the flags flutter, and the bells jangle, and the roundabout creaks, and the girls giggle and scream affectedly; all save two,—Trine, who is wrapped in a dull dream of pleasure, and her companion who is watching the boy, with ever-growing indignation and disgust swelling her breast, causing her to clench her thin hands.

Each time she looks, the heavy lids seem to droop more, the tongue to loll longer, the face to wax paler. Save for the strap the scarcely human form would topple over with weariness. A whip is leaning up against the frame-work.

'Why should I see it?' she cries inwardly with passionate resentment, 'why should I always pitch on the rotten spot in the fruit? Will the thing never stop? O my God, that poor wretch!'

She scans her schoolmates, laughing carelessly with their mouths filled with chocolates, 'leckers,' and kookjes; at the nuns with their spotless guimpes and their hands primly folded inside their long sleeves, and when she passes at the next round she shuts her eyes with a shiver.

'They don't see, they don't see,' she cries to herself. 'I alone see. My God, is that to be my fatal dowry, to go through life and always see? Oh, how I hate it! Made in God's likeness! Is that God's likeness, that poor, half-bestial thing with the lolling tongue and misshapen frame? Or that German with the bulbous nose and sensual lips who owns him, and perhaps uses the whip to goad him on!'

'Polly Witfoet, Polly Witfoet, lallallallallala!'

'Oh, stop! Will that wretched air never stop? Ha! ha! ha!'—with an hysterical laugh—'Oh, that poor creature! I am only seventeen, and is that what I shall find in the world to come—some poor idiot turning the organ for all the luckier born to dance——?'

The roundabout stops with a long-drawn groan, and they all dismount, and an eager throng of smaller girls struggle to get places. She clambers down on the inner side, and peers into the gaily-striped pagoda. He has laid down his monstrous shock-head on top of the hurdy-gurdy, and is drawing his breath in hard, shuddering gasps; but the swollen hand with the knotted fingers still grips the handle with a convulsive tension, ready to grind again.

She flees from the spot, forcing a passage through a slit in the canvas tent, and almost runs through the street of the prim little village; flees up the dusty road, utterly reckless of the penalty in store for leaving the nuns.

She throws herself breathlessly down at the foot

of a great tree, and bursts into tears, not sorrow-
ful tears, but heaving, rebellious sobs against the
All-Father for His ordering of things here below.

' Oh, that poor thing! that poor thing! You
needn't have made him ; God, I tell you, you
needn't have made him! You knew from all
time he'd be there, and why should he be? Why
should he grind music for all those selfish brutes
to ride? Oh! oh! oh! why should he?' She
bruises her poor little clenched fist against the
gnarled roots as she emphasises her words, and
shakes it up at the silent sky, with the featherets
of delicate lemon relieving the grey, the silent
sky—that is always dumb.

' Oh, poor thing, poor thing! I wanted to love
you, God ; indeed, you know I did, but I can't, I
can't, I can't. I love all those poor things of your
creation far more, and oh, I hate to live ! I don't
want to—always I see the pain, the sorrow, underneath the music—and I tell you '—with a burst of
passion—' if I were a great queen I would build a
new tower of Babel with a monster search-light to
show up all the dark places of your monstrous
creation. I would raise a crusade for the service
of the suffering, the liberation of the idiots who
grind the music for the world to dance—— '

She lays her hot, tear-stained cheek to the cool
lap of Mother Earth, and the slender girl-frame
shakes with deep-breathed sobs, and away from
the tent under the shadow of the spire that points
like a futile finger upwards, the tender breeze
comes rustling through the jaundiced foliage, and

scatters the dying leaves like golden butterflies
that bear no message, bringing the refrain of the
common tune :

'Polly Witfoet, Polly Witfoet, lallallallallala !'

III.—THE WOMAN

LONDON that is west of Piccadilly Circus is
virtually empty ; town looks jaded ; the very
mansions wear a day-after-the-fête air. The men
who look some way so effete, so weak-kneed in
their town dress, have gone to shoot grouse or
lure a salmon, gone in obedience to the only
honest passion left in them—the lust to kill. The
stalls in such theatres as are open have a show of
soiled frocks, and the jaded young women of the big
shops grow paler in the chaos of the autumn sales.

A man came out of the National Conservative
Club and stood in the doorway, drawing his hand
slowly through his beard. He was evidently
weighing a question of some moment, for an
acquaintance sauntering by greeted him with a
jovial 'How are you?' (he was Irish), and a
fellow-member, likewise an acquaintance, passing
in, uttered a stereotyped 'How d'ye do?' (he
was English), without eliciting a responsive look
or greeting. At length he raises his head and
looks about him. A lady is passing with two
children, pretty, blue-eyed, golden-locked, well-
kept little ones. One of them looks up at the big
man as she trips sedately by, and a smile lurks

in her eyes and dimples her cheeks. His face changes, and an irresolute expression crosses it. The spirit of evil that hovers round men and their destinies nearly loses her game, but she calls a quean to her aid, and saves it by the odd trick. The man's eyes with their softened expression are following the child, when a high-heeled French boot, with a liberal display of silk-covered calf above it, stepping on to the kerbstone attracts him. He looks up the figure and stops at the head of its owner. Her hair glistens metallically in the autumn sunlight, and her blue eyes throw him a challenge through their blackened lashes. He repays it with interest, and winks insolently as she tosses him a second glance over her shoulder. The cynical hardness returns to his face stronger than before, and he hails a passing hansom.

'British Museum!' He tilts his hat over his eyes and leans back, but he evidently wavers still, for he pulls out some loose money, and, selecting a sovereign, thrusts back the rest.

'Heads I do, tails I don't!' he mutters, and he spins it up and catches it on his open palm, and covers it with his left hand. The diamond in his ring seems to sparkle with a mocking light, like the eye of the jade who went by, he thinks. He lifts his hand—her Gracious Majesty the Empress of India in ugly Jubilee presentment! Who can say if he were not sorry? His face looks darker, and a more cynical smile flits over it, a tribute to the spirit of evil and the chance that favours his game.

About the same time as the man left his club, a
girl sitting at a desk near 'dictionary corner' in
the reading-room of the British Museum looks up
at the clock. A shadow of some emotion difficult
to define waves across her face and leaves her
paler. She takes up two books, mounts the step-
ladder and replaces them reluctantly on the top
shelf; puts on her hat, takes her gloves and some
copy-books, and walks slowly out of the great
room. When she reaches the door she turns and
stands there, an unconsciously pathetic figure. She
takes a long look—why? She does not know
herself. She looks up at the great dome, at the
tiers of books circling one above the other, the
strange medley of men and women, and the skull-
capped head of her favourite official. She has a
kind of affectionate feeling for the great room ; it
has been her oasis in a vast desert. There she has
forgotten the cravings of physical hunger and soul
thirst ; struggles, weariness, almost despair. She
has found strong meat and perennial springs from
which to draw nourishment ; has mixed with a
right goodly company of the wittiest and best of
dead men and women. She has laughed over
poor Dick Steele's letters to his dear Prue ; envied
Rahel the rare charm that held her young husband a lover always ; visited Heine with La
Mouche—forgotten her lack of living acquaintances in the richer companionship of her dead
friends. The tears fill her eyes as the door swings
behind her, and she draws on her gloves sadly as
she goes out. She turns to the left and goes

through the King's Library—she has a fancy to circle the ground-floor. But to-day she walks on with drooping head ; she never glances at the quaint books of the Virgin in the cases, nor the rare samples of the forgotten art of binding. She goes up the stairs wearily and down again, and stops at the entrance to the Egyptian Room ; she looks up at the head of her friend Rhameses.

She has a peculiar fondness—nay, more, a close sympathy—with this old-time monarch of unforgetable features, with the thin curving lips and inscrutable smile lurking perpetually on his face.

She knows naught of him nor his dynasty, but she always says that he has whispered many wise things to her. Sometimes when the burden of life has pressed heavier than usual upon her frail shoulders, she has gone and sat down on the wooden bench and looked up to him for counsel. He has seen so much, looked down on so many races, well he may sneer at the struggling toil of the earth-ants that crawl over God's great dust-heap in futile effort to leave a lasting mark to make themselves known to posterity. 'You know it all,' she used to whisper, nodding up to him ; 'what do you teach me ? Endurance ! To meet the world with a granite face and a baffling smile, and smile always, come bad come good ; and when all is done lay my own speck of dust on the heap for another speck of dust to stumble over.' She smiles up to him with moisture dimming the soft bird-like brightness of her questioning eyes, and walks down the long room. Its very size is a delight to her, and she halts before the perfect little black Apollo with the white eyeballs. He always responds to some artistic sense in her; perhaps her art inclines to originality of expression; she has at least no standards, she likes what she likes. She was much astonished once when some one told her that she was plagiarising Mr. Ruskin, when she said that Moroni's tailor was her ideal portrait—indeed he was the only tailor she ever pined to know. But she astonished her informant equally when she dared to say that she disagreed with the great authority on many points; and that, besides, her own liking or non-liking was the only criticism worth a doit to her. She has found life a hard battle, but there have been beautiful books and beautiful pictures to worthen it, and, best of all, a free spirit and a free heart to fight the demons; but now, perhaps—for she has a strange fore-feeling that she is singing the swan-song of her peace of soul, as she stands and takes a last look—now, perhaps, she is to go into bondage. A legend of the Finn gypsies flits across her memory. A true spirit dwelleth in the sun. Every child-girl can look up at it until she counts twelve summers, a few later. They can stare right into the glowing heart of the mid-day sun in search of the God-spirit without blenching, for they are white in soul; but as soon as they lose their innocence, as soon as they learn the mystery of life that men call sin, they lose the power, and when they try to see him they are blinded and tear-drenched by his fierce rays. A queer legend with a deep meaning. Ay, she has been able to look each man and woman in God's world in the face; heart and soul have been free and untrammelled as a gypsy child's; and what awaits her to-day?

She cannot shake off the dread feeling of an evil destiny drawing near to punish her for the pride in herself that has kept her steps light to carry her over the muddy places. She rises wearily to her feet and goes out; the pigeons flutter aside from her path, and, as she avoids treading on the joins in the flagged path, another great yard rises before her visual memory, and she looks down.

Ay, there is the curl of orange-peel and the crumpled paper, but something is lacking—she tries to recall it—what can it be? Ah! a bit of pencil! As she steps out through the entrance-gate a hansom pulls up with a jerk, and he advances to meet her. She has something in each hand, perhaps purposely. The driver notes her shabby serge gown, and the little patched shoe that shows beneath it, and looks for some startling set-off in the way of face or figure; but they are not of the kind to strike the common eye.

They turn up Bedford Place and walk silently on. He watches her face through his half-closed lids.

'Well!' he says, 'you are not very communicative.'

An underlying threat lurks in his tone; she feels it and flushes.

'There is not anything to say that I have not said before.'

'Indeed! You might, for instance, say that you are glad to see me—that it is awfully good of me to fag up to this beastly God-forsaken hole when I might be cruising round the Isle of Wight. You don't think you could bring yourself to tell even the conventional fib, eh?'

'Why should I? I have told you as often what I *do* think as I have begged you to let me be. One is as useless as the other,' with a touch of weariness.

They have reached Tavistock Square; a nurse-maid has just come out. He winks at her and slips her a florin; she unlocks the gate again; the place is almost deserted. He chooses a seat sheltered by some shrubs, and sits down. Clasping his hands on the top of his stick, he watches her with a strange mingling of affection and dogged determination.

'You look ill, thinner, more hungry-looking than when I saw you last, you obstinate little devil!'

'I am all right, if you would but let me be.'

'And that is just what I can't do; I want you, little woman, I want you more than anything else in the whole world; I'd let everything else slide for a soft word from you.'

'Which you have no right either to give or demand.'

'Oh, for the Lord's sake, don't harp on that string again. You've told me all that before. I am married, very much married, I owe all to my wife, etc. etc. Let us stick to facts—the great fact —you! If you only knew how much good you might do me, what an influence you have over me, how straight you could keep me. But you are like all the rest of your sex, selfish to the heart's core. You'd let a man go to perdition before you'd sacrifice an iota of your infernal purity—let him blow his brains out, because you hold your good name more worth than a man's life. Your good name, ha! ha! Who knows anything about you, or what are you to speak of? Take your own people; in a few years the young ones will be grown up and not care a merry damn about you, and as for your——'

She checks him by the passionate ring in her low voice, with its singularly clear enunciation :

'Leave them alone! What they are to me, or I to them, you are the last person in the world able to judge. I doubt if you ever had a clear unselfish feeling in your life. Say what you will to me, but leave them be'—with passion—'I won't bear it!'

'How you love them! And I have tried every way with you, coaxed as no mortal man ever coaxed before, bribed you all I know—it only remains to threaten you.'

She looks at him steadily; there is stinging contempt in her tone :

'I expected that from your letter; indeed I might have expected something of that kind from you in any case.'

'You drive me to it. I have tried to overcome your scruples—I have studied your wishes, endeavoured to meet you half way——'

'There is no half way for a woman. There is one straight, clean road marked out for her, and every by-road is shame. Grant that it is absurd that it is so, that does not help her. She has to walk that one way unless she is prepared to give every man and woman a right to throw a stone at her ; and history tells us they don't stay their hands. I am putting it on the very lowest grounds ; you '—with a fine scorn—' would fail to grasp a higher argument for her virtue.'

'Pah ! No one need know anything about it. I 'll buy you a little place ; make it over by deed of gift ; or you can go and study abroad. I 'll settle so much on you. I can always make an excuse to get away. You could see your dear home-folk just the same. *I* won't say anything for my own sake ; and who will be the wiser ?'

'*I* would !' Her eyes are blazing and her voice is beyond her control. ' Do you think, if I consent, if I am forced for some reason to go with you, that I would do that ? Do you think I would lead a double life of lies, that I would make living a pretence of goodness ? Go home and tell them fancied tales of my life, kiss them '—with a choked sob—' buy them with your money the trifles I take them now out of my earnings, look into their eyes, hear them tell me '—the tears are hanging on the ends of her lashes—' I am good and brave and dear, feel how proud they are of me, and know in my heart that I was a thing not fit for them to touch ; play a part, lie with eyes and lips and life ? No, rather sever every connection with them by one sharp blow ; die to them at once and trust to their love and mercy to judge me in the after time.'

'Pshaw! heroics! You'd make a capital emotional actress; wonder you never tried it.'

There is a long silence.

'Well, now that you have cooled down a bit, what is your final say?'

'Great God, I tell you I won't! I can't! Oh leave me be, do leave me be!'

'Yes, you can, little woman; or rather, yes you must, and you know it. You are no fool, you err rather on the side of brains. You know that if you had dared you would have refused to meet me long ago, but your intuition told you I had a card in reserve, a trump card to play when you drove me too far, and now I am going to show it to you.'

He is opening a pocket-book.

'Show it to you, do you understand? not such a fool as to let you get it between your little brown hands, ha! ha!'

He takes out a letter; it is a little soiled. She is very white and scarcely draws her breath; once she looks at him, and her eyes are kindled with a deadly hate. He points to the name of the receiver and to the signature. He holds it so that she can read it, opens it; there is a soiled, crumpled receipt in acknowledgment of money pinned inside. She reads with whitening face; a hurdy-gurdy outside the railings is grinding out

'Polly Witfoet, Polly Witfoet, lallallallallala!'

She starts, knitting her brows in vain endeavour to find what the tune brings back to her.

'Well!' he says, 'have you seen enough? I have a few more letters from the same hand. Now,

if I know you as I fancy I do, you will count any
individual shame—mind that is your own term for
it—as a small thing in comparison with the disgrace that will fall if I take any step about this
little matter'—he is putting it carefully back—
'and you will come!'

The wind rustles through the trees and scatters
a shower of tinted leaves over them. They flutter
on to her tightly-locked hands and shabby little
hat, and rest on her lap like flecks of blood; and a
great cry rises up in her breast of rebellion against
the Creator of men. If she could only steal away
to some quiet wood and lie down and die! let
the brown leaves, with their deep stains, blood
stains, cover her gently and hide her for ever!
Surely it would not be very hard to die? She has
often felt her heart beat, she knows exactly where
it is, a good long hat-pin would reach it.

He is watching her face intently.

'You are just in a mood to shoot me, or put an
end to yourself, where's the good? You force me
to be hard to you. You can't escape. I swore to
have you. "All means are fair in ——." You
know the rest. If you put an end to yourself, I'll
put this thing through, so help me God I will.
You may as well give in. I'll make arrangements
to go abroad, as your sensitiveness revolts against
the more sensible arrangement and courts a scandal. I'll let you know.' He gets up and some
remnant of remorse stirs in him. He is angry, not
with himself but with her for forcing him to speak
and act as he has done. She is very pale, and her

step is heavier than when she flitted through the
museum ; something buoyant has left her. She
droops her head as she walks, she will never carry
it in quite the old way again ; insolently the
women called it who disliked her, but it was the
insolence of fearless integrity. He is sorry for
her, and, now that he has gained the point he has
been striving for, for the best part of a year, a little
gnawing worm of a doubt begins to worry. Is it
worth it all ? Shall he let her off ? Be bested by
a woman ? And this particular woman, whose
love or liking he cannot gain, and whose affection
he fancies he craves for more than that of any one
he has ever known ? No, he 'll be hanged if he
will. Kismet ! it is written. And the hurdy
gurdy grinds on white-footed Polly's polka.

.   .   .   .   .

He who has not seen Paris in May has not seen
la belle in her freshest and prettiest guise ; lilac-
scented, and flower-crowned, with a fragrant chestnut spike for a sceptre. Late one afternoon in
this sweetest of months, the girl of the foregoing
scene enters a private sitting-room in an hotel in
the Rue de Rivoli. It is a drawing-room furnished
in modified Louis quinze style. She has come in
from a long drive in the Bois, and she who used to
notice external things so closely has lain back in
the hotel carriage, and let the vehicles with their
freight of pretty occupants, parisiennes, in all the
freshness of dainty spring toilettes, the bonnes,
the flâneurs, on the pathway, all the radiant glad
crowd in whom the sensuous witchery of spring is

working insidiously, pass her by, a blur of motion and colour, as a stage scene may appear to a short-sighted person. She throws her bonnet, gloves, and the parasol with dainty enamel and gold handle on to a couch, and sitting down in a chair at the window, closes her eyes wearily.

She has changed greatly in the between time. After all is said and done there is a great excuse for women's craze for dress. There is no beauty, except the beauty of absolute nude perfection that is not enhanced by it. Wholly beautiful women are rare things, but a woman who knows how to accentuate her good points and tone down her defects by skilful blending of colours and choice of material may pass as a beauty all her days, may exact the homage of the sons of men, and excite the envy of the daughters; and is not this the salt of existence to many? To students of character she would have been at any time attractive; now she would hold the eyes of men of commoner stamp. She looks a personage. She is a finished study in the art of taste in dress, and she is one of the women who pay for the trouble; it is impossible to vulgarise her.

There is an expression in her eyes and set of mouth that was not there when she stood and bade good-bye, with a touch of humoursome sadness, to her friend Rhameses. She has passed through her ordeal by fire, and the sear of the iron is there in ineffaceable traces. In repose her face is a mask to the inner woman, one would be loth to disturb it; there is something unapproachable about her. Sitting there motionless, a casual observer would say she is asleep, a nicer one would note how ever and again the delicate brows contract in thought. He was as astonished and proud of the transformation clothes effected in her outwardly, as disappointed at their effect on her inner self. She chose the right things in obedience to an innate sense of beauty and fitness, and wore them with the same ease as her old serge frock.

She accepted everything with the same irritating indifference. It stung him into efforts to impress her, with the disconcerting result that she made him feel underbred. She left him no fault to find, the things that irritated him most in her were rather praiseworthy than otherwise. She might have filled the position of a legitimate duchess, but as a mistress she was not amusing.

She remarked that some jewellery he brought her was vulgar, palais-royal, suitable for a cocotte. He took it back, and she evaded choosing any other on a plea of fatigue. She found fault with an *omelette au chasseur* at the Maison Dorée, and he had to allow she was right. She remarked, in reply to his taunting query as to where she got her fastidiousness, that a course of tea-dinners in aërated-bread shops did not necessarily blunt one's palate or deprave one's discriminate appreciation in finer feeding. He was forced to acknowledge that a man may pay too dearly for having his own way.

Once only she had made what he called 'a scene'; it was at St. Raphael. An American family, pleasant cultured people of the kind one meets seldomer in Europe than America itself, were staying at another hotel. They took a fancy to her. She touched on general subjects in such a bright individual way, with a passing gleam of humour, that it made her remarks worth listening to. But she avoided them when possible, especially the daughters. They put it down to 'inherited side' rather than a phase of individual temperament, and persisted in seeking her. They made up a party to visit the old Roman remains in the neighbourhood, and he desired her to join it. The American man 'knew a thing or two' about solid investments in western mortgages, and was worth cultivating. She refused point blank; commands and threats alike failed to move her, and she ended the discussion by saying: 'You can make what excuse you will. I made no bargain to deceive any one, and I will not go. I have tried to avoid them; when that was not possible I have been as pleasant as it is left in my nature to be. If you send her up to persuade me I shall simply say, "Madam, I am not this man's wife, I am his mistress." Do you think then she will be anxious to continue the acquaintance?' He struck her on the side of the face, and he excused her on the score of migraine.

Late in the evening their high-pitched laughing voices, and the odd drawl that fits itself so well to a smart saying, rang up to her from the gardens below. They sent her a fragrant tangle of flowers with pretty regrets for her absence. She laid them gently aside.

She is kneeling at the open window, gazing out over the rustling woods and the white châteaux with the gaily striped awnings at the long windows; the thread of river, where the women bathe the linen, and gossip in voluble tones, winding its way to the quick sea.

What are *they* doing, who are never out of her thoughts? How do they think of her? Have they taken her photo out of the prettiest frame in the shabby old room, with the untidy litter of writing materials and paint brushes? She can see every detail in it: Molly's old work-basket, with the frayed silken lining, and the pile of cheap socks that work into holes so quickly. They are in the midst of fogs, and she is surrounded by rose-tangled banks. Roses, ay! But the red spider gnaws at the rosebuds too. A rose bush they saw once comes back to her with a new meaning. She remembers how all the tender shoots were covered with the crawling cinnamon red insects, how they ate into the heart of the buds, how she had watered, syringed, and taken a delight in killing the nasty things, with their thread-like legs, because Molly felt sorry for the roses. How plainly she can see her, with her clear true eyes, odd tender face, and pathetic droop of mouth. She used always to take her flowers, only a few narcissi or golden 'daffys,' a pennyworth from the street corner; country thoughts astray in the vile streets of the modern Sodom. How she used to delight in them, talk to them, poor pretty things, as if they lived and understood! A fancy of hers

from child days, when she looked for elves in the
bluebells, and never plucked the 'fairy fingers' for
fear of the good people's pinches. And now,
great God! she is lost to them—ay, worse lost
than if she were out there fathoms deep—smothered
in the sand that the sea rolls in unceasingly. If
she could only explain! but that she cannot ; only
crawl in once, and lie down like a stray cur.
Cats and dogs and waifs of all kinds always sought
shelter with them, and shared their scanty haphazard happy meals. Happy? No, no longer.
They are surely miserable. That *she* has done ;
but what is their misery to hers? She meets her
teeth in her arm, it is a sort of relief to counteract
the agony of her soul by a pang of physical pain.
The mild evening breeze, the monotonous note of
the sea, the shiver of leaf, scent of night-plants, all
seem to accentuate her misery, to bite the picture
of the well-known room, peopled with the beings
who are more to her than all the world beside,
into her heart, so that the smart of it is almost
intolerable. She rocks herself to and fro, and then
looking up into the vast purple canopy overhead,
as if trying to pierce the gloom, she cries with
sobs, 'Oh God! Christ God! if it be that in guise
of a little mortal child you grew to manhood in
the midst of poor suffering toiling humans, shared
their poverty, saw their sins, their crimes, their
mistakes ; if you were weary as they with the
heat and toil of daily labour, surely you will
understand and have pity on my poor ones!
Dear God-man! you who laid your hand on the

head of the Magdalen in tender human pity, and forgave her because she loved much, help them! Let them forget me, even if their forgetfulness add to my Gethsemane! Oh, if there be any merit in anything I have ever done, I offer it up for them.'

And the leaves just rustle, rustle, and the sea croons on, and the great blue canopy stretches away impenetrably, and no voice answers the poor trembling words wrung out from the heart that is sore and torn with the strongest affection of her life, and she finds relief in merciful human tears, the first she has shed since she has left them.

.   .   .   .   .

That night seems years ago, and the prayer echoes as the voice of a dead acquaintance. A knock at the door rouses her, and a German waiter enters with a card on a salver.

'Ze shentleman wish to speak with you, madame!'

Mr. ALOYSIUS GONZAGA O'BRIEN.
7 *Bachelor Walk, Dublin.*   90 *Marine Parade, Dalkey.*

'Are you sure, Karl, that he asked to see me, not monsieur?'

'Oh yes, madame, ze shentleman have seen monsieur zis mornin' in ze shmokin' room, it is madame he vish to ze!'

She controls a start of surprise.

'Well, show him up here, Karl, in five minutes.'

One of her presentiments has come to her. With the swift intuition that is almost second sight with some women, she knows the objects of his visit. She looks at the card again. It is characteristic

of Dublin, and a damning satire as a cognomen
for the man who bears it. She knows that he is
his man of business for Ireland. She has a difficult
part to play, she must summon all her inwit to her
aid, for he has not yet redeemed his promise to
give her those fateful papers. She shivers, and
her temples beat with hard quick throbs, but at
his sharp knock she nerves herself to bid him
'come in' with steady voice. He enters with a
swagger. He is not the man to see any need of
deference to a woman for womanhood's sake, and
surely not to one who is in an anomalous position.
Now when he had the honour of an interview with
the Countess of Derryguile about a lapsed tenancy,
he was obsequiously prepared to kiss her ladyship's number seven shoe. And he could not do
justice to her second best sherry, so eager was he
to stammer 'yes, your ladyship' to every remark.
But there was reason in that. She remains seated,
inclines her head a little, and looks at him in a
way that disconcerts Aloysius Gonzaga O'Brien,
lineal descendant of Brian Boru, with the blood of
Milesian kings in the remoter past, and of his
grandfather the pawnbroker, and his grandmother
the chandler's daughter, who died in the odour of
sanctity and left one thousand pounds for masses,
coursing through his veins in the nearer present.
It arrests his familiar greeting; it was not thus
he had mapped out the scene when thinking of it.

'You wish to see me?' She has an uncomfortable way, at least so he feels, of letting her eyes
rest on him; a way that does not tend to set him

more at ease. 'Won't you sit down?' pointing to a chair.

He draws one over to the table, and she notes the contrast between the chair with the delicate posies and fluttering love-knots of its brocade, and this man who twists his leg awkwardly round one of its dainty gilded legs. She notes his flushed porous skin, his heavy pink lids, half concealing eyes cunning as a hedge-hog's, his fat jaw and gaping slit of a mouth with the protruding under-lip and slight red shade on his shaven chin. With the quick sensitiveness of perception of every Celt, he feels that her thought of him is unflattering, and he anathematizes her mentally in racy epithets gleaned in early days when he played 'tip cat' in Meath Street. Neither schooling at Tullabeg, the shades of the Four Courts, nor mixing in such polite society as his success in Dublin has procured for him has deprived him of the ugliest Dublin accent and a tendency to clip the ending of his words.

'I suppose yer wonderin' at my wantin' to see ye. Well,' as she makes no reply, 'there's no use batin' about the bush, I might as well say I came over to Paris for that purpose. Ye know I transact a dale of business for Mr. St. Leger in Oireland, an' I may say'—twisting a crested signet on his little finger—she wonders if it has three balls—'I have his interest intoirely at heart.'

'Of course, coupled with your own ; that is your business.'

'What's that?' She does not repeat it, only watches him calmly.

He flushes a deeper red : 'Well, as I waz sayin', I had an interview with her solicitors in London, an' she—they—we consulted and agreed I should try to see if we couldn't come to some arrangement. She is disposed, an' I think it very handsome of her, to overlook everything uv he goes back. Otherwise there'll be a divorce an' a scandal ; an' so I came over.'

'Yes. But why to me? You saw Mr St. Leger!'

He looks at her curiously. Now, is she making a shrewd guess in order to trip him into an admission, or does she know? It is safer to distrust people always.

'Yes, I saw him about another matter, sure ye know, I had to make an excuse.' A face given to open expression does not readily change, and a gleam of comical disbelief waves over hers. It stings him, he raises his voice a little. 'Well, anyhow, ye know this business can't go on ; it 'ud just be his ruin intoirely. Yer clever enough to see that. Just look at the facts. Suppose she divorces him and he marries you . . . well, he'd lose a power of money, an' you yerself wouldn't be much the better for it. *All the water in the Seine wouldn't wash ye white again, sure ye must know that !*'

She grows very pale, but otherwise she makes no sign, the same inscrutable expression that seems now to be a subtly blended part of her features gathers on her face. It flashes through her mind,—did she read it?—something about an act of parliament having been necessary to stamp an attorney a gentleman. It would take more than that to effect the apotheosis of Aloysius Gonzaga O'Brien. 'That is rather an opinion for individual judgment, Mr. O'Brien. Surely it was not to tell me that, you came over to Paris. Would it not facilitate matters to come to the point?'

'Oh, faith I've no objection,' with an insolent laugh, 'it's just how much will ye take?'

There is a long silence in the room; the sun stole in and lit up a group of porcelain Watteau shepherdesses and ogling swains on a cabinet behind him, so that it showed out in high relief, one distinct object in the swirling red confusion of all things that surged in her brain in the minutes that seemed so long to her. It brought her back to actual life; the simpering beaux and ridiculous Chloes with rose-ribboned crooks and rosetted hats on one side of their carefully coiffured heads strike her as a farcical note in a moment of tragedy, but never more will she be able to say: 'I don't understand how any one can commit a murder.'

'I am perhaps dense, but I must ask you to explain more clearly what you mean.'

There is a sharper note in her voice, and mistaking her paleness for fear he grows in insolence.

'Oh thin, it's plain enough! They don't want any scandal, an' if ye just take a fixed sum an' sign a guarantee that neither you nor your people'll come up after with an action for seduction or the like, the whole matter's settled straight off, an' there's no more to be said.'

'No, there's not much more to be said. Only I think it was *he* who authorised you to make that proposal to me, not her men of business, they would hardly have chosen you for an emissary!'

'Well, iv id was so, what is that to you? Ye know yer own position, an' if ye get, say, one thousand pounds, ye can't complain that ye didn't get divilish lucky out of id. Yer a clever woman wid a stoile of yer own, for them that likes it'—filling his eyes brutally with the grace of her figure—'an' there's many ways of starting in life wid a sum like that.' Deceived by her quiet, he continued with a leer : 'Ye might set up an——'

'An establishment in St. John's Wood perhaps?'

''Twas something like that I meant.'

'You do my capabilities too much honour.'

She is fighting a brave fight, the nerve force that comes to her inexplicably in such times, making her strong as a man, stands to her. She rises and presses the electric bell. Karl answers it.

'Find monsieur, and say madame wishes to see him.'

She remains standing on the hearth, the logs are ready for lighting, and fir cones are mixed with them; she wonders if they come from the Ardennes; if little children in sabots laughed as they gleaned a resinous harvest, and if they too called them 'crows' prayer-books,' as she and her playmates did in childhood days, when the trees and the flowers and the beasts had each a message and the world was a wonder world. He enters and exchanges a rapid look with the other man, who is obviously ill at ease.

'I cannot congratulate you,' she says, with smiling contempt, 'upon the finesse of your man of business. If I were you I should not employ him in future in affairs requiring delicate treatment—in which you didn't wish to be given away.'

He flushes, throws his half-smoked cigar into the grate, and tugs nervously at his beard. 'Eh? I don't—I don't quite——'

'Understand? I will explain to you. As far as *I* understand, your wife is anxious to smooth this over, and you yourself, having weighed the profit and loss, think it best to agree. That I expected; I knew it must come sooner or later. But I didn't expect you to employ a common cad to tell me so. Perhaps you think'—with a passionate catch in her voice—'with him, that it is now impossible to insult me. But knowing what he can't know, I think you ought to have chosen a different means of conveying your wishes, been a little nicer in your choice of an instrument. Was it by your orders that he informed me that not all the waters in the Seine will wash me white— suggested a comfortable course of genteel vice as a future to me? Or did you merely suggest the thousand pounds and cry quits?'

He turns from the gaze of her eyes that seem to pierce his soul and vents his discomfiture on his tool.

'Damn it, O'Brien, of all the thick-headed, infernal Irish asses, you——'

'You couldn't change the man's nature,' she interrupts. 'I have only one thing to say before I request Mr. O'Brien to leave the room, and that is, I make no terms—I require no bribe to buy me off, I am glad to go. You know why I came, and how ill you have kept your part of the bargain. Keep your promise, and you are free to leave me now if it suit you—but I touch no money of yours. I have no intention of sinking lower than you brought me in the eyes of conventional people, and you can be equally sure I shall not molest you. Bid him leave the room now, a few words will settle everything between you and me!'

Both men go out. He returns shortly; she has not stirred. He is vexed that she should have probed the truth; relieved at the prospect of parting; for she shames him daily, and her presence is a constant reproach. Virtues that would be tiresome in a wife are doubly so in a mistress! He strives to carry it off easily.

'You have a stinging tongue; O'Brien won't forget you in a hurry; I'll remind him of it when he shows an inclination to put on side.' He touches her hair in awkward attempt at a caress; he tells himself that he really was fond of her, but she wouldn't let him; she wouldn't be reasonable, all women are contrary devils.

'There's no use in saying I am sorry now, that I wish to God I could undo the thing, is there?'

'No; it won't undo it, will it?'

He thrusts his hands into his pockets and tries to find an introduction to what he wants to say. He finds himself watching the toe of his patent boot instead. In despair he plunges boldly to the point.

'Look here. About this money. You've got to take it. I'll lodge it in Glyn's bank and you can draw it as you like.'

'That won't make any difference. I have never changed any you gave me yet. What I have will pay my way.'

'Where are you going? I suppose you have settled?'

'Why let that concern you? You can be sure I shall neither add to my own sense of shame, or your need for remorse. You need not fear. Neither I nor mine will give you trouble.'

'I know that. I told O'Brien so. But it seems such a queer wind-up—I meant it to be so different, 'pon my soul I did. Anyhow, stay till to-morrow morning for the look of the thing—I'll cross in the evening with him. Is there anything I can do—I——'

'Yes, one thing. You made me a promise when I came with you—I ask you to keep it now that we are going to end our—episode. Give me those papers!' She says it so quietly that he does not dream that she is almost faint with suspense. It stings him that she always harps on that, that no thought of him occupies her.

'Well, I don't mind,' taking out his pocket-book, 'now that we are going to cry quits, I may as well let you have them. You paid rather a big price for it, eh?' He holds them high above her head and looks tantalisingly at her; things have gone more smoothly than he imagined; he is in good humour. 'Give me a kiss into the bargain; one of your own accord; you are not as generous with your gifts as I was with mine.'

It says much for her strength of will that she masters the hysterical desire that prompts her to scream. She looks up at him, nay, more, puts her arms up round his neck and kisses him with a wan smile. It crosses her mind that Delilah must have smiled that way. He hands her the papers, closing her other hand over them with a softened amused look. She folds them with trembling eager fingers into spills and, lighting the wax candles, holds them to the flame, watching them curl into grey black ash. She sears her nails and there is a smell of singed horn; she rubs the last bit of ash between her fingers and bursts into a laughing sob of relief. For the first time she realises how great and long the strain has been, and how racking a pain she has in her head.

He has been leaning back in a chair watching her with a flickering smile. 'Well, are you satisfied now?'

She cannot reply at once, the desire to laugh and cry at once is choking her.

'Yes, I am satisfied now. In a few hours I shall have looked upon your face for, I hope, the last time. I have been waiting for these or I should have gone long ago.'

'You are a tenacious little devil! and so I have no hold more on you—I suppose you'll go in the morning?'

'I'll go in the morning!'

'Well, I'll leave the hotel the same time; I can leave my traps in the cloak room. Are you going to cross?'

'No; I am not going to England!'

'Haven't you,' he asks it with a kind of fierce impatience, 'one atom of regret? I haven't treated you badly whilst you have been with me, have I?'

She smiles her odd amused smile, but says nothing. He takes up his overcoat and goes to the door and hesitates; comes back and stands beside her:

'Well, Kismet! I'll go. I fancy you'll like that best. Won't you shake hands, little woman?'

She puts out her hand. 'Oh yes, and I wish you no ill.'

He looks at her regretfully and goes out, opens the door again and puts in his head, saying:

'I'll order dinner for you, and tell Karl to put up my things—and God bless you!' The door closes quickly, and so the every-day follows the tragedy, and dinners must be eaten even if lives are wrecked.

.   .   .   .   .   .

She has finished packing, and her travelling hat and cloak and bag lie ready waiting. She has declined dinner and ordered some tea; the tray with the pretty china is still on the table. She is flushed with the excited sense of relief that fills her whole thought. She has made no plans as to where she will go or what she will eventually do. She has a well-defined idea as to the course of action that will guide her future life, but she has not studied details. The Finn legend occurs to her again. Well, she can no longer look fearlessly into the eyes of the day god ; there will always be a shrinking fear of hurt. All the blind faith in a beautiful future, the golden hopes that made climbing the hills such an easy task, have left her. Her dream of a White Knight waiting for her, if only she keep her spirit free and her heart clean, has been dispelled by her own action ; she has smirched her white robe : never more can she stand waiting to meet her knight with fearless glad eyes. Foolish fancies of a girl, perhaps, but the sweetest and best of life lies in its fancies. If it were not for them the dead weight of life would crush us in early youth. She utters her thoughts aloud, as if finding comfort in her own voice. She opens the long window and steps out into the balcony, and gazes out into the twilight, and up to the stars that shine faintly over the beautiful city. She is glad to be leaving it ; she has a strange sensation of breathing an unclean atmosphere in it. She wonders if it is peculiar to her. Sometimes men, women, even streets, affect her that way. She has often conceived a repugnance to the very houses in an unknown street, to the faces of the women peering out from the windows; a loathing dread of the men who leered at her as they met her; and if she asked, 'What is

such a street ? ' the answer would explain her
feeling. Beds in hotels and places have sometimes disturbed her in the same way, so much so
that she has started up and rolled herself in her
rug and slept in an arm-chair, because the sense of
evil thoughts that never come to her otherwise
seem to impregnate her as if the very bed held
them ; and she, highly sensitive as she is to the
psychometrical influence of things, cannot but feel
it. Paris, though it has been a dream of hers to
visit it, to revel in the art treasures of the people
of all dwellers on the globe most gifted with an
artistic sense of the fitness of things, disturbs her
in a curious way. She remembers how once in
the private collection of an art connoisseur she
came suddenly upon a tinted ivory Aphrodite, so
perfect, so exquisite a piece of carving, that one
could almost see the rounded bosom rise and fall
with the breath that seemed to tremble through
the parted lips ; the roseate tinge of toes and
palms, the play of light, the warmth of shadow in
the beautiful curve of back, quickened the ivory
into throbbing life. She recalls this woman
smiling through her half-closed lids under the
shade of a modern hat cocked insolently upon the
ripples of hair that crowned her classic head. She
remembers the outraged feeling of shame that
sent the blood rushing to her face as she realised
for the first time how vile a thing false art could
become. She has never forgotten the effect it had
on her : the stained ivory, the beauty of the limbs,
the marvellous reality of the curled feather, the

genius of the artist who debased his art to produce just a nude woman, an Aphrodite of the Boulevards. She has the same feeling here in this lovely city. It is as if she has a diabolical intuition of corruption underlying its beauty ; the men sipping absinthe outside the cafés inspire her with dislike ; the shifting green and opal changes of the liquid remind her of snakes' eyes, mocking *reflets* of ancient evil. She will seek some quiet sea village amongst a strange people, simple working people. She has an intense longing for a good sea-breeze, to blow away the atmosphere of the city. She feels so bruised, so shamed, and yet she asks herself, Why shame ? Is not that, too, a false conception based on custom ? No, not in her case. Her soul-soiling is not because she lived with him, but because she lived with him for a reason other than love—because it involved a wrong to another woman.

There is a knock at the door.

' Entrez ! ' she calls, stepping back into the room. A tall, massively-built woman comes in. She is a splendid creature, with deliberate, sensuous movements, of the type which has what is vulgarly called ' a fine presence.' A fur-trimmed cloak falling loosely back shows her black silk dinner gown ; it is cut square, and is an admirable setting for her handsome throat and neck, that is white with the whiteness of flesh peculiar to red-haired women. Her forehead is broad, dazzlingly white and unlined, and the masses of her hair are waved loosely back from it, and twisted with a

burnished copper crown at the back of her broad
head. Her heavily moulded face is unemotional,
expressionless in its sullen calm; the thin red
lines of her lips droop at the corners, and her
grey eyes look steadily, coldly out, with an air of
weary inquiry.

The two women face one another, finished exponents of opposing types: one, insistent with
nervous energy, psychic strength manifesting itself
in every movement of her frail body, every fleeting
expression on her changeful face; the other, a
model of physical development, with a face and
eyes admirably adapted to conceal rather than
reveal her feelings or passions.

She is about to tell her visitor that she has
mistaken the room, when she is stayed by a feeling
that such is not the case. Fleeting images of
forgotten scenes cross and clash through her inner
vision—out of the chaos recognition must come—
an anæmic girl with drawling voice and Dublin
accent—ah! now she knows. She does not heed
the outstretched hand, a large, soft hand, with
fingers that curl back at the tips and a managing
thumb, she only flushes painfully.

'You remember now,' says the other. Her
voice is thin, flutelike, odd, coming from such a
throat. 'I knew you at once; you are too distinctive to change.'

'I did not at first, I could not place you; it is a
long time, and you have changed greatly.'

'Yes, in more than appearance.'

She makes no reply. She scarcely knows what

to say. Her position is a difficult one. She feels
the grey eyes searching her face ; their owner puts
an end to her perplexity, saying :

' May I sit down ? I saw you come in yesterday ; I was in the hall. I have been trying to see
you ever since.'

' To see me ? ' Now the release is near, the strain
of the last months is telling on her ; she resents
the intrusion. ' I think you would not if —— '

' I knew, you mean ! You are not changed.
But I do know, that is just why. O'Brien is a
connection of my husband's ; he told me why he
came over here. Your—they have all three gone
to some place, something rouge—— '

' Moulin rouge ? '

' Yes, that 's the place. I wanted to see you for
myself.'

The girl looks at her with a touch of defiance,
and her eyes burn sombrely. The remembrance
of a [letter received a few days before stings her
anew. Is this to be part of her punishment ? Is
every proper woman she ever knew to come and
anoint her wound with well-meaning, bungling
fingers, and advise her what ointment to employ ?
No, a thousand times no ; she will stop it at once
and for ever ! There is a new sharpness in her
voice as she remarks :

' Under existing circumstances I am at a loss to
know why. There can be but one reason—a kind
intention on your part to persuade me to repentance. The day before yesterday I got this letter,'
she selects it from a heap of papers she has been

sorting, and twists it in her feverish fingers, 'from Mary O'Mahony, you know, the Queen's counsel's wife. She enclosed a medal and an introduction to a convent where they receive Magdalens of a better class, with means enough, in fact, to indulge in genteel contrition. They find them occupation, and, I presume '—with bitterness—' white sheets to stand in. No doubt she meant it kindly ; but I fail to see why she or any other woman should stand in judgment over me. What can such a woman as Mary know of motives ? reared in a convent school, married at seventeen with absolutely no knowledge of life ; and who has spent her time ever since in nursing babies and going to missions, and never reads a book except under the direction of her father confessor. If you are actuated by any such motives, I beg you to spare yourself and spare me. You do not know my reasons, and I shall most certainly not explain them.'

There is silence ; the little timepiece chimes out ten silvery peals. She is standing near the fireplace ; the logs are glowing from red to white, and the fir-cones sputter and fill the room with an aromatic smell. She is very pale, her eyes seem sunken, and one expression chases the other with baffling quickness.

The woman in the chair is holding her face in the palm of one big white hand, resting her elbow on the table. Her eyes dwell on the other's face, and there is a soft wistfulness in their expression. The pupils are larger ; as a rule they narrow into a speck when she looks at any one. She says slowly :

'You are wrong then ; I had no such intention. I heard you were leaving to-morrow, and I wanted to see you. I have never forgotten you ; you were younger than I was, but you influenced me——'

The girl interrupts her incredulously : ' I ? '

'Yes, you. I never forgot that scene in the old school at Rathmines. I told you you were a fool, do you remember ? That was the outcome of home training ; in my own heart I envied you your courage. When O'Brien told us, I had heard a rumour about it before I left, I '—with hurried speech and softening rush of vowels—' I envied you. I envy you now, though I don't understand why you did it, or why you are going away from him. Yours isn't the face of a woman leaving a man for whom she has sacrificed all because she loved him ; I think you are glad. Maybe you wonder at the word I use, but I say it again, I envy you the self-reliance that gave you courage to do it—and courage to face life again after having done it—alone, as you mean to do. Sure, I could make two of you '—rising to her feet and stretching out her magnificently modelled arms, whilst her words trip one another with tremulous passion —' and I haven't a spark of your courage. I am a coward, just a soft thing beside you. I would give all I ever dreamt of to have it or your truth. I am a living lie, acting a lie daily, and even if I could, I wouldn't change it ; I am afraid of public opinion. Do you remember how you used to laugh at things and say : " Bother what people say " ? I used to study you and wonder if you really meant it, or if it was only for bravado's sake. You knew papa, and our home. You knew our life. We were scrupulous in the performance of religion, and bigoted to our souls' core ; we gave to charities, when there was a subscription-list in the papers, and slunk by our poor relations in trade. We toadied and slandered, and the biggest ambition we had in life was to move to Fitzwilliam Square, and be presented at the Castle. No snubbing was cutting enough to deter us from trying to attain it. Bah, you know so-called Dublin society better than I do ; you know girls who go year after year to the Drawing-Room in cotton-backed satin trains ; pinch and save at home to find dresses for dances ; walk Kingstown pier season after season and set their caps at every stray military man, and when their good looks are going and regiment has followed regiment without success, they fall back on an attorney at home with a decent practice, and pretend they loved him all the time. We are no better than the rest ; you made me think first ; I used to want to write to you, but mamma discouraged it—you were not well enough off to make it worth while. Papa got on well ; he stood in with the Cardinal in politics, and didn't offend the other party. When I was twenty I went to an aunt in Liverpool ; she had money. There I met the man I cared for. He was only first officer on board a steamer, and a Protestant into the bargain. I was very happy as long as it lasted ; but he wrote home and my father came and fetched me, and I was bundled back as if I were a girl of twelve ;

sent to Rathfarnan Convent on a visit (it was
Retreat week), and I hadn't courage to rebel.
Nuns and priests and family clutched at me as if
I was a lost soul ; you would have laughed at it,
but I had not read or thought then as I have
since, to quiet my misery. A Protestant of no
family and no means, a heretic who couldn't buy
a dispensation to marry in this life, and was bound
to peril my soul and certainly lose his own in the
next. Is there such fanatical bigotry anywhere
under the name of religion as with us ? And sure
I knew so well that if he had money or high county
connections, they 'd have jumped at him, ay, even
if he had been a fire-worshipper. I used to
think of you sometimes, I was so lonely, and I
knew so well what you would have done. He
wrote to me, and after that my mother stayed
home from Mass to open his letters whilst I was
out of the way. Then he came over, and she never
left me alone a second with him ; and he was going
out to Brazil. Then I got courage, and I wrote to
him myself, but I never got an answer. I know
since; it was stopped.'

How the woman is changed ; her grey eyes are
gleaming with light, and her great white chest is
heaving with a passion of resentment.

' Papa and mamma and the priests made up a
match, and I was married to a man I detested and
detest still. But all Catholic Dublin came to the
Cathedral ; I have never put my foot in it since.
The Cardinal married us, and there were seven
priests at the sacrifice, and the nuns sent me pious

congratulations and a crochet quilt. It made me
sick of the very form of religion, of life, of everything. I hate their shams and the snobbery of the
people I meet, but what could I do? Two years
ago my aunt left me her money. There is great
power in money to a woman, and I knew more
than before—I knew how to use it. The marriage
laws as to separate property for women in Ireland
are as good as void, because few women care to
insist on them. The priests don't encourage independence in women ; when they lose this hold
on them they'll lose their hold on humanity. A
farmer's wife in country parts of Ireland would
find it difficult to lodge or draw money without
her husband's signature, the fools! And no Zulu
strikes a harder bargain for cows with his prospec-
tive father-in-law than the average Irishman for
the girl's dowry. They are huckstered and traded
for, and matches made up for them, just the same
as they bargain for heifers at a fair. The fortune
is handed over to the husband to use as he pleases,
and the priests get an ample percentage on it. I
made it understood that no penny of mine would
go out of my keeping. I refused to share in any
dealings. I am a good business woman now. My
babies died, and at my death neither family nor
husband nor church'll benefit ; every penny of it
will go to him or his. That's my satisfaction. My
case is not an uncommon one in Ireland. Most of
the women find their consolation in piety, and a
few in drink, and neither stops a mortal heartache.'

She has dropped into her seat again, and, leaning down her head on her arms, begins to cry with deep, quiet sobs. The girl goes over ; she has not once interrupted her passionate torrent of words. She smoothes the thick hair that waves so richly up from the white neck. It strikes her that there are some very handsome things about this woman as she lies there with her face concealed, and only her quivering white throat and grand heaving shoulders, and little pink ears, that sit so prettily to her head, visible.

'Poor thing, poor big woman, perhaps you will feel better now that you have told some one. I think you came to me because you thought that I too loved as you do, and that I had courage to put all aside for it. I do not know if I would '—gravely —' I have never been tried. It was not for that. Why, it concerns no one to know ; excuses and apologies are always a mistake. The best is to bear bravely the consequences of one's acts ; that is the only way to spare others from suffering for them. Ssh ! there, there, don't sob so ! Don't ! Did you think I could help you perhaps ? '

The red-crowned head bows in assent.

' I am afraid I know of no silver slippers to walk the thorny way. My own doctrine is a hard one. Endure, simply endure. Forget yourself, live as much as you can for others, get a purchase of your own soul some way, let no fate beat you. In a few years what will it all matter ?—not one cent, whether you have loved or been loved, been happy or unhappy. We have all got to thole our assize of pain. Perhaps everything is for the best, though one can't see it. Just think! Is not my lot a harder one than yours? Remember, for all my life to come I have to carry the loathing of one portion of it with me ; it will sour the bread and bitter the drink of all my days. But I will not let it beat me for all that. I would not talk of myself to you now but that it may be in hard hours to come you will, as you say you have done in the past, think of me ; and it may help you to forget your own fate to realise another's harder one.'

The older woman looks up out of her red-rimmed eyes at the grave face, with its strange half smile, of the younger, and smoothes the slim hand between her large ones ; she does it awkwardly as if caressing is rare to her fingers.

' I have always thought that each man or woman should bear as far as possible the entire effect of his mistakes or sins. It used to be a fancy of mine that if I were unfortunate enough to bring an illegitimate child into the world I would never disown it or put it away. I suppose it is my lack of orthodox belief which makes me unable to see that a bastard is less the fruit of a man and woman's mating than the child of a marriage blessed by priest or parson. To my poor woman's logic the words of the clergy have nothing to do with the begetting. I know men think differently ; they don't seem to realise that their physical and mental peculiarities, their likeness, body and soul, is stamped on the one as well as on the other. They rarely give them so much as a thought, at best seven shillings a week. And yet they will strive and toil, love, ay, sin, for the puniest specimen of humanity assigned to them by religion and law. If I had such a child'—with a lightening of eyes—'I would call it mine before the whole world and tack no Mrs. to my name either. I would work for it, train it up to respect and love me, explain to it, as soon as it had understanding enough to grasp my meaning, the wrong I had done it in men's eyes, teach it to bear its part bravely in the world, and hold its head high amongst men, to laugh at the want-wit inconsistency that forgives the man that begat the brat and treats with pitiless scorn the helpless result of his fathering. It is an unwritten law of society that the woman who strays from the narrow path assigned to her shall never walk again in the way of honour. And if nowadays she has no scarlet letter tacked to her gown to mark her from her sisters she is none the less doomed. Doomed to choose between two roads. Either she must be a hypocrite and play the penitent Magdalen and be driven to despair by the sanctimonious pity of zealous women of second-rate virtues and untempted honour or . . . Believe me, the Magdalen at Christ's feet had an easy road to repentance. But think of the poor soul who tells her sins to His vicar on earth or his wife. Think of the dismal platitudes tinctured with the world's opinions, the exhortations to repentance pointed with a hint to keep her place as a sinner. If she is of the kind to rebel at the dreary road Christian charity indicates to her, she is free to seek the broad road to destruction as a pleasanter alternative. She is a prey to every man who thinks she has given him a pre-emptive right to her person, a target for every woman to shoot at with arrows dipped in the venom the best of them have in their nature.

'You look questioningly at me? Your eyes query which road I shall take ; why should I tell you, why should I talk to you at all? I seek pity, help, friendship from no one. And yet because you understand me well enough to offer me nothing but simply to come to me as a woman to a sister woman, I will tell you. I shall take neither. I shall apologise to no man, court no woman's friendship, simply stand by my own action, and I defy them to down me, and that is what I would teach every woman.'

'Is it true you refused to accept any——?'

'Terms? Yes, it is true. Do you think I fear? Not one whit. No power on earth, no social law, written or unwritten, is strong enough to make me tread a path on which I do not willingly set my own foot. The world owes every man born into it bread, and no more ; no man need starve, but the hungry man or woman must buy his bread at the world's terms—work. I cannot demand the place I would have sought in it before ; my character or want of it, *comme vous voulez*, is against me ; but I can get a living and I mean to. I know more than the average woman, ay, more than the average man ; and I have intuition—he hasn't. My fingers are as deft at woman's work as the most conventional jade's who ever trimmed a

bonnet. I can do most things I try to. I never
yet met ten men or women together without finding that five of them either knew less or were
weaker in will or personal magnetism than I am.
Those five will give me a living. I shall get it
honestly, give them more for their money than
any one else, and when it is a question of value to
be received, believe me, the character of the giver
is of mighty little consequence to those who are
the gainers. That is the story of the world.
There is no power strong enough to crush a man
or woman determined to get on, or who knows
how to die if needs be. It is a stale truism
that nothing succeeds like success.'

'But that is all so hard, dear; don't you want to
be happy?'

She smiles sadly back to the tear-drenched grey
eyes with their look of pitiful questioning.

'Happy, what is happiness? The most futile
of all our dreams, the pursuit of a shadow,
the legacy of a forgotten existence bequeathed as
a curse to lure men from peace to despair. The
nearest approach to it is absolute negation of
self, to think, work, live for others round each day
as if one is to close one's eyes at night for the last
time. Life is far too short, dear woman, to run
after happiness. Stand on your own feet, be a
burden to no man, find your work and do it with
all the might of your being, and men will give you
a full measure because you neither need nor ask it
of them, for that is their nature. Do you know I
don't think people realise how much of the world

belongs to them. All that has been written, or said, or sung, or lived, has been lived for us of to-day. It is ours. No monarch yet has been powerful enough to hold a monopoly of a sunshine, of the varying beauty of the seasons, the sheen of moonlight on rippling water, the stain on the leaves at fall-time, the dappling shadows in the woods, the laughter of little children. All that is best, and strongest, and most beautiful, because most love-worthy'—smiling triumphantly—'in the world is a common inheritance, and I mean to take my share of it. The world is full of pictures that no Czar can confine to a gallery, full of unwritten comedy with the smiles trembling in the balance, with the tears and tragedies deeper than any ever staged by managing mummer. If men are miserable it's because they pursue the shadow and leave the substance, run like the old crone in the fairy tale all round the world in search of the sunshine instead of opening the windows of their souls to let it in. We are all so busy building up wretched little altars to hold the shabby gods of our devotion, that our years pass away and we are laid to rest without ever having tasted life for the span of a day. No Russian peasant bows more humbly to his ikon than does the average man and woman to the mangy idols of respectability, social distinctions, mediocre talent with its self-advertisement and cheap popularity. Great God! think how many miss a glorious sunset they might see from the doorstep because it is genteeler to peep over the window-screen! I wish I could start a crusade and preach a new gospel to all my weaker brethren, who have suffered and sinned and are being driven to despair for the sake of their pasts. I would make them arise with renewed hope; teach them to laugh in the faces of the hackneyed opinion of the compact majority who are always wrong; stir them to joy of living again; point out to them well-springs of wisdom and love, that no speculator on the world's change has power to make a corner in; prove to them that the world is to each of us if we have canning, or cunning, enough to take our share of it; and that when all is said and done there is no particular kind of maggot to feed on the king any more than the peasant.'

Her voice has dropped to a whisper. She has been clothing the thoughts of months into words and she has completely forgotten her audience of one. The latter is looking at her with eager eyes and parted lips, and when the girl, roused from her thoughts, smiles at her, she draws her down and holds the throbbing head to her heart.

'You see,' she says, lifting her head, 'I can't help you. You must find yourself. All the systems of philosophy or treatises of moral science, all the religious codes devised by the imagination of men will not save you—*always you must come back to yourself.* That is your problem, and one which you must solve alone. You've got to get a purchase on your own soul. Stand on your own feet, heed no man's opinion, no woman's scorn, if you believe you are in the right. If every human being settled his own life there would be no need for state-aided charity. Work out your own fate, and when your feet are laid together, and your hands folded, and perhaps a silver piece laid on each eye, and those to whom you have stood nearest will hasten in all decency to lay you out of sight, the best they will know to say of you will be: "She never troubled any one." Go, big woman, and if you find other women weaker, teach them to be sufficient to themselves—give of your largesse, but hold your own soul in the hollow of your hand and give no man a mortgage on it. It is getting late; they may come back.'

'And they're welcome to. I am glad I came to you. I was hungry for some word stronger and warmer to my heart than I get out of books, that bothered me with the virtues and woes of dead saints and never touched the living woman within; that told me to trample on the natural feelings of my being as if existence is a crime and human love a sin. Oh! you dear little soul, am I not to know where you'll be at all? I'd like to tell you how I get on. And if you are sick, or perhaps want some one, I would like to do something for you.'

'Would you?'

'Ah then I would!'

The girl rises and takes a leather photograph case out of her bag. She points to one.

'If I give you her address, will you go to her and tell her of me? Say I will write in some weeks' time.'

'I will.'

'Thank you. There is the address, if you can go to her. And now let us say good-bye. I am tired, and to-morrow I have my journey before me. I shall sleep in that chair. Thank you for coming, you big, soft, foolish woman. And I used to think you a hard girl! Don't you be afraid for me, I am not afraid for myself. There are no dragons in the world nowadays that one cannot overcome, if one is not afraid of them, and sets up no false gods.'

'Good-bye!'

She nestles with tears in her smiling eyes into the big woman's arms, kisses her back, and pushes her gently out of the room.

The meeting has touched her, helped her to formulate her vague ideas, given her, as it were, a friendly set-off on her way.

The fire has burnt out, and the grey ashes lie in a heap on the tiles. She turns to the window; the still night has a fascination for her. The city clocks are booming out the death-knell of the day in deep tones, and the one in the room chimes out a silvery accompaniment like the laugh of a woman through a chorus of monks.

She wraps herself in a shawl and sits watching. One great star blinks down at her like a bright glad eye, and hers shine steadily back with the sombre light of an undaunted spirit waiting quietly for the dawn to break, to take the first step of her new life's journey.

HER SHARE

HAS it ever happened to you that, may be sitting on a stile on a summer's day, when the whole world about you basks in sunshine, and the gladness of the time whispers round you in the fields, and the trees hold long talks together in the woods, and the mystery of it speaks to you and works in you in some subtle way so that you too feel summer in you, a sudden shadow waves across the landscape ; a chill puff of wind sets all the leaves fluttering into a surprised murmur ; the tolling of a dead-bell floats across to you from the belfry in the neighbouring village, and a feeling of sadness grips your soul and oppresses it ; the more keenly by contrast with your feeling of insouciant well-being—as a mocking whisper of relentless fate?

It was as the echo of the slow knell of a passing-bell on such a day, that her story struck me.

I was in the first flush summer of my new-found happiness. I wanted to get away by myself, to think, to dream it over again, to thrill at every recollected touch, to re-see every long look, to repeat every word shyly, to live it over and over again in thought. I wanted to escape from congratulations, questions, sympathy ; they jarred on me as when an ass brays suddenly when one sits listening to the nightingales. I had a song in my own heart so wondrously new and strange that I was jealous of every disturbing note.

There was a clear week to our next meeting, and the arrival of an elder sister, whose own unhappy marriage made her a very Cassandra with regard to the fate of others, strengthened my desire for solitude. I resolved to run down to the country on my bicycle, to get out into the fields and listen to the birds singing, to match the melody in my own heart. I arrived one afternoon in early July at a little town in Buckinghamshire, and turned into the cobble-stoned yard of a quaint old inn, to find another 'bike' in the yard before me.

I was tired from the hills, parched with heat, and glad to wash off the dust before tea. I went downstairs, humming for very gladness, to the commercial room. It was a big, cool room near the old-fashioned kitchen, but somehow the clatter of the cups and saucers and the persistent 's's'ss' of an ostler in the yard, washing the legs of an old bay mare, seemed to belong to the atmosphere of the place.

There was another visitor in the room when I went in, a tall, thin woman standing with her face to the window, lost in thought. Her cycling dress proclaimed her as the owner of the other machine. I was glad it was a woman—just then the world held only one man. She was leaning against the side of the window, with her hands clasped behind her back. There was nothing to be seen but a piece of ivy-covered roof, and a patch of blue sky, and the door of a loft, yet there she stood gazing at them ; perhaps she did not see them, there was a suggestive pathos in her attitude.

The maid came in and laid tea for two ; she never stirred. I wondered what her thoughts could be ; she struck me as quite middle-aged from the glimpse of cheek and neck I had.

'What nice fresh watercresses!' I said to the girl.

'Yes 'm ; a little too late for Buckingham folks' (with the air of a connoisseur), 'city people finds 'em good.'

The woman turns round ; she has a nervous face, and her hair is nearly white at the temples. There was a strange quiet wistfulness in her eyes that made me sorry for her ; but then she smiled, and somehow I thought of sun-slants, and violets, and it struck me that if one were lonely one would forget it as one met her look.

'Ah! do they still' (pointing to the cresses) 'make the local calendar? You must know' (to me) 'that everything is reckoned by the coming and the cutting, the laying and cleaning of the beds; and now I believe it has reached the dignity of an industry.'

'You know the town, then? I fancied you were, like myself, a visitor on wheels.'

'And that is all ; I have not been here for fifteen years, but I was born here thirty-eight years ago and to-day is my birthday ; I had a fancy to see it again——'

She takes up her old position at the window.
My own joy kept singing in me and I felt as if I
had tenderness enough for all the world, and I was
drawn to this woman with the lonely face and
wistful voice. I wanted her to be glad as I.

'Are you going on a long tour?' I ventured
to ask.

'No, I return to-morrow morning; I can never
get away for long; my work is waiting for me
when I return——'

'Tea is ready, 'm!'

We sit down and enjoy it as only women can;
she does not say very much, but she encourages
me to talk, and I feel drawn to her. I show her
my ring, and I tell her half shyly of my great
happiness, and how I had wished to get away
to realise it quietly—and she smiles in response,
saying:

'Yes, I know that feeling: that is why I came
down to-day.'

There is such a peculiar resigned note in her
voice that the idea comes to me that perhaps she
may have ridden down to visit the grave of some
one, and I forbear to ask. Besides, I have a sort
of respect for her, she seems so old to me in my
throbbing youth. But when tea is over I follow
an impulse and put my hand caressingly on her
arm. I ask her if I may go out with her, and she
assents with a smile.

We walk up the cobble-stoned streets with the
narrow houses, their quaint windows with the
curiously wrought iron hasps, and the wonderful

geraniums and calceolarias in the rows of pots pressed against the diamond panes. We turn past the clear river with the lads walking through it on stilts, and the swallows darting in aerial circles with shrill squeals as they skim it fly-snapping ; past the old church and the little vicarage, nestling amidst trees, and an ugly row of pretentious little modern houses, with dispro-portionate bulging bow-windows like a paste stud in a paper shirt-front.

'They were not here in my time,' she says, and she stands and looks about her as a person receiving a shock at some change wrought in his absence. We pass through a laneway, skirt a copse, and turn into a clover field on a slope. The vicarage with its gabled roof, the grey church, and the great hedge of clipped yew, smooth as shaded velvet, and older than the oldest man in the town, she tells me, are clustered at the end of it. I feel subdued by the emotions that cross her face like shadows and I follow her in silence.

We pause and gaze around us. To our right is a field of oats ; the grey-green stipples of the ears quiver on their slender sap-green stalks, with blotches of blood-red poppies in between. Roses climb over every hedgerow and dabs of elder bloom seem thrown amongst them. And our feet sink in clover blossoms, pink and white and yellow and purple, with feathery stems of grass nodding lightly above them. We drink in the exquisite smell that is as the distilled sweetness of all that is good in

summer, in long greedy breaths, and sit down and
bury our faces in the fragrant balls.

'O God, how sweet it is!' she says, with an
undercurrent of passion breaking her voice. 'How
it brings back things! How honey-sweet it is!
O God, I would like to die in a clover field!'

There is such hopeless regret in her voice that
I more than wonder what it is that brings it there.
We sit in silence, she lying with her face in the
clover; myriads of fragrant censers swing in the
evening breeze. The metallic rattle of a mowing
machine sounds in the distance, the songs of larks
overhead, and a bird in a gorse-bush at our back
keeps calling with a long-drawn, wheezy 'ch-e-e-s-ze
ch-e-e-s-ze.'

'It makes you sad, it hurts you; I am so sorry,'
I say.

'Shall I tell you why?' she asks. I nod.

'And yet, there is so little to tell. It is only
now, sitting here, that I realise how barren in all
that is best the years have been. Do you see
that gable window where the roses are thickest?
that was my room from childhood to girlhood.
There I had most of my dreams, my illusions;
there I used to beat my wings as a lark in a cage
against the loneliness, the monotony of my life;
and when my uncle died, and I had to go to the
great weary city and struggle for existence, it was
to there my thoughts used to fly when the seasons
changed and the city was dreariest and the burden
of work was heaviest. I think one feels things
more as one grows older, one dwells on them

more. Youth is elastic, and its pain is hot and
sharp while it lasts, but it never cankers as it does
in later years. Now a measure of success has
come to me, and comparative comfort, and I
thought I would be at peace, and yet . . . The
clover brings it back, brings back one face out of
the blankness of the past. Strange I don't think
until to-day that I have ever quite realised what it
meant. It stands out now vividly in my memory
as the recollection of an unheeded signpost on a
lonely road flashes across the mind's eye of a
wayfarer, showing him how he has missed the
path. I seem lately to be having a sort of Indian
summer of the senses. Vague feelings of disturbance that I used to have in early girlhood—you
know them?—that have been hushed to quiescence
in the years between, thrill in me now at a sensuous note of music, the coo of a baby. I have
learned to blush again.' (With a shy flushing.) ' It
is a pity hearts and souls do not always grow old
with their bodies. I don't know that there is
much to tell you; now that I come to think it
over, it is scarcely a story. I can tell back the
years as the beads of a brown rosary, always
sombre in hue. I am thirty-eight to-day, and no
man has ever kissed me.

'It is twenty years ago now, this time of year
too, Squire Raymond came back in the spring—
you can't see the Hall, it is behind that wood—
and brought home a foreign wife, a Roman
Catholic. There was an old chapel at the Hall
disused since the Reformation, and he promised

her to have it restored, the old carvings replaced, and the wooden statues—they had been partially burnt at one time. The railway has made great changes, and spoiled much, as it always does. Down there, where the telegraph pole stands behind that copper beech, there used to be a cottage, and between it and the vicarage a meadow. A lane led from it—Lover's Lane. I was coming through it late one evening—I had been to a croquet match, and I was singing to myself as I sauntered home—when I ran against a stranger at the turn. He raised a slouched hat and said, 'Your pardon, miss,' with a soft foreign accent and a grace that was strange to me then. I remember I stood still after he passed on, and I carried home the expression in his eyes, and when I woke in the morning it was the first thing I recalled, and I closed my eyes again to gather it into my mind and fix it. It haunted me through all the days that followed, and something kept me from speaking about him, although all the affairs of the county were known at the vicarage. I learned somehow that he was only a foreign workman brought over to restore the carvings.

'Some days afterwards we went to call on Squire Raymond, and he took us into the chapel to see how the work got on. *He* was up on a scaffolding, he had on a linen blouse, and a lot of tools stuck in his belt; and I hardly dared to look at him, my eyelids seemed weighted. I remember the resentment that blazed up in me when my uncle spoke to him in the same patronising way he used to talk to Bunker the saddler, and I lingered behind them to say a good-day to him, but he never looked down, though I felt he saw me. He lodged in the cottage I spoke of, and I gave Goody Thornton some sewing to do just to have an excuse to go there. I remember perfectly, as if it were yesterday, how I stood in that window one day and watched him go to the village, and how I slipped out, ran down the lane, and raised the latch, and went into the funny little kitchen. I wonder where all the quaint furniture has gone. His room was at the side of it. I know every detail of it: the clear-starched curtains, the patchwork quilt and equally wonderful piece of crochet representing Ruth gleaning, and the stiff row of flower-pots in the window. I remember how oddly I was stirred, and how shyly curious I was to see his things. Goody said he was as particular as a gentleman. A long row of books was arranged on the chest of drawers; I felt guilty as I opened them and read the name on the fly-leaf; it had a Slav ending; I copied it later on into my note-book. I remember the odd thrill of pleasure I felt as I read such of the titles as I could make out. My uncle was a good linguist, and had given me a smattering of foreign languages, at that time enough to give me a reputation as a blue-stocking. There was an old edition of Shakespeare, another of Spenser, several volumes of Heine, Max Stirner, "Der Einzige und sein Eigenthum, 1844"—I got it since in the British Museum—and some German metaphysics, and several volumes of poetry in a Slav tongue.

'There were long pipes, such queer shapes, and a pouch embroidered with beads and silken letters, a rack with carving tools, and a velvet cap and coat. Do you know, when I am alone in the dark I can see every one of the things that belonged to him in that room. I unrolled a housewife on his table; it was filled with needles and skeins of thread and pins of foreign make, and it was exquisitely embroidered with fairy-like wreaths of flowers and a heart with a dart through it, and a basket with tiny ribbon roses. A sudden unreasoning jealousy rose in me at the sight of it, and I can remember perfectly well saying over and over again, as if to convince myself, " It was his mother made it, do you hear, it was his mother!" I was delighted Goody stayed for a gossip; I liked to be there, I liked to touch his things. It was like a page out of the great, wonderful outside world. I remember when I was quite little a show came, with camels and elephants and other wild things in cages, and how I dreamed of them for nights, and longed to run away with the showman. His things roused the same feeling in me. There was a carved crucifix lying on his pillow, and the first rosary I had ever seen, and on the end of his bed an old violin with sorghum red wood in a carved case. They spoke to me in a strange way; there was an enchanting flavour of mystery about them that spoke of southern lands and sunshine. I felt vaguely that somewhere in under my pink and white English skin there lurked a brown spirit that responded to their influence. I often stole in there after that until I knew the names of the books by heart; and sometimes, as I saw the carving progress, a dull pain—I did not then realise what it meant—used to gnaw at me ; and once I laid my face against his velvet coat as it hung on the door ; it smelt of tobacco, and I cried without knowing why, and a knot of ribbon I wore at the neck of my gown caught in a button and hung there—and I left it there. . . . I had a reckless wish that he should know I used to go there, and sometimes I left a flower. . . .'

' How very strange ! And did you never speak to him ? '

' No, he was a workman in every one's eyes, and I was the vicar's niece.'

I try to see her as she must have looked then, but it is hard to picture her as anything but a faded, disillusioned woman with a weary, lovable face and wistful eyes ; she looked like a fruit that has grown to maturity in the shade and withered before it ripened properly.

' Squire Raymond came to see us one day, and spoke of him as a genius, a wonderful woodcarver and modeller in clay, an artist but a Socialist. Socialism in those days was looked upon much as Anarchy to-day, if not worse : it was not a thing to be taken into consideration by state parties. That meadow then was planted with clover as this is now. My uncle could barely recognise the

National Anthem, and Goody was deaf, and there
were no houses ; so evening after evening all
through that glorious June month, I used to play,
and he used to answer me with an improvised
echo of whatever I played to him.   It was a
strange secret duet, to which no one had a clue.
One night he played to me—ah ! how can I tell
you of it ?—music such as I had heard in dreams,
or in mad hours when the restless spirit worked in
me ; music as if all the hearts in the world were
being pierced with swords that cried out their
anguish as they slayed.   I walked up and down
the garden in my white gown ; he could see me
from his window, and he drew my soul with his
bow as one winds silk out of a cocoon, and he
bent it across the strings of his violin, and sent it
flitting out as a sigh into a world of pain, just to
wile it back and croon it to rest in himself in
a last soft note.   My girl friends used to look
curiously at me, and men took more notice of me,
for I blossomed suddenly into a kind of beauty
that belongs to every woman once in her life.   I
scarcely dared tell myself what it meant.   I know
that all that summer there was a thrumming on
an unknown chord in my innermost being, a
wonderful by-song in my heart that I alone
heard.   Intense joy has its element of pain.   The
days were too short, and at night I used to creep
out of bed and kneel at the window and cry for
no known reason.   Then one night I awoke with a
strange feeling as of some one laying a hand
upon my forehead, and I rose and went to the

window as usual. Something shivered through
me, and I saw a stir in the shadow of the great
copper beech on the road below, and my heart
fluttered as a fledgeling trying its wings for the
first time, and I knew he was there, and I understood all at once why I used to wake with that
feeling of being watched. His voice stole in to
me with the smell of the clover on the night
breeze ; not singing, rather whispering in song,
so that only he and I and the soft-bodied moths
and the big white owl that flitted heavily across
the road could hear it. . . .'

She has forgotten me ; it is as if she is reading
aloud the pages of a book that has been shut up
in herself for so long that the story is new to her.

' The words he sang were foreign, but the melody
spoke passionately, warmly, caressingly, with a
chord of despair that turned my heart to water
and touched the most secret fibres of my being,
hurting me with love. I felt as if I were in a
trance and he were singing my requiem over me.
Then he changed the air and sang a little tender
thing with a refrain that said plainly in this strange
tongue, " I love you ! " I tried to hum it back
to him, but no sound issued through my lips ; I
felt as if the fingers of fate were clutching my
throat, choking down the sound ; I made the most
strenuous efforts to shake them off; the blood beat
in my temples ; I struggled and strained, but no
sound came. I watched him with a dull despair
come forward into the silver white moonlight on
the white road ; as his voice died out in a sigh,

he looked up at me.   I snatched a rose that was
nodding drowsily, with all its pink leaves crumpled
up like a baby's fist, and I put my lips to it and
flung it down with a groan.   I saw him catch it
and raise it to his, and then a cloud-drift scudded
across the moon and a night-jar shrieked hoarsely,
and still the fingers clutched my throat, and though
I groaned his name with all my being, though my
whole self was one utterance of his name, no sound
other than his vanishing footsteps and the shrill,
pained shriek of some little beast in the clutch of
a stoat broke the stillness of the night.   And for
years after, ay, even now, I wake and hear the
steps growing fainter and fainter down that white
road . . .'

There is a long silence.   'Yes?' I query at
length.

'Well, the rest of that night is blank, and when
day came I knew before I went to Goody's that he
had left.   He had left a parcel for me—a box
carved as a book ; I peeped at it, and then hid it
till night came.   The hours of that day dragged
like years, but when at last it came, I locked myself
in my room and looked at it.   I cried to think how
he must have worked at night to finish it, and my
heart swelled with pride, for it was the work of an
artist.   The story, if it is a story, is carved on the
lid in wonderful tracery—a female figure with a set
face, mocking eyes, and inexorable mouth, " Fate "
written on her girdle, has her hand on the bolt of
a prison window.   Behind the bars a man's face,
his face, stares out with hopeless yearning—and

do you know, when I saw it I set my teeth in my arm to relieve the pain it gave me ? And tumbling down the prison walls are roses that seem to live in the wood—their very petals are loose as if a breath might shake them, one great blossom nods tantalisingly before the gaze of the man; and when I looked I marvelled, because growing out of the trailing roses I saw myself—my hair, my face, my hands. It is like one of those puzzle-pictures. I was only suggested by a curl of petal, a twist of leaf or stem, and yet there was no mistaking it (though you would fail to see a likeness now); the story was told. Ah, if he only knew! The other side is a sea, suggested with a few lines ; an endless desolate sea, with a raft and a solitary figure floating out towards the horizon. All the beauty of my life was on the cover, and my life has been as the empty wooden box with a date in it.'

The sun has gone down long since, and the birds have hushed them, her voice fits into the twilight.

' I have cried so often over it when the loneliness of life has touched me sorely, that the wood is stained and smoothened.'

She has risen to her feet as she speaks, with a bunch of clover in her hand, and we turn towards the town.

' The smell of the clover and the sound of his voice are always associated in my senses, and perhaps, perhaps—for the dream is always greater than the reality—it is best so ; but'—with soft sadness—' it is of him I will think when I am dying, and death may come easier for the thought.'

GONE UNDER

ONE forenoon in late autumn an outward-bound steamer lay close to a wharf in New York. She lay quietly waiting for the signal of her departure, in which few seemed to take an interest. There was a lonely note in her waiting. No telegraph boys bearing God-speeds to much-initialled citizens, no loquacious interviewers, no crowd of friends and relatives with floral offerings boarded the gangway of the *Portugal*, for she was only a third-rate steamer carrying a live freight of cattle to London, and her score of passengers either studied economy, absence of scrutiny, or a longer spell of sea.

The last of the weary, harassed beasts was packed closely under decks, but their presence was betrayed by uneasy lowing and a warm smell that made an Irish dock-labourer think, with tears in his eyes, of a thatched cabin on a Kerry hill-side, and his old mother, with the rent coming due ; made him brace his back to the work anew and croon an old Irish melody, because of the ten dollars saved to send her.

A girl leaning over the side smiles as she hears him ; she has a grave, tender face, plain at a first look ; but her eyes are the changeful hazel that lighten with mirth or darken with thought, as when cloud-rifts or sun-slants flit across a turf-fringed tarn.

She has no 'style,' and her clothes are plainly made and rather shabby; she is going home on a free pass.

She has been working for two years in New York, and is glad to go back, even if it be only to seek fresh work amongst her own people. She has read much, thought much, worked hard, and lived clean—been necessarily lonely. She has observed closely during her stay in this polyglot city of striking paradoxes, this monster dollar-mint, this gigantic sieve through which the surplus of the old world is silted over the new; city of many sects and blatant atheism; narrow prudery, and naked vice; where foreign literature is emasculated, and native newspapers are as broad as the Bible, and filthy as Sterne.

She has suffered physically under the mighty throb and high pressure hustle of a life that rolls on like a mighty steam-roller, crushing the sap out of the men before their prime, making the women the most consciously sexless, and unconsciously selfish, on the face of the globe.

She has learnt strange lessons in social economy; understands how sealskin 'saques' and imported hats can be bought on a salary of six dollars a week; has lost most of her illusions.

She is watching idly a man and a woman who have driven up in a closed carriage. They have seated themselves on a bench on the wharf and are talking earnestly. The woman has her back turned to the boat; she is very tall, her figure is superb, her waist too round and too small. The sunlight mates with the golden knot of hair under her crimson toque. She wears a plaid woollen gown in which cream predominates, and a red satin bodice, and carries a useless silk parasol to match. She is dressed for a garden-party, and, save for the new travelling-bag, ulster, and rug lying next her on the wharf, shows no signs of fitness for a perhaps rough voyage.

The man seems to be trying to reassure or convince her, but she shakes her head as she listens, and her shoulders heave, and she wipes her eyes impatiently.

The girl wonders vaguely in what relationship they stand to one another, and if she will be a passenger, and why in that gown.

A laughing party troop up the gangway and divert her attention. Most of them are members of a stranded burlesque company, and they have come to say good-bye to the leading girl.

The doctor joins them, and the quiet girl, who takes life too seriously, listens with a touch of wistfulness to their chaff and quaint slang. She even admires the effect of their smartly cut clothes, and is not feminine enough to see how cheaply it is gained.

She is a great child in spite of her knowledge, and she envies these girls their gift of repartee and the ease with which they turn aside foolish compliments. She has had little experience of men—

she does not get on with them very well. She has started with old-fashioned ideas as to their superiority ; she is so desperately in earnest that she takes them too seriously, she fails to see how comic they are, and they find her a bore. She is having a lesson now, and she tells herself musingly: ' This is the secret : look pretty, laugh *à pleine gorge*, if you have white teeth or dimples ; smile up through your lashes if they are long ; don't tax them, don't ask them to take you seriously ; just amuse them, that must be the great thing, to amuse them.'

Meanwhile the bustle has increased ; the odd people that crowd the deck of outward-bound vessels troop down the gangways. The cattle-jobbers laugh lustily and bandy jokes with friends on the wharf ; the steam falls in feathery spray, with a suspicion of oil in it ; and ear-splitting whistles call responsive bellows from the penned beasts below, and echo through the creak of grain-elevators and giant cranes, and the thousand vagrant sounds of the harbour.

The woman with the red bodice comes on deck ; she steps to the girl's side and waves her hand to the man below. He raises his hat and goes, looking back as the carriage turns.

She is younger than a back view alone would lead one to think ; she cannot be more than five and twenty ; but there are fine lines about her eyes, they are circled with heavy indigo stains, and her lids are swollen with tears. She is dazzlingly fair, and the blue veins show in delicate tracery at her temples, her lips are crimson, and the under one is full, but her chin runs softly into her white throat.

The girl, endowed as she is with the passionate worship of beauty and the imagination that belong to Celtic ancestry, feels attracted to her, and yet repelled.

Off at last! She has watched the scene too often during her luncheon hour from the top of the great building in which she has worked to see any novelty in it; she goes down to find her cabin. It is dark, small, near the pantry, as befits a shabby girl who travels free. She arranges her few belongings and goes on deck. The smell of the cattle, for it is hot down there, and the hatchways are open, oozes forth and mingles with the briny smell of the sea, recalling childhood scenes —stretches of sandy dune melting into the grey-green sea, red-tiled homesteads, and lowing kine going home to be milked; and she realises that she has been home-sick unawares; that the old world has a glamour for her in its reverend age, far beyond the crude green youth of the new—the witchery of its great past, and the wonderful host of its living dead—its dead in some of whom she has a share, who still live in her, making her what she is.

The first days pass as usual on a steamer of the kind; she sees nothing of the fair woman, but notices that the stewardess brings many empty bottles out of her cabin. It amuses her to watch people, it is almost like a play in which she is sole audience. Two maiden sisters take a fancy to

her and have a daily talk. The little actress sings and plays, and the men cluster round her, but the doctor is first in favour.

Then the wind changed, places got vacant, and the 'fiddles' appeared on the table, and early one morning they ran into the boisterous clutches of an autumn gale. Her cabin became unsupportable, the nauseous smell of paint and bilge-water made her sick; all the plate and crockery in the pantry next her seemed to shiver into atoms, and wash about her very ears; and sometimes the little silvery thread of light in the pear-shaped globe would dwindle to a red thread to plunge her suddenly into total darkness. She fought through her dressing, and the fresher air of the saloon revived her, and she crept up on to one of the lounges.

Stifled cries from the state-rooms mingle with the rattle of chains and howl of the wind. The steamer strains and groans like a huge beast in labour, and the screw rises and falls with a desperate thud. A second of suspensive quiet, and they sink into darkness with a sickening dive that turns her hot and cold with a feeling of melting; and the screw pops out of the water, and the steamer shudders, until they float up again, and it is struck by a giant wave with a crash like the deafening report of mighty cannon, terrific after the ghastly silence. A rush of hurried steps mingled with confused hoarse shouts overhead, and the trickle of water finding its way out again adds to the feeling of excitement.

The doctor passed through, and paused to give

her a word of praise for her pluck, but a shout
down the companion-way hurried him off to a man
crushed in the cattle-pens. Sometimes in a lull
in the tumult of wind and waves she fancied that
she could hear terrified groans from the prisoned
beasts. Then the stewardess disappeared, and
the second steward answered the bells instead, and
crept along the floor balancing brandy and biscuits.
She fell into a troubled sleep to wake with a start,
as if some one had called her. She sat up and listened; it is colder, darker, and the steamer labours
more; the electric light is out, and a few lamps
swing dismally to and fro. A stifled groan reaches
her, and a voice moans in a cabin near her:

'O God, will no one come to me, I guess I'll
die, my God, my God!' She got down and
managed by waiting for the uprising swell to creep
on her hands and knees towards it.

She pushed aside the curtain and went in; the
golden-haired woman lay moaning in the lower
berth; the bed-clothes had fallen into a confused
heap upon the floor, and she was uncovered,
shivering with cold, her hair streaming out like
amber drift-weed at every lurch; a trickle of blood
ran from one of her white wrists. A diminutive
pair of boots, an empty champagne bottle, frag-
ments of glass and china, and an upturned tray
slid noisily to and fro on the floor; an unopened
bottle is propped with towels in the basin. The
girl caught the empty one as it rolled towards her,
and thrust it, with the other loose things, into the
empty berth.

The woman is utterly helpless with terror and sickness, and the girl had to exert all her strength to lift her into a better position ; she bound up her wrist and tucked the bedclothes and rug about her, and knelt down, holding fast to keep herself from slipping ; but the smell of stale champagne and the closeness of the air made her feel faint, and she touched the bell.

The second steward answered it, muttering angrily as he pushed aside the curtain, but checked himself on seeing her there :

' Can you tidy up a little ? ' she asks hesitatingly, ' mop up the floor and straighten things ? '

' I 'll have a try, miss ; the stewardess has sprained her wrist, and every one 's ill. You just leave her to me, I 'll fix her up, she 's boozed '— with contempt—' that 's wot she is.'

' Don't leave me ; O God, don't leave me ! ' whimpers the woman in terror, and her blue eyes stare wildly ; and the girl, who has flushed at his words, pauses irresolutely and then goes back and kneels again.

' It can't matter,' she says to the youth ; ' the poor thing is frightened, and perhaps I can do her some good.'

He tidies in silence, and later he brings her some sandwiches and tells her the galley fires are out, and some men hurt, and one man washed overboard, and that the night promises to be no better than the day. He fixes her some cushions for her to kneel upon, and fetches a striped blanket and tucks it respectfully round her, with a look of ill-concealed disgust at the woman and resentment for her own sake. For her face reminds him of a little girl with whom he kept company down Wapping way, one whole glorious summer, until she got 'saved' and joined the 'army,' and gave him up as unregenerate.

The woman moaned and cowered in terror, and once when there was a crash, and they were plunged in darkness, she put out her hand, and clutching the girl, besought her to pray.

The night passed slowly, but towards morning the gale abated, and the steamer rolled with long steady swings, and the woman fell asleep holding the girl's hand. The latter is cramped by her crouching position and nods wearily, but it never occurs to her to leave her post. At length she dozes and has a dream, in which dragons and leviathans fight bloody battles, churning red-stained foam as they hurl islets at one another in their rage, whilst a mermaid with streaming golden tresses urges them on with a shrill voice like the scream of sea-mews.

The lad comes in the early dawn with some coffee, and tells her the worst is over. She forces the woman to eat a little, and then finds a hair-brush; it is silver-backed, and brand new, as everything is, even the night things she is wearing, as if bought for the journey. She brushes the wonderful hair into a long shining braid, parts the fringe, and the uncurled hair, soft as raw silk, frames the temples chastely; the head and forehead and drooping white lids and pencilled brows

have the delicacy of a Madonna by Ary Scheffer;
but the mouth cannot lie—the pout of the wine-
red lips, the soft receding chin, and the strange
indefinable expression that lurks about them
rather fits a priestess of passion.

'I would paint her as Helen,' thinks the girl,
'I wonder who she is, and why she sets out on a
journey with a satin bodice and lace-flounced
petticoats, and how old she is?' Her forehead is
a child-girl's; her mouth a courtesan's of forty.
She unclasps the hand that prisons hers, and considers it: hands tell age better than faces. It is
white, pink-palmed, and satin-soft, the nails are
manicured and polished as agates—twenty-five.
She has been so alone that she has acquired a
habit of observing closely things that happier
women barely understand. She speculates and
weaves stories about the people she meets; they
strike her fancy as the characters in a book or picture, and interest her always. She is saved, not
knowing them, from finding their limitations.

The forenoon has dragged through before the
woman awakes from her long restful sleep; she
smiles up at the girl, and then a burning flush
stains her face, and she turns it aside, and when it
has ebbed away she looks back searchingly into
the girl's grave eyes, and taking her hand kisses it
closely and holds it to her cheek.

'You are better now, I can leave you, I am very
tired,' says the girl.

'Yes,' letting go her hand; then with an
impulse: 'Will you——?'

'Yes?' a silence.

'Will I——?'

'Will you?—ah, no matter—thank you—I guess you'd best go ——,' and she turns her face to the wall.

The girl creeps to the top of the companion-way for a breath of fresh air. The sea still washes the after-deck, and sometimes a sheet of spray dashes over the bridge. A dismantled barque rides erratically on the right, and a piece of wreck-age dances on the waves. Deep groans and a pained lowing rise from the hold, and a smell of steaming beasts blows with the wind; some sailors, in shining oilskins, are tipping a dead ox overboard. Her vivid imagination calls up horrid scenes of broken limbs under heavy swaying bodies, gored sides, and gouged eyes amongst the penned beasts below; and she descends with a shudder. She visits most of the cabins, and in an unobtrusive way shortens the time for the other women, but she does not go near the only one that really awakes her interest.

Two days pass, and then the little actress appears in a fascinating tea-gown; she is better, for she has curled her fringe and koholed her lashes, and the doctor is radiant. The maiden sisters come out with knitting-bags and Testaments, and the woman who travels in embroidery silks follows, and the man who quoted 'Rocked in the Cradle of the Deep' the first evening, and sang nautical songs (in which 'yeo-ho' was the only intelligible word) in a brave manner, and collapsed at the first roll. They congratulate her as the only passenger with 'sea-legs,' and are very friendly, but when she speaks of the sufferings of the other woman, they purse their lips, look virtuous, and change the subject.

The girl is sitting in her favourite corner, and presently the woman, Mrs. Grey on the passenger-list, comes out with a novel and seats herself near her. In reply to the girl's shy query she flushes a little, says she is well, and begins to read; her eyelids are pink and swollen, her whole face is puffed as with much weeping.

The little actress plays for them, enthralls them with the spirit of music that is so often a birthright of the children of Israel, witches, and warms, and saddens them, as Miriam in olden days. They beg for their favourite songs, and once in a pause the woman, it is the first time she has spoken to any of them, asks for a serenade of Kjerulf. There is a dead silence, every one looks round—the little actress very slowly—then, drawing herself up to her full height, she lets her black eyes travel coldly from the woman's head to her feet and up again, with the well-known air of affronted scorn with which she is wont to annihilate the villain in her best part, and turns away without replying.

The woman winces, the girl has winced more; she moves nearer and speaks to her, but the woman makes no reply; keeps her eyes on her book, and tries to brave it out. When a few minutes have passed, in which every one talks together, she goes back to her cabin; the bell rings sharply, and the steward answering it comes out calling to the second steward :

'A bottle of fizz for Mrs. Grey !'

She is seen no more that day.

Late the following evening the girl is up on deck watching the phosphor froth in the steamer's wake, and the moon playing hide-and-seek through a feathery maze of clouds. She is roused by *her* voice beside her :

'Have you heard when we arrive ?'

'Yes, Saturday, if all goes well.'

'And this is Wednesday, oh, my God, my God, pity me !' (under her breath). 'If I were not such a coward '—with passionate emphasis—' I 'd just jump over right here into the middle of that shining streak. It would make a lovely shroud wouldn't it ?' (with a laugh). She rests her hand on the girl's shoulder, and then her head, and rocks her shoulders as if in pain. The girl smoothes her hair silently.

'Why are you so good to me ?' she asks suddenly.

'I don't know, because you are a woman, I suppose, as I am ——'

'I believe I 'll go mad,' she cries, ruffling her hair back from her lovely wretched face. 'I must tell some one, my head is bursting ; come down to my cabin later on, will you ?'

'Yes, if it will help you in any way, yes.'

The head steward has been standing near them. He saunters up to the girl as the woman leaves her, and makes some remark about the fineness of the night; but he keeps his cap on, and has a cheap cigar stuck between his teeth; there is a familiar note, too, in his voice. Her look of grave surprise disconcerts him, and he moves off with a swagger. She has been conscious of a difference in her treatment for some days, a shrinking on the part of the women, a touch of insolence in the glance of the men. It hurts her a little.

It is late when she seeks the woman. She finds her crouched on the floor, with her head resting on her arms, that are crossed on the plush seat. She looks up as the girl enters.

'I don't know why I asked you to come,' she cries, 'except that I am so wretched, and you seem so sure of yourself. I am very miserable.'

'Poor woman'—with tenderness—'don't tell me anything on impulse. Can't I help you without? Aren't you going to friends?'

She groans and buries her face in her hands.

'Is your husband in London, don't you want to go to him?'

'O, no no,' she writhes, 'I am afraid. O God, what *will* I do?'

'But why? Listen to me, Mrs. Grey,' she says persuasively.

The woman lifts her head, her breath smells of brandy, and says:

'My name is Edith.'

'Isn't it Grey as well though—I thought——'

'No, I am called so, I am not really married——'
There is a pause.

'Well, no matter. He looked upon you as his

wife, didn't he? He was good to you or you wouldn't be going to him.'

'He cabled for me, I have to go.'

'And you don't want to?' with a puzzled look. 'Don't you care about him?'

'I did when I was with him, but he left me. He shouldn't have, I implored him not,' with a wild gesture. 'Now he is angry, and I am afraid,' sobbing.

'But why, dear woman, what have you done? Tell me'—with hesitation—'is it because of this?' pointing to a bottle.

The question seems to strike the woman in some ludicrous way, for she stifles an hysterical inclination to laughter, and replies shamefacedly:

'No, oh no, he does not know I take anything, it isn't that.'

'Why do you? It shows so plainly, and people notice it, and it spoils you—you are so beautiful, it's such a pity——'

'I can't help myself—I want to forget—I used to nearly go mad, and so I began it, and now I can't do without it. I wasn't meant to be what I am, do believe me'—with a pleading in her voice. 'I am not bad at heart, I don't care about it really, but I can't help it. I was only sixteen when he took me, I was a silly fool of a girl, and I had no one belonging to me. I thought it was a grand thing. Even his relatives didn't know I wasn't married to him. He petted and spoiled me, and dressed me like a doll, and whenever I wanted to learn anything he laughed at me. There

were times when I wanted something better, I
used to tire of it all : but I was always a little
afraid of him ; the set we mixed in was a fast one,
and I learnt no good, and the women I met were
worse than the men——'

'But he was really fond of you ?'

'Yes, in a way. He loved my beauty, he was
proud of my figure, and the admiration other men
had for me.   I had a very good time, and I enjoyed
life, except sometimes when a fit came over me.
I suppose I should have gone on like that for
ever, only—I don't know why I should tell you
this—there is something in you draws it out of
me—well, one day'—there is a sharper note in
her voice—'I found I was going to have a little
child. He was away when I discovered it, and I
was just crazy with delight—I played with dolls
until I was fifteen, you know. I used to sit and
think about it, and I wished he would come home.
I never was so glad. They're such cunning little
things, with such cute little ways, and,'—there is a
touching pathos in her tear-stained face—'when he
did come I flew to tell him——'

'Yes ?'

'He was as angry as ever he could be ; it was
as if he struck me sharply in the face. He said it
would spoil me ; he didn't want it ; it would make
complications ; he had no intention of marrying
me, we were quite well as we were—we had a
dreadful scene—he—well—I defied him for the
first time—I could have killed him, I hated him
so—I was almost mad, I wanted to run away, to

be safe. Then he pretended to be sorry, and I let him fool me '—clenching her hands—'fool me into thinking it was all right. He took me to a quiet place in the country, asked me not to write to any one about it, and I was to stay there till the time came. I was quite content, I used to go into the woods and listen to the birds, I was just as happy as ever I could be. Then the time drew near, and we went up to town. He took me to Madame Rachelle's. I thought it a little strange, I had heard so many stories about her establishment ; but he said I should be well taken care of, and I was a fool in his hands, and too happy to trouble——'

Her face is set and her voice is bitter.

' They gave me some anæsthetic, and when I came back to myself, as it seemed to me out of a rush of swirling waters, I was lying, too weak to lift my hand, too confused to call. But suddenly I did ; it all came back to me in a flash of consciousness, and I sat up and screamed, for I had a presentiment of what it meant ; and I beat with my hands and called for my baby,—and that she-devil, curse her ! rushed in and held me down, and put a handkerchief over my face, and I lost myself again, but not altogether. I heard his voice, and I pretended to be unconscious. My brain was in a whirl, and I fancied '—her voice has sunk to a whisper, it is as if she is muttering to herself—' I could hear *it* cry, and that it wanted me so ; I felt its tears on my breast, it was only my milk had come, and *that* made me think of the little baby head ; and I felt as if my brain and heart would burst. I nearly went crazy. I got cunning, and when she bent over the bed I lay quite still and held my breath. She thought I was unconscious, and I watched her ; she went into the dressing-room, and then a nurse called her hurriedly. She had many patients,'—with a laugh—' and she went away with her. I got up quickly, and by holding to things I managed to crawl to that room. I *had a feeling it was there.*' There is such a frenzy of passion in her voice, such a seal of despairing remembrance on her face, that the girl holds her breath in suspense.

'I got there and crawled in, . . . there was a bundle there——.' She chokes down a sob and her eyes flash fire ' I felt my heart stop. . . . I snatched it up and unrolled it, and God curse them ! it was my little one. I couldn't believe it was dead. I kissed it and tried to warm it, and I put it inside my nightgown between my breasts ; and then I heard voices, and I rushed out and down the stairs. A nurse met me and tried to stop me, but I screamed and bit her hand. Then more came, and I felt everything grow black around me, and my little one melted like a lump of ice on my heart, and I knew no more.' There is a silence, both women are pale. ' When I came to my senses I was back in the country, and they told me I had been ill for months, and that I could never endure him to come near me.'

'You poor thing, you poor woman,' cries the

girl ; 'the brutes ! I would have had them up for murder. I would never have rested——'

'So you think, but I guess you wouldn't. Money can do everything ; the certificate of death said it was stillborn, and it was signed by a medical man. It was only last year the death of a schoolgirl of good family caused such scandal that the place was closed ; but too many big people were implicated to make a fuss, and Madame Rachelle escaped. I went back to town and threw myself into every dissipation. He was glad ; I *seemed* reconciled, but it haunted me. I could feel it at night groping about for me, and the chill of its poor little hands clung to me, and I used to drink to get warm again and forget it. I used to wonder if it cried when it came into the world, and if they hurt it. Can you think '—with piteous, hiccoughing sobs—'how any one could hurt a little thing like that ? or can you wonder I drink ? I would have loved it so—I wanted something better than I had. I wasn't meant to be bad ; you don't think I was—say you don't '— gazing eagerly into the girl's face, that is blanched by intense feeling.

'No, you poor woman, you were not meant to be bad. I think you were meant to be *very good*. I have known many women, and I think the *only divine* fibre in a woman is her maternal instinct. Every good quality she has is consequent or co-existent with that. Suppress it, and it turns to a fibroid, sapping all that is healthful and good in her nature, for I have seen it—we had many girls in the office. . . . Every woman ought to have a little child, if only as a moral educator. I have often thought that a woman who mothers a bastard, and endeavours bravely to rear it decently, is more to be commended than the society wife who contrives to shirk her motherhood. *She* is at heart loyal to the finest fibre of her being, the deep, underlying generic instinct, the " mutterdrang," that lifts her above and beyond all animalism, and fosters the sublimest qualities of unselfishness and devotion. No, indeed, you poor woman, you are not bad ; you are, perhaps, just as God intended you ! '

Her cheeks burn with the vehemence of her words, and a tear hangs on her lashes.

' But drink will not help you, believe me ; work might—— '

' But what could I do? I can't put a stitch in my clothes. I haven't learnt a single useful thing. I know how to attract men '—with bitterness—' that is all.'

' Have you ever told him how you felt, spoken to him frankly? After all, he was good to you in a way ; he must be touched by it. Try it when you meet him, dear ! Let him see the real woman, as you have let me ! '

Her words have a startling effect ; the woman's face changes, a look of terror and the remembrance of something momentarily forgotten gathers upon it ; she hides her face, and rocks impatiently with moaning cries.

' It 's no use, no use ; it 's too late. My God,

what is to become of me? You don't know all;
you could never understand; you are strong, you
don't know what reckless passion means—if you
only knew you would go away, you wouldn't
touch me. O God! O God!'

She has slid on to the floor, and kneels, wringing her hands and crying, the girl looking helplessly down at her.

'Try me,' she says, 'I promise you I won't go
away. What are you afraid to tell him? what
else is there?'

'What else?' she groans, stretching out her
hands, 'the worst that could be. He had to go
to Europe a year ago. I begged him to take me
with him. I knew how it would be if I were left;
I had no occupation, and the child haunted me!
I drank to kill it; it made me reckless, and he
was the only check. But he said he couldn't take
me; he wouldn't. I tried to tell him what I felt,
but I was afraid. And now a letter was written
to him about me, and he cabled to me to sail by
this steamer—my passage was taken—or never
see him again. I was not at home; the cable was
sent after me; I had only time to catch the train
for the boat, without clothes or anything. I wired
for my things to be sent, but they did not come in
time, and I had to get some before I came on
board. I know him so well; he will never forgive
me, and I am afraid to face him, and I have hardly
any money.

'But I don't understand. What was written to
him? Who wrote?'

'Oh, a woman, of course! she got to know things; she likes him.'

'Well, but can't you explain? isn't it something you can tell him?'

The golden head shakes a dismal denial; and a tortured moan is the only reply.

'Tell *me*, then; two heads are better than one.'

'You saw'—the girl has to stoop and catch the words—'that man who came with me?'

'Yes.'

'He is my husband's cousin; he owes everything to him. Well, it . . . it . . . *was with him* —he used to come to see me; he didn't admire me . . . not a bit. . . . I was lonely and wretched, and I don't know what madness possessed me— you can't understand. One just gets insane, and lets oneself be carried away. I think the devil gets hold of one. I tried to attract him; there was a kind of excitement in it, . . . and . . . well, we let ourselves drift . . .' —she has grown calmer as she speaks—'and afterwards, when we thought of him, we felt like shooting ourselves. He cried like a child and cursed me, and I hated him; but that soon passed over—we grew reckless, and sometimes we quarrelled and said good-bye; then we felt miserable, and sought one another again, and'—with a musing air—'all through there was a kind of fascination in the danger, though we didn't really care a bit for one another.'

The girl is dumb with pained realisation; it is her first actual contact with a problem of such a nature, and so little does she grasp it that she says:

'It's dreadful, but you must tell him the truth.
You see he sends for you in spite of all, and,
besides, he first taught you to . . . to . . . be as
you are ; he must remember that. He shouldn't
have left you to yourself ; you were beautiful and
wretched ; you must tell him——'

The woman cowers lower ; her hair has come
undone and covers her shoulders like a tawny
golden garment.

'I can't,' she groans hoarsely ; '*that was a year
ago . . . since . . .* Oh, I can't tell you—I can't !
Better go, far better go ! you can't help me—no
one can——'

'*Since ?*' repeats the girl, with stark-white lips
and horror-filled eyes, '*since ?*'

'*There was some one else.* You don't know
what it is to have nothing to hold one back. I
had no control over myself, something used to
possess me ; it is always like that, *one stifles the
memory of the first with the excitement of the
second.* Afterwards I wanted to kill myself straight
away, that is God's truth, but I was afraid.'

There is a long silence, only the woman cries
with stifled groans of crushing misery ; and the
girl listens as if in a confused, horrible dream to
the sobs that shake the bowed figure at her feet,
for she has risen, and is standing at the door,
holding the curtain with one hand. Something
in the crouching figure, with the rippling waves of
hair falling about her in a glory of colour, recall
to her the beautiful story of tender pity for such
another ; and the simple great words of it repeat

themselves in her inner soul, and the lesson comes
home to her, and she goes back, and, stooping,
clasps her arms about the heaving shoulders of
the woman at her feet, and says, with her heart
breaking her voice :

'Hush, hush, Edith, sister ! look at me !'

The woman obeys with incredulous look, and
then buries her face in the girl's lap, saying :

'I am not worth it, indeed I am not. I am
sure you——'

'Think nothing. I have no right to sit in judgment ; I have never been tempted. I simply can't
understand it. I am as ready to help you now as
before, if I only can——'

'You say that, but'—lifting her head and
searching the grave white face—'would you
kiss me ?'

The girl bends her head, but the woman drops
to the floor with a sharp 'No, no,' and hides her
face in the girl's gown, with the tears streaming
down her cheeks.

They talk late, and the girl soothes her. She
promises not to drink for the remaining days, and
a spark of hope flickers up in her weak soul, and
the girl, to whom no one any longer speaks, spends
most of her time with her.

Saturday morning early they go up on deck and
watch the fleet of fishing smacks, with their ochre-
red sails, and the low land, shrouded in silver
mists, that looks as if a big wave might wash it
away. And the sound of bells floats out to them,
and further up the river the blast of foghorns, and

the shriek of whistles, and the rumbling hum of
the city mingle in a great symphony. The beasts
below divine the nearness of land in some subtle
way ; perhaps they scent the brackish grass, for
they low deeply ; and the steamer creeps steadily
up the Thames with the warehouses looming at its
waters' side, as the spectre buildings in a land of
shadow.

They watch it together. Her long travelling
cloak barely covers her light gown, though the
girl has pinned it up. Tears and emotions have
chastened her face and effaced the traces of passion
and debauch. She is filled with good intentions
and the hope of a chance to do better. She
trembles a little as they near the dock, and scans
the little crowd that awaits them.

'No,' she says, 'he is not there!'

A youth, a typical London clerk, with knowing
eyes and assured manner, is one of the first to
come on deck. He inquires for Mrs. Grey, hands
her a letter and waits. She turns her back to the
inquisitive gaze of the stewardess and women,
opens it and reads; and the girl watches her with
a feeling of trouble. It crosses her mind as she
watches her, that she has often scoffed at novelists,
when they spoke of people turning to stone,
but that now she realises the meaning ; for there
is a curious change in the woman's face ; it is
grey, and hard, as if every atom of life and feeling
are being killed by the action of some petrifying
fluid, working from inside ; and the gold of her
hair seems to stand out from it as a wig on a

stone face, and her flesh changes to what children call 'goose skin.'

She folds the letter carefully ; turns, grips the girl's arm, and says thickly :

'It's no good, I can't do it—I know myself too well, it is impossible—I am lost. This letter, this simple written thing, has damned me as surely as if I were already in hell. If,'—with a sudden gust of passion shaking her from head to foot—'if I knew the address of a good fast house, I'd drive straight to it ; you are a good, good woman, but say good-bye to me now, and God, if there be such a being'—with a little laugh—'bless you! But if ever you meet me, if ever you see me in the street or elsewhere, never speak to me, or try to stop me, for if you do, by Christ, I'll throw myself under the first horse's feet.'

'Come downstairs, Edith, I can't let you go so,' pleads the girl, and she leads her by the hand. They pass through the crowd that scans their stricken faces curiously, and the girl takes the letter and reads it. It is cold, pitiless, the letter of a man with iron will, wounded in his pride. She is to go with bearer to his lawyer's, he will tell her what she is to do. She need not write to him, for he will be on his way to China when this reaches her. All her future good treatment will depend on her implicit obedience. She will be driven to rooms and supplied with all necessities ; but, she is not to write to any one, or see any one, neither must she go out except under the escort of the woman in charge of her ; and if she require money she must state in writing to his solicitor for what purpose.   If at the end of three months, her behaviour has been satisfactory, he will consider what steps to take for her future.

No fanatical inquisitor of the middle ages, acquainted with the secret recesses of the human soul, knowing where to touch the most sensitive place, could have calculated more fiendishly.

The girl's heart burns as she reads ; she knows it is the death sentence of the woman standing with the hardness of despair on her set face.   She has probed into the depths of her nature, and she sees the impossibility of it.   Yet she says, feeling the want of conviction in her own words :

'You must try to do it—it is hard—cruelly hard, but you must try to endure it.'

And for answer the woman laughs, and at that the girl breaks down and pats her cold hands, only to drop them and throw her arms round her, pleading :

'When you have seen this man, if you can't do it, wire to me, won't you promise me, Edith dear? Promise to send for me, I'll come, indeed I will, no matter where you are.   I'll wait all day and Monday too for a message, only promise !'

The woman takes her face, and framing it with her hands says :

'Forget me, little sister, good, kind little sister, except when you pray.   And now kiss me good-bye.'

They kiss one another, the girl with tears drenching her face, and the woman goes up, and she and the youth walk down the gangway and

she never looks back once, though the girl strains
her eyes to see the last of her. And when the
weary customs have been gone through, the women,
seeing the girl had bidden her good-bye, come
and advise her for her good to be careful. She
repulses them savagely, for she is unstrung and
her heart burns hotly ; but when the little maiden
ladies come timidly, with chaste tears in their
eyes, perhaps for the sake of these she says more
gently to them :

'She is a lost soul, *I* tried to do what I could
for her. You are old, the others were married,
you had nothing to lose, and yet you held back.
It is good, untempted women like you, whose
virtue makes you selfish, who help to keep women
like her as they are.'

. . . . .

She waited anxiously for a message; none came.
Gradually her new work engrossed her thoughts,
only sometimes when the bus that carried her home
after a late day's work pulled up in Leicester
Square, that rendezvous of leering, silk-hatted
satyrs and flaunting nymphs of the pavement,
where the frou-frou of silk mingles with the ring
of artificial laughter, the glitter of paste with the
hectic of paint, where the very air is tainted with
patchouli, and souls sensitive to the psychometry
of things shiver with the feel of passional atoms
vibrating through the atmosphere of the great
pairing ground of this city of smug outer propriety;
sometimes there, where the foot-walk is crowded
with the 'fallen leaves' of fairest and frailest

womanhood, like wild rose leaves blown by a
wanton wind into a sty, she would think of her
again ; then she would scan fearsomely the faces
of the women who thronged there with dreadful
asking eyes ; and every gleam of golden hair
would set her heart throbbing, to recognise with
relief it is not *hers*. The dreadful problem of her
fate, and the ultimate fate of all these others would
weigh on the soul of the girl ; and the question of
the justice of the arrangement beat insistently
in her tired brain, and the hateful query force
itself, With how many of them is this life just
selection ?

And so three years passed on and brought her
a measure of success, and the content patient
work sometimes brings.   People said she was
better looking—she was simply better dressed.
She was not the less lonely, not the less sad, for
her sympathy with human suffering was no wise
blunted, her sense of its inevitability perhaps increased.   Fanciful folk who met her in the streets,
such as poets and painters and Irishmen, drew inspiration from her sombre gaze and tender mouth.

Then one bitter winter's day as she stands waiting for her bus in Cornhill, a novelty vendor, a
man with a strident voice, shrieks in her ear : ' 'Ave
you seen the larfin' baiby ?   Only one penny !
See the larfin' baiby !   They *all* larf ! 'ow to maike
the baiby larf !   Wot a baiby ! '

She boards her bus with the words ringing in
her brain, and out of the jangled echoes a memory
rises, bringing *her* face.

'Perhaps I shall see her,' she muses, for it is odd that when a person one has forgotten completely crops up in one's mind, and one wonders why one thinks of them on this particular day, a turn of a street corner sometimes brings an answer in person.

Late that night she says good-bye to a friend at the door of the College of Medicine for women, and turns her steps towards her lodgings. It has been raining, and the streets are encrusted with glass-like particles of frozen snow, a searching north-east wind rattles the blackened branches of the skeleton trees, and chills the thinly clad to the marrow. A fit of desperate coughing draws her attention to a woman holding on to the railings opposite ; the abject misery of the shaken figure awakes her keenest pity. As the last hollow cough dies out in a moan, the woman clutches her breast and groans out a curse on her misery and shuffles on. Her rain-soaked skirt clings to her legs, a piece of torn frill at the back drabbles in the mud, and slops round her feet at every step. The tattered remains of a smartly cut summer jacket is her only wrap, except a dishevelled rag of a feather boa that flutters futilely in the wind, and yet there is a trace of the peculiar grace that accompanies perfect proportion of limbs.

Obeying an uncontrollable impulse, the girl turns back and follows her. As the woman passes the gates of the old graveyard where a daughter of Cromwell sleeps under a conical stone, and children peg tops round forgotten graves, the hanging lamp of the Baptist Chapel next the entrance flickers over her, and the glint of golden hair under a ragged old toque catches the girl's eye and sends her heart fluttering to her throat. She hurries on, determined to pass her, to make sure, and then wait for her ; she is breathless with suspense, she sees her plainly as she pauses under the lamp at the corner of Compton Street, and a stifled cry of horror bursts through the girl's lips.

What a wreck! What a face! What a mask of the tragedy of passion, and sin, and the anguish of despair! Phthisis and drink have run riot together ; have wasted her frame, hollowed her cheeks, puffed her eyelids, dried the dreadful purple lips and soddened the soul within. The girl follows the shambling steps with dry wide eyes and painful heart thud. A loafer at the other corner says something to the woman as she passes, she answers him with a toss of head, and a peal of ribald laughter, that is worse to hear than a tortured cry ; it brings on another fit of coughing, and the pity of it stirs the girl's heart again, and the feeling of sudden loathing that has possessed her gives way to a diviner impulse of compassion.

She hurries on, crosses over, and, turning back, meets her ; there is barely a yard between them, her face is alight with tender feeling ; the woman looks up and sees her ; she pauses for the space of a second with a vivid brightening of her dull eyes, as when one strikes a light in a darkened room ; then, as the eager ' Edith, sister ! ' reaches her, she flings up one arm wildly to hide her face, thrusts

out the other to ward the girl off and sobs out,
'Oh, oh, no not that!' with a wailing moan. Then
she swerves quickly into the street, still shielding
her face, and breaks into a mad run; her wet
skirt impedes her wavering steps and her poor rags
flutter in the sharp wind, and, maddened by
memory perhaps, she utters a shriek that startles
the passers-by and brings faces to the upper
windows, and cuts into the girl's soul to haunt it
ever more like the fancied echo of the laughter of
hell.

A policeman at the turn to Harrison Street
walks towards her as he hears it; she screams
hoarsely at him with the defiance of reckless despair,
twice, thrice, never slackening her speed; further
on, at a turning near Gray's Inn Road, she stumbles,
and falls heavily, but she picks herself up with
lightning speed and scuds on again with a cough-
broken curse; the girl halts when she reaches the
corner where the woman fell in her flight, and
peers down the dark street. It seems to her that it
yawns like a long narrow grave or the passage to
a charnel house. The only sign of life in it is a
famished cat scraping at something in a rubbish
heap. She has disappeared into the night as she
came, into the night of despair that leads to death;
and as the girl stepped back her foot struck
against something, and stooping she picked it up—
a frayed, mud-soaked, satin shoe—it is small, and
once was a delicate rose.

To her to whom life had brought a deep understanding of its misery and makeshifts, it is a mute

epitome of a tragedy of want; and through her great agony of distress the narrow practical question forced itself in a comically persistent way : Had the poor weary foot without this frail covering even the sorry shelter of a stocking to protect it ? And facing homewards through the biting wind, with the lamp gleams shining through the dusky mists of the London night, like gorse blooms when the valley is in shadow, she holds it to her breast. What fell upon it as she turned ? A raindrop or a tear ?

WEDLOCK

Two bricklayers are building a yellow brick wall to the rear of one of a terrace of new jerry-built houses in a genteel suburb. At their back is the remains of a grand old garden. Only the unexpired lease saves it from the clutch of the speculator. An apple-tree is in full blossom, and a fine elm is lying on the grass, sawn down, as it stood on the boundary of a 'desirable lot'; many fair shrubs crop up in unexpected places, a daphne-mezereum struggles to redden its berries amid a heap of refuse thrown out by the caretakers; a granite urn, portions of a deftly carven shield, a mailed hand and a knight's casque, relics of some fine old house demolished to accommodate the ever-increasing number of the genteel, lie in the trampled grass. The road in front is scarcely begun, and the smart butchers' carts sink into the soft mud and red brick-dust, broken glass, and shavings; yet many of the houses are occupied, and the unconquerable London soot has already made some of the cheap 'art' curtains look dingy. A brass plate of the 'Prudential Assurance Company' adorns the gate of Myrtle House; 'Collegiate School for Young Ladies' that of Evergreen Villa. Victoria, Albert, and Alexandra figure in ornamental letters over the stained-glass latticed square of three pretentious houses, facing Gladstone, Cleopatra, and Lobelia. The people move into 26 to the ring of carpenters' hammers in 27, and 'go carts,' perambulators, and half-bred fox terriers impede the movements of the men taking in the kitchen boiler to 28.

One of the men, a short, wiry-looking man of fifty, with grizzled sandy hair and a four days growth of foxy beard on his sharp chin, is whistling 'Barbara Allen' softly as he pats down a brick and scrapes the mortar neatly off the joinings. The other, tall and swarthy, a big man with a loose mouth and handsome wicked eyes and a musical voice, is looking down the lane-way leading to a side street.

''Ere she comes, the lydy wot owns this 'ere desirable abode. I want 'er to lend me a jug. Wo-o-a hup, missis! Blind me tight if she ain't as boozed as they makes 'em! Look at 'er, Seltzer; ain't she a beauty, ain't she a sample of a decent bloke's wife! She's a fair sickener, she iz. Hy, 'old 'ard! She dunno where she are!' with a grin.

But the woman, reeling and stumbling up the lane, neither hears nor sees; she is beyond that. She feels her way to the back-yard door of the next house, and, rocking on her feet, tries to find the pocket of her gown. She is much under thirty, with a finely-developed figure. Her gown is torn from the gathers at the back and trails down, showing her striped petticoat; her jacket is of good material, trimmed with silk, but it is dusty

and lime-marked. Her face is flushed and dirty ;
her light golden-brown fringe stands out straight
over her white forehead ; her bonnet is awry on
the back of her head ; her watch dangles from
the end of a heavy gold chain, and the buttons of
her jersey bodice gape open where the guard is
passed through ; she has a basket on her left arm.
She clutches the wall and fumbles stupidly for the
key, mumbling unintelligibly, and trying with all
her might to keep her eyes open. The tall man
watches her with ill-concealed disgust, and tosses
a pretty coarse jest to her. The sandy man lays
down his trowel and wipes his hands on his apron,
and goes to her.

'Lookin' for yer key, missis ? Let me 'elp yer ;
two 'eads is better nor one enny day !'

'Ca'an fin' it. M'm a bad wom—a bad wom—
um,' she says, shaking her head solemnly at him,
with heavy lids and distended pupils.

Meanwhile he has searched her pocket and
opened the basket—nothing in it except a Family
Novelette and a few gooseberries in a paper bag.
He shakes his head, saying to himself : ' Dropped
her marketing. It ain't here, missis ; sure you took
it with ye ? '

She nods stupidly and solemnly three times.

' Got the larchkey o' the fron' door ? ' queries
the other.

She frowns, tries to pull up her skirt to get at
her petticoat pocket, and lurches over.

' Old 'ard, missis, 'old 'ard. Throw them long
legs o' yourn acrost the wall, maite, an' see if ye

carn't let 'er in !' says the little man, catching her
deftly. The other agrees, and the key grates in
the lock inside and he opens the door.

'She took the key an' lorst it, that's wot she
did. She's a nice ole cup o' tea; she's a 'ot
member for a mile, she iz, an' no mistaike !' and he
takes up his trowel and a brick, singing with a
sweet tenor.

The little man helps her into the house through
the hall into the parlour. He unties her bonnet-
strings, pulls off her jacket, and puts her into an
arm-chair.

'Ye jist 'ave a sleep, an' ye'll be all right !'

She clutches at his hand in a foolish sort of way,
and her eyes fill with tears.

''Ands orf, missis, 'ands orf, ye jist go to sleep !'

He halts in the kitchen and looks about him. It
is very well furnished; the table is littered with
unwashed breakfast things on trays—handsome
china, plate, and table-napkins, all in confusion.
He shakes his head, puts some coal in the range,
closes the door carefully, and goes back to his
work.

'Well, did ye put beauty to bed?' laughs the
big man. 'I'd rather Jones owned 'er nor me.
'E picked a noice mother fur iz kids 'e did ! Yes,
them three little nippers wot come out a wile ago
is iz.'

''E must be pretty tidy orf,' says the little man ;
'it looks very nice in there, an' seemin'ly the 'ole
'ouse is fitted up alike—pianner an' carpets an'
chiffoneers.'

'Oh, Jones iz all right. 'E's a cute chap iz Jones. 'E's got a 'ell of a temper, that's all. 'E's bin barman at the Buckin'am for close twenty year; makes a book an' keeps iz eyes peeled. Bless ye, I know Jones since I woz a lad; iz first wife woz a sort o' cousin o' my missis—a clever woman too. 'E took this 'un 'cos 'e thort e 'd maike a bit out o' gentlemen lorgers, she bein' a prize cook an' 'e 'avin' the 'ouse out of a buildin' society, an' be a mother to the kids as well. She'll keep no lorgers she won't, an' she's a fair beauty for the kids. If she woz mine'—tapping a brick—'I'd bash 'er 'ed in !'

'Maybe ye wouldn't !' says the little man ; 'thet iz if ye understood. Wot if it ain't 'er fault ?'

'Ain't 'er fault ! Ooze iz it then ?'

'That I ain't prepared to say, not knowin' circumstances; but it might be as it runs in 'er family.'

'Well, I'm blowed, I often 'eerd' (with a grin, showing all his white teeth) 'o' wooden legs runnin' that way, but I never 'eerd tell o' gin !'

'Ye ain't a readin' man I take it,' says the little man, with a touch of superiority, 'I thought that way onst meself. My ole woman drinks.' (He says it as if stating a casual fact that calls for no comment.) 'It woz then I came acrorst a book on "'ereditty," wot comes down from parents to children, ye know, an' I set to findin' all about 'er family. I took a 'eap o' trouble about it, I did, I wanted to do fair by 'er. An' then sez I to meself : "Sam, she carn't 'elp it no more nor the colour of

'er 'air, an' that woz like a pine shavin' in sunshine.
'Er gran'father 'e drunk 'isself dead, an' then iz
wife she reared my girl's mother for service—she
woz cook at an 'otel in Aylesbury. Well, she
married the boots ; they 'ad a tidy bit saved, an'
they took a country public with land an' orchard
an' such like an' they did well for a long time.
Then 'e took to liquor. I never could find out iz
family 'istory ; maybe as 'ow 'e couldn't 'elp it
neither. 'E woz a Weller, an' she jined 'im arter
a bit, which considerin' 'er father woz to be expected. My ole woman often told me 'ow she an'
'er brother used to 'ide out many a night in the
orchard. Well they bust up an' 'e got notice to
quit, an' wot does 'e do but goes an' 'angs 'isself
to a willer next the well, an' she goes out to git a
pail o' water an' finds 'im. That set 'er orf wuss
nor ever, an' then she went orf sudden like with a
parrylittic stroke. Some laidies took the children
an' put 'em to school.' (He works steadily as he
speaks.) 'Well, one bank 'olliday twenty-eight
year come Whitsun' same date izzackly, I went
down with a mate o' mine to an uncle of 'iz in
Aylesbury ; 'e 'ad a duck farm, an' I seed 'er.
She woz as pretty as paint, an' there woz as much
difference atween 'er an' city girls, as new milk
an' chalk an' water. I woz doin' well, times woz
better ; I 'ave three trades, when one iz slack I
works at another. I got work down there an' we
kep' company, an' got our 'ome together, an' woz
married, an' woz az 'appy az might be for six
year. Then our eldest little lad 'e set 'isself afire

one day she woz out, an' they took 'im to the
infirmary, but 'e died in a 'our, a' wen we went
to fetch 'im 'ome 'e woz rolled in wite bandages
most like one o' them mummies in the British
Museum. It went to my girl's 'eart like, for she
couldn't seem to recognise 'im nohow. An' 'twoz
arter that I begin to notice she took a drop. At
fust I woz real mad, I gave 'er a black eye onst;
but then I came acrorst that book—I woz allus
a man for readin'—an' I found out about 'er folk,
an' I see az 'ow she couldn't 'elp it. It got worser
an' worser an' arter two years we come up to town;
I couldn't stand the shame of it. Then I went
down to my ole mother; she woz livin' with a
widowed sister in Kent, an' I up an' told 'er: I sez,
"Mother, ye got to take the kids. I ain't goin' to
'ave no more with the curse on 'em, an' I ain't
goin' to 'ave 'em spoiled," an' I took 'em down an'
sent 'er money regular, bad times same az good.
She went on dreadful at first; I gave 'er a fair
chance, I took 'er down to see 'em, and sez I:
" Knock off the drink, ole girl, an' ye 'az 'em back ! "
She tried it, I really believe she did, but bless ye
she couldn't, it woz in 'er blood same az the
colourin' of 'er skin. I gave up 'ome then, wen
she gets right mad she 'd pawn everything in the
show; I allus puts my own things in a Monday
morning an' takes 'em out a Saturday night, it
keeps 'em safe. The landlady looks arter 'er
own, an' so she ain't got much to dispose on. I
carn't abide liquor meself, though I don't 'old
with preachin' about it; an' that 's wy they call

me Seltzer Sam, and wy I gets my dinner in a
cookshop.'

The little man is laying his bricks carefully one
on top of the other.

'You spoke sort o' sharp to your missis to-day,
cos she woz a bit laite, an' I thort as 'ow ye woz
uncommon lucky to 'ave 'er come nice and tidy
with it—it's twenty years since I woz brought me
dinner in a basin.'

There's a silence.   The big man looks thoughtful, then he says suddenly :

'Well I couldn't do it, I couldn't do it, that's all
I sez.   Wy don't ye put 'er away someweres ? '

'I did, but lor, it woz no manner o' good.   I
allus fancied she'd set 'erself o' fire or fall in the
street or somethink an' get took to the station on
a stretcher with the boys a' callin' " meat " arter
'er, an' I couldn't sleep for thinkin' of it, so I
fetched 'er back.   We woz very 'appy for six
year, an' thet's more nor some folk az in all their
lives, an''—with a quaint embarrassment—' she
were the only woman as ever I keered for, right
from the fust minute I seed 'er 'oldin' a big bunch
o' poppies an' that grass they call " wag wantons "
down there, in 'er 'and, as pretty as a picture—an'
I *didn't marry 'er cos she could cook*, that's no
wearin' reason to marry a woman for, leastwise
not for me.   An' I wouldn't 'ave the children—I
call 'em children, though, lor bless yer, they're
grown up and doin' well—I wouldn't 'ave 'em
think I'd turned their mother out o' doors—no'
—with an emphatic dab of mortar—' no, 'er fate's

my fate, an' I ain't the kind o' chap to turn the ole woman out for what she can by no manner o' means 'elp!' and he puts another brick neatly on the top of the last and scrapes the oozing mortar.

The big man rubs the back of his hand across his eyes, and says with a gulp :

'Shake 'ands, mate, damme if I know wot to call yer, a bloomin' archangel or a blasted softy.'

. . . . . .

The woman lay as he left her, with her feet thrust out in her half-buttoned boots, and her hands hanging straight down. The sun crept round the room, and at length a clock chimed four strokes up on the drawing-room floor. A woman sitting writing at a table between the window looks up with a sigh of relief, and moistens her lips; they are dry. A pile of closely written manuscript lies on the floor beside her; she drops each sheet as she finishes it.

She is writing for money, writing because she must, because it is the tool given to her wherewith to carve her way; she is nervous, overwrought, every one of her fingers seems as if it had a burning nerve-knot in its tip; she has thrust her slippers aside, for her feet twitch; she is writing feverishly now, for she has been undergoing the agony of a barren period for some weeks, her brain has seemed arid as a sand plain, not a flower of fancy has sprung up in it; she has felt in her despair as if she were hollowed out, honeycombed by her emotions, and she has cried over her mental sterility. Her measure of success has come to her, her public waits, what if she have nothing to give them? The thought has worn her, whispered to her in dreams at night, taken the savour out of her food by day. But this morning a little idea came and grew, grew so blessedly, and she has been working since early day. Her landlady has forgotten her luncheon; she never noticed the omission, but now she feels her frail body give way under the strain; she will finish this chapter and have some tea. She has heard steps below. She writes until the half-hour strikes, then drops the last sheet of paper with a sobbing sigh of relief. She pulls the bell sharply and sits waiting patiently. No one answers it. She rings again; there is a crash downstairs as of china falling with a heavy body, and a smothered groan. She trembles, listens, and then goes down.

The woman is lying in the doorway of the sitting-room, a small table with broken glass and wax flowers on the floor near her. She hides her face as she hears the light step.

'Did you hurt yourself? can I help you?'

She drags her up, supports her into the bedroom and on to the unmade bed, and goes out into the kitchen. A look of weary disgust crosses her face as she sees the litter on the table. There is a knock at the back door, she opens it; three children peer cautiously in, keen-eyed London children with precocious knowledge of the darker sides of life. They enter holding one another's hands. The eldest signs to the others to sit down, steals up the passage, peers through the slit of the door, and returns with a satisfied look and nods to the others.

'Your mother is not well, I am afraid,' the woman says timidly, she is nervous with children. The three pairs of eyes examine her slowly to see if she is honest.

'Our mother is in heaven!' says the boy as if repeating a formula. 'That's our stepmother, and she's boozed!'

'Johnny!' calls the woman from the inner room. The boy's face hardens into a sullen scowl, and she notices that he raises his hand involuntarily as if to ward off a blow, and that the smaller ones change colour and creep closer to one another. He goes to her—there is a murmur of voices.

'She sez I'm to get your tea!' he remarks as he comes out, and stirs up the dying fire. 'Ain't *you* 'ad nothin' since mornin'?'

She evades the question by asking: 'Have you children had anything?'

'We took some bread with us.' He opens a purse.

'There's nothin' in it, an' father gave 'er 'arf a sovereign this mornin'!'

'I will give you some money if you come upstairs, and then you can get my tea.'

The boy is deft-handed, prematurely cute, with a trick of peering under his lashes. It annoys her, and she is relieved when she has had her tea and got rid of him. She is restless, upset, she feels this means moving again. What a weary round a working woman's life is! She is so utterly alone. The silence oppresses her, the house seems filled with whispers; she cannot shake off this odd feeling, she felt it the first time she entered it; the rooms were pretty, and she took them, but this idea is always with her.

She puts on her hat and goes out, down the half-finished road and into a lighted thoroughfare. Costers' carts are drawn up alongside the pavement; husbands and wives with the inevitable perambulator are pricing commodities; girls are walking arm in arm, tossing back a look or a jest to the youths as they pass. The accents of the passers-by, the vociferous call of the vendors, the jostling of the people jar on her; she turns back with tears in her eyes. Her loneliness strikes doubly home to her, and she resolves to join a woman's club; anything to escape it. She pauses near the door to get her latchkey, and notices the boy at the side entrance. He draws back into the shade as he sees her. She stands at her window and looks out into the murky summer night; a man comes whistling down the street; the boy runs to meet him, she sees him bend his head to catch the words better and then they turn back. She lights the gas and tries to read, she dreads the scenes she feels will follow, and she trembles when the door slams below and steps echo down the passage.

There is the low growl of the man's voice and
the answers of the woman's, then both rise discord-
antly—a stifled scream and a heavy fall, footsteps down the passage, the bang of a door, and
both voices raised in altercation, with the boy's
voice striking shrilly in between—a blow, a crash
of china and glass, then stillness. She is breathless with excitement; the quiet is broken by a
sound of scuffling in the passage; he is going to
put her out. Drag, and shove, and the scraping
of feet, and the sullen 'you dare, you dare' of the
woman, in reply to his muttered threats. She
goes to the top of the stairs and cries:

'Don't hurt her, wait until morning to reason
with her, don't hurt her!'

'Reason with *'er*, miss! There ain't no way of
reasoning with the likes of 'er, chuck 'er out is the
only way. Would ye, would ye? Ye drunken
beast!——'

The woman and the man sway together in the
passage and her bodice is torn open at the breast
and her hair is loose, and she loses her footing
and falls as he drags her towards the door. She
clutches at the chairs and brass umbrella-stand
and drags them down; and the woman, watching,
rushes upstairs and buries her face in the sofa
cushions. Then the door bangs to and the
woman outside rings and knocks and screams;
windows open and heads peer out; then the boy
lets her in and there seems to be a truce.

A charwoman brings her breakfast next morning, and it is tea-time before she sees *her*. She

has on a clean pink cotton gown and her hair is
nicely done and her skin looks very pink and
white; but her eyes are swollen, and there is a
bruise on one temple and a bad scratch on her
cheek. She hangs her head sullenly and loiters
with the tea-things; then she goes over to her and
stands with her eyes on the ground and her hair
glittering like golden down on the nape of her
thick neck in the light from the window at her back.

'I am sorry for yesterday, miss, it was bad of
me, but you won't go away? I won't do it again.
Take it off the rent, only forgive me, won't you,
miss?'

She is flushing painfully; her face is working,
perhaps it seems worse because it is a heavily
moulded face and it does not easily express
emotions. It has the attractive freshness of youth
and vivid colouring.

'We won't say anything more about it. I am
so sorry; I am not used to scenes and it made me
quite ill; I was frightened, I thought you would
be hurt.'

The woman's face changes and as she raises her
heavy white lids her eyes seem to look crosswise
with a curious gleam in them and her voice is
hoarse.

'That little beast told him, the little sneak!
But I'll pay him for it, I'll pay him!'

An uneasy dislike stirs in the woman; she says
very quietly:

'But you can't expect a man to come home and
find you so and then be pleased.'

'No, but he shouldn't——' she checks herself
and passes her hand across her forehead. The
other woman observes her closely as she does
most things—as material. It is not that her sym-
pathies are less keen since she took to writing, but
that the habit of analysis is always uppermost.
She sees a voluptuously made woman, with a
massive milk-white throat rising out of the neck
of her pink gown; her jaw is square and prominent, her nose short and straight, her brows traced
distinctly; she is attractive and repellent in a
singular way.

'You don't know what works in me, miss——' She
says no more, but it is evident that something is
troubling her and that she is putting restraint on
herself. Late in the evening, when the children
are in bed, she hears her go up to their room;
there is a sound of quick blows and a frightened
whimper; and the next morning she is roused
from her sleep by a child's scream and the
woman's voice uttering low threats:

'Will you be quiet?' (whimper) 'will you be
quiet? I'll teach you to make a row' (more
stifled, frightened cries), and she feels in some
subtle way that the woman is smothering the
child in the bed-clothes. It worries her, and she
never looks up at her when she brings her breakfast. The latter feels it and watches her furtively.
At lunch time it strikes her that she has been
drinking again; she musters heart of grace and
says to her:

'You promised to be good, Mrs. Jones. It

seems to me to be such a pity that you should drink, why do you ? You are very young !'

Her voice is naturally tender, and her words have an unexpected effect; the woman covers her face with her hands and rocks her shoulders. Suddenly she cries :

' I don't know ; I get thinkin'; I 'ave 'ad a trouble. I never knew a woman drink for the love of it like men, there 's most always a cause. Don't think me a bad woman, miss, I ain't really, only I 'ave a trouble.' She talks hurriedly as if she can't help herself, as if the very telling is a necessity. 'I 'ad a little girl' (dropping her voice) ' before I was married—she 's turned three, she 's such a dear little thing, you never seen such 'air, miss, it 's like floss silk an' 'er eyes are china blue, an' 'er lashes are that long '—measuring a good inch on her finger—' an' 'er skin is milk-white. I keep wantin' 'er all the time——' The tears fill her eyes and splash out. 'I was cook in a big business house, an' 'e was the 'ead of it—I was cruel fond of 'im. Then when my time came I went 'ome to my step-sister an' she nursed me. I paid 'er, an' then when I went out to service again she took 'er. I used to see 'er onst or twice a week. But she was fonder of 'er nor me, an' I couldn't bear it, it made me mad, I was jealous of every one as touched 'er. Then Jones, 'e woz always after me, 'e knew about it, an' 'e promised me that I could 'ave 'er if I married 'im. I didn't want to marry, I only wanted 'er, an' I couldn't 'ave 'er with me, an' 'e promised '—with resentful emphasis—' 'e swore as 'ow I could 'ave 'er. I took 'im on that an' 'e kep' puttin' me off, an' when I went to see 'er, 'e quarrelled, an' once when she was ill 'e wouldn't let me send 'er any money though 'e 'ad wot I saved when I married 'im—it just made me 'ate 'im—I see 'er so seldom, an' she calls *er* mammy, it most kills me—I feel my 'ead burstin' —an' 'e laughed when I told 'im I wouldn't 'ave married 'im only for 'er sake!'

'Poor thing, it is hard, he ought to have kept his promise to you when he made it. Haven't you told him you wouldn't drink if you had her with you?'

'Where's the good? 'E says 'e never meant to keep it; as a man ain't such a fool as to keep a promise 'e makes a woman just to get 'er. 'E knows it sets me off, but 'e's that jealous that 'e can't abear 'er name. 'E says I would neglect 'is children, an' 'e called 'er names an' says 'e won't 'ave no bastard round with 'is children. That made me 'ate 'em first, nasty yellow things——'

'Yes, but the poor children are not to blame for it?'

'No, but they remind me of 'er, an' I 'ate the very sight of 'em.' There is such concentrated hatred in her voice that the woman shrinks. 'I ain't 'ad any money to send 'er this long time, but my sister's 'usband is as fond of 'er as 'is own; they 'ave seven of their own. I 'ate to see things in the shop windows, I used to keep 'er so pretty. I got a letter a while ago sayin' she wasn't very

well, an' that set me off. You 've spoken kind to
me since you 've been here, that 's w'y I tell
you, you won't think worse of me now than I
deserve.'

She clears away the things sullenly, with her
jaw set, and the strange oblique light flickering in
her eyes. It oppresses the other woman; she
feels as if she is facing one of those lurid tragedies
that outsiders are powerless to prevent. This
woman with her fierce devotion to the child of the
man who betrayed her; her marriage, into which
she has been cheated by a promise never meant
to be kept; and the step-children fanning her
fierce dislike by the very childish attributes that
waken love in other circumstances. She stays a
week longer, but every whimper of the children,
every fresh outburst wears upon her, and she
leaves, not without speaking with all the earnest-
ness and sympathy of her nature to the woman
of whose fate she has an oppressive, inexplicable
presentiment.

The tears in her eyes at leaving have touched
the girl, for she is little more, and she has promised to try and be better, as she childishly puts
it. Things have gone pleasantly for some days,
and she has been patient with the children. One
of them has been ill and she has nursed it, and
to-day she has made them an apple-cake and sent
them to the park, and she is singing to herself
over her work; she is cleaning out her bed-room.
It is Derby Day. He has the day off, and has
gone to the races. He gave her five shillings

before he started in the morning, telling her she might send it to the 'young 'un.'

It touched her, and she brushed his coat and kissed him of her own accord. She has felt kindly to him all the morning for it. She notices a button dangling off his working coat and takes it out to the kitchen to sew it on ; he seldom brings it home. There is nothing in the pockets except a slip of 'events' cut out of some sporting paper ; but the lining of the breast-pocket is torn, and as she examines it, the rustle of paper catches her ear. She smiles ; what if it is a 'fiver'? She knows all about his betting. She slips two fingers down between the lining and works it up—a telegram. She still smiles, for she thinks she will find a clue to some of his winnings. She opens it, and reads, and her face changes; the blood rushes to it, until a triangular vein stands out on her forehead like a purple whipcord. Her throat looks as if it would burst ; a pulse beats in her neck ; her upper lip is completely sucked in by the set line of her under one, and her eyes positively squint. A fly that keeps buzzing on the pane rouses her to such a pitch, that she seizes a boot off the table and sends it crashing through the pane of glass into the yard, liberating the fly at the same time. Then she tries to re-read it, but there is a red blaze before her eyes. She goes out, up the lane, towards the unfinished houses, to where the bricklayers are at work, and hands it to the little man, saying hoarsely :

'Read it, I'm dazed, I can't see it rightly.'

The big man stops whistling and looks curiously
at her.   She is perfectly sober; the flush has
ceded to a lead-white pallor, and her face twitches
convulsively.   She stands absolutely still, with
her hands hanging heavily down, though she is
devoured with impatience.   The little man wipes
his hands, and takes out his spectacles, and reads
slowly:

'Susie dying, come at once, no hope.   Expecting you since Saturday, wrote twice.'

A minute's silence—then a hoarse scream that
seems to come from the depths of her chest; it
frightens both men, so that the big man drops a
brick, and a carpenter in the house comes to the
window and looks out.

'Since Saturday!' she cries, 'to-day is Wednesday.   When was it sent, tell me!' she shakes
the little man in her excitement, and he scans the
form slowly, with the deliberation of his class:

'Stratford, 7.45.'

'But the date! the date, man!'

'The 20th.'

'To-day,' with a groan, 'is the 22nd.   So it
come Monday, and to-day is Wednesday, an' they
wrote twice.   It must 'ave come when I fetched
'is beer, an' 'e kept it.   But the letters?—that
little cub, that sneak of 'ell!   Aah, wait!'   She
calls down curses with such ferocity of expression,
that the men shiver; then crushing the fateful
paper inside the bosom of her gown, she rushes
back, and in a few minutes they see her come out,
tying on her bonnet as she runs.

'Well, this 'ere's a rum go, eh?' says the big man, regaining his colour, 'an' ooze Susie?'

The little man says nothing, only balances a brick in the palm of his hand before he fits it into its place, but his lips move silently.

. . . . . .

In the parlour of one of a row of stiff two-storied houses, with narrow hall-doors in a poor street in Stratford, a little coffin painted white is laid on the table that is covered with a new white sheet.

There are plenty of flowers, from the white wreath sent by the grocer's wife, with a card bearing 'From a Sympathiser' in big silver letters, to the penny bunch of cornflowers of a playmate.

Susie has her tiny hands folded, and the little waxen face looks grey and pinched amongst the elaborately pinked-out glazed calico frills of her coffin lining. There is the unavoidable air of festivity that every holiday, even a sad one, imparts to a working-man's home. The children have their hair crimped and their Sunday clothes on, for they are going to the burial-ground in a grand coach with black horses and long tails, and they sit on the stairs and talk it over in whispers.

The men have come in at dinner-hour silently and stolidly, and looked at her, and gone out to the 'Dog and Jug' for a glass of beer to wash down whatever of sadness the sight of dead Susie may have roused in them.

Every woman in the row has had a cup of tea,
and told of her own sorrows ; related the death of
every relative she has ever possessed, to the third
and fourth degree, with the minuteness of irrelevant detail peculiar to her class. Every incident
of Susie's death-struggle has been described with
such morbid or picturesque addition as frequent
rehearsals, or the fancy of the narrator, may
suggest. Every corner of the house is crammed
with people, for the funeral is to leave at three
o'clock.

'Looks like satin it do, it's as pretty as ever I
see!' pointing to the pinking, says one woman.

'Yes, Mr. Triggs thought a 'eap o' Susie, an' 'e
took extry pains. 'E's a beautiful undertaker, an'
'e's goin' to send the 'earse with the wite plumes!
Don't she just look a little hangel?'

So they stream in and out, and in the kitchen
a circle of matrons hold a Vehmgericht over the
mother.

'She's an unfeelin' brute, even if she iz yer arf
sister, Mrs. Waters,' 'says a fat matron, 'to let that
pretty, hinnocent hangel die without seein' 'er, not
to speak o' buryin', I 'ave no patience with sich
ways!'

The roll of wheels and the jingle of tyres cuts
short her speech, and the knocker bangs dully.
Heads crane out in every direction, and one of
the children opens the door, and the woman steps
in.

In her pink gown! when every one knows that
not to pawn your bed or the washing-tubs, or any-

thing available, to get a black skirt or crape bonnet, or at least a straw with bugles, is the greatest breach of propriety known to the poor, the greatest sticklers for mourning etiquette outside a German court. The half-sister is a quiet woman with smoothly parted hair and tender eyes, and a strong likeness to her about the underhung chin. She goes forward and leads her to the room; the women fall back and talk in whispers.

'W'y didn't you send?' she asks fiercely, turning from the coffin.

'We wrote Friday, an' then, when you didn't come, we wrote Sunday. Jim couldn't go, an' I never left 'er a minute, an' Tiny an' little Jim 'ad the measles, an' Katie 'ad to mind 'em; but a mate o' Jim's went to the 'Buckin'am' on Monday mornin' an' told 'im, an' then we sent a tellygram, an' we couldn't do more, not if she were our own.'

There is a settled resignation in her voice; she has repeated it so often.

''E kep' the letters an' 'e never told me, an' I only found the tellygram this mornin' by accidin'. When 's she to be buried?'

'At three o'clock,'—with a puzzled look at the set face.

'Leave me along of 'er then; go on!'—roughly.

The woman goes out, closes the door, and listens. Not a sound comes from the room, not one, not a sob nor cry. The women listen in silence when she tells them; they are used to the fierce passions of humanity, and jealousy is common amongst their men. After a while one of the children says,

with an awe-struck face, ' Ma, she 's singin'.' They
go to the door and listen ; she is crooning a nonsense song she used to sing to her when she was
quite a baby, and the listening women pale, but
fear to go in.　For a long hour they hear her talking and singing to it ; then the man comes to screw
down the lid, and they find her on the sofa with
the dead child on her lap, its feet, in their white
cotton socks, sticking out like the legs of a great
wax doll.

She lets them take it from her without a word,
and watches them place it amongst the white
frills, and lets them lead her out of the room.　She
sits bolt upright in the kitchen, with the same odd
smile upon her lips and her hands hanging straight
down.　They go without her.　When they return
she is still sitting with her hands hanging, as if she
has never stirred.

' Mother, w'y did they plant Susie in the ground ?
Mother, carn't you answer ; will she grow?' queries
one of the children, and something in the question
rouses her.　She starts up with a cry and a wild
glare, and stares about as if in search of something—stands trembling in every limb, with the
ugly flush on her face and the purple triangle on
her forehead, and the pulse beating in her throat.
The children cower away from her, and the sister
watches her with frightened, pitying eyes.

' Sit down, Susan, there 's a dear, sit down an'
'ave some tea ! '

' No, I 've got to go—I 've got to go—I 've got
t——' she mutters, swaying unsteadily on her feet.

The words come thickly, and the end of the sentence is lost.

'She'd be better if she could cry, poor thing!' says the fat matron.

'Give 'er somethink belonged to the young 'un!' says a little woman with a black eye. The sister goes to a drawer in the dresser and turns over some odds and ends and finds a necklet of blue beads with a brass clasp, and hands it to her. She takes it with a hoarse cry as of an animal in dire pain, and rocks and moans and kisses it, but no tears come; and then, before they can realise it, she is out through the passage, and the door slams. When they get to it and look out, she is hurrying wildly down the street, with her pink gown fluttering, and the roses nodding in her bonnet, through a drizzle of soft rain.

.   .   .   .

Six o'clock rings; the rain still falls steadily, and, through its dull beat, the splash of big drops on to the new boards in a roofless house, and the blows of a hammer, strike sharply.

'Comin', mate?' queries the big man. 'No? Well, so long!' He shoulders his straw kit and turns up the collar of his coat and goes off whistling. The little man puts his tools away, fastens a sack about his shoulders and creeps into a square of bricks—they had thrown some loose planks across the top earlier in the day as a sort of protection against the rain; he lights his pipe and sits patiently waiting for her return. He is hungry, and his wizened face looks pinched in the light of the match as he strikes it, but he waits patiently.

The shadows have closed in when she gets back, for she has walked all the way from Liverpool Street, unheeding the steady rain that has come with the south-west wind. The people maddened her. She felt inclined to strike them. A fierce anger surged up in her against each girl who laughed, each man who talked of the winner. She felt inclined to spit at them, make faces, or call them names. Her dress is bedrabbled, the dye of the roses has soaked through the gold of her fringe and runs down her forehead as if she has a bleeding wound there. The gas is lit in the kitchen, and her tea is laid and the kettle is singing on the stove ; a yellow envelope is lying on the top of the cup ; she opens it and turns up the gas and reads it :

' Been in luck to-day, going home with Johnson, back early to-morrow evening.'

She puts it down with a peculiar smile. She has the string of beads in her hand ; she keeps turning them round her finger ; then she steals to the foot of the stairs and listens.

The little man has watched her go in, and stands in the lane-way looking up at the house. A light appears in the top back window, but it must come from the stairs, it is too faint to be in the room itself. He bends his head as if to listen, but the steady fall of the rain and the drip of the roof on to some loose sheets of zinc dominate everything. He walks away a bit and watches a shadow cross the blinds; his step crunches on the loose bricks and stones; a woman rushes down the flagged path of the next house and opens the door.

' Is that Mr Sims ? '

' No, ma'am, I 'm one of the workmen.'

She has left her kitchen door open, and as the light streams out he can see she is a thin woman with an anxious look.

' I thought it was Mr. Sims, the watchman. My baby is threatened with convulsions. I wanted him to run for the doctor at the end of the terrace; I daren't leave him, and my sister 's lame. Will you go ? it isn't far ! '

She is listening, and though he hears nothing, she darts off calling, ' There he 's off, do go, *do go*. Say Mrs. Rogers's baby, Hawthorn House, No. 23.'

He stands a moment irresolute ; the shadow moves across the blind, and a second smaller shadow seems to wave across it ; or was it only the rising wind flicking the blind ? and is it fancy, or did not a stifled cry reach him ; and was it from that room it came or from Mrs. Rogers's baby ? The little man is shaking with anxiety ; he feels as if some malignant fate in the shape of Mrs. Rogers's baby is playing tricks with him, to bring about a catastrophe he has stayed to avert. He is torn both ways ; he can offer no excuse for not going ; he dare not explain the secret dread that has kept him here supperless in the rain watching the house where the three motherless children sleep. He turns and runs stumbling over the rubbish into the side street and arrives breathless at the corner house where the red lamp burns at the gate—rings—what a time they keep him—it seems ages, and visions keep tumbling kaleido-scopically through his brain; the very red of the light adds colour to the horrid tragedy he sees enacted in excited fancy.

'The doctor is out; won't be back for some time; there's a Dr. Phillips round the corner,' explains the smart maid—the door slams to.

'Yes, Dr. Phillips is in; you must wait a minute,' ushering him into a waiting-room. He sits on the edge of the chair with his wet hat in his hand. Two other people are waiting: a girl with a swelled face and a sickly-looking man.

A door opens, some one beckons, the man goes in. He looks at the clock—five minutes pass, seven, ten—each seems an hour—fifteen—and the woman's face as she went in, and the frightened children (his mate questioned them at tea-time), and the shadow on the blind of the room they slept in! Why should Mrs. Rogers's baby go and get convulsions just this particular night? seems as though it were to be—seventeen; no, he won't wait any longer. The strange, inexplicable fear clutching the little man's soul gives him courage, though the well-furnished house awes him; he slips out into the hall, opens the door, and rings the bell. The same girl answers it.

'Well I never! W'y, I just let you in. Carn't you wait yer turn—the *idea*!'

A pale young man with spectacles coming down the stairs asks:

'What is it you want, my man?' The girl tosses her head and goes downstairs.

'I can't wait, sir; Mrs. Rogers's baby, 'Awthorn 'Ouse, No. 23 Pelham Road, round the corner, got the convulsions. She wants the doctor as soon as 'e can.

'All right, I'll be round in a second.'

The little man hurries back, trying to add up the time he has been away—twenty-five minutes, it must be twenty-five, perhaps twenty-seven. The yard door of Mrs. Rogers's house is open, and a girl peers out as he runs up the lane.

'The doctor woz out; Dr. Phillips is comin' at onst!' His eyes rest on the window of the next house as he speaks. It is dark up there and silent. He pays no heed to the thanks of the girl, and he hears the tap of her crutch up the flagged path with a gasp of relief.

What has happened whilst he has been away on his errand of mercy? Has anything happened? After all, why should this ghastly idea of a tragedy possess him? He climbs on to a heap of loose bricks and peers over the wall — darkness and silence. He goes down the lane and round to the front of the house. A dim light shines through the stained glass over the door showing up the name 'Ladas,' that is all, yet the little man shivers. The rain has soaked through his coat and is trickling down his neck; he scratches his head in perplexity, muttering to himself, 'I'm afear'd, an' I dunno wot I'm afear'd on. I meant to wotch; maybe arsk 'er for a light. It ain't my fault if

Mrs. Rogers's baby came atween—but twarn't no wearin' reason to marry for,' and he goes down the road and faces home. The rain ceases, and a tearful moon appears, and the water drips off the roof with a clucking sound. Upstairs in a back room in the silent house a pale strip of moonlight flickers over a dark streak on the floor, that trickles slowly from the pool at the bedside out under the door, making a second ghastly pool on the top step of the stairs—a thick sorghum red, blackening as it thickens, with a sickly serous border. Downstairs the woman sits in a chair with her arms hanging down. Her hands are crimson as if she has dipped them in dye. A string of blue beads lies on her lap, and she is fast asleep; and she smiles as she sleeps, for Susie is playing in a meadow, a great meadow crimson with poppies, and her blue eyes smile with glee, and her golden curls are poppy-crowned, and her little white feet twinkle as they dance, and her pinked-out grave frock flutters, and her tiny waxen hands scatter poppies, blood-red poppies, in handfuls over three open graves.

VIRGIN SOIL

THE bridegroom is waiting in the hall; with a trifle of impatience he is tracing the pattern of the linoleum with the point of his umbrella. He curbs it and laughs, showing his strong white teeth at a remark of his best man; then compares the time by his hunter with the clock on the stairs. He is florid, bright-eyed, loose-lipped, inclined to stoutness, but kept in good condition; his hair is crisp, curly, slightly grey; his ears peculiar, pointed at their tops like a faun's. He looks very big and well-dressed, and, when he smiles, affable enough.

Upstairs a young girl, with the suns of seventeen summers on her brown head, is lying with her face hidden on her mother's shoulder; she is sobbing with great childish sobs, regardless of reddened eyes and the tears that have splashed on the silk of her grey, going-away gown.

The mother seems scarcely less disturbed than the girl. She is a fragile-looking woman with delicate fair skin, smoothly parted thin chestnut hair, dove-like eyes, and a monotonous piping voice. She is flushing painfully, making a strenuous effort to say something to the girl, something that is opposed to the whole instincts of her life.

She tries to speak, parts her lips only to close them again, and clasp her arms tighter round the girl's shoulders; at length she manages to say with trembling, uncertain pauses:

'You are married now, darling, and you must obey'—she lays a stress upon the word—'your husband in all things—there are—there are things you should know—but—marriage is a serious thing, a sacred thing'—with desperation—'you must believe that what your husband tells you is right—let him guide you—tell you——'

There is such acute distress in her usually unemotional voice that the girl looks up and scans her face—her blushing, quivering, faded face. Her eyes are startled, fawn-like eyes as her mother's, her skin too is delicately fair, but her mouth is firmer, her jaw squarer, and her piquant, irregular nose is full of character. She is slightly built, scarcely fully developed in her fresh youth.

'What is it that I do not know, mother? What is it?'—with anxious impatience. 'There is something more—I have felt it all these last weeks in your and the others' looks—in his, in the very atmosphere—but why have you not told me before —I——' Her only answer is a gush of helpless tears from the mother, and a sharp rap at the door, and the bridegroom's voice, with an imperative note that it strikes the nervous girl is new to it, that makes her cling to her mother in a close, close embrace, drop her veil and go out to him.

She shakes hands with the best man, kisses the girl friend who has acted as bridesmaid—the wedding has been a very quiet one—and steps into the carriage. The Irish cook throws an old shoe after them from the side door, but it hits the trunk of an elder-tree, and falls back on to the path, making that worthy woman cross herself and mutter of ill-omens and bad luck to follow; for did not a magpie cross the path first thing this morning when she went to open the gate, and wasn't a red-haired woman the first creature she clapped eyes on as she looked down the road?

Half an hour later the carriage pulls up at the little station and the girl jumps out first; she is flushed, and her eyes stare helplessly as the eyes of a startled child, and she trembles with quick running shudders from head to foot. She clasps and unclasps her slender, grey-gloved hands so tightly that the stitching on the back of one bursts.

He has called to the station-master, and they go into the refreshment-room together; the latter appears at the door and, beckoning to a porter, gives him an order.

She takes a long look at the familiar little place. They have lived there three years, and yet she seems to see it now for the first time; the rain drips, drips monotonously off the zinc roof, the smell of the dust is fresh, and the white pinks in the borders are beaten into the gravel.

Then the train runs in; a first-class carriage, marked 'engaged,' is attached, and he comes for her; his hot breath smells of champagne, and it strikes her that his eyes are fearfully big and bright, and he offers her his arm with such a curious amused proprietary air that the girl shivers as she lays her hand in it.

The bell rings, the guard locks the door, the train steams out, and as it passes the signal-box, a large well-kept hand, with a signet ring on the little finger, pulls down the blind on the window of an engaged carriage.

.   .   .   .   .   .

Five years later, one afternoon on an autumn day, when the rain is falling like splashing tears on the rails, and the smell of the dust after rain fills the mild air with freshness, and the white chrysanthemums struggle to raise their heads from the gravel path into which the sharp shower has beaten them, the same woman, for there is no trace of girlhood in her twenty-two years, slips out of a first-class carriage ; she has a dressing-bag in her hand.

She walks with her head down and a droop in her shoulders ; her quickness of step is due rather to nervous haste than elasticity of frame. When she reaches the turn of the road, she pauses and looks at the little villa with the white curtains and gay tiled window-boxes. She can see the window of her old room ; distinguish every shade in the changing leaves of the creeper climbing up the south wall ; hear the canary's shrill note from where she stands.

Never once has she set foot in the peaceful little house with its air of genteel propriety since that eventful morning when she left it with him ; she has always framed an excuse.

Now as she sees it a feeling of remorse fills her heart, and she thinks of the mother living out her quiet years, each day a replica of the one gone before, and her resolve weakens; she feels inclined to go back, but the waning sun flickers over the panes in the window of the room she occupied as a girl. She can recall how she used to run to the open window on summer mornings and lean out and draw in the dewy freshness and welcome the day, how she has stood on moonlight nights and danced with her bare white feet in the strip of moonlight, and let her fancies fly out into the silver night, a young girl's dreams of the beautiful, wonderful world that lay outside.

A hard dry sob rises in her throat at the memory of it, and the fleeting expression of softness on her face changes to a bitter disillusion.

She hurries on, with her eyes down, up the neat gravelled path, through the open door into the familiar sitting-room.

The piano is open with a hymn-book on the stand; the grate is filled with fresh green ferns, a bowl of late roses perfume the room from the centre of the table. The mother is sitting in her easy chair, her hands folded across a big white Persian cat on her lap; she is fast asleep. Some futile lace work, her thimble, and bright scissor are placed on a table near her.

Her face is placid, not a day older than that day five years ago. Her glossy hair is no greyer, her skin is clear, she smiles in her sleep. The smile rouses a sort of sudden fury in the breast of

the woman standing in her dusty travelling cloak
at the door, noting every detail in the room.   She
throws back her veil and goes over and looks at
herself in the mirror over the polished chiffonnier
—scans herself pitilessly.   Her skin is sallow with
the dull sallowness of a fair skin in ill-health, and
the fringe of her brown hair is so lacking in lustre
that it affords no contrast.   The look of fawn-like
shyness has vanished from her eyes, they burn
sombrefully and resentfully in their sunken orbits,
there is a dragged look about the mouth ; and the
keynote of her face is a cynical disillusion.   She
looks from herself to the reflection of the mother,
and then turning sharply with a suppressed exclamation goes over, and shaking the sleeping woman
not too gently, says :

'Mother, wake up, I want to speak to you !'

The mother starts with frightened eyes, stares
at the other woman as if doubting the evidence of
her sight, smiles, then cowed by the unresponsive
look in the other face, grows grave again, sits still
and stares helplessly at her, finally bursting into
tears with a

'Flo, my dear, Flo, is it really you ?'

The girl jerks her head impatiently and says
drily :

'Yes, that is self-evident.   I am going on a long
journey.   I have something to say to you before I
start !   Why on earth are you crying ?'

There is a note of surprised wonder in her voice
mixed with impatience.

The older woman has had time to scan her face

and the dormant motherhood in her is roused by its weary anguish. She is ill, she thinks, in trouble. She rises to her feet ; it is characteristic of the habits of her life, with its studied regard for the observance of small proprieties, and distrust of servants as a class, that she goes over and closes the room door carefully.

This hollow-eyed, sullen women is so unlike the fresh girl who left her five years ago that she feels afraid. With the quiet selfishness that has characterised her life she has accepted the excuses her daughter has made to avoid coming home, as she has accepted the presents her son-in-law has sent her from time to time. She has found her a husband well-off in the world's goods, and there her responsibility ended. She approaches her hesitatingly ; she feels she ought to kiss her, there is something unusual in such a meeting after so long an absence ; it shocks her, it is so unlike the one she has pictured ; she has often looked forward to it, often ; to seeing Flo's new frocks, to hearing of her town life.

' Won't you take off your things ? You will like to go to your room ? '

She can hear how her own voice shakes ; it is really inconsiderate of Flo to treat her in this strange way.

' We will have some tea,' she adds.

Her colour is coming and going, the lace at her wrist is fluttering. The daughter observes it with a kind of dull satisfaction, she is taking out her hat-pins carefully. She notices a portrait in a

velvet case upon the mantelpiece ; she walks over
and looks at it intently. It is her father, the
father who was killed in India in a hill skirmish
when she was a little lint-locked maid barely up
to his knee. She studies it with new eyes, trying to read what man he was, what soul he had,
what part of him is in her, tries to find herself by
reading him. Something in his face touches her,
strikes some underlying chord in her, and she
grinds her teeth at a thought it rouses.

'She must be ill, she must be very ill,' says the
mother, watching her, 'to think I daren't offer to
kiss my own child !' She checks the tears that
keep welling up, feeling that they may offend this
woman who is so strangely unlike the girl who
left her. The latter has turned from her scrutiny
of the likeness and sweeps her with a cold criticising look as she turns towards the door, saying :

'I *should* like some tea. I will go upstairs and
wash off the dust.'

.   .   .   .   .

Half an hour later the two women sit opposite
one another in the pretty room. The younger one
is leaning back in her chair watching the mother
pour out the tea, following the graceful movements of the white, blue-veined hands amongst the
tea things—she lets her wait on her ; they have
not spoken beyond a commonplace remark about
the heat, the dust, the journey.

'How is Philip, is he well ?' The mother
ventures to ask with a feeling of trepidation, but
it seems to her that she ought to ask about him.

'He is quite well, men of his type usually are; I may say he is particularly well just now, he has gone to Paris with a girl from the Alhambra!'

The older woman flushes painfully, and pauses with her cup half way to her lips and lets the tea run over unheeded on to her dainty silk apron.

'You are spilling your tea,' the girl adds with malicious enjoyment.

The woman gasps: 'Flo, but Flo, my dear, it is dreadful! What would your poor father have said! *no wonder* you look ill, dear, how shocking! Shall I—ask the vicar to—to remonstrate with him?——'

'My dear mother, what an extraordinary idea! These little trips have been my one solace. I assure you, I have always hailed them as lovely oases in the desert of matrimony, resting-places on the journey. My sole regret was their infrequency. That is very good tea, I suppose it is the cream.'

The older woman puts her cup on the tray and stares at her with frightened eyes and paled cheeks.

'I am afraid I don't understand you, Florence. I am old-fashioned'—with a little air of frigid propriety—'I have always looked upon matrimony as a sacred thing. It is dreadful to hear you speak this way; you should have tried to save Philip—from—from such a shocking sin.'

The girl laughs, and the woman shivers as she hears her. She cries—

'I would never have thought it of Philip. My

poor dear, I am afraid you must be very unhappy.

'Very,' with a grim smile, 'but it is over now, I have done with it. I am not going back.'

If a bomb had exploded in the quiet, pretty room the effect could hardly have been more startling than her almost cheerful statement. A big bee buzzes in and bangs against the lace of the older woman's cap and she never heeds it, then she almost screams :

'Florence, Florence, my dear, you can't mean to desert your husband! Oh, think of the disgrace, the scandal, what people will say, the '—with an uncertain quaver—' the sin. You took a solemn vow, you know, and you are going to break it——'

'My dear mother, the ceremony had no meaning for me, I simply did not know what I was signing my name to, or what I was vowing to do. I might as well have signed my name to a document drawn up in Choctaw. I have no remorse, no prick of conscience at the step I am taking ; my life must be my own. They say sorrow chastens, I don't believe it ; it hardens, embitters ; joy is like the sun, it coaxes all that is loveliest and sweetest in human nature. No, I am not going back.'

The older woman cries, wringing her hands helplessly :

'I can't understand it. You must be very miserable to dream of taking such a serious step.'

'As I told you, I am. It is a defect of my temperament. How many women really take the man nearest to them as seriously as I did! I think few. They finesse and flatter and wheedle and coax, but truth there is none. I couldn't do that, you see, and so I went to the wall. I don't blame them; it must be so, as long as marriage is based on such unequal terms, as long as man demands from a wife as a right, what he must sue from a mistress as a favour; until marriage becomes for many women a legal prostitution, a nightly degradation, a hateful yoke under which they age, mere bearers of children conceived in a sense of duty, not love. They bear them, birth them, nurse them, and begin again without choice in the matter, growing old, unlovely, with all joy of living swallowed in a senseless burden of reckless maternity, until their love, granted they started with that, the mystery, the crowning glory of their lives, is turned into a duty they submit to with distaste instead of a favour granted to a husband who must become a new lover to obtain it.'

'But men are different, Florence; you can't refuse a husband, you might cause him to commit sin.'

'Bosh, mother, he is responsible for his own sins, we are not bound to dry-nurse his morality. Man is what we have made him, his very faults are of our making. No wife is bound to set aside the demands of her individual soul for the sake of imbecile obedience. I am going to have some more tea.'

The mother can only whimper:

'It is dreadful! I thought he made you such an excellent husband, his position too is so good, and he is so highly connected.'

'Yes, and it is as well to put the blame in the right quarter. Philip is as God made him, he is an animal with strong passions, and he avails himself of the latitude permitted him by the laws of society. Whatever of blame, whatever of sin, whatever of misery is in the whole matter rests *solely* and *entirely* with you, mother'—the woman sits bolt upright—'and with no one else—that is why I came here—to tell you that—I have promised myself over and over again that I would tell you. It is with you, and you alone the fault lies.'

There is so much of cold dislike in her voice that the other woman recoils and whimpers piteously :

'You must be ill, Florence, to say such wicked things. What have I done? I am sure I devoted myself to you from the time you were little; I refused—dabbing her eyes with her cambric handkerchief—'ever so many good offers. There was young Fortescue in the artillery, such a good-looking man, and such an elegant horseman, he was quite infatuated about me; and Jones, to be sure he was in business, but he was most attentive. Every one said I was a devoted mother; I can't think what you mean, I——'

A smile of cynical amusement checks her.

'Perhaps not. Sit down, and I'll tell you.'

She shakes off the trembling hand, for the mother has risen and is standing next to her, and pushes her into a chair, and paces up and down the room. She is painfully thin, and drags her limbs as she walks.

'I say it is your fault, because you reared me a fool, an idiot, ignorant of everything I ought to have known, everything that concerned me and the life I was bound to lead as a wife; my physical needs, my coming passion, the very meaning of my sex, my wifehood and motherhood to follow. You gave me not one weapon in my hand to defend myself against the possible attacks of man at his worst. You sent me out to fight the biggest battle of a woman's life, the one in which she ought to know every turn of the game, with a white gauze'—she laughs derisively—'of maiden purity as a shield.'

Her eyes blaze, and the woman in the chair watches her as one sees a frog watch a snake when it is put into its case.

'I was fourteen when I gave up the gooseberry-bush theory as the origin of humanity; and I cried myself ill with shame when I learnt what maternity meant, instead of waking with a sense of delicious wonder at the great mystery of it. You gave me to a man, nay more, you told me to obey him, to believe that whatever he said would be right, would be my duty; knowing that the meaning of marriage was a sealed book to me, that I had no real idea of what union with a man meant. You delivered me body and soul into his hands without preparing me in any way for the ordeal I was to go through. You sold me for a home, for clothes, for food; you played upon my ignorance, I won't say innocence, that is different. You told me, you and your sister, and your friend the vicar's wife, that it would be an anxiety off your mind if I were comfortably settled——'

'It is wicked of you to say such dreadful things!' the mother cries, 'and besides'—with a touch of asperity—'you married him willingly, you seemed to like his attentions——'

'How like a woman! What a thorough woman you are, mother! The good old-fashioned kitten with a claw in her paw! Yes, I married him willingly; I was not eighteen, I had known no men; was pleased that you were pleased—and, as you say, I liked his attentions. He had tact enough not to frighten me, and I had not the faintest conception of what marriage with him meant. I had an idea'—with a laugh—'that the words of the minister settled the matter. Do you think that if I had realised how fearfully close the intimacy with him would have been that my whole soul would not have stood up in revolt, the whole woman in me cried out against such a degradation of myself?' Her words tremble with passion, and the woman who bore her feels as if she is being lashed by a whip. 'Would I not have shuddered at the thought of *him* in such a relationship?—and waited, waited until I found the man who would satisfy me, body and soul—to whom I would have gone without any false shame, of whom I would think with gladness as the father of a little child to come, for whom the white fire of love or passion, call it what you will, in my heart would have burned clearly and saved me

from the feeling of loathing horror that has made
my married life a nightmare to me—ay, made me
a murderess in heart over and over again. This is
not exaggeration. It has killed the sweetness in
me, the pure thoughts of womanhood—has made
me hate myself and *hate you*. Cry, mother, if you
will ; you don't know how much you have to cry
for—I have cried myself barren of tears. Cry over
the girl you killed '—with a gust of passion—' why
didn't you strangle me as a baby ? It would have
been kinder ; my life has been a hell, mother—I
felt it vaguely as I stood on the platform waiting,
I remember the mad impulse I had to jump down
under the engine as it came in, to escape from the
dread that was chilling my soul. What have these
years been ? One long crucifixion, one long sub-
mittal to the desires of a man I bound myself to
in ignorance of what it meant ; every caress '—
with a cry—' has only been the first note of
that. Look at me '—stretching out her arms—
' look at this wreck of my physical self ; I wouldn't
dare to show you the heart or the soul underneath. He has stood on his rights ; but do you
think, if I had known, that I would have given
such insane obedience, from a mistaken sense of
duty, as would lead to this ? I have my rights
too, and my duty to myself ; if I had only recognised them in time.'

' Sob away, mother ; I don't even feel for you—
I have been burnt too badly to feel sorry for
what will only be a tiny scar to you ; I have
all the long future to face with all the world

against me.   Nothing will induce me to go
back.   Better anything than that ; food and
clothes are poor equivalents for what I have had
to suffer—I can get them at a cheaper rate.   When
he comes to look for me, give him that letter.   He
will tell you he has only been an uxorious husband,
and that you reared me a fool.   You can tell him
too, if you like, that I loathe him, shiver at the
touch of his lips, his breath, his hands ; that my
whole body revolts at his touch ; that when he
has turned and gone to sleep, I have watched him
with such growing hatred that at times the tempta-
tion to kill him has been so strong that I have
crept out of bed and walked the cold passage in
my bare feet until I was too benumbed to feel anything ; that I have counted the hours to his going
away, and cried out with delight at the sight of the
retreating carriage !'

'You are very hard, Flo ; the Lord soften your
heart !   Perhaps'—with trepidation—'if you had
had a child——'

'Of his—that indeed would have been the last
straw—no, mother.'

There is such a peculiar expression of satisfaction
over something—of some inner understanding, as
a man has when he dwells on the successful accom-
plishment of a secret purpose—that the mother
sobs quietly, wringing her hands.

'I did not know, Flo, I acted for the best ; you
are very hard on me !'

.   .   .   .

Later, when the bats are flitting across the moon,

and the girl is asleep—she has thrown herself half-dressed on the narrow white bed of her girlhood, with her arms folded across her breast and her hands clenched—the mother steals into the room. She has been turning over the contents of an old desk ; her marriage certificate, faded letters on foreign paper, and a bit of Flo's hair cut off each birthday, and a sprig of orange-blossom she wore in her hair. She looks faded and grey in the silver light, and she stands and gazes at the haggard face in its weary sleep. The placid current of her life is disturbed, her heart is roused, something of her child's soul-agony has touched the sleeping depths of her nature. She feels as if scales have dropped from her eyes, as if the instincts and conventions of her life are toppling over, as if all the needs of protesting women of whom she has read with a vague displeasure have come home to her. She covers the girl tenderly, kisses her hair, and slips a little roll of notes into the dressing-bag on the table and steals out, with the tears running down her cheeks.

When the girl looks into her room as she steals by, when the morning light is slanting in, she sees her kneeling, her head, with its straggling grey hair, bowed in tired sleep. It touches her. Life is too short, she thinks, to make any one's hours bitter ; she goes down and writes a few kind words in pencil and leaves them near her hand, and goes quickly out into the road.

The morning is grey and misty, with faint yellow stains in the east, and the west wind blows with a melancholy sough in it—the first whisper of the fall, the fall that turns the world of nature into a patient suffering from phthisis—delicate season of decadence, when the loveliest scenes have a note of decay in their beauty ; when a poisoned arrow pierces the marrow of insect and plant, and the leaves have a hectic flush and fall, fall and shrivel and curl in the night's cool ; and the chrysanthe-mums, the 'good-bye summers' of the Irish peasants, have a sickly tinge in their white. It affects her, and she finds herself saying : ' Wither and die, wither and die, make compost for the loves of the spring, as the old drop out and make place for the new, who forget them, to be in their turn forgotten.' She hurries on, feeling that her autumn has come to her in her spring, and a little later she stands once more on the platform where she stood in the flush of her girlhood, and takes the train in the opposite direction.

THE REGENERATION OF TWO

'Love is the supreme factor in the evolution of the world.'
—PROF. DRUMMOND.

IT is mid-June one hot forenoon in Christiania.
The air seems to vibrate audibly with heat, to
gasp for coolness. The sun rays play 'hide and
seek' amongst the tombstones in our Saviour's
graveyard. Sable-clad figures move about with
spades. A few sit and do fancy work, and spend
a thoughtful hour at the resting-place of some near
one passed through the gates of Sleep. The roses,
such roses, hang their heads with faintness as the
sun becomes more insistent in his wooing, and the
fragrance of a thousand plants fills the air with
the glory of summer.

The long French windows of a villa overlooking
it are thrown wide open. The lace curtains hang
limply, for there is not a breath of wind. It is a
pretty room, with evidences of taste and wealth.
Its only occupant is stretched in a weary attitude
in a low rocking-chair. She is swaying slowly to
and fro ; a book lies on the carpet near her, as if
thrown there ; her slippers are kicked aside ; she
has taken off her rings, and they are glittering on
her lap, and as she rocks from shade to light, and
light to shade, the sun strikes gold and ruby,

emerald and diamond and sapphire flashes. She yawns wearily and stretches up her arms behind her head, then clasps her long hands—they are well formed, with a yellow whiteness and a look of delicate strength about them—round her knees, and looks at her own reflection in a mirror opposite. She is not unlike an illustration in a dainty magazine ; she has an æsthetic appreciation of the effect of her black silken-clad ankles and the froth of white lace flounces on her petticoats, the cool tones of the broad lilac and white stripes of her muslin morning gown, and the chic of the black rosette at the waist.

She is scarcely beautiful, but she is undeniably striking. There is a tantalising irregularity about the face, with its bored expression. Her mouth is large, but no man would wish it smaller, with its firm, tender curves and deep-set corners ; her brows are delicately marked ; the orbs of her wonderful eyes, with their changeful lights, are large ; there are weary lines about them, the lids are heavy with bistre stains ; her skin has an anæmic tinge, and to-day it looks shrivelled like a waxen flower with the first touch of wilting over it ; the little touch of rouge, though it is artistically applied, only heightens this effect. As she leans back, her throat looks singularly strong for such a small head ; her hair is curled loosely about her forehead ; the moulding of her temples is fine ; taking her altogether, she is seductively attractive, a thing of piquant contrasts—the attractive artificiality, physical lassitude, and irritable weariness of a disillusioned woman of the world, and the eyes of a spoilt child filled with frank petulant query. She yawns wearily as she rocks, and looks at the coquettish bows on her pretty shoes—she fancies they have a dejected look. A door opens; she calls irritably, 'Jomfru!' and a stout woman with quiet eyes and repressed mouth enters the room.

'Does Fruen want anything?' She speaks respectfully, yet there is the note in her voice that one uses to a child or an invalid; indeed, she is on terms of companionship with her mistress.

'I'm awfully thirsty, I want something tart.'

'Fruen had better have saft' (fruit juice) 'and seltzer.'

She leaves the room to return with a tray and a long glass; the seltzer rises in little silver pearls through the rose-coloured liquid; she watches them idly for a moment, then drinks it greedily with a sigh of satisfaction.

'Shall I rub Fruen's feet?' the woman asks, drawing forward a footstool. Without waiting for a reply she takes them on her lap and rubs gently, shaking her fingers after each time as if she is scattering away something she has drawn out of them.

'Can't Fruen read?'

'No, my head aches; I feel much more as if I want to scream. Don't you ever?'

'Fruen isn't well.' Then with a sort of hesitation: 'At times—at night I do feel as if I could just cry without knowing why. I suspect all

women do—it's part of our nature. Fruen ought
to do something.   Fru Hohlsen, with whom I
lived before, used to sew for poor children for the
missionary fund, and I know English ladies have
many interests——'

'Bah! bah! I don't believe in that, Aagot.
What on earth's the good of sewing flannel petticoats for poor little niggers in Zanzibar? I am
sure it's much nicer for them to roll their little
brown bodies in the warm sand, I wouldn't mind
doing it myself. It's'—with a humorous twitch
of mouth—'an æsthetic sin to send them out
Christian fig-leaves in the shape of hideous—the
patterns always *are* hideous—garments sewn by
pious fingers at home here. I have too much
respect for the poor little beggars' individual
liberty ; and then in such a climate, too! Phew!'
She undoes her gown and draws a deep breath.

'But in Fruen's country I have read of ladies
doing all sorts of things.'

'Yes, so they do ; they go in for suffrage, social
reformation, politics, all sorts of fatiguing things.
I thought of doing something of that kind myself,
of having a mission ; but it would last just as long
as it was a new sensation.   Besides, I didn't care
much for any of the advanced women I met, they
were so desperately in earnest, they took it out of
me so. I am too selfish, I am afraid, Aagot!
Do you know, I think philanthropy is a masculine
attribute ; you don't find woman as a rule lavish
her affections on man in the abstract.   Love
narrows rather than broadens her, unless she is

"crossed" in it, then she sometimes dispenses it in particles. I *want something for myself!*'

'Fruen could go into society, there is life in London, theatres, balls——'

'Psha! There's more real life here, or at least you see it more plainly. It's too big, Aagot. Friendship in London costs a tremendous lot, you have to pay very dearly for your social whistle, and it's only a tin one when you get it. I used to have the feeling at an afternoon sometimes, that I was one of a company of marionettes, and that some malicious demon was pulling a string in me, making me say things utterly unlike myself—and it wasn't even amusing. The men have the best of it. If a man is bored he puts on his hat and goes out, and looks for a man or a woman to help him to get rid of himself. Why can't we do the same? I wish I knew what to do with myself?'

'Yet Fruen has much to be thankful for. She had a rich husband and——'

'Buried him,' she interrupts cynically. 'Yes, there is a measure of thankfulness in that.'

The woman says nothing in reply, but her lips twitch and her lids drop.

'Yet Fruen likes gentlemen's society, likes to be admired, has many friends!'

'Ugh! I like talking to them, Aagot, in a way, like them to admire me, there's excitement in it; but when they want to come nearer I get a kind of dislike to them, a sort of resentment. They interest me, until they want to be more than a pastime; then, if they persist, I hate them. I am jealous of myself, one sees such a lot of animal in them when they are in love. Sometimes I get sorry for some one and ask, "Could I marry him?"— then I shudder. It's all horrid unless one has what some one calls "the white fire of love" to burn out the animalism, to consecrate it in a way. You see I know it, Aagot,'—with a serious air, 'because I married without understanding anything about it; I never cared for the master. He just came when I was in one of my affectible moods, and I was too ignorant to understand why I felt like that. He was good to me, without understanding that I had anything more in me, good in a "man of the world's" way. You were there, Aagot, and it is a terrible thing to say'—sinking her voice—'but the strongest feeling I had when he was dying or dead, though I was sorry in a way, and dreaded the loneliness, was a fierce inward whisper of exultant joy that I belonged to myself again. I fancy there must be many marriages like that in which the woman feels a dull resentment against the man because her love does not go with herself. Were *you* ever in love, Aagot?'

The colour mounts slowly to the other woman's dull fair hair.

'Yes, Frue, at least I think so. There was some one once, but there is very little to tell. I went a voyage with father; he used to take us girls in turns; that time it was to Spain. I always wanted to go to Spain.'

'You northerns always do; "Spanish" seems to convey an idea of romance, of beauty to you folk up here.'

' Perhaps, Frue. Well, we went with a cargo of deals to Barcelona ; father had a mixed freight to bring back, and we stayed there three weeks. There was a big Swedish barque at anchor next us. The captain had died in hospital and the first mate was going to take her home. I met him at a Norwegian ship chandler's ; it was a great house for all the northern skippers to meet. I met him several times. Then one evening I was going down to the quay by myself and there was a troop of asses with panniers trotting down one of the narrow streets, and there was a fearful row going on between some sailors and a woman, and when I saw knives flash I got frightened and ran down an alley. A fellow leaning against a doorway said something to me in Spanish and caught hold of me, and I screamed ; and *he* came up and sent him flying into the gutter, and took my arm and led me away. I felt faint and couldn't answer him, and it wasn't because I was frightened, but because there was something that came from him to me and paralysed me and made my legs fail me. I often met him after that, and he was always just the same, laughing, joking, mischievous, never serious, and sometimes that hurt me ; and one day I saw him leaning against a counter talking to a Spanish woman with just the same look as when he spoke to me, and I went on board and didn't go on shore for three days. Father thought it was the heat was too much for me ; and one evening when he had gone in to a dinner with a Danish captain, *he* rowed over and came on board and

talked to me. He wasn't feeling well, he said he
had missed me, asked me where I lived in Norway,
if I was engaged. We sat and listened to the
castanets ringing out from a dance house near the
wharf, and I was very happy. He said when he
was going, that he would likely be skipper after
the next voyage and that he wanted to settle down,
and that he would come and see mother after
he got home. Two days after, he was dead—a
sort of cholerine, they said. That is why I go out
to service. The winter after that I stayed at home
and it nearly drove me mad. I like to work; when
I am idle I can hear the castanets and the air of
the dance they played—work is the best.'

'But you are going to marry a cousin, aren't
you?'

'Yes, Fruen, that is to say a cousin's widower.
He is a cripple, he got a stroke, and he has three
little children. I love the children, I went to
school with her—and you see—he is quite helpless.'

'Hum! will that satisfy you?'

'I think so, Fruen; I don't want a husband—I
should hate it. The one I wanted lies out there
under the olive-trees in the Catholic churchyard.
I just want the children; little Henrik has a smile
like his.' There is a long silence; a bee buzzes
in and fills the room with the drone of summer.

'Perhaps you are right,' says her mistress, 'you
have the melody of the air he played in you. No
man ever played on me. I am like a harp that
has lain away until the strings are frayed, and no
one ever called out its deepest music.'

'Fruen ought to go out,' she replies ; and she slips on her shoes, and rises with no touch of sentiment in her stolid face, and busies herself in the next room.

The woman in the chair gets slowly up, and goes into her bed-room—there is a delicate smell of violets about it. She takes off her loose gown and begins to dress. She is far above the average height, and as she lifts her rather long, bare arms to reach down a gown, every action is full of grace. She has sloping shoulders and a long, deep chest ; she looks slight of hips, and yet her frailness is more apparent than real ; her muscles show under her delicate skin as she moves. She dresses slowly, and stamps her foot impatiently when she lets anything drop out of her hand, which she seems to do often in her nervous irritability. She looks at herself in the long glass with a kind of satisfaction, rubs off a final dab of powder with a soft piece of chamois, lifts up her gown and looks at her feet in the glass, turns slowly round to get a back view, and then gives a pleased nod over her shoulder at her own image.

Quarter of an hour later she is on her way to the landing-stage, for she has decided to go to Bygdo, that prettiest of Christiania surroundings.

The city is almost given over to tourists. A party of Cockney 'Cookies' are standing outside Torstrup the jeweller's window. She smiles as she passes them, for they have evidently anticipated a polar temperature. 'What guys!' she laughs, hurrying on, for they are making unflattering remarks, at the top of their voices, on some of the idiosyncrasies of national costume, with a characteristic disregard of the fact that every second Norwegian understands them. She turns with relief to look at a group of pretty girls and students, town residents probably. Their fresh laughter touches her in some way. She is affected to-day by every change in the world about her.

She finds a comfortable seat on the little steamer, and settles down to languid enjoyment of the scene. It is too early for a crowd, and she is aware of a strange feeling, of a presentiment of coming change as they steam out. The fanciful idea strikes her that all the flags fluttering from the different poles are flying gaily in honour of some special event in her life. The very breeze blowing freshly from the sea seems to whisper of a vague change. The mountains lie blue in the distance, and she watches idly the water drip off the oars of the rowing boats they pass—looks as if they scattered a shoal of little silvern fish at each dip, she thinks. Students' and girls' and children's laughter, and the murmur of voices about her, reach her without conveying any sense to her ; she feels inclined to close her eyes and just sleep.

When they reach Bygdo she hurries past the tables, the waiters with seidels of beer, and what an Irish acquaintance wittily calls 'bread and butter and trimmins,' bends round the cove and up to the wood. The witchery of the surround-

ings begins to affect her. The resinous smell of
the pines does her head good. The fir-trees stand
sturdily, as if listening to the gracile silver birches
bending their delicate branches in airy persiflage.
A wren alights for an instant on a blossom of
dwarf honeysuckle, then darts under a tuft of
wild thyme. The lace of her parasol throws patterns on the grass, and the quick trab of horses
coming round the bend of the road startles her,
and she slips quickly aside. An officer, a civilian,
and two ladies ride by. She recognises one of
them, the young wife of a painter ; scandal con-
nects her name with the man at her side. How
whitely her teeth gleamed through the crimson
curve of her lips as she laughed, thinks the woman,
and a story she heard lately about her flashed
through her memory. Some way the meeting
jarred on her ; she wants to get away by herself,
away from the memory of town scandals and
town people. She almost regrets she did not
take a droschke out to the country. She turns
down a side-path towards the water. She sits
down under a tree on the slope. The cove forms
a horseshoe to the right ; in the centre lie the
landing-stage and bathing-house. She can see
heads bobbing in the water from where she is
seated. To the left the fjord stretches, dotted
with islands and boats, and further still she can
see a villa, and a flag fluttering from a white staff
against a background of pines. Groups of people
are scattered about. Two Hallelujah lasses in
neat uniform pass her with Norsk versions of the

War Cry under their arms; a soldier, with a hat like a forester's, with the addition of a horse's tail, is chaffing them. A little below her, two lovers are sitting oblivious of passers-by; his arm is around her waist, and her head is on his shoulder. The expression on his otherwise stupid face disgusts her, and she hurries further round the cove and seats herself again. She is tired, flushed with the exertion, and she sits watching lazily the dip of the sails, and the midges as they whirl before her against the background of blue sky, in ever-recurring giddy circles, always two, an aerial wooing.

There is no one to be seen, yet she is not at ease: she experiences the odd feeling one has sometimes of not being alone, and her heart throbs with quick thuds that seem to dominate over the little, whispering, flute-like prattle of the water against the rock. She looks round as if expecting to see eyes peering down through the firs at her back. The conviction grows upon her of the nearness of some one. She has felt eyes on her back before, has felt strange presences with some sense that lies outside her ordinary senses. She gets up and walks down towards a blue-grey boulder with a clump of dried bracken next it, to look behind it, and as she reaches it she is stopped by a yawning whine that ends in an unmistakable growl. A dog, *genus* cur, a rough, yellow-coated dog, crouched on the grass a yard ahead, is looking up at her; she has honest, tawny eyes, and a ragged ear torn in some old fight, and she is studying her attentively. She looks back at her bravely enough, although she draws a quick breath, and the lace on her bodice flutters as her breast heaves. Something else, too, is working in her: a hypnotised sensation, making her limbs heavy; it isn't fear, it is purely physical. She snaps her fingers, and pats her knee coaxingly, and is answered by a yawn that reassures her. She walks on; this time the growl is only feigned, and she becomes aware of a man lying on the bracken in the hollow below the boulder. She stops at once, and the blood rushes to her face in a hot flood. She looks down at him, and a kind of wondering, interested look succeeds her surprise. The man at her feet is not a tramp, and there is something in the unconscious helplessness of his attitude that appeals to all that is womanly in her; perhaps it is just the unconsciousness. It reminds her too, with the thrown-up arm and hand loosely clenched, of a little brother, dead so many years that he is barely a memory; besides, the fellow's head is striking, and he sleeps with his mouth shut. It isn't given to every man to look beautiful in his sleep, even though he may pass for a handsome chap enough in his waking hours; faces tell tales in sleep, one's subliminal consciousness is apt to play mean tricks with one's expression. This man's face has a sorrow-worn, spiritualised look, a sternness about the mouth; he is clean-shaven, and his hair is longer than the men of his set wear it, but it is dark and soft and silky. She wonders vaguely what colour his eyes are. He looks, she thinks, as if he has gone through some of God's mills and got hurt in the grinding. She is conscious of a wonderful sudden change in herself; her depression is melting away, she only feels a ridiculous kind of buoyant reaction against it, a sense of rest after disturbance, the quiet after a rain gust. She hardly knows why she remains standing there, looking down at the sleeping man; she tells herself the proper thing to do is to go. She is about to do so, not, she recognises with some astonishment, without reluctance, when the dog, perhaps awakened to a sense of having failed somewhat in her duty, protests by catching her dress in her teeth, letting it go, growling and frisking round her. Now, fear is not exactly a part of her nature, but regard for a pretty gown is. She stands still, and whispers soothingly to the beast. It has a certain effect. She lets go, but seizes her again every time she takes a step forward. The ludicrous aspect of the matter strikes her, and she laughs softly. She stands still, doggie likewise a little distance away. Finally, the latter lies down with her forepaws stretched out, keeping her quizzical eyes fixed on the woman. This grows monotonous; she says to herself, ' I wonder if I may venture to sit down.' She bends slowly, keeping her eyes on the dog; the latter growls softly. She sinks on one knee; it is not an easy manœuvre, encumbered as she is with a parasol and a book; however, she accomplishes it successfully, with one foot under her. Doggie is satisfied with the compromise, so she gets into a better position. She has a side-view of the sleeping man, and she examines him with a woman's attention to details. His clothes are rough blue serge, the unstarched collar of his linen shirt is scrupulously clean, a soft felt hat is lying on the grass near him, and a canvas knapsack; his shoes are worn, one of them is patched. She speculates on his calling—a painter, a poet, a Bohemian of some sort—likely. A 'pillar of the State,' a churchwarden—unlikely. Meanwhile the sun creeps round, and slants through a tree right on to his face. How tired he looks! there is a weary droop about his mouth. She flushes, hesitates, looks at the dog—she is asleep, with her black snout on her paws; she moves very softly, and contrives, by leaning back, to stand her open sunshade so that it shades his face. Its lace and knots of ribbon flutter and throw fantastic shadows over him, and she laughs, for it reminds her of a furbelowed bassinette. The little dog creeps up to her, gives her wrist a lick, trots down to the water's edge and laps eagerly, comes back and nestles down at her knee. She takes off her glove, and scratches her behind her ears and rubs her head. 'You are a bit of a vagabond, I think,' she whispers. There are many old scars, and one ear is split, and, when she cocks it, the half of it flaps in a comical way. So she sits with an unwonted sense of drowsy well-being; the mingled smell of pine-trees and brackish water, the lap and sparkle of the waves that wash gently in the sunshine, the rustle of foliage and the trickle of

runlets finding their way to the fjord, act soothingly. She is affectible to-day, stirred in the
depths of her nature, in the underlying wholesome woman that is there, uncalled to life, for the
warp is only external.

How long she sits there she heeds not; a
little breeze rises and a shrill whistle sounds
in the distance. She looks at her watch, almost
five o'clock. Chiff, chiff, chuff, chuff, and the
steamer by which she has intended to return passes
by with its freight of gladsome people towards
the landing stage. She is loth to go, it is so good
to sit thus bathed in silken air; besides, she feels
as if she is infused with some mystical elixir that
is filtering down to the underlying strata of her
being. Let chance decide! She unloosens a
penknife from her chatelaine, and spins it smartly
on a flat stone in the moss beside her: 'points to
me, I go!' She catches her breath, and sets her
teeth in her lip, as the silver and pearl glisten as
it revolves slower, slower, a-ah, she closes her lids
involuntarily—opens them—one little turn more;
the point rests fjordwards. She feels inclined to
clap her hands; she recalls having experienced
precisely the same relief once years ago, when, in
a fit of childish passion, she had thrown a stone
at a playmate and it just missed her temple.
Why should she feel so, now? she asks herself;
well, why analyse? She has two hours more
until the next steamer! She feels unreasonably
glad, as glad as when, a little child, she sat in the
meadows and wove daisy chains, twenty golden

years ago. The steamer has left again, and up in the sky above its track two clouds are meeting; now they fuse and turn into a chariot tipped with silver, and soar upwards. 'Why can't,' she says softly, 'his soul, and my soul, and the doggie's soul loosen ourselves and float away in soul communion out of the barren loneliness of this old earth here?' The band up in the 'umbrella' strikes up the opening bars of a 'Huldretanz,' a weird, witching thing with a want in it, and someway it brings her back to earth again. She laughs at herself, and pats the dog's head and says: 'No, I wouldn't sail over the clouds if I could, I'd rather be you, doggie, and curl up under the caress of some one's hand.

She considers herself as she sits there. Her patent shoes are made by the best man in London; her muslin gown, with all its apparent simplicity, is fitted by Parisian fingers; and her hat is an inspiration of blossoms and lace from the Rue de la Paix. Her gloves are delicate to sight and smell and touch; and yet she would give all she possesses for one hour's real happiness.

Suddenly the quiet is broken, a troop of boys and girls playing 'hide and seek' come rushing round the slope, and one of them holds a handful of pine cones. She throws them with uncertain aim at the lad following her, and darts up through the trees with a giggling scream; the tan cones pelter with a rattle on to the sunshade and over the sleeper. He wakes, not drowsily, but all at once wide-awake, with eyes black on awakening, grey as the pupils close with the light, steel-grey, as a lake without sunlight.

He sits up, looks at the cones, at the sunshade, at the woman. She is uncomfortably conscious of his steady, cool scrutiny. It flashes through her that he is not in the least impressed, and that he will judge on first impressions. She flushes angrily, and stammers:

'Some young people playing threw those things, and they fell on my parasol.'

The man's face softens; he says directly and simply:

Did you put it here to shade me?'

'Yes, the sun was fearfully strong, and it struck directly on your head.'

'Thank you, it was very kind of you. I must have slept a long time.'

He takes out a clumsy, old-fashioned silver watch in a crystal case such as peasants wear.

'You were asleep when I came three hours ago,' she interjects.

He examines her with new interest, frowns as he takes her in, as if puzzled at himself, or some sudden idea.

'That is odd, for I never can sleep if any one is near me, never.'

She feels, for her senses are sharpened in some subtle way, that there is disapproval of her in the look. It is a new sensation, she wonders why she finds it more hurtful than amusing.

'Your dog objected to my going in the first

instance,' she says, with a touch of restraint. A pained disturbance is replacing the unreasoning sense of joy that has possessed her, her head throbs, and a feeling of faintness overpowers her. The sun-filled air, the music, water, all the thrumming sounds of summer seem to fuse into a gigantic gold-green disc, that revolves first quickly, then with ever-slackening turns, around her, until she loses herself in the slow swirl. A voice coming to her from ever so far away rouses her, saying, 'Drink this!' The cold of metal touches her lips, and the disc whirls the other way round with sickening swirls, ever quicker and quicker, until it stops with a jerk, and she comes to full consciousness of herself and her surroundings. He is holding the top of a flask to her lips, watching her with eyes in which the dominant expression is impatient disapproval. It strikes her as supremely funny, she can't help herself, and she bursts into an hysterical, uncontrollable fit of laughter. It has a true unaffected ring in it, and it is unrestrained as a child's; coming from her, it is as if one of the figures in a fashion plate in a lady's paper were suddenly to change its simper into a natural smile, and let its waist expand. The man's face relaxes, and he stands up remarking:

'You are better, Frue; it was the heat, no doubt and you gave me your parasol.' A pause. 'Why did you?'

She blushes through her powder, and tells the simple truth.

'I don't know. You looked someway helpless, like a child, in your sleep.'

She pales again ; he draws his brows together impatiently, and says somewhat ungraciously :

'Can I get you anything?'

'Yes, if you don't mind calling to a waiter, please ; or, perhaps, I shall be all right in a moment, I will go myself.'

He has put on his hat, and picked up the sunshade ; the impatient look leaves his face again as he hands it to her.

'What does Fruen want—coffee, lager?   I am at her commands.'

'Coffee, please, and I am very hungry'—meekly.

He has gone, followed by the dog, trotting first to the right, then to the left, at his heels.

She bursts into another fit of laughter, and diving her hand into her pocket, takes out a little ivory case with a glass in it, and looks at herself.   It strikes her as never before, that the powder accentuates her lines and makes her look horribly haggard.   She wipes it off carefully. The utterly non-admirative look in the man's eyes is burning into her, as the recollection of some *bêtise* one has committed will strike one afterwards with a double sense of discomfiture.   If she were not afraid of his coming back, she would go down to the fjord and wash her face.   It has grown natural to her to exact homage from every man, and it piques her, rouses a devil-may-care mood in her.

A waiter comes down the slope with a tray, a

coffee-service, and some sandwiches. A shade crosses her face as she sees that he is alone; but she reassures herself, as she sees his knapsack and stick still lying there.

Whilst she is picking out the little nickel coins in her purse, she inquires with an effort at carelessness for the gentleman who ordered it. The waiter has in the meantime been examining her clothes, and he is puzzled. He says doubtfully, 'I brought for two, Frue; the gentleman only said, "take some coffee and something to eat down to where that lady is sitting," pointing Fruen out.'

'Oh, that is all right, keep the change.'

The man goes away smiling. She buries the coffee-pot in a clump of bracken and waits. The band is playing a waltz, the whole atmosphere is filled with a murmur of leafage and laughter, whispers of wind and wave. It seems to her a long time since he went; she is thirsty and starts at every step and looks around. At length his voice sounds behind her:

'I hope Fruen got all she wanted?' He asks it politely; the doggie trots and looks wistfully at the tray. 'Fruen hasn't had anything yet! She has been waiting—— ?'

She disinters the thick white coffee-pot from its nest in the bracken. The sun flicks rainbow sparks off the rings on her ivory-tinted hands as she sets the cups to rights. 'You were a long time!'

She does not look up to see in what way he takes her remark, she is half afraid of the new side of herself that is prompting her to recklessness.

She hands him his cup with a demure tightening of lips, and then passes the sugar basin.

'Well, when ladies will!' he says, and there is a mocking note in his voice. Her lips quiver and there is a mute reproach in her look; it touches him as her laughter before, and he changes his tone and says 'thank you' simply.

It crosses her mind that some of her acquaintances, a certain little lawyer with very keen eyes, might easily pass, and put her in an awkward position. She pours some cream into a saucer for the dog.

'Does Fruen often have these extempore picnics?' with the intonation that hurts her.

She looks him steadily in the face.

'This is the first time, and you are the first man I have ever spoken to without a formal introduction and'—with a quiver through her voice—'I don't know why I am doing it now. It's not that you are too—too amiable.'

There is a silence that seems long, and the man pushes back his hat with an impetuous, nervous movement and runs his hand through his hair and says:

'But, dear lady, don't think so; I scarcely understand, I mistook—I—I am sorry. You see I am not used to women, to ladies—to any one lately. I am not much used to kindness, I resent it rather; I am a solitary kind of fellow, a bear, a boor, anything you like; you must overlook it.'

'Have some strawberries?' is her only reply, and she heaps a plate with the tiny wild berries and smothers them with cream, adding mischievously : 'They are rather uncultivated too, but they are nice for all that, far better than the garden ones.'

He laughs responsively, his eyes glow warmly when he laughs, as if they catch and keep the sunlight. She heaps the things carefully on the tray, stands up and waits in an undecided way, swinging her sunshade :

'Don't you hate seeing the remains of a meal?' she asks.

He laughs. 'I am afraid I am sometimes so glad to see the meal that those hyper-refinements are lost upon me.'

She walks round the slope skirting the water's edge ; he follows, shouldering his knapsack ; they go further into the wood, where the last year's fir needles carpet the ground with a warm brown ; and she finds a place where the evening sun is sending golden slants to the water's edge. She throws down her shawl and sits down ; looks up at him, and he cedes to whatever of mute invitation may have been in her brief glance.

He stretches out his hand to feel in the pocket of his knapsack, hesitates and draws it back. She divines his intention and says : 'I don't mind, at least in the open air.' He lights his pipe and she sees a package of closely written papers in the pocket. She would like to ask him where he is going, but fears he might resent it ; she never remembers before to have taken the man's feelings into consideration ; she has simply dwelt on her own as of primary importance.

'Does Fruen live in Christiania?'

She feels he asks it more for the sake of saying something than from any real interest in her.

'At present. I have an estate on the south coast, I came up for a change.'

'Does Fruen like the city?'

'I don't like any place much: they are all the same. And you?' with timidity.

'I, Fruen? I'—with a grim humour—'I am the most fruitless of all things; the thing of least commercial value to the state—a poet. I belong nowhere, the whole world is mine! Poor in all the world counts of value, and yet I am rich in all she has of best—in myself—in freedom.'

She scarcely knows why, but a shadow falls on her heart at his words. This strange man who is so self-sure, who is unaffected by her presence as no man before; to whom she is almost afraid to talk; who looks dreamily ahead at some mental picture in which she has no part, seems even as a shadow unseizable—what does she know of the working of his soul, how reach him? Her temples throb, she is unconsciously concentrating every effort of her will to draw his spirit to hers.

Suddenly there is a tremulous stirring and whispering in the foliage, a ripple across the water, a susurrus in the air, the disturbances one feels just before sundown, as if some unseen spirit is soaring across the land announcing the sun's good-night.

The silent man watches Sol's masterpiece, the silent woman watches it and him. Before them a stretch of swart green land lies low against a distant background of purple mountains, a purple almost black in its intensity. And above it a scattered mass of brazen gold clouds, flecked with vivid purple, is tossed in heaps, as if flung by some Titan's hand against the sky of aurous green—a sky that suggests a veil of filmy golden tissue dropped smoothly over a background of lettuce green. The veil is jagged at the ends and the green becomes fainter and fainter and blends into the tint of a wren's egg, changes into opal, warms again suddenly and melts into the sea in delicate misty rose. And further to the left a great bold sweep of opaque salmon and orange, and orange-pink cloud spattered with audacious violet flecks, darts upwards from the horizon to resolve into transparent nebulous filaments of colour overhead. They both give a sigh as the last wave of colour fades. An exultant feeling masters her soul, because she knows that for the space of the gorgeous colour-change they have felt together, and the knowledge brings an odd shyness with it. The dog licks her wrist in a friendly way and goes over to her master and snoozles her snout into the palm of his hand. She makes one more desperate effort, not without a sense of shamed wonder at herself, to approach him :

' Why do you say a poet is the most fruitless of all things ? '

He looks puzzled for a moment, then recalling his own remark looks at her with a fresh gleam of interest.

'Because he sees too much. Because his soul is a harp hung up in the market-place of the world. Every passer-by strikes a chord on it, most of them roughly. Because he is cursed with a dual nature, flesh and spirit always warring in him; because the very harmony of his creations springs from the discords of his temperament. Does Fruen never think? I mean think of things outside the circle of her own immediate desires?'

There is more than sarcasm in his voice, there is a wish to probe under the surface of her 'make-up,' as he puts it to himself: to get at the woman under that infernal corset.

'Sometimes!' she replies; she is not surprised, neither is she offended; he is a new type of man and she is attracted powerfully. 'I read more, I have got into a way of letting other people think for me. I used to think more when I was a girl than I do now. *A quoi bon?* Life is a bore.'

'So? why should it be? isn't that your own fault?'

'No, I don't know that it is, quite. The things I have don't satisfy me. People seldom interest me for long, and the more one thinks, the more discontented one gets.'

'But you do get discontented. That is a hopeful sign. With yourself or things?'

'Both!' With a sudden inspiration: 'Tell me something: what do you see when you get that absent look? You had it a while ago.'

He flushes this time. 'Only thoughts, Frue; thoughts that find words and glide into verses, mayhap into print, to lie on a shelf—perhaps wrap butter!'

'Oh, poetry, I hate poetry!' He turns and looks at her. 'Except folk-songs. I'd much sooner read prose. I hate bothering with metre and dodging about after the verb; one gets at the heart of the thing—at least I do—best in plain prose. I don't believe that women as a rule do like poetry as well as men. I believe we have really much less sentiment in us. No,'—with a coaxing intonation—'tell me what you see in plain prose; tell me the truth!'

He smiles, and she marvels at the softening of the stern lines and the new tone in his voice.

'The truth? Does Fruen think she could stand the truth? Truth doesn't wear a fig-leaf!'

'Fruen will try.'

There is a long silence, and then he says, half-musingly:

'Close your eyes, Fruen, and look down over all the cities of the world—look with your inner eyes, try to pierce to the soul of things; what do you see? Shall I tell you what *I* see? A great crowd of human beings. Take all these men, male and female, fashion them into one colossal man, study him, and what will you find in him? Tainted blood; a brain with the parasites of a thousand systems sucking at its base and warping it; a heart robbed of all healthy feelings by false conceptions, bad conscience, and a futile code of morality—a code that makes the natural workings of sex a vile thing to be ashamed of; the healthy delight in the cultivation of one's body as the beautiful perfect sheath of one's soul and spirit, with no shame in any part of it, all alike being clean, a sin of the flesh, a carnal conception to be opposed by asceticism. A code that has thrown man out of balance and made sexual love play far too prominent a part in life—(it ought to be one note, not even a dominant note, in the chord of human love)—a code that demands the sacrifice of thousands of female victims as the price of its maintenance, that has filled the universe with an unclean conception of things, a prurient idea of purity—making man a great sick man. Divide him into units again, drop them into their separate places, and look down at them : a hungry, ignorant crowd swarming like flies over a dust-heap in search of enough to keep them alive for the day. Look down to the market-places of the world and watch the jugglers at play ; the jugglers of religion and morality. What a motley crowd of followers each one can claim, and how they applaud with satisfaction as the gilded balls are tossed before them ! Look at the domes and spires and minarets of the houses of worship ; listen to the preachers shrieking from the pulpits, listen how their voices roll out and are lost in the chink of the money-changers' coins, and the clamour of the bourse in the great squares. See, there comes a procession headed by cardinals who spend their lives in deciding theological quibbles as futile as the famous one of " how many angels can dance on the point of a needle " ! And as it passes on with its mitres and costly robes and swinging censers, and waxen lights in silver candelabra, and trappings worth a prince's ransom, the crowd cry " Alleluia " for the space of a second, only to return to their bartering and their " Buy, buy, buy !" and the last chant of the choir is drowned by the raucous voices of the latest novelty vendor. " I am the only true church, in me seek salvation ! anathema maranatha be to him who believeth not in me ! " cry the heralds of the older creeds of the state, and their words are swallowed by a crash of cymbals, rattle of tambourines, and the swell of brass instruments and voices singing in hysterical frenzy of Jordan rivers and golden streets to the latest music-hall air. *You*, deafened by the many voices, ask which is the true belief? and a feeble voice replies to you and says : " Do good for good's sake, without thought of heaven or fear of hell," and, stepping forth, he cries that the balls are gilded ; points to the cracks in the pedestals upon which the gods stand ; and the exponents of the creeds look frightened, and the partisans of each rally round and cry their particular " Crucify him ! " There is a volley of stones, a rush of hurrying feet, a little blood, a few grey hairs, and the voice is silenced—so much for religion. And I look to the rulers of the world, and I see an emperor hold up a withered hand, and yet in that hand the threads of the destinies of nations are held as an old wife curls the flax for her distaff ; and he tangles them into a ball, and throws it down with his gauntlet to the other nations, and

says, " Fight for it ! "   And trumpets call, and the
hand trembles under the beat of marching feet and
rings with the clangour of arms ; and men leave
their ploughs, and the hammer ceases to ring on the
village anvils, and dust covers the sawdust beneath
the carpenter's bench ; and the group at the door
of the village inn is made up of red-eyed women
with tear-worn cheeks, forsaken sweethearts, senile
greybeards, and half-grown youths—thirsting for
tidings of the men who have marched from them ;
and away on the battlefields where the brethren of
Christ, the Peacemaker, meet as foes, the brown
earth is soaked with blood, and the vultures, with
gore-dripping beaks, flap heavily from dead horse
to conscious men, alike their prey ; and I see
factory doors open and troops of men and women
and children, apologies for human beings, narrow-
chested, stunted, with the pallor of lead-poisoning
in their haggard faces, troop out of them ; and as
they laugh wearily their teeth shake loosely in
their blue-white gums, and they are too tired to
wash the poison off their hands before their scanty
meals.   And I see great monopolies eating away
the substance of the people, and magnificent
chapels built in memory of railway kings who
ruined thousands of women and children, and I
say, " So much for the rulers."

' And I said to myself, " Salvation lies with the
women and the new race they are to mother."   I
sought out women I had heard of whose names
were identified with advancement ; and I found
them no whit less eager to employ every seduc-

tion at their command to win men over to their particular narrow cause, than their frivolous sister to keep him at her beck and call. And she who flaunted the white banner of purity calculated the cut of her evening frock, and enticed men to walk under her banner by the whiteness of her breast. And underneath it all I saw vanity, the old insatiable love of power that is the breath of most women's nostrils, or the physiological necessity for excitement that belongs to the wavering cycle of her being; and I found no woman, to whom, if I had said: "Love is a divine gift, it is the strength of the game of life! Come with me, work with me, be the mother of my children to come, let us try to live the broad life purely, and soberly, in like freedom for the development of the best in each of us," who would have placed her hand in mine with the courage of womanhood, sure of herself, and come. I had illusions in those days. I sought my Rachel well, I would have served my time for her patiently, but I found her not. Sometimes I thought I had found her, but it was only a mask with sawdust at the back of it; for if I buried my face in her neck to smell the sweetness of herself—faugh! she reeked of distilled perfumes and scented powders; if I uncoiled her hair it came off in my hand and the roots grew dark to mock the gold of its length; and when I spoke to her of little children she looked bored, for little children spoil one's figure and dim the lustre of one's eyes; and when I saw how skilled they were in converting their bodies into targets for men, I said: man need not trouble to woo woman, for she can calculate to the finest point the cut of her gown on her hips, the flutter of lace on her bust. She knows how to reach him at his worst by deliberate caculation of dress—and then sell herself or her daughter to the one who can pay the most for trappings to set her off. And I went amongst the advanced women—some on platforms, some in clubs, some buttonholing senators in the lobby of the senate, or cooing politics or social economy over afternoon tea ; and I knew that in hovels and cellars in the dens of the " angel makers " the foredoomed fruit-age of human mating wailed pitifully on heaps of reeking straw, sucking their lean thumbs hungrily; and no woman of the crowd of reformers had courage enough to cut the father if she knew him to be amongst her acquaintance. And still I sought amongst the petticoated crowd, I conned the inscriptions upon the banners—suffrage, purity, equal wage ; I looked underneath and I said that with some it was a pastime, but with most "suppressed sex " was having its fling ; I turned from them and went into a lighted square, and the rippling laughter of women's voices fell softly as the churring of ringdoves in my ears, soothing after the chattering shrieks of "wrongs" of the women I had left—and I was surrounded by women ; some just crossed girlhood, some alluring in the ripeness of womanhood, some old, painted into fictitious youth, making age despicable. The frou-frou of silken skirts, the tap of little heels on the pavement, the heaviness of perfumes, the touch of their hands as they slipped them under my arm or searched my pockets enervated me ; dark eyes smiled at me, and blue eyes grew deeper as they met mine, and I had to wrench myself free to save myself; asking as I fled: " With how many of these is it just selection ? Surely here is the place to begin, here, where women are on sale in a public mart." And I saw men hurrying past the place I had just quitted, with tender girls on their arms, and these all had bandages over their eyes, and I asked, " Why are they blindfolded ? " for I noticed that many peeped out under the bandages when a male step passed by, and that in all a morbid curiosity gleamed. And the men made answer : " I would keep her from eating the tree of knowledge, for she is my one ewe lamb ; I would keep her from the understanding of evil until to-morrow, when I deliver her into her husband's hands—an ignorant virgin." Her betrothed hastened up, and he too shielded her from the wanton crowd on the pavement, and as one, more bold than the rest, pressed towards the girl, he shoved her brutally aside, so that she fell and cut herself sorely ; and the women with the banners marching by that way passed her with cold indifference, for they too must be protected and kept clean at all cost ; and I marvelled anew, thinking " Verily, the price is great ! " But the Jezebel whom he had struck staggered on to her feet again, and, stepping near to him, whispered with a triumphant smile on her cracked lips : " *You* can open the book of life for her ! fitting exponent of

the text of evil! for have I not taught you? Have
not I given you a bridal gift for her and her children and her children's children, a fatal crimson
flower with far-reaching tendrils?—the *flower of
revenge* of me and my sisters. I know you well.
You have forgotten me, for I was but one of the
many embraced in a night of passion and forgotten
with the dawn of the day. Go to your unsoiled
dove; were her eyes not blindfolded, she would be
loth to take you." So much for women!

'I was but a youth, but my heart burned in me
at the problems that presented themselves to me,
and I returned home to my native place, and I
wrote down these things, and I unveiled the
hushed truths that carry betterment, and they
deprived me of my office in the state; and
woman, being a creature appreciative of the concrete, shunned me. For I had thrown aside a
chance of endowing her with a social position;
and men called me "a crack-brained poet," a
madman, and now I have learnt to lean on
myself——'

She draws a long breath that is half a crying sigh.

The band is playing a wild Hungarian dance,
and the beat of whirling feet comes down to them,
and the laughter of men and women's voices, and
away at a great distance a bell is tolling, and a
dog barking with a sharp, excited yap, yap; but it
seems to her that she is inside a circle, and that
his voice alone reaches her. She feels her corset
press her like an iron hand; she is shamed to the
depths of her soul. The spots of rouge on her

cheeks seem to sting as a sharp blow from a freshly gathered nettle; and she is conscious that she who has all her life let men care for her, and closed her eyes without thought of their trouble or what she may have done to them; that she, who would have laughed at their presuming to find fault with her, only cares now because this one 'crack-brained poet,' outcast, what you will, is the first man who has touched the underlying fibres of her nature; and she is the epitome of this class of women he lashes with his scorn! She cringes inwardly, and a dull pain stirs in her, and she queries impatiently, as so many others have done before her : What is this feeling, and from where does it come, making us the playthings of the inexplicable?

'Are you not ever lonely?' she asks.

'Yes, when I am ill. The only natural companion for man is woman. I seek now in nature what I failed to find in her. I lay my heart on the brown lap of earth, and close my eyes in delicious restfulness. I can feel her respond to me; she gives me peace without taxing me for a return. I sought that in woman, for I thought to find her nature's best product, of all things closest in touch with our common mother. I hoped to find rest on her great mother heart; to return home to her for strength and wise counsel; for it is the primitive, the generic, that makes her sacred, mystic, to the best men. I found her half-man or half-doll. No, it is women, not men, who are the greatest bar to progress the world holds.'

Her thoughts have been clamouring for words
as he speaks, and as his voice dies away she asks,
half defiantly, half timidly :

'Perhaps more of us than you think recognise
the truth of what you say. In our girlhood we
perhaps ask, but such questions are not easily
answered ; one seeks to spare youth from disillusion. And don't you think'—there is a shake
in her voice, and the man watches her, shading
his eyes with his hands—'that you are rather hard
on—us dolls? Perhaps we too have our lonely
hours, hours in which we ask ourselves what it is
we need to complete us? Perhaps we seek a key
to the enigma of our own natures, we try man
after man to see if he hold it. Do you think,
taking them on an average, that they could give
it to us? You are hard on us'—with a touch of
sadness—'for perhaps we are merely the playthings of circumstances ; contradictions, leading a
dual life, . . . our varying moods bound up with
the physiological gamut of our being. We have
been taught to shrink from the honest expression
of our wants and feelings as violations of modesty,
or at least good taste. We are always battling
with some bottom layer of real womanhood that
we may not reveal ; the primary impulses of our
original destiny keep shooting out mimosa-like
threads of natural feeling through the outside
husk of our artificial selves, producing complex
creatures.' Her voice vibrates with feeling, and
she marvels at her own words, and where she
finds expression for her thoughts. 'One layer in

us reverts instinctively to the time when we were
just the child-bearing half of humanity and no
more, waging war with the new layers that go to
make up the fragile latter-day product with the
disinclination to burden itself with motherhood.
And our powder and our paints! Aren't they
rather tributes to the decay of chivalry in your
own sex? It's not to woman but to pretty
woman man pays deference. So much'—with
bitterness—'for the dolls, as you call them, . . .
and the desexualised half man, with a pride in
the absence of sex feeling, reckoning it as the
sublimest virtue to have none, what is she but
the outcome of centuries of patient repression?
Repress and repress—how many generations has
it gone on? You must expect some return for
it—if you get the man-woman as a result! Well,
I have known some feminine men too. Isn't
feminisation a result of all civilisation, and isn't'
—with desperation—'it that perhaps you resent
most?'

She has risen to her feet, and is leaning against
a slender fir-tree; she is quivering with excitement. The man still watches her under his hand.

'I have been a coward because I have half felt
these things, but I never knew till to-day that I
could put my thoughts into words, and may be
after to-day I shall turn over a new leaf, and put
more into my life, or more of myself into it.'

Her voice is steady now, and her eyes are
shining. The man has risen to his feet, and
the steamboat passes towards the landing-stage.

They seem to have changed places, for he is watching her, and she only thinks of herself. She feels as if her inmost soul is laid bare, as if she cannot face the people, possible acquaintances on the boat, in her present mood. She is so stirred that she forgets the man near her, forgets everything save the new conception of life forming in her, her mighty need of being alone to sift the thoughts that are crowding in upon her. She lifts her gown and turns up the slope, crosses the road, crowded with chatting people, and is only then aware that he and the dog are following her. She passes the standing-place where the droschke drivers are grouped waiting for their fares, and takes the road leading back to the town. The man scans her face with surprise; somehow it seems different to him; he tries to recall the first impression it made upon him, but cannot. He is acutely conscious of the rustle of her gown, the swing of her hips, and the varying expressions that chase one another across her face. Something of her disturbance communicates itself to him. An empty droschke comes slowly up to them; as it reaches them she holds up her hand and stops it; the driver pulls up and waits. As she stands still she notices that three little white pebbles form a triangle at her feet, and that the driver is a man who has driven her before. She is searching for something to say to this man beside her, and an unreasoning anger against herself, against him, and against the mysterious forces that make it possible for an unknown vagabond—she repeats the epithet to herself, it seems to mitigate her self-shame—to disturb her; forces that she feels it is useless to struggle against, because one has no key to their origin. She notices that she is as tall as he is, and that now when she can examine him closely, he looks nervous and suffering, as if the sword is wearing the scabbard, and she feels sorry; her face softens; she smiles as she says:

'Adieu then, and thank you for everything you said.' She stoops and pats the little beast's head, and turns towards the shabby old droschke. He opens the door for her and waits, hat in hand. She steps in, and he shuts it.

'Thank you. A pleasant journey.' The wheels give one turn. 'I hope you'll find that perfect female!' she adds mischievously; it is the parting flippancy of her old self.

'Au revoir, Fruen,' is his only reply. The driver jerks the reins and urges the horse on with the peculiar noise Norsk horses seem to expect as a right. She looks back. He is still standing with the cur at his side, and something in the lonely figure standing in the quiet evening touches her. She feels a warm rush of feeling for him, a desire to be good to him. She waves her hand, and watches until he becomes a tiny speck in the twilight of the pearl-white summer night.

II

SNOW everywhere! A white world wrapped in
a snowy shroud, under a grey-white sky. What
a feast the gods are preparing; the last down of
the wild geese breasts falls softly, silently, caressingly down, as when death comes to a little child
in its sleep. A twig crackling in the wood, the
brittle snap of a branch under its weight of snow,
the rattling rush of icicles as it crashes to the
ground, the hoarse startled call of capercailzie;
every sound is as crisply distinct in the clear
stillness, as a sibilant whisper in a hushed room.
Every touch of colour, the crimson in a little lad's
muffler, as he drags his newly-painted kjelke
(hand-sled) up the hill, strikes warmly to one
as the light in the window to a wayfarer on a
murky night, or one's name on the lips of a
sleeping lover.

A great white house nestles in the hollow like
the mausoleum of a Titan under a white pall.
The sun strikes discs of light off the window
panes, and the steam of the beasts' breaths and
skins waves out from the stalls into the frosty
air to fall in feathery flakes to the ground. Every

outline is sharply defined ; there are many shades in the whiteness of the world, silver-white, golden-white, white with a grey, and white with a green in it. The sea is frozen near the land into glass-grey ridges, and further out the waves wash over the serrated edges of the last freezing ; the 'sprint' of beast, and the tell-tale impression of birds' claws mark the snow in all directions, and the heaviest animal goes with a padding step.

It is Christmas Eve ; a Sabbath stillness lies over the place. The sound of men's voices and the laughter of women float across the stillness from the farm yard. Two men are running a sheaf of wheat to the top of a pole for the birds' Christmas treat. In a country where every man is more or less a sailor, and where the driest notary can tie a 'Turk's head,' most things are done in a seaman-like way. They break into a shanty as they hoist it up. She is standing looking at them, she has on a red ski (snow-shoe) costume, hussar-braided jacket, full-pleated skirt, and knickerbockers tucked into the top of her sealskin boots. Her hair gleams brightly under her crimson cap, and her cheeks are glowing with cold and exercise. She looks a different being from the anæmic woman of three summers ago. There is a restrained energy in the very way she stands watching them. The Jomfrue is holding a little lad by the hand ; for the cripple is dead, and the children board in the village. They hoist up two more sheaves, and then one of the men asks :

'Will Fruen see how I have put up the wreaths?'
They go up to a big spare room over the bakery
and brewing houses. It has been scrubbed clean
with silver sand, and the walls are festooned with
green wreaths and flags. A monster Christmas
tree is planted in a huge feeding-tub, it is covered
with tinsel balls bobbing on elastic, fairies, and
angels, and tapers. A pile of packages are heaped
round the base.

'It's very nice, Jensen, you have made it very
pretty, you must light the tapers at seven.' And
Jensen, most daring of pilots on the coast, who
would have been a pirate in older days, laughs
with a boyish pleasure. He knows every port
in the world, spins wonderful yarns of girls who
broke their hearts for him in Boston, niñas who
stabbed themselves in Barcelona, lassies who pined
away in Glasgow, and never gets a girl in his
own town to believe him. She goes to the store-
room, praises Jomfrue's waffles and the great
pile of 'fleadcakes,' varying in tints from golden-
yellow to biscuit-brown, looks with a smile into
a big room where some women are dressing the
children for the evening, and then goes into her
own room. She has not stilled her heart-ache,
nor has she forgotten him, but she has found
a use for herself. She has turned the many spare
rooms of her big house into dormitories, where
a limited number of waifs and strays, generally
nameless, find a temporary or permanent home.
At first her friends laughed at her 'new freak,'
and gave her till Christmas to go on with it,

but when the new year went, and the summer followed the spring, and the year ran its circle, and she only paid flying visits to the city, looking stronger and bonnier each time, they allowed there might be something in it. That she would be eccentric in her way of carrying out her scheme was only to be expected, and there were both smiles and headshakings when she espoused the cause of all women, without reference to character or exhortations to repentance. It began when Captain Sörensen turned his pretty daughter out of doors. She took her in, and kept her until the trouble was over, and when Morten Ring went up to read to her, and she found the girl shaken with sobs, before the scathing power of his ranting eloquence, she took him by the collar of his coat and put him out of doors, with a definite intimation to keep off her property. Then a gypsy woman brought her newly-born in her apron, and craved admission, and so the thing grew of its own accord. It gave rise to much concern amongst the orthodox members of the various orthodox beliefs in the commune, and the pastor, as representative of the state church, felt compelled to broach the subject of service to her. He chose a sunny forenoon when the hum of early summer filled the air to ask if there was no morning service.

'No morning service!' she replied, with her great eyes dancing with mirth. 'No morning service! Why, it began at eight, and it is going on now.' And she took him out to a large bright

room in an outbuilding. Half a dozen women
sat at spinning-wheels, two worked at weaving
machines in the end of the room, and some
children rolled about the floor on rugs, and fought
and chuckled as children will. And the rhythmical
tread of the women's feet, and the whirr of the
wheels, mingled with the wooden beat of the
weaving machine, and the twitter of the birds
through the open windows from the wood at
the back. And she swung the children up in
her long strong arms, opened a great press, and
showed him neat piles of linen and flannel, towels
woven after the old patterns, that are better than
the new ; flax from Russia, and balls of fine yarn,
and a ledger with orders for work.

'To-day is Wednesday, Herr Pastor, your
church has been closed since Sunday, except
for the christening of a baby, and the funeral of
a granny ; mine is open every day, and all day,
and my sinners laugh and sing, and find new
hopes and self-reliance in measure as they better
their work, and then chicks will grow up to be
proud of their mothers. For'—with a mischievous
smile—'the fathers were only an accident. I can
trust you and society to look after them, to
welcome the erring rams to the fold; the mothers
are my look out. Fathering is a light thing to
the man, as light as the plucking of a flower by
the wayside ; he enjoys its colour, its perfume,
then flings it aside, and goes his way and forgets
it. The act of the butterfly that flits from flower
to flower, deposits the pollen on the blossom, and

flies to another. The flower withers and dies, and the seed bursts the ovary, and drops into the kind earth, sleeps through the winter, and wakes to life with the kiss of spring. But the human flower has to live and carry the burden of its conception through months of fear, winters, and summers, and springs of disgrace. Yet she is the flower of humanity; he, but the accessory. Yes, I know what you are going to say, Herr Pastor, I see it on your lips, it's a stock church phrase, "Man is the head of the woman, etc." St. Paul had something to do with that heresy, hadn't he—well, I don't believe him a bit. Her maternity lifts her above him every time. Man hasn't kept the race going, the burden of the centuries has lain on the women. He has fought, and drunk, and rioted, lusted, and satisfied himself, whilst she has rocked the cradle and ruled the world, borne the sacred burden of her motherhood, carried in trust the future of the races. And, if she has sometimes failed in it?—well, she was lonely, and there was no one to point her a way. The only sign-post man ever raised for her was: " Please me, that is the road to my heart ; curb the voice of your body, dwarf your soul, stifle your genius and the workings of your individual temperament, ay, regulate your conscience in accordance with mine and my church, be good, and I will feed you and clothe you in return for your services ; what more can a woman desire ? " And if sometimes the untamed spirit looked out of a woman's eyes, and she spurned his offer, he took care to cry: "She is a traitor to the sex I have moulded in my hand for centuries!" And if her own sex joined in the cry, small blame to them to curry favour with their bankers. Spinning is a good thing for women, they always want something to keep time to their vagabond thoughts, for in measure as they possess the dear old devil, in the same measure they need excitement. Monotony is the biggest trump card in the hand of the devil when his design is the seduction of woman.'

'But does Fruen think it is wise to encourage them in, in ——'

'Promiscuous mothering? Fie, Herr Pastor, you know I don't, but you would be a much more clever man than you are, and I a much more clever woman, if you could allot the measure of blame or responsibility. Take Strine. A lump of emotional inclination, without a grain of reasoning power or resistance; the daughter of a drunken father and an epileptic mother; at times affectible as an aspen leaf to a wind-puff—and yet not a bad mother. What do you and the commune do for such as she? You give her a few pence a week, place her in the poor-house in an atmosphere of evil talk and worse associations, or let her tramp the roads or sink to beggary—and insinuating tinkers. I think music and dancing and laughter and work lead to decent living; a fig for your stool of repentance! I know you don't agree, Herr Pastor, but we are doing very well; my colony of sinners almost pay for themselves—

Svendsen '—the pastor gasps with horror—'is a good ploughman, not half a bad carpenter, and he makes decent boots for the chicks. You never could do anything with him, because you preached temperance at him and gave him his tobacco rolled up in a tract. He gets his ale and his tobacco here in payment for his work.'

The pastor is only a mortal man, with a very plain wife and a large family, and when she turns the battery of her luminous laughter-lit eyes on him, he may be forgiven for forgetting his homily; besides, her offering is the biggest in the parish.

' Will Herr Pastor take Fruen some peas and a couple of ducks ? ' and the pastor was evasive in his replies to the inquiries of his female parishioners as to how she took his advice.

' Poor man, he 's very susceptible ! ' she says to Aagot with a laugh, as they watch his white ruff vanish down the path.

She is justly proud of her success ; the whirr of wheels and the laughter of children, the farm upon which they all work in the brief harvest time, the necessity of watchfulness, fill her life. There is a sense of power in directing it. And if in quiet hours, when the swallows wing southwards, or the storm lashes the waves into leaping white-crested horses, and the rain beats against the windows of her house, she may have felt a kind of loneliness creep over her, some call upon her time is sure to disperse it.

She goes up to her own room ; nothing reveals

a woman's character more fatally than her bedroom. There is the room that is almost ascetic in its bareness ; the room that has a smell of clean linen and lavender, the very ornaments of which are treasured from girlhood, the old workbox, water-colours and girlish souvenirs ; attachment to things for association's sake, explaining the expression of youth that is still in the face of the matron who owns it. Then there are rooms all mirrors and Cupids, rose-silk quilts and lace, and ribbons, and heavy perfume, like the stage bedroom of a cocotte, so that one longs to open the window and thrust out one's head and draw a long breath. Her room is a large room with four windows looking south and west ; her arm chair is turned to the southern windows looking seawards and roadways as if some day some one might come that way. Everything in the room is white, from the narrow white bed to the big white wardrobe with glass doors, showing the shelves with their store of dainty underclothing and the row of boots and shoes on the lower shelf. There is something odd about it, a sort of frank revealing of the woman's self ; it is spotless, and clean, and attractive.

There is a writing table between the windows, and a man's head in a frame. It has been cut out of a magazine and mounted. Her crack-brained poet ! His last book of vagabond ditties and a pile of reviews are lying on her desk. She looks at it wistfully and then dresses and goes down. Many sleighs will dash up with a merry jingle to share her Christmas cheer. A magistrate from a neighbouring district, a young doctor, a solicitor, and a big timber merchant, all bachelors with a keen appreciation of the comfortable income of the lonely Frue with the estate on the fjord. The daylight is fleeting rapidly, the curtains are drawn, and the birch logs are sizzling in the great white porcelain stove with a fragrant wood-wild smell. She slides back the door and lets the firelight dance into the dim room; everything in it is old, for she has merely added to the antique furniture she found in it, and it holds treasure dear to any antiquary. A case is filled with silver quaint bridal cups and rings and marvellous filigree brooches; the flame dances over the gold dragons on some leather chairs. There are spoils in it from all the ports of the world. She looks very big in her crimson gown, with its long full folds and tiny border of sable. It is spun and woven on her own place, and she is very proud of it; she has put sheep on a rocky bit of land and the wool is dyed after an old recipe. She is pleasantly tired, for she rises early and her self-imposed duties are many. Her thoughts go back to that midsummer day, three years and a half ago, when the contemptuous words of a strange man stung her to self-scrutiny. She can see a gorgeous glowing picture of that summer scene, the water and rocks and trees, the man and the cur, in the heart of the fire. She looks back to herself and laughs softly at her discontent and weariness and the trouble she used to take to find amusement. She has not reached her present stage without

weariness and discouragement, but considering the
time the result is marvellous. It has cost her
pains and anxiety to set her scheme for helping
wretched sisters out of the mire. She had to cut
down many luxuries to set it in working order;
and she has discovered that the very qualities that
made her social success, her personal magnetism,
have stood to her here. She has witched the men
of the district to help her in many ways and been
indifferent or politely disagreeable when the
women interfered. She has found scope for the
varied sides of her nature. Her man of business
croaked of expenditure and disaster, and she
laughingly promised to reconsider her refusal of
himself and his flourishing concern when bankruptcy came. He is forced to acknowledge that
the thing almost pays for itself and that his
chances are remoter than ever. Jomfrue has been
her loyal companion; she is cautious and not
emotional, and it takes tact to find work fitted for
each.

She has looked out eagerly for every scrap of
news about him or his books. Men have come
and wooed and ridden away; something tells her
to wait, just wait. She scarcely knows what she
expects, sometimes she tells herself nothing—and
yet better so. Sometimes at night she wakes and
a shadow drops on her soul and weighs her down,
and in the gloom she can see his face staring
wildly, wild-eyed, pale-lipped, with dank, tossed
hair. She has a fancy that she gets nearer to him
in her sleep, that her spirit finds his and draws

him to her by force of will and love. But not
always sadly : once she dreamt that she was out
in a boat with him, out in a sunlit harbour, he and
she alone, and as they looked back to the land, a
crowd of people were there, and the women called
her names and beckoned to him to go back.
Their sail was shaped like a silver crescent and
every rope was twined with moss and roses, and
their oars were like the forked pinions of a giant
white bird ; and they sailed out through the
breakers and the rocks, and his face was lit with a
strange light as if his fancies burned through it as
light through a crystal cruse ; and the dream look
stole over it, and he began to improvise a song, a
wild exultant song of self, the glory of solitude,
individual life and the love of one woman ; forgetting aught else. And she was forced to take
the helm and steer through the shoals, out with
the wind to the open sea towards an island of
delight. When they came there she cast anchor,
a golden anchor, and threw out a net that gleamed
like spiders' webs in the dew of morning, and she
hauled in a shoal of silvern fish with scales glittering as mother-of-pearl and opals ; and once when
it was too heavy she asked his help and he gave
it, marvelling at what she had done ; forgetting to
thank her in the inspiration of a new song of
Home. And when they had eaten and sat resting in a grotto, he was still singing, and she was
the goddess of his muse, the quell of living waters
out of which he drew fresh strength for new lays.
And the sea-birds dipped and mewed over the

waters, and one hovering near her cried : 'I am older than many cycles, I have seen much, I have followed many ships and dipped in many harbours. I have flown with the brent geese before the north wind and exchanged tales. It was I who whispered Hans Andersen the tale of the Fisher Maiden as he sat on the strand one day. He got the credit, but it was I who told him, for I knew her. I knew her when she dived 'neath the waves, a glad sea-child, and I saw her the morning she waded on shore with her pretty new feet, and I saw her wince as the knife-dart pierced them at each step, for the love of the Earth-prince. Many a night when the shadows danced in the moonlight she stole from his side and laved her feet in the sea of her childhood ; as women dream of girlhood days before sorrow came with the burden of their love. And your poet too is an earth-prince, and the price you pay will be even as great as the Sea Maiden's, for that is the toll women pay to poets—they are the sheep that are shorn of the wool that the poet weaves into a web of fanciful hues——'

Then she woke and laughed with moist eyes, for she knows that it is only in her dreams that such fancies come to her ; in her waking hours she is a practical creature with little imagination. The dusk draws closer round the room, and she is filled with tender, regretful thoughts of the man who woke her out of her blind sleep; she wonders where he is spending his Christmas, and whether any one will think of a gift for him ; she fancies him alone, when the Christmas tree is lit in all the homes, and a yearning tenderness fills her heart ; she steps to the window and looks out into the gloom ; no moon is visible, but many lights gleam across the snow, and she remembers that the Christmas candles are lit in the windows above, and the tapers must be soon kindled in the tree ; so she gathers him into her heart again, for she has laid aside dreaming, and goes out to the kitchen where Aagot reigns supreme. She looks in without being seen. Jensen has a child on each knee, singing :

> 'An elephant sitting on a hickory stick,
> Picking his teeth with a horseshoe pick,
> And a by baby by——'

He gives a rather free translation of it in Norsk, adding, 'I learnt that from a Boston lady,' an exclamation which is met with shouts of laughter and a broadside of witty chaff from the cattle-girl. She is in gala dress, and wears all her quaint silver ornaments ; she is stirring the Christmas porridge with a 'spirtle,' made from a tiny fir tree. Aagot is brewing ale posset, for servants and guests share alike this evening. Her heart warms as she looks round her big kitchen, filled with people all dependent on her in some way, and she steps forward into the light to be greeted by the cooing of the children.

. . . . .

The third Yule day has drawn to a close. There has been no need of a snow plough, for the sleighs coming and going with jingling bells have kept the roads clear. She has held open house, and had little time for thought. There will be no regular work until the New Year has gone, and it is just at such times her people need looking after. It is late, and they have all gone to bed ; she and Aagot have been talking, and the latter has just gone up stairs. She has pulled up the blind ; there is a bright moon, and every bush looks as if fretted in silver. She is disinclined to go to bed, and paces up and down the long room ; she keeps listening for something, and a feeling, not the inexplicable dread that chills one's flesh and makes one's heart throb with a sick beat in lonely rooms, rather a suspensive presentiment, oppresses her. Suddenly she stops, with a stifled scream, in the middle of the room, and stares at the window ; two gleaming eyes meet hers. She is too frightened to stir ; then there is a whine and a scratching of paws as the dog—she sees now it is a dog— slips back off the frozen snow on the low window sill.

She steps to the window and raps on the pane ; the dog answers with a yelp, and looks up with one ear flapping. She catches her breath, and a sick fear seizes her ; she runs to the garden room, unbolts the door and whistles ; the dog comes trotting up lamely. There is a bit of paper tied to its collar, she undoes it and reads : 'Send kariol to old road through wood beyond church on K—— road.' 'Seven miles away, he must be hurt ; why did the dog come to me ?' There is one farm and the posting station between. They may have gone to bed at the farm, and there is a savage dog at the posting station; he probably kept the little brute off. She stoops to pat her, and the little beast trots backwards and forwards and whines; she tries to seize her, but she shows her teeth and snarls. She runs upstairs to Aagot's room, the latter is half undressed. She explains rapidly. Aagot says, taking up her skirt:

'I'd best go down and rouse up Henrik, he can take the dog with him.'

'No, no, I am going myself. I know who it is; come down and help me to put in a horse, and get a blanket, and some brandy, and a hot water tin; oh, do hurry, Aagot!'

She is the woman again whom Aagot has grown to look upon as a memory, for she is quivering with excitement and impatience. The stolid little woman eyes her with grave disapproval.

'Fruen must not go alone; take Henrik; it is late, and there are often rough tramps!'

'We are losing time as it is, Aagot! I tell you I know who it is, it's the man in the picture in my room. Supposing your Swede were lying there, *you* wouldn't hesitate! It would be quite twenty minutes before you could rouse Henrik. Give the dog something whilst I get on my things and light the lantern.' Something of her eagerness communicates itself to the other woman, and a few minutes later they are crossing the yard towards the stable. The dog keeps trotting restlessly about, whining pitifully.

'Take Brownie, Fruen—she's sure-footed—and

the double sleigh!' She holds up the lantern as they search for the harness. They both start as a voice calls sharply :

'Who's there, who's in the stable?' and the cattle-girl appears at the door with a lantern slung round her neck, armed with a two-pronged fork. She grins and shows all her white teeth as she sees them: 'O Fruen, I thought it was thieves; that Henrik had left the door unbolted. I am sleeping in the stall to-night. Brindle has dropped a calf; Fruen is lucky to have a heifer calf so early, a fine stout calf, and the mother is doing well.' She has been getting down harness as she talks on, from a kind of delicacy to avoid appearing inquisitive.

'You are shaking, Frue. We'll do this if you go in for the things,' says Aagot. 'Lord! what creatures we women are! The Lord send her safe back!' she prays as she strives with buckles and straps. The cattle-girl is as strong as a man ; she pulls out the sleigh, backs the horse, and fastens the nose of the great bearskin to the front of the sleigh, and the claws at the back.

'Come here, Bikkje' (little bitch), she calls to the dog ; her quick intelligence has grasped something of the case. 'You're a queer bred 'un, you are, but you might be as true as the best of 'em !' she calls in her odd dialect.

'If Fruen is going alone, best slip Bulldoggen ; he'd frighten the devil with that ugly snout of his!'

'Ay, Gunhild, you might do that ; but the Bikkje ?'

' He won't harm her if I pat her ; here, Bikkje; here, little woman ! '

She comes out and steps in ; Gunhild hands her the reins, and Aagot fastens the bearskin, and the dog limps alongside, and the bulldog follows, and they are off. The two women watch her till she turns round the wood. The Jomfrue's lips move : ' The Lord guide her safely through the dark places ! '

' Go in, Jomfrue, and keep up the fires ; I 'll warm my coffee kettle, and give me a bottle of ale for Brindle. Ale is the best thing for a lady in her condition. Go in and don't be foolish.'

．　　　．　　　．　　　．　　　．　　　．

She drives as in a wild dream through an enchanted world, such as one has read of in fairy tales, a world in which the snow-queen and the frost-king and the rime-elves reigned and the woods are witched. The snow glistens as if tons of diamond dust had been scattered over it, and the moon shines full on the sea to the left, then the road swerves to the right, and winds through the wood. The firs and pines grow thickly on each side of her. There is not a whisper in the air, for the runlets are frozen, and hang in crystal spikes over the rocks and boulders that lie here and there. Each tree stretches out its arms laden with snow, with a fringe of green underneath and crystal bugles of glistening ice. A funeral has passed that way, and branches of fir and ivy leaves lie at intervals on the white road. It touched her painfully, and she gave a great deep sob, and sent the whip smartly across Brownie's flanks. They dart ahead, and when they reach the foot of the hill a pitiful howl reaches her, answered by a deep bark from Bulldoggen. She looks back away down the white road; a yellow brown speck toils wearily on three legs; she stops, and when the faithful little beast reaches her, she stoops and seizes her by the scruff of the neck, and drags her up on to her lap. She whines and resigns herself, and they dash on again.

The bells jingle merrily as they glide past the sleeping farm on the left, past the posting station, where a hound bays deeply as they glide by, past the ferry where the fjord is frozen over— a strange quiet drive, skimming along with the horse's feet sinking noiselessly into the soft over-snow, and the straight pine trunks rising like the masts of ice-bound ships in a frozen sea. She stoops and kisses the top of Bikkje's head; she grudges Brownie a breathing spell. At length they reach the wood, and she can see the ruins of the old church sacred to Mary in pre-Lutheran times; the snow is blown by the wind into fantastic shapes about the tombstones, as if the dead beneath had risen and found it cold, and huddled to sleep in their shrouds again. The old road leads to the right. Bikkje is getting excited.

'All right, little one!' she whispers; 'we'll soon be there!'

The disused road is uneven, and the sleigh goes down on one side; there is not a sign of a footstep. She lets Brownie find her way, and fastens one end of a long silk scarf to the dog's collar. Her heart is beating painfully, surely he must be near here, she is sick with suspense, and she keeps her eyes on the dog. There is a way to the right in summer, and there is a heap of timber and brushwood piled into a stack in there. Turning will be impossible if she goes further, she halts and holds the dog by the end of the scarf; the latter is bristling with impatience, and makes frantic efforts to get loose. She undoes the skin and gets down, her ankles sink in the loose snow, the dog strains, and as she advances she can see the mark of her paws, so she lets her go and darts forward herself, knocking against the branches in her haste, and scattering the icicles with a clatter like hailstones, and in a second she is on her knees beside him. He is sitting with his back to the brushwood, fast asleep, with his chin buried in the collar of his fur-lined coat.

His face looks ghastly under his peaked cap, Bikkje is licking his hand, and she moans and croons over him, and tries to rouse him; she shakes him, he moans stupidly, and half opens his lids only to close them again. She springs up to run for her flask, when she notices that one boot is lying next him, he has taken it off and wrapped his foot in a plaid muffler. 'That explains it,' she reasons as she darts back, 'he wrenched his foot and took off the boot; how will I get him into the sleigh?' She plunges into the snow, seizes Brownie's head, and strains and pulls, and turns the sleigh and backs it as near the path as possible.

Bikkje is licking his face, and he lifts one hand in feeble protest. She kneels and forces some spirit through his lips; it makes him cough and rouses him. He looks up stupidly, with the tears running down his cheeks. 'Drink!' she says, and this time he takes it and drains the cup. She is afraid the drowsiness will steal over him again; she says slowly and distinctly:

'You must lean on me, and try to get to the sleigh, do you hear?'

'Yes,' but he makes no effort to rise. She shakes him, Bikkje growls. He tries to rise, but presses on his sore foot, and falls back with a moan.

'My God!' wringing her hands. 'What shall I do?'

She picks up his boot, valise, and stick, and runs back to the sleigh; the moon has gone in behind a cloud, and the wood is dark and shadow-filled, and there is no sound save the jingle of the bells when Brownie shakes her head or stamps her feet. She unclasps her cloak and throws it on the seat, and darts back as a crimson shadow through the gloom.

He is lying as she left him, she stoops, and seizing him by the shoulders, turns him round; the ground slopes towards the sleigh, but it is a good way, and she is going to try to drag him there. She crosses the hurt foot over the other ankle, gets him into a sitting position, and puts her arms under his and begins to drag him down. The blood rushes to her face, she thanks heaven it is over snow. She strains patiently, looking back over her shoulder to see that she does not get out of line with the sleigh ; props him against it, goes round to the other side, gets in and bends over him. He groans, and she forces some more brandy through his teeth ; he drinks, the movement, possibly the pain, has roused him ; he turns his head and tries to see her ; Bikkje barks excitedly.

'Try to get in, the sleigh is very low, don't try to stand, try to sit up on it, then I'll manage.'

She puts her arms under his armpits and tries to raise him ; he does succeed in getting in, he sees what is wanted of him, and manages to get on to the seat. She puts the blanket and valise under his feet, fastens the skin on his side; Bikkje has got in of her own accord. He leans back exhausted. She leads Brownie to the end of the road, turns her head homewards, gets in and gathers up the reins. The moon is out again weaving light as with a silver shuttle. She looks at his face; the outlines are sharp as bleached bone, the eyes are sunken, and the same helpless childlike expression that touched her the first time is more accentuated than ever. Brownie needs no guiding, she scents home, and knows every turn of the way. She throws back her cloak from her shoulders, and passes her arm round him and draws his head on to her shoulder. 'Tzuk, tzuk, Brownie, old girl!' she urges, without looking up.

'He must have been ill,' she thinks, and she croons over him. 'Oh, my poor love, my poor, poor love !' She remembers how she has wished

all through the changing moons that have waxed
and waned since they parted in the twilight of
that eventful white summer night, wished with a
strength that was prayer to have him again.
Some of the strange dread of fate, the fetich fear
that lies deeper in our souls than our new religion
or civilised codes, wakes in her, and she whispers
to herself, with a dread chilling her heart : ' Have
I wished him, willed him harm, by wishing him to
myself, wished another fate than destiny held in
store.'   And she makes a sort of bargain with
fate to suffer anything if only he be spared her ;
this vagabond, lost on a summer night and found
in the moonlit snow ; and a hot tear splashes from
her lashes on to his face, she bends and rubs it off
with a caressing touch of her cheek, telling herself
he will never know.

It is warm under her cloak, and her body is one
glow of heat; his half-frozen limbs sting him as he
begins to thaw again.   They pass the ferry :
' Tzuk, tzuk, Brownie, old girl !'   Soft little flakes
are beginning to fall, they touch her face like shy
cool fingers, and she feels in her heart that she
would gladly drive on for ever thus with his head
on her breast.   The idea comes to her, ' if her
sleeping friends could only see her,' and she laughs
an odd exultant laugh as she thinks how they lie
tucked under their eider downs, whilst she is
gliding through the white woods to the rhythm of
bells and light of moonbeams in crystal lustres,
with her prince asleep on her heart.   He stirs,
she looks down, his eyes are wide open, and gaze

wonderingly up at her. There is no recognition in them. She is glad, and yet there is a little sting of pain in the knowledge. She forgets that she looks big and bonny, with clear eyes and glowing cheeks, and that the waves of her hair under her fur-trimmed cap are frosted with rime. He rubs his cheek against the fur, and smiles drowsily.

'Are you the Snow Queen?'

'Perhaps. Shut your eyes and sleep, and when you wake you'll know.'

'I do know lillemor' (motherkin), 'only I forgot.'

Her joy changes to alarm; he is wandering back to snow queens and the little mother of early childhood. She urges on the mare with sharp jerk of rein and encouraging cries, and she answers and flies ahead scattering the loose snow like foam. A light gleams at the turn of the wood near home, and as she nears it Gunhild cries, with a tone of relief in her voice:

'God be praised, Frue, I was going to leave Brindle and take the road after you.'

She springs on to the back of the sleigh with her lantern swinging at her waist. 'Jomfrue has been on her knees ever since,' she says, as they drive up to the door.

Aagot rushes out; the cattle-girl gets down.

'I'll take Brownie out, Frue, she's very warm; he won't hurt to wait a second!' She unharnesses the mare and leads her to the stable, they can hear her talk to her as she bustles about.

They wait in silence until she comes out and unfastens the bearskin.

'His foot is hurt, Gunhild, mind it!'

'No fear, Fruen, I'll take his shoulders.' She passes her strong arms under him; she is as used to handling animals as other women babies, to moving great tubs of mash and carrying huge trusses of hay.

Jomfrue takes his feet and they carry him in. She follows, her shoulder is cramped and her hand has gone to sleep, and her head throbs when they get into the warm air. They carry him upstairs, and the blood rushes to the cowgirl's face, and she breathes a bit hard when they reach the top. She makes an effort and lifts him on to the small bed. A bright streak of flickering light darts across the floor from the oven and the sizzle of wood and smell of spiced wine fill the room pleasantly. Some blankets are warming near the stove.

'He's a long fine-built chap, if he had any flesh on his bones!' she remarks, drawing a long breath with her hands on her hips and the eye of a connoisseur in beasts; then turning to Aagot:

'You see to Frue, she mustn't take cold, she'll be wanted by-and-by. I'll see to him,' with a significant look. They leave the room and she unrolls the plaid, cuts off his sock with the scissors hanging to her belt, and feels his ankle like a bonesetter:

'Ai yai! that was a bad wrench.'

She feels it with the tip of her fingers, he winces and groans:

'So oh, lad, so oh, that's better, he's coming to.'

Living alone among beasts as she does, she has a habit of talking aloud. She lifts his head and forces some of the spiced wine through his teeth. She is more decisive than tender, and some of it runs down his chin and neck; it rouses him and he drinks eagerly.

'That's the man, drink it up, and then we'll get you into the blankets.' She is taking off his clothes.

'Lean on the other foot and help yourself! Uf! men are like calves, if they've got a limb they mustn't use, that's the one they'll want to put to the ground.' She pulls him up and gets off his coat; he stares about vacantly.

'Where am I, how did I get here? Hey, Bikkje!'

'You're where the calf was when he got in the clover field. Pull out your arms, man. Lord! you're a skinful o' bones like a calf after the scour. You must have had water gruel for your Yule cheer.'

The wine with its fume of cardamoms and nutmeg, the strong smell of cows and stable from her clothes, and the shooting pain confuses him; he does not answer, only fights feebly against her. She laughs and handles him like a young kid, strips him stark naked without paying the slightest heed to his remonstrances and rolls him unceremoniously in a blanket.

Jomfrue enters just as she is picking up his shirt from the floor.

'Lord sake, Gunhild, I put a shirt out of the poor cupboard.'

The cow-girl laughs : 'Not a shirt he wants yet awhile. I'll come and put one on if you're shy about it. Get some strips of old linen and dip them in cold water and wind round his foot. I'll see to Brownie and put up the sleigh and Henrik nor no one need know how he got here. Send for the old doctor by the six boat. He's more like a vet than a doctor for creatures, but he can hold his tongue. I know the old doctor. He swears by Fruen, and he's worth ten of that other whipper-snapper.'

She steals downstairs. She rises with the dawn and she has done the round of her work each day ; drunk her share of raw spirit in honour of the Yule ; danced vigorously each festival evening and had no sleep for two nights. Yet she makes no complaint; she is true to her nature with its splendid loyalty, sturdy independence and stubborn pride, and about as much understanding of conventional morality as the first best cow amongst her flock. She is never in the house except when the big bell rings to meals, and she brooks no interference ; it is only on rare occasions where strength is wanted that she lends a hand, and she is proud of the reliance placed in her. She comes up at five with some coffee and rusks to Jomfrue ; some bits of hay are sticking in her hair, for she has lain down with the newly-arrived calf for a brief sleep.

She stands and looks down at him, looks at the

palm of one of his hands, but makes no remark, and only whispers:

'Did Frue leave the note ready? That's right, I'll send Henrik. Is she asleep?'

The big house is alive with the bustle of the day. The adze rings in the wood-shed, the Swedish gardener is whistling at his carpenter's bench, for that is his winter work, and the women sing as they spin.

The jingle of bells sounds through the clear air and the doctor's kariol dashes up. He is driving a wicked black mare from the Hallingdal, half thorough-bred, that no one else can handle. He must harness, unharness and hold her while she is groomed, and once when he was away she held the yard at bay for two days, tore up two sacks of oats, and roused the village with her wild whinnying. And when he tried his first breaking, she bit off two of his fingers; and they tell yet how he and she fought it out for a day and a half and how the old doctor laid a spell on her. There is the usual scene of tramping and plunging, tossing mane and streaming tail, dogs barking and men calling: 'Look out!' before Zwarten (Black one) is safe in a stall. She watches the scene from the bedroom window and goes to the door to meet him.

'Well, what have we here? Where's your colour?' pinching her cheek. The old doctor does as he pleases. He looks down at the man in bed; his face is flushed and he is tossing his head from side to side. He feels the foot.

'That'll get all right in time! This is more serious'; he listens to his breathing, covers him up and takes out his thermometer.

'He's in for pneumonia, and by all tokens he's not long out of it. Hey, Bikkje! What the deuce are you doing there? You go down and get me a glass of that old port of yours, and a boy to ride back with me and I'll have a talk with Jomfrue about the patient.' He pushes her gently outside the door; she goes down and stands at the window looking out at the winter scene; she does not hear him come in.

'Well, Princess, who is he?' She utters his name with a rush of colour, and the old doctor purses his mouth into a whistle! 'Phew! that wild eagle, well he's like Zwarten, every one mightn't care to tackle him, but there's race in the fellow, and that's everything. There's no reckoning on women; they give the mitten to a fellow with a solid banking account, and set their hearts on a fellow that flashes like a comet and is about as seizable.'

'Well, it's like some men's taste in horseflesh, doctor!'

He laughs genially. 'True, dear lady. How did he get here? He couldn't put that foot to the ground, and he wasn't fit for much walking when it happened.'

She gave him the facts in outline.

'I know the place. How did you get him into the sleigh?'

'Dragged him!'

'The devil photograph me, did ye now! Ay, what did the old doctor tell ye : throw aside those infernal stays, take exercise and you'd be a grand woman !—and so you are—I'll come back to-night. Trust the old doc. to pull your crazy poet through for you! Only patience!'

. . . . . .

The new year has come and gone ; twice death has poised on its sable wings over the great house, and then flapped heavily further, seeking its prey elsewhere.

The place has been hushed in silence, the spinning wheels stilled, and the women have worked in whispers, and the sleighs have dashed by like phantom vehicles without their bells. Gunhild has told them how Death came once before in the time of a mad Englishman, who had the estate before Fruen's husband came in for it : related strange tales of his death and great funeral. But now he is coming back to strength. He is beginning to ask questions ; the old doctor parries them adroitly, but he has teased more out of Jomfrue than she imagines. What is that whirring sound ? he asks, and his eyes sparkle as she tells him of the women and children, and the school Fruen is going to have when they are bigger, and how everything possible is to be made on the place, and how they grow most of their own food, and how Fruen hopes to revive many of the old home industries. And for the twentieth time he asks how did he get here ? It was a chance, for he and a chum used to send Bikkje down from their mountain hut with messages to the farms in the valley.　Did she come here, and who fetched him? and Jomfrue evades a reply.　He has asked so often, and to-day he is to see this gracious lady. This description of the colony of women managed by a woman, going their own way to hold a place in the world in face of opinion, has fired his fancy—a wonderful song is singing in him, the rhymes fit and the verses round off, and he marvels at it himself as it works out.　He fancies this song is the silver key to a golden casket, in which a rare conception waits, the best thing he has ever done, a great poem, 'an epic of the new'; and he feels a stream of sunlight flood his inner soul, and he is watching it, when a knock at his door rouses him.　She enters, tall and gracious and strong, in her crimson, homespun gown, with large clear eyes shining steadily, and her clear skin flushed, and Bikkje at her heels.

She has pictured this meeting hundreds of times, fancied it on a steamer, at a friend's house, up on some fjeld tour—fancied how his eyes would light up with astonishment at the transformation in her, and how she would tell him that his words had acted as the tap of a wizard's wand, and now she is face to face with her 'crack-brained poet,' whose head has been pillowed on her shoulder all through a witching white drive (she has felt it ever since), over whose pillow she has watched, catching the strange stray words of his delirium; she has had to pause outside the door to still the beating of her heart before entering, and his eyes meet hers without a trace of recognition. He looks very wan and white, with his cheek and jaw bones showing sharply, and his great eyes sunken.

'Words won't thank you, dear lady, for all you have done for me. I don't understand it, I am not used to——'

She disengages her hand gently.

'To attempting an impossible walk, getting nearly frozen in the snow and catching cold, and doing all manner of foolish things. Now I should have thought those were quite characteristic of you.'

He flushes and smiles with quaint embarrassment. She has brought a bundle of papers and reviews with her.

'Now that you are better, I thought perhaps you would like to look at these, and I wondered if you wanted to write to any one. You must tell Aagot anything you want.'

'I hope I won't need to trespass on Fruen much longer——'

'You won't stir till you are quite well—you would only get a relapse, and we are quite proud of our patient. Ah, here comes the doctor!'

She goes to the window, and something in her attitude strikes a chord in his memory; he tries to recall it, and afterwards, when she turns laughingly to the doctor, he notices it again; it worries him, makes him nervous.

Downstairs the doctor turns her sharply to the light and scrutinises her face. Her eyes meet his

fearlessly . . . he feels her pulse and says, quiz-
zically :

'That's right, Princess, one bundle of nerves in a
family is quite enough. What are you going to
do with him now that he is on the road to re-
covery ? There is good stuff in the fellow, but he
wants ballast.'

She colours vividly and says :

'What can I do, doctor ?'

'A-ah, that's not for me to say. Women are
kittle cattle, but — you've got a queer one to
manage up there. I know his kith and kin.
Yes,' in reply to her start of surprise, 'I knew his
mother, and I guess his father, and there is race in
the lad, and heart—and brains, judging from the
way the penny-a-liners go for him. But they
were queer ones to drive, and devils to go off at a
tangent. If you take him in hand, you've got to
give him a loose rein and leave the stable door
open. He'll come home all right ; but don't put
the curb on. I've got a soft spot,' patting her
shoulder, 'in my heart for you, Princess, and I
know the breed.'

He buttons up his fur-lined coat, and lifting his
glass, 'Skaal! your luck!' and his keen grey eyes
twinkle under his bushy brows, and his rugged,
coarse-grained old face is softened for a spell.

Next day, when the afternoon was drawing to a
close, Aagot came to her :

'Wouldn't Fruen go up and read to him for a
while? He is as restless as a new-weaned child,
he keeps asking about Fruen. My head is light

with his questions, and he's working himself into a fair fever.'

She knocks, and goes in ; the papers are tossed over the bed and floor, his eyes are feverishly bright and his face is flushed, and the pillows are awry. He smiles like a pleased child when he sees her.

'I hear from Aagot that you are misbehaving, and I have come to scold,' she says, standing next the bed.

'I don't mind'—with a touch of petulant audacity—'that is better than not seeing you at all.'

She tries to look severe, and arranges the pillows without reply.

'Don't be vexed with me, dear lady'—with sudden penitence—'but Jomfrue Aagot, good as she is, is not entertaining, and the time is long, and I can't sleep!'

'Shall I read to you?'

'Oh no, talk to me. Tell me about this scheme of yours. Jomfrue's version is a fairy tale.'

She sits and tells him of her plans, dwells on the humorous phases of its development until the room is filled with shadows, and she has an uncomfortable sense of his nearness. She rises, saying:

'To-morrow you must come downstairs, I believe you will be better there.'

'Must you go, Fruen?'

'Yes, I must go my rounds, see women and chicks, and finish the day. Now, good-night—Aagot will bring the light—sleep well!'

Early the next afternoon he is helped down, and propped on the couch with pillows. He looks round the big room.

'I am like the beggar boy who wandered into the castle of the Fay. Where is the Princess? Aagot, thou woman of the silent tongue, thou inscrutable keeper of the secrets of the Princess, where is she?'

'If ever I saw such a restless thing! You'll hurt your foot and be another three weeks.' (There is a significant stress in her voice.) 'You were anxious enough to get off a while ago, I couldn't keep you quiet—now lie still, there are lots of books; ring the bell if you want anything.'

'But, Aagot,' catching her gown, 'dear, good Aagot, where is the Frue? isn't this her room? Aagot, you are the unkindest of kind women!' wriggling a pillow on to the floor.

'Fruen went away early this morning; she won't be back till later on—no, I must go.'

Half an hour later she answers the bell.

'Move me nearer the window, Aagot!'

He lies there watching the children slide down the slope, one little lad and one little maid always toil up and glide down together, tumbling into the soft snow beneath.

The shadows lengthen and the early gloom gathers, and a crescent moon, the last half, rises silently over the white world; and then the jingle of bells reaches him, and a sleigh with a pair of horses creeps round the fringe of the wood and up the drive. He sits up eagerly and watches—

watches the quiet way she handles her reins, and the firm face, touched by the moonlight, with the glisten of rime on her hair. 'A silver witch,' he mutters, 'a great strong silver witch, riding to the music of silver bells.' He listens intently, hears a door slam, and women's voices, the barking of dogs, then steps overhead. Her room perhaps. He wonders what it looks like.

Half an hour glides by, he feels an unreasonable sense of disappointment, almost of injury, as she does not come. She might in common courtesy have looked in and asked how he fared. He recalls the caress in her voice as she said goodnight, the look in her eyes, as she bent over his bed, and anathematizes her for a coquette ; all women are alike. Then reproaches himself for ingratitude, recalls his position, tells himself that she too must know it, he is public property, she must know that he is dependent on his pen, on his sheaves of verse that look so bonny in the growing and bear so little corn for daily bread. His mood darkens, his thoughts embitter, the silver witch of a while ago becomes the embodiment of the social force that crushes him. He chafes, he must leave, he curses his foot, his friends to whom he has written for funds, his penniless condition—for he was going to meet the coast steamer when the accident happened. The captain is an acquaintance and would have given him a ticket. He fumes and works himself into acute distress. The sound of women's laughter and the barking of a dog in play comes

into the now dark room—Bikkje's bark, ay, even
the little bitch has deserted him.   His temperament is as wax to receive impressions, and he
sinks into despair; he starts, surely that is her
voice in the next room ; there is a rush of cool air,
and she enters.

'All in the dark! Aagot has been so very
busy, two of the children are ill ; why didn't you
ring ?'

She slides back the stove door and stirs the
logs into a blaze that lightens the room and
flickers gaily through it.

'But why are you over there in the cold ?   You
must be frozen.'

His eyes are gloomy and his face tired—how
like that first day, she thinks with concern.   She
turns aside the rugs that lie between him and the
fireplace.

'I am going to move you, the couch is on
rollers, and I am very strong,' stretching out her
arms with a frank pride in them.

'Ssh,' as he sits up with a remonstrance, 'I
always have my own way here.'   She stands at
its head and taking him by the shoulders pulls
him gently down again and wheels over the
couch.

'Now isn't that better?   I am going to have
some tea, I want it badly.'   She leans back as
she speaks in a low chair, the glow of the logs
lights up her face.

'Fruen has been for a long drive ?'

'To Arendt.'

'To Arendt? Why, that is fourteen miles away; alone?'

'Yes.'

He makes no further remark, she wonders what is working in him and says:

'You are very silent, what is it? You look worried, sad, tell me——'

She disturbs him rarely, he moves restlessly and pushes his hair off his forehead—she notices that his hand trembles. She goes over and lays her hand upon it—it is burning—she feels his forehead.

'Why you are in a fever, this will never do—I shall have to send for the doctor if you go on like this. What has upset you, what is it?' There is a caress in her voice.

'Many things, dear lady, I am a fool, this amongst the rest!' pointing to a review on the end of his couch.

She takes it up and reads it, holding it in her left hand, leaving her right on his forehead. It is a notice of his latest book—an almost cruelly personal attack by a well-known critic—a cold man of keen brilliant intellect with a pen like a lancet and a faculty of biting sarcasm that wounds sensitive souls like a hornet's sting. Having no temperament himself, every thing of personal jars on him; the touch of egotism that one gladly pardons for the sake of the warm human blood flowing through the pages, the sympathy one feels lies in the writer's nature, offends some canon of taste peculiar to him. Every word of praise is

ceded grudgingly, and accompanied by a sneer.
It makes her indignant as she reads it, and she
throws it aside and sits down next him.

'Why should you mind that? I wouldn't let it
cost me a thought. I fancied you were above
that, that you never cared, that you always went
to nature for comfort, that you had made friends
with the great god Pan, that you despised the
opinions of the ruck, that you had found yourself and with that peace—or didn't it work?'

He starts and stares at her, and the same
puzzled expression crosses his face.

'How did you know?'

'Perhaps—I guessed. I know your books and
all about you this long time. I read a good deal,
you see. Once you helped me. Nothing I have
done for you would ever begin to discharge my
debt.'

'Helped you, Fruen, *I* helped *you*—I don't
understand——'

'Yes, you helped me to find myself!'

The shadows are deep about the room, but the
light from the sizzling wood in the great porcelain
stove streams out across them, and shows her
hands folded in the lap of the crimson gown.

'To find yourself?' he asks softly, with a boyish eager wonder in his voice.

'Yes, you drew a picture of women, you told
me some unintentional home-truths, you hurt
me——'

'But, dear lady!——'

'Men had never done that before, at least I was

too blind to see that much of their courtesy was the worst possible compliment to my best self. It was not to their minds or souls that I appealed, but to their senses, and their admiration sprang from that. You stung me to analyse myself, to see what was under the form into which custom had fashioned me, of what pith I was made, what spirit, if any, lay under the outer woman. To see what significance the physical changes in my body had from where the contradictions of my nature sprang—to find myself. I closed the book of my soul and what I had read there made me sorrow. I was sorry for myself, resentful because I had been reared in ignorance, because of my soul-hunger, but I had found myself all the same, and I said: From this out I belong body and soul to myself; I will live as I choose, seek joy as I choose, carve the way of my life as I will. Aagot has told you of our life here. It has cost me much effort, but I am pretty sure of myself now. It is you men who are the dreamers. Once a girl or a woman is kissed out of the sleep of her ignorance by love or suffering—they are generally synonymous—she gets a grip on reality, she seizes the concrete in life.' She looks at him for the first time since she has spoken and adds: 'In teaching me to find myself, you taught me more than you thought, and what you taught me I am trying to teach to others. A feminine 'Umwerthung aller Werthe,' a new standard of woman's worth. Woman has cheapened herself body and soul through ignorant innocence, she must learn to worthen herself by

all-seeing knowledge. I have begun low down on
the social scale, but I hope the seeds I am plant-
ing will grow into big trees with wide-spreading
roots. Most churches and all social law have
tended to cheapen woman, and in some measure
woman has been the greatest sinner against
woman by centuries of silence.'

Her voice died away and there is silence; only
his quick breathing comes from the dusk of the
couch, and it seems to him that in all the world
only they two exist. Her speech has taken him
aback, his perceptions are in chaos. She appears
to him as the embodied figure of a dream, dreamt
at some past date, and he cannot place her. He
once 'hurt' her, when? He tries to think what
he could have written that touched her.

'But, lady, that I should hurt you, I don't
understand.'

'Ah, that is a thing of the past; now I am for-
tified against hurt, because I know I am in the
right. I owe you a thank-you for that'—her cool
hand meets his nervous shaking one and grasps it
firmly—'and I mean to give it you when I can.'

She rises and lights the lamp and rings:

'They have forgotten me on the children's
account!'

A maid brings in the tray with an apology from
Aagot. She pours out some tea and waits upon
him, and as she leans forward and says, 'Sugar?'
the same tantalising memory rises to puzzle him.
It makes him silent, it gets between him and his
thoughts, irritates him.

She takes his empty cup and puts the small table away.

'Would the whirr of a wheel irritate you?'

'No, Fruen, no,' he says absent-mindedly, he is exerting his whole will to try and find the clue. She has an old black spinning-wheel, with ivory knobs; she moves her foot with steady rhythm, and she feeds it with the ivory white curls of well-carded wool with a beautiful action of hands. He watches her with a kind of fascination, and the song of the wheel sings soothingly in his thoughts.

'Few ladies spin now,' he remarks.

'No; I am not very good at it, I am only learning. The wool in my gown holds all my first attempts—I like it; I span an awful lot of thoughts into it, much of my old self, and when it was finished I was new.'

He makes no reply; he is still endeavouring to find the clue. Bikkje supplies it; she patters with tapping claws across the waxed floor and rubs against her; she stops to pat her, the little beast licks her wrist and then trots over to him; their eyes meet, she flushes, and the whole scene comes back to him in a flash—lapping fjord, music of water and trees, and the woman with the laugh of a child, who looked so like a fashion-plate. He sits up in his astonishment, crying:

'Now I remember—but is it possible? No; it can't be. You are so changed; and yet now you smile I see it plainly, and marvel I did not see it before. And that is what you meant by "hurt"

—I was rough, I remember,' with a sort of hesitation——

'Go on,' she smiles encouragingly.

'You irritated me, I was hurt, I was bitter—I
am always getting hurt and getting bitter,' with
rueful humour. 'You embodied that section of
society that had discarded me . . . you—' with
desperation—'powdered and painted, and your
waist was absurd—but your eyes, your eyes and
your smile are the same—that is why I have been
puzzling—it is wonderful, like a fairy-tale, and
even now I do not understand.'

'That your words should have worked so great
a transformation, no,' remembering the why *his*
words more than another man's, she adds softly,
'no, perhaps you do not quite understand that!
But it is none the less true ; but you, all this time
I have been finding myself, how is it you have
grown less secure, how have you lost your grip of
mother nature? Did your philosophy go lame
on the journey?' She has risen and is moving
about the room, drawing the curtains closer. His
eyes follow her, her hair shines so in the light, her
supple figure sways as she moves.

'No ; but, dear lady, I cannot stop looking at
you, it is so strange. You have grown, I believe.
Your bust is fuller, your hips—ah, your corset is
gone. You look so strong, so capable—you are
half a woman, it is wonderful—*I begin to fear
you !*'

She throws back her head and laughs, stands
with her hands clasped behind her back, perhaps

conscious of the lines of her own grand figure, and looks at him.

'Methinks, Poet, the pupil has distanced the master!'

'Ah, that is sure! I must have been blind not to see!' his eyes fill, and she forgets everything but that; and goes over and kneels next him and says:

'Tell me why it is you seemed so sure then, and now you look as if everything had gone awry with you. Even your books have less of joy, less of truth in them, less of grip at the world's heart, the grip that made them touch mine and got you a name.'

He is won by her frank appeal and bares his heart, perhaps for the first time, even to himself. All that has lain smouldering there through lad years and man years till now. She marvels at the strange tangles of his poet nature, the child, and man, ay, the woman in it—at the dreams of the man ; the cobwebs spun over the ore ; and he little dreams, as he tells her, that she is weighing her life as it is, as it may be, with possible sorrows and joys deliberately in the balance, and that she chooses her course.

'Have you ever told this to any one?'

'No, dear lady, I have few close friends.'

'You want a home, you are not fit to be alone. Your body and spirit wage war. The scabbard is too frail for the sword. Yet you need freedom, freedom to go when you will, but you ought to have a place to return to. There must be no

more waiting in the snow,' with a tender smile,
that sets his pulses stirring. 'Now you are tired,
and must talk no more, and I need to think before
I tell you my plan. Hush! lie still, and I will
play for you.'

.   .   .   .   .

Some days later he is hobbling from room to
room on a crutch. Aagot wishes him away, that
is sure. He leans against the window, looking
out at the snow; the sun is bright to-day,
and he is thinking of something she said in the
morning. She asked him point-blank to go into
the disused smoking-room when some ladies came
up the drive. It set him thinking, and he realises
he must leave. He has had a glorious rest, but he is
still weak, and the world outside looks less invit-
ing than ever. That she cares for him he knows;
that he touched her in some way acutely at that
first meeting, her whole life since shows; but is
she not less approachable in her new womanhood
than ever? She has found fresh interests, new
duties, an ambition, and, if he judge her rightly,
no love will ever satisfy her wholly; it will never
be more than one note; true, a grand note, in the
harmony of union; but not the harmony. The
whole man in him is touched by this new creature
his stray words have waked into life: this grand,
fearless, wholesome woman, with a clear head and
sure hand to guide the great house and its many
inmates. He is proud of her, she is the woman he
dreamt of; but what has he to offer her instead?

In a dream it was easy for her to say: 'Come with me, woman,' but come to what?—beggary?

He knows the place, her ambitions, her plans. He can't say: 'Let me share it!' He has nothing to offer her; he remembers their first meeting, he would give all he has ever dreamt of to try and show her how he thinks of her now; but he must go. How he dreads the loneliness, the bare room in some cheap lodging house, the feeling of loss. It must be, he shrinks from it because he is still ill. Aagot comes in for him to sign the receipt of a registered letter. She looks significantly at him. He reads her unspoken thought; she hopes he will go now that his money has come. He sits still and reproaches himself for his cowardice, and yet is he not now, at the supreme moment of his life, swayed as much by conventional considerations as the pettiest bourgeois stickler for usage. If she care, does he not insult her by thinking his poverty would weigh with her? Well, he will tell her in his verse, he will glorify her as no woman before, but she must, if she is to be his queen, exercise her prerogative and speak—it is hard—he will give himself this one day, and to-morrow he will leave.

She has been thinking over it, she knows what is working in him, for love makes a woman as wise as a serpent. No consideration of outside people or his circumstances has any weight with her; she is only weighing the effect of it on her own life and work; she is not willing to leave the plough she has set herself to guide. She realises well that his love, no matter if it be his whole love, will not fill her life completely ; she has seen too many marriages not to know that every woman, except the few that go to prove the rule, chafes at the narrowness of the horizon that is simply confined to attending to one man's needs. She recalls the words of a cynical woman friend of hers : 'Nothing is so conducive to make a woman content with her husband as a platonic friendship with a decent other fellow, or a hobby of some sort. It gives her an interest, saves her from being bored to extinction by his fidelity.'

She sees his faults clearly, she knows that marriage with him will bring her a measure of happiness such as she has never held before ; but she is not willing to go into old - fashioned bondage. She has no illusions about him ; she is too thoroughly a woman to take him very seriously ; she laughs as she thinks of him, laughs tenderly and softly, her comic great child, child in his greatest moments, with a little of the child's desire for praise, a little of the child's 'show-off,' happiest when fooled for his own good, capable of being driven along the roughest road, if only the reins are silken—she feels a desire to make the world good for him ; she will go and look for him.

He turns as she enters the room ; their eyes meet, for she is tall as he.

'Dear lady, I must go to-morrow, I ought to have gone before !'

'Why ?'

'Because I ought to have considered you—people——'

She laughs, such a light caressing laugh, and goes nearer to him.

'Have you been well content here? And is that the only reason? *I* care nothing for them, that care is a thing of the past.'

He looks at her with shining eyes.

'Am I more to you than the world's opinion?'

Her eyes drop.

'Put on your things, they are in the hall, and I will show you!'

She speeds away like an arrow, and he hears her voice outside and her step overhead, and presently she comes down in her crimson cloak and fur-trimmed cap, and she hands him a great soft fleecy, silk scarf, so fine and sweet-smelling that he handles it fearsomely; she takes it out of his hand with a laugh, throws it over his head and fastens it under his coat, without looking at him; he feels as if she has taken the power to breathe from him, as if her own soft warm arms are about his neck and her breath on his breast. He follows her and seats himself without a word in the sleigh next her, but he has a feeling as they drive off, that curious looks are following them, and he looks at her to see if she too is conscious of it. Her cheeks are vivid with colour, her lips are parted as if uttering the words of some inner song. When they reach the end of the wood, she swerves sharply to the left and drives towards the village, draws in the horses and drives slowly.

Already her intention has its effect. A woman pops out her head over a half door, vanishes to reappear with another head behind her.

'Frue,' he says, and his voice shakes, 'dear lady, is it wise of you?'

She turns and reads his eyes searchingly.

'It only rests with you to make it foolish.'

After that he gives himself up to the exultant gladness that surges up in him; he neither sees the curious glances of the men in the street, or the eyes of the women in the windows as they return, he only knows that he is bound on a wonderful white journey, through a glorious white world, to the chime of silver bells, a betrothal journey with his queen. Neither of them speaks, but both look up to the house as they dash past the gate and smile, and then on through the wood. It is a strange silent drive, as if both hearts are too full of a sacred, wonderful music they fear to disturb by common words. He feels as if the sun in his soul is so warm that it might transform the winter landscape into summer, radiant, passionate summer. At the old road she turns, and they drive silently back; the sun burns like a dull red globe as it hangs suspended in the grey sky, shedding a shiver of red across the grey space. And it is dark with the sudden fall of the winter night when they reach home and the lights stream to meet them in welcome from every window. She meets Aagot on the stairs and stoops and kisses her, for the very love of every human thing welling up in her soul for his sake.

Why should she trouble what the world says —after all one's world is only as big as one can grasp it—why worry over the rule of waiting to be wooed ; a relic of the days of capture by force. She owes the world not a thank-you, why wound him by a silence for a convention's sake?

She pauses a moment before she goes into the room. She has changed her gown for a long soft white woollen one with quaint silver clasps ; it is open and shows her strong white throat. There is something about her makes him stand up as she enters. She waits with a quaint proud shyness for him to speak.

'What does it mean, dear lady? what does it mean? I am dazed.'

'As much or as little as you will.'

'Are you sure?'

'I am quite sure.'

'And if I should tire, and the song in me stifle, and the curse of my restlessness come over me again——'

'You will go and I will wait, until you weary and come home again!'

'And if my fancy waver—if I seek new eyes and new lips——' His eyes pierce her soul ; she pales white as her gown and the ruby in the heart-shaped pendant on her breast flashes as it rises.

'You will be free to go.'

'Free man?'

'Free man '—with pride—' and free woman!'

'And what do you ask me for this?'

'Has any woman in the world a claim on you,

have you any wrong to right, is there any child
who has a right to call you father?'

'No, no, dear lady!'—with exultant pride—'not
one.'

'Then I ask you nothing!' It seems to him
that she is like a tall pillar of white flame. 'For I
am sure of myself, proud of my right to dispose of
myself as I will, to choose——'

She looks him full in the face as she speaks and
her changeful eyes are glorious with a fire that is
too clean, too strong for shyness. 'And even'—
there is a break in her voice—'if I mistake you, to
feel not one pang of false shame at having spoken
as my heart tells me. Man, I love you!'

There is one moment's absolute silence, silence
as when Death is felt stealing to a bedside, and
they both appear to one another in the glow of
some magic light; then the exultant cry of the
man, who has found a dream realised, a dream
half doubted as a poet's fancy, trembles through
the room to fill it with echoes that sink into her
heart and make melody there for evermore. He
drops at her feet and hides his face in her gown,
and when he raises it to her, his eyes are bright
with tears.

'Now you are a whole woman; the woman I
have seen flit as a silver shadow through the woods
on moonlit nights; whose smile I have caught in
the sparkle of wine and the colour of flowers;
whose voice whispered to me in every strain of
music, every bird's note, every sigh of the winds;
who sang in my blood in boyhood, whom I have

felt in my dreams, and who has filled my soul with an unstilled want; whom I sought in crowds and found not; the woman of whom every woman was but a fragment; the woman to whom I could kneel as I kneel to you, to whom I could go for rest, to whom I could give myself, whom I could gladly serve, O my queen, my love, my dear love!'

And outside the snow falls softly and the darkness gathers, but inside the music of women's voices singing at their work and the patter of children's feet and cooing laughter fill the house in which love is making a carnival of roses.